kristina ohlsson

THE CHOSEN

Translated by Marlaine Delargy

SIMON & SCHUSTER

London · New York · Sydney · Toronto · New Delhi

A CBS COMPANY

First published in Sweden by Piratförlaget under the title *Davidsstjärnor*, 2013
First published in Great Britain by Simon & Schuster UK Ltd, 2015

A CBS COMPANY

1 3 5 7 9 10 8 6 4 2

Simon & Schuster UK Ltd
1st Floor
222 Gray's Inn Road
London WC1X 8HB

www.simonandschuster.co.uk

Simon & Schuster Australia, Sydney
Simon & Schuster India, New Delhi

A CIP catalogue record for this book is available from the British Library

TPB ISBN: 978-1-47114-879-8
EBOOK ISBN: 978-1-47114-881-1

Typeset by Hewer Text UK Ltd, Edinburgh
Printed and bound in Great Britain by CPI Group (UK) Ltd, Croydon, CR0 4YY

THE
CHOSEN

Fear came with the darkness. He hated the nights. The distance between his own room and the safety of his parents' bedroom seemed immense. Many times he had chosen to hide under the covers rather than venture out onto the dark landing outside his door.

He could see that his mother was worried about his night terrors. He would scream out loud when he had bad dreams, and she always came running. Stroked his forehead and whispered that everything was all right. Switched on the bedside lamp and opened the blind.

'There's nothing here, David. Nothing that could hurt you. Come and have a look, and you'll see that there's nothing to worry about.'

Like all parents, she wanted him to look for himself, see that there were no dangers lurking outside.

But David wasn't afraid of something you could see with the naked eye. He was afraid of something you weren't aware of until it was too late. Of dangers that moved with the darkness as their protector and silence as their companion. David was afraid of the danger against which there was no defence.

It was Avital who had told him the story. Told him about the boy who hated children, and who waited for them in the barren landscape around the village where they lived. The Paper Boy.

'He sleeps during the day and wakes up when the sun goes down,' Avital said one day when they were hiding in his tree house so that David wouldn't have to go home. 'He picks out the child he wants, then he takes them.'

David felt his stomach turn over.

'How does he choose?' he whispered.

'No one knows. The only thing we know is that no one is safe.'

David tried to swallow his fear.

'You're making it up.'

The floor of the tree house was hard, and the wind was so cold. He was wearing only shorts and a short-sleeved top, and he was starting to shiver.

'I am not!'

Avital had always been more daring. He was never scared, and he was always ready to fight for what he thought or what he wanted. But he was also a true friend. David's father had said more than once that Avital would be a good man and a good soldier when he grew up, the kind of man who always did the right thing, who stood up for his friends and his people. He never said what he thought about David, but David assumed he had a very different opinion of his own son.

'He comes at night, when we're asleep. He waits outside the window, and when we least expect it, he comes in and grabs us. So don't sleep with the window open,' Avital said.

Those words penetrated David's brain like nails and were impossible to remove. From then on his window had to remain closed.

But when summer came and the dry heat rolled in across the country, his mother had had enough.

'Being too hot can make you ill, David. You have to let in the cool night air.'

He allowed her to open the window, then waited until she had gone to bed. When the house was silent, he tiptoed over and closed it. Only then could he get to sleep.

Although you could never be completely sure.

Avital explained this to him a little while later.

'When he gets angry, he becomes very strong, and then there are no doors, no walls, no windows that can keep him out. The only thing you can do is hope.'

'What do you mean?'

'Hope he chooses someone else.'

That did it. From then on, David's fear of sleeping alone was greater than his fear of making his way across the landing. Every night he crept into his parents' room; they sent him away only if his little sister had got there first.

'In you come, sweetheart,' his mother would whisper as he slipped under the covers.

But he slept for no more than an hour or so as dawn was breaking, and that created more problems. He had just started school, and was nodding off during lessons. The teachers were worried; they called his parents, who took him to the doctor.

'The boy is exhausted,' the doctor said. 'A few days' rest and he'll be as good as new.'

David was allowed to stay at home, and Avital came round after school with his books to tell him what they had been doing. David wished the teacher would send someone else. He had been trying to avoid Avital so that he wouldn't have to listen to any more of his terrifying stories, but it was as if he wasn't meant to escape. As Avital zipped up his rucksack and got ready to go home, he said:

'Have you seen him yet? At night?'

David shook his head.

'I think he'll come soon,' Avital said.

It would be a while before his prophecy was fulfilled.

Many years passed. David and Avital left the village where they had grown up, and by chance ended up on the same kibbutz.

And then he came. The Paper Boy. A child went missing from the kibbutz. For ten days and ten nights they searched for him – adults, police officers, soldiers. Eventually they found his body, so badly mutilated that they didn't want to tell the other children what had happened to him.

But they knew anyway.

David and Avital, grown men by this time, looked at one another in silent understanding. They knew what had happened to the boy.

The Paper Boy had taken him.

And it was only a matter of time before he returned.

CONCLUSION

FRAGMENT I

The woman who still does not know that hell is waiting around the corner is walking briskly along the pavement. Snow is falling from the dark sky, settling like the frozen tears of angels on her head and shoulders. She is carrying a violin case. It has been a long day, and she wants to get home.

Home to her family.

To her sleeping children and to her husband, who is waiting with wine and pizza.

Perhaps she even feels a sense of peace, because a drama that has been going on for a long time seems to have reached its conclusion. Only now is she aware of how much it has been weighing her down. Being able to put it behind her will change so much.

She strides out, speeding up as she gets closer to home. It is time to allow herself to rest. To recover. Gather her strength.

She can't wait, and starts to walk even faster.

And then she hears it. The sound that slices through the winter silence and hits her like a hammer blow.

Screaming sirens, blue lights. The engines roar as they catch up with her and race past.

And suddenly she knows where they are going.

To her home.

She runs faster than she has ever done before. She runs for her life as she moves towards death. Her footsteps are silent in the snow, her breath is like thick smoke. She rounds the last corner and sees the blue lights pulsating against the neighbouring buildings. There are people everywhere. Men and women in uniform, on the pavement and on the road. Loud voices, agitated expressions. Someone is openly weeping, and someone else yells at a driver, telling him to fucking park somewhere else.

Then they catch sight of her.

She is a freight train hurtling down a straight track; no one can stop her. Someone makes a futile attempt but misses her by a millimetre. She hurls herself through the open door of the building and races up the stairs.

And that is where she stops.

She slams into another body and she falls down. She tries to get up but is pinned down by arms that think they are stronger than a mother under threat.

'You can't go in there right now. You just need to wait a little . . .'

But she will not wait. She doesn't even understand how it happens, but she takes him down with a single blow to the crotch, gets to her feet and carries on running. She hears his voice echoing through the stairwell:

'She got away! Stop her!'

Soon she has reached the top of the stairs. Soon she is standing outside her own door. Soon she will find out what has happened.

That her husband and her children are dead.

That there is no one left.

She will stand in silence on the threshold of the room

where they are lying, observe the frantic activity going on around them in an attempt to save whatever can be saved, in spite of the fact that it is too late. That is how all those present will remember the scene.

They will remember her standing in silence in the doorway, with snow on her coat, and a violin case in her hand.

EARLIER

The First Day

WEDNESDAY, 25 JANUARY 2012

Efraim Kiel had arrived with two tasks to accomplish. The first was to identify and recruit a new head of security for one of the Jewish associations in Stockholm, the Solomon Community. The second task he preferred not to think about too much. Once both had been fulfilled, he would return home to Israel. Or move on elsewhere. He rarely knew how long his journeys would take.

It shouldn't have been so difficult. It wasn't *usually* all that difficult. How many times had he been sent off on a similar mission? Countless times. And how often had he come up against problems like this? Not once.

The Solomon Community in Stockholm had made the decision to approach contacts in Jerusalem. A series of worrying incidents had occurred over the past year; the community had been the target of a sabotage campaign. In several cases this had involved direct attacks, and the community's school had also been targeted. No one knew why the situation had changed in Stockholm in particular, and that was largely irrelevant. The important thing was to assess their current position and to see how security could be improved.

It had been decided that one part of the solution was to employ a head of security who was better qualified, and Efraim's task was to find such a person.

He knew what he wanted.

A good leader.

In order for a team to work well, it was essential to have a clear, energetic leader, someone with integrity and the ability to prioritise, to make strategic decisions. But above all they must have someone who would command respect. No qualities in the world could compensate for character traits that evoked contempt in those he or she was supposed to guide and co-ordinate.

So far they had found it hard to track down a person who possessed the necessary skills and attributes. There was always something missing, usually integrity and sufficient operational experience. One applicant after another was discounted, and now time was running out for Efraim Kiel.

'But we've got the perfect candidate – why can't we employ him?' The query came from the general secretary of the Solomon Community, who was sitting opposite Efraim.

'Because he can't take up the post until summer, which is too late. You can't be without a head of security for six months. That's out of the question.'

Efraim looked over at the window and saw the snow falling from the dark clouds, covering the ground with white powder. Stockholm in January was very different from Tel Aviv, where he had been sitting outside drinking wine just a few days ago. The Swedes had their own customs and rituals, of course. Efraim had realised that they sometimes sat outdoors in the snow, grilling sausages and sipping hot chocolate. Even allowing for the fact that he didn't eat pork, and that it would never have occurred to him to mix milk and meat, he still thought it was a bizarre tradition.

'We need to find someone else,' he said, making an effort

to maintain a diplomatic tone of voice. 'Someone with a broad range of experience who can start right away.'

The general secretary shuffled through the pile of applications on the desk in front of him. There weren't very many, but from a purely numerical point of view there should have been enough to find someone. Efraim knew that the general secretary had had a lot to deal with over the past few months. Both the Solomon Community and the school had moved to new premises in buildings directly opposite one another on Nybrogatan. They hadn't moved far from their previous home on Artillerigatan, but it had still taken time and energy. Everyone needed a period of peace and quiet.

If only their preferred candidate could take up the post earlier.

Efraim was open to a solution that involved a temporary appointment to fill the gap until the summer, but they still needed a solid incumbent. A community without a head of security was naked and vulnerable.

He couldn't explain why, but Efraim had the distinct feeling that this particular community wouldn't be able to cope for very long. He reached for the pile of applications, in spite of the fact that he knew them off by heart by now.

'Actually, we had another application today,' the general secretary said hesitantly. 'Several, in fact. From a consultancy firm that specialises in strategic security work.'

Efraim raised his eyebrows.

'And?'

'I'd say that only one of the candidates is worth looking at, but then again the application arrived too late, and I'm not really sure if the person in question is suitable for the post.'

Efraim didn't care whether the application was late or not, but the issue of suitability was more interesting.

'Why is he unsuitable? Or she?'

'He. And he's not one of us.'

'You mean he's a gentile?'

'Yes.'

A non-Jewish candidate for the post of head of security within a Jewish community.

'Why are you mentioning his application if you think he's no good?'

The general secretary didn't answer; instead he got up and left the room. He returned with a sheaf of papers in his hand.

'Because he has certain qualities and a level of experience that made me curious, especially in view of the fact that we may need to make a temporary appointment. I checked out his background and found several important elements.'

He passed the documents to Efraim, and reeled off a brief summary.

'An ex-cop, almost forty years old. Wife and two young kids. Lives in Spånga; they moved out of the city when he lost his job. Did his military service with the Marine Commandos, and seems to have flirted with the idea of becoming an officer, as he stayed on for a while. Got into the Police Training Academy and made rapid progress in the police service. Promoted to the rank of Detective Inspector at a very young age, and spent only a few years in the sticks before he was handpicked to join a special investigation unit in Stockholm. Led by a DCI by the name of Alex Recht.'

Efraim looked up.

'Alex Recht. Why do I recognise that name?'

'Because he was in the papers back in the autumn when that plane was hijacked. His son was the co-pilot.'

'That's it.'

Efraim nodded to himself. The hijacking had also featured in the Israeli press. He focused on the documents in his hand once more. The information the general secretary had just given matched what the man himself had said in his application. However, there was one piece of information missing.

'You said he lost his job.'

'Yes.'

'And you're still considering taking him on? Don't you realise how much you have to fuck things up to lose your badge in a country like Sweden?'

Yes, the general secretary did realise.

'However, I would say there are definitely extenuating circumstances in this case.'

'Go on.'

The general secretary paused for effect.

'They kicked him out after he shot the man who murdered his brother. And it happened in the line of duty.'

Efraim stared at the man opposite for a long time, then looked down at the application once more.

Peder Rydh. Could he be the person they needed?

The meeting was interrupted by the general secretary's PA, who knocked on the door and walked straight in.

'You have to come,' she said. 'Something terrible has happened. I've just had a call from the Solomon school to say that one of the pre-school teachers has been shot.'

The call from the Solomon school in Östermalm didn't make any sense at first. A pre-school teacher had been shot. In front of children and parents. Probably by a sniper who must have been on a roof on the other side of the road.

Incomprehensible.

As far as DCI Alex Recht was concerned, the Solomon Community was a closed book. He knew it was one of Stockholm's Jewish communities, but that was all. He couldn't understand why the case had landed on his desk. If the motive was anti-Semitism, then it should be investigated by the National Crime Unit's specialist team who dealt with hate crimes. Maybe the National Security Police, Säpo, should be involved. But why Alex's team, which had only just been formed and wasn't yet ready for a major challenge? And even more importantly, who the hell would have a reason to shoot a pre-school teacher in broad daylight in front of a group of adults and kids?

'Her new partner,' Alex's boss said, tossing a computer printout onto his desk. 'This is no hate crime, although that's how the internet editions of the papers are reporting it. This is linked to serious organised crime, and if you look under a few stones I'm sure you'll discover that the poor little schoolteacher who got shot in the back isn't quite as pure as the snow she's lying on.'

Alex picked up the printout, which was an extract from the serious crimes database.

'This is her partner?'

'Yep.'

The words in front of him were all too familiar. Drugs-related offences. Unlawful threats. Assaulting a police officer. Resisting arrest. Aggravated theft. Armed robbery. Procurement.

'Anything on the teacher herself?'

'Not a thing. She isn't even in the suspects' database.'

'In which case she might be as pure as the driven snow after all; perhaps she just has particularly poor judgement. And bad luck.'

'I'll leave it to you to look into; find out if this is about her or her boyfriend. Or possibly both of them. And don't hang about.'

Alex looked up.

'Are we in a hurry?'

'The Solomon Community is very energetic when it comes to security issues. If they don't get answers from us fast enough, they'll start their own investigation. Whatever happens, they're bound to demand major input from the police, and they'll do it very publicly.'

Alex ran a hand over his chin.

'Maybe not if we tell them that their teacher was living with someone who has a criminal record as long as your arm,' he said. 'Surely that will give the impression that they're recruiting potentially dangerous individuals, which won't be very good for their image.'

His boss was already on his way out of the door.

'Exactly. So make sure you get in touch with them as soon as possible. Go over there and have a chat. Take Fredrika with you.'

'She's not in this afternoon, but I'll call her tonight and let her know what's going on.'

His boss frowned.

'That's up to you, of course, but don't you think you ought to call her now and ask her to come in? If she's in town, that is.'

'She is in town, and of course I can call her, but she probably won't answer.'

'Has something happened?'

'She's rehearsing with the orchestra.'

'Orchestra? What does she play?'

'The violin. And it makes her feel good, so I'm not going to interrupt her.'

After being away from the police for almost two years, Fredrika Bergman was back at last. Back at Kungsholmen. Back with Alex. Which was exactly where he had always thought she should be, so he had no intention of quibbling over the odd rehearsal.

He would make a start on the investigation himself. The teacher had been living with a man who had been in a hell of a lot of trouble, so that was the obvious place to begin.

'So why am I dealing with this?' Alex asked. 'Serious organised crime isn't in my remit.'

'The Östermalm police have asked for back-up in the initial stages,' his boss explained. 'I promised you'd give them a hand. If there's a clear link to organised crime, just pass the case on to the National Crime Unit.'

It sounded so simple. Just pass the case on through the system. God knows how easy that would actually be. Alex thought back to the unique team he had led previously, drifting like a jellyfish between the National Crime Unit, the local forces and the Stockholm City police. On paper they had been part of the Stockholm City police, but in reality they had served several masters. Alex had liked it that way, and if it was up to him, the new team would be no different.

'I'll send a car to bring in her partner if he's at home,' Alex said. 'I want to hear what he has to say, see whether we can eliminate him as a suspect.'

'I shouldn't think he did it himself,' his boss said. 'It's too crude.'

'I agree. It sounds like revenge or some other crap. But we still have to talk to the guy. I'm sure he must know who shot her in the back.'

Only an hour had passed since Fredrika had left Police HQ in Kungsholmen to go to her rehearsal. One hour, but the job no longer existed. Nor did her family or her friends. Not within the vacuum that was created when she settled her violin in the correct position between her chin and shoulder.

The music carried her as if she had wings. She was flying high above everyone else, pretending she was alone in the universe. It was a dangerous thought. Soloists rarely did well in an ensemble, but for a moment – *just one moment* – Fredrika Bergman wanted to experience a taste of the life she had never had, to catch a glimpse of the woman she had never become.

It was the third week of the new, yet familiar era. All her adult life Fredrika had mourned the career as a violinist that she had never had, and would never have. Not only had she grieved, she had searched hard for an alternative future. She had wandered around like a lost soul among the ruins of everything that had once been hers, wondering what to do, because as a child and a teenager, she had lived for music. Music was her vocation, and without it life was worth very little.

Things never turn out as we expect.

Sometimes they're better, but often they're worse.

Occasionally the memory would resurface, as unwelcome as rain from a summer sky. The memory of a car skidding, ending up on the wrong side of the road, crashing and turning over. With children in the back, parents in the front, skis on the roof. She remembered those cataclysmic seconds when everything was torn apart, and the silence that followed. The scars were still there. Every day she could see them on her arm, white lines that told the story of why she had been unable to put in the necessary hours of practice every day. In despair and emotional turmoil she had buried her violin in the graveyard of the past, and become a different person.

And now she was playing again.

It was her mother who had found the string ensemble and told her: 'This is your chance, Fredrika'. As if Fredrika, who was married to a man twenty-five years older than her, with two small children, had endless hours at her disposal, just waiting for something to fill them.

But seek and ye shall find, as they say, and for the past three weeks music had been back in her life. For the first time in twenty years, Fredrika felt something that might just be harmony. Her husband and children made her heart whole. She was happy in her work, for once. Reaching this point had been a messy process. The case of the hijacked plane a few months earlier had been the key. Her employer in the Justice Department had sent her back to work with the police on a temporary basis, and Fredrika had realised where she felt at home, where she wanted to be.

In the police service. On the first of January, she was back. Working with Alex Recht as part of a new investigative team, which was very similar to the one she had been a part of a few years ago.

Very similar, even though so much had changed.

Harmony. A word that would have made her feel queasy just a couple of years ago. But not now. Now it had acquired a new meaning; it wrapped itself around her soul like cotton wool, and lit a spark in her eyes. Fredrika Bergman had found peace.

For the time being, at least.

There had once been a Jewish bloodline in Alex's family, but it had been broken several generations ago. Since then, none of his relatives had any links to Judaism, and the only trace that remained was his surname. Recht.

Nevertheless, he felt that the name gave him certain advantages as he set off for the Solomon Community in Östermalm, as if its Jewish origins would be enough to bring him closer to a people he had never felt part of.

The air was cold and damp as he got out of the car on Nybrogatan. Bloody awful weather. January at its worst.

The Östermalm police had cordoned off the area around the body. Huddles of curious onlookers were leaning over the plastic tape. Why did blood and death attract so much attention? So many people shamelessly gravitated towards misery, just so they could feel glad they hadn't been affected.

He quickly made his way over to the cordon where he could see several younger colleagues in uniform. He had once been like them, young and hungry, always ready to put on his uniform and get out there to keep the streets safe. He was rather more disillusioned these days.

One of the officers introduced him to the community's general secretary, a man weighed down by a tragedy that was only a few hours old. He could barely speak.

'None of the witnesses is allowed to leave,' Alex said, placing as much emphasis on the first word as he could muster. 'As I understand it, a number of parents and children saw what happened. No one goes home until we've spoken to them, or at least made a note of their contact details.'

'Already done,' one of his Östermalm colleagues said tersely. Alex realised that he had overstepped the mark. Who was he to come marching onto their turf issuing orders? They had asked him to help out, not take over.

'How many witness are we talking about?' he said, hoping that he had managed to soften his tone.

'Three parents and four children aged between one and four. And of course various people who happened to be passing when the incident took place. I've asked those who came forward to stick around, but of course I can't guarantee that's everyone.'

It shouldn't be a problem; Alex had been told that the school entrance was covered by CCTV, so it would be fairly straightforward to get an idea of how many people had been passing at the time of the shooting.

'Who's your head of security?' Alex asked, turning to the general secretary.

'We don't have one at the moment. Our security team is running itself until we fill the post.'

Alex looked over at the body. The falling snow was doing its best to bury the scene of the crime, but without success. The warm blood that had poured out of the woman was melting the snowflakes as effectively as if they had landed on a radiator. She was lying on her stomach, her face on the ground. She had been shot in the back as she turned towards the open door of the school to call to one of the children.

Alex thanked God that the bullet hadn't hit one of the little ones instead.

'According to the parents, there was just one single shot,' said his colleague from Östermalm.

Alex looked at the body. Clearly one shot was all that had been required.

'Shall we continue inside, where it's warmer?' the general secretary suggested.

He led the way into the building, where another man appeared and introduced himself as the headteacher of the Solomon school.

'I need hardly say that we are devastated by what's happened, and that we expect the police to give this matter the highest priority,' the general secretary said.

'Of course,' Alex said sincerely. Shooting someone down in broad daylight in the middle of the city wasn't exactly common.

They sat down in the general secretary's office. The walls were adorned with pictures of various places in Israel arranged in neat rows – Jerusalem, Tel Aviv, Haifa, Nazareth. Alex had visited the country several times, and recognised virtually every location. In the window an impressive menorah spread its seven branches: one of the classic symbols of Judaism. Alex wondered if he had one at home; if so it must be in one of the boxes in the loft.

'Tell me about the woman who died,' he said, trying to remember her name. 'Josephine. How long had she been working for you?'

'Two years,' the headteacher replied.

'Which age group did she work with?'

Alex knew nothing about the way pre-schools were

organised, but he assumed that children of different ages were separated into groups. His own children were grown up now, and parents themselves. Sometimes when he listened to their talk of day care and school and dropping off and picking up, he wondered where he had been when they were little. He certainly hadn't been with them, at any rate.

'Early years – one to three. She and two colleagues were responsible for a dozen or so children.'

'Have there been any threats directed against Josephine or the school in the past?'

The headteacher looked at the general secretary, waiting for him to respond.

'As I'm sure you know, there are always threats against Jewish interests, irrespective of time or place, unfortunately. But no, we haven't received any concrete threats recently. Unless you count all the vandalism, that is. Which we do, even if it isn't directed against individuals.'

'I know you keep a close eye on people moving around outside your premises; have you noticed anything in particular that you'd like to share?'

Once again the answer was no; everything had been quiet.

'What about you?' the general secretary said, leaning across the desk. 'I realise that the investigation is at an early stage, but do you have any leads that you think could prove interesting?'

There was something about the man's tone of voice that made Alex suddenly wary. He decided to answer a question with a question, which he directed to both the headteacher and the general secretary.

'What do you know about Josephine's private life?'

A pale smile flitted across the headteacher's face.

'She was twenty-eight years old. The daughter of two members of our community who have been close friends of mine for many years. I've known Josephine since she was little. She was a lovely girl.'

But? There was always a but.

'But?'

'She was a little . . . wild. It took time for her to find the right path in life. However, I had no hesitation in giving her the job. She was fantastic with the children.'

A little wild. That could mean anything from 'She robbed a bank but she didn't mean any harm,' to 'She hitched her way around the world twice before she decided what she wanted to be when she grew up'. Alex didn't understand words like 'wild'. It was new a invention, coined by a generation with too many choices and skewed expectations of life.

'I'm sure you're right,' he said. 'Given that you know her parents so well, I assume you're also aware that she was living with a man fifteen years older than her, with convictions for a series of serious crimes?'

Their reaction took him by surprise.

They hadn't had a clue. Or had they? Alex gazed at the man who looked the least surprised: the general secretary. But he was also the person who had most to lose if it appeared that he had no idea what was going on within his community.

'There must be some misunderstanding,' the headteacher said. 'We didn't even know she was living with someone.'

Alex remembered that they had been co-habiting for only a few months, according to the records.

'Surely her parents must have known who she was sharing her home with?' he said.

'You'd think so, but then I don't know how much they saw of her,' the headteacher said.

Alex immediately decided that he needed to speak to the parents.

'Where can I get hold of Josephine's mother and father?'

'They have an apartment on Sibyllegatan, but I know they were keen to get to the hospital as soon as she's taken there; they want to see her. Or whatever the procedure is.'

You saw. You felt. You understood.

You went under and fell apart.

'Any brothers or sisters?'

'She has a brother in New York.'

So at least the parents still had one child left. That always gave him some small consolation – not that he thought it was possible to replace one child with another. He had almost lost his son just a few months ago, and nothing could have compensated for such a loss.

Nothing.

Alex hated remembering those hours when everything had been so uncertain and no one knew how it would end. And it was almost more painful to remember the aftermath of the hijacking, which had cost him so much. All those weeks of frustration, all the footslog that had been necessary to bring his son home; exhausting marathon trips to the USA; endless meetings with government officials who were unwilling to let him out of the country.

He shook his head. That was all behind him now.

'I'm assuming that you will treat the information I have given you with the greatest discretion,' he said, getting to his feet to indicate that the meeting was over.

'Of course. Please don't hesitate to contact us if we can

help in any way,' the general secretary said, holding out his hand.

Alex shook it.

'I'll be in touch,' he said.

'So will we, actually,' the general secretary said. 'As I said, we're in the process of recruiting a new head of security, and one of the applicants has given your name as a referee.'

'Really?' Alex was slightly taken aback.

The general secretary nodded.

'Peder Rydh. But as I said, we'll be in touch.'

Peder Rydh.

It still hurt to hear that name.

He still missed his former colleague.

A little while later Alex was standing on Nybrogatan, wondering why he felt so uneasy. It was as if the snowflakes were whispering to him.

This has only just begun. You have no idea of what is to come.

The falling snow was like confetti made of glass. Simon suppressed an urge to stick out his tongue to let some of the crystals land on it. The cold made him stamp his feet up and down on the spot. Why was Abraham always late? He was the kind of person who thought punctuality just didn't matter. How many hours had Simon stood waiting for him in bus shelters, outside the school, outside the tennis centre, and in a million other places? If he added it all up, and he was good at that kind of thing, he had probably spent days and days being annoyed with his friend who was incapable of turning up on time.

Who never apologised.

Just smiled when he eventually showed up.

'Have you been waiting long?' he would say.

As if he hadn't a clue about when they were due to meet, or the fact that they had agreed on a specific time.

The humiliation bothered Simon more often than he was prepared to admit. He no longer knew why it was simply taken for granted that he and Abraham should be friends. Their parents no longer saw as much of each other as they had in the past, and in school they belonged to different groups. When he thought about it, tennis was really the only thing they had in common, although that had changed too in recent weeks. They still went along together, but ever since the coach had taken Simon to one side and said that he thought it would be worth putting in a few extra hours of training to help him move forward, Abraham had begun to withdraw. They no longer played against each other, but against other boys.

Simon was careful to avoid a direct conflict with Abraham, mainly because his friend couldn't deal with losing in any way. It didn't matter whether it was in a tennis match or in school; Abraham always had to be right.

At any price.

And now Simon was standing here with his tennis racquet on his back in the bus shelter on Karlavägen, waiting for his friend yet again.

Five minutes, he thought. If he's not here in five minutes, I'm going.

To his surprise he realised that he meant it.

He had had enough. He had already waited for Abraham approximately a hundred times too often. Even his own father had told him he ought to draw the line.

The minutes crawled by as the snow came down, heavier and heavier. It was windy too. And cold. Really cold.

'Excuse me, do you have the time?'

The voice came from the side, and belonged to an elderly lady wearing a big purple woolly hat. She looked nice.

Simon found his watch in the gap between his sleeve and his glove.

'Five past four.'

'Thank you. I'm sure the bus will be here in a minute,' the woman said.

She was probably right, and Simon would be getting on

it. He straightened his back and his breathing slowed down. He was going to do it this time. Just get on the bus and go. He would look at Abraham with the same nonchalant expression he had encountered so often, and he would say something along the lines of:

'Oh, did you think we were supposed to be going together?'

A few minutes later he saw the bus approaching. The woman in the hat looked relieved, and stepped forward. But Simon didn't.

His determination ebbed away, seeping into the snow beneath his boots. Was it worth arguing about a few minutes here or there?

His cheeks burned with embarrassment and self-loathing as the bus pulled up and the doors opened. He didn't move; he just stood there as if he was frozen to the pavement.

He was so weak.

No wonder Abraham despised him.

He kicked angrily at the ground as the bus disappeared in a cloud of snow, leaving Simon feeling tired and furious.

Then he saw the car. It was moving so slowly that it almost seemed to be floating towards him. Someone was waving from the front seat. Hesitantly, almost cautiously.

He looked around in surprise, but there was no one else nearby. The hand must be waving to him.

It was only when the car pulled up in front of him that he saw who was in the passenger seat.

Abraham.

The window slid down and Abraham looked out.

'Sorry I'm late,' he said. 'We've got a lift – hop in.'

Simon was lost for words. He couldn't see who was driving.

'Hop in,' Abraham said again.

Or was he pleading with Simon?

Simon wasn't sure. His friend's voice was so shrill, his face so stiff.

'Come on, Si!'

The window began to slide up. Another bus appeared a few hundred metres behind the car.

Simon felt the weight of his sports bag on his shoulder, and thought that it would be nice to have a lift. But most of all he thought that Abraham didn't seem to want to be alone in the car, so he opened the door and slid into the back seat.

It was only when the car began to move that he realised what had just happened.

Abraham had said 'Sorry I'm late'.

Sorry.

A word Simon had never heard him use before.

He was overwhelmed by a feeling so strong he could almost touch it.

Out of the car. They had to get out of the car.

Nybrogatan, just after six o'clock in the evening. Dark and almost deserted. The call had come less than an hour ago. A man who spoke English had introduced himself as the person responsible for human resources at the Solomon Community in Östermalm; it was about the post of head of security. Was Peder able to attend an interview that same evening?

Absolutely. Peder Rydh had become the man who never said no.

Once he had had everything. Now he had virtually nothing.

Here comes the king of sand; here comes the king of nothing at all.

Unless you counted Ylva and the boys, which he did, of course. Every day Peder thanked his unlucky star that he had at least been allowed to hold onto his family, even though he had almost lost them too.

After he had lost his job with the police, things had gone downhill. Fast.

He had ended up in an abyss he hadn't even known existed, rolling in filth in a way not even a pig would have considered. He had staggered home drunk at four in the morning and thrown up in the children's shoes. Collapsed on Ylva's lap and wept until there was nothing left. She had leaned forward and whispered in his ear:

'You can try as hard as you want, Peder, but I'm not leaving you. Not again.'

Counselling had been good, but expensive. It had formed part of his package on leaving the police, thank God. At least they hadn't chucked him out at thirty thousand feet without a parachute.

He still found it difficult to sleep, and only occasionally slept right through the night. He had spent many long hours lying there wide awake, staring up at the ceiling.

Could he have done anything differently?

Had he really had a choice?

He always reached the same conclusion. No, he couldn't have done anything differently. No, he hadn't had a choice. And therefore there was no room for regret.

'Why don't I feel guilty?' he had asked his counsellor. 'I shot a man in cold blood. Three times. Two of the bullets went into his heart.'

'You do feel something,' the counsellor had said. 'That's what differentiates you from the man you killed. You know you did the wrong thing.'

No one who knew Peder regarded him as a murderer. He had been confused; he couldn't be held responsible for his actions. The court had agreed; the man who had been killed had to carry his fair share of blame for the way things turned out. The prosecutor hadn't been happy. He had appealed against the verdict of the Magistrates' Court, determined to see Peder convicted of manslaughter or premeditated murder, but the Crown Court had acquitted him as well.

Things had been different when it came to the police. They couldn't simply disregard the fact that he had voluntarily placed himself in the situation which led to the shooting of a suspect. His actions showed a lack of judgement which, combined with a whole load of other old crap, was enough to lead to his dismissal, as they put it.

Perhaps he could have appealed.

Alex had suggested it, and Peder should have listened. But Alex also said quite a lot of other things. He thought it was time Peder pulled himself together and stopped brooding. Those demands had come much too soon after what had happened; it was as if Alex expected Peder to function like some kind of machine. He couldn't do it.

Sorry to disappoint you, Alex. I have a heart and a brain, I can't just stop feeling the way I do.

To hell with the police, there were other careers for someone with Peder's background. The private security industry was growing, and there were plenty of jobs. It hadn't been difficult to get a foot in the door; at the moment Peder was working for two agencies who took it in turns to provide him with assignments. One of them had put his name forward for the post of head of security with the Solomon Community. Peder had no objections; admittedly he knew nothing whatsoever about the community, but stuff like that always became clear once you were on the spot. If you weren't happy, you just moved on.

Alex helped Peder by acting as a referee, and whatever had happened between them in the past, Peder almost always got the jobs he applied for. So Alex must have said something good about him.

Hopefully he would do the same this time.

Peder had already heard that a teacher had been shot dead outside the Solomon school in Östermalm, and had tried to read as much as he could in the media before he went to the meeting. There had been very little concrete information in the flow of news: a young woman, shot in the back. No trace of a suspect so far.

He had briefly considered calling one of his former colleagues to ask for more details, but he had a feeling it was far too early for that. Besides which, he didn't know who to call. It was a long time since he had had a handle on who was dealing with what.

When he arrived it was clear that he was expected. A security guard asked him for his ID, and he had to pass through a metal detector before entering the building. He could see a police cordon on the opposite side of the street, and officers trudging around. The body had been removed, but he could still see blood on the snow.

Red snow.

Unusual in Stockholm. Unusual anywhere, perhaps.

Peder was shown into a small office where two men were waiting for him. One of them was the man who had called him.

'Efraim Kiel – thank you for coming at such short notice.'

'No problem. I realise it's urgent.'

The other man was the community's general secretary. Peder was surprised at the title; he had thought it was only major organisations like the United Nations that had a general secretary.

'You've heard what happened?' Efraim said.

Peder nodded.

'How far have the police got?' he asked.

A flash of approval in Efraim's eyes.

'That's exactly what we're wondering. Perhaps that's not

entirely fair; we think we've established a good relationship with the police, and it seems as if they already have an idea of the direction in which they're going to start looking for the perpetrator. So far, we're satisfied.'

'Who's leading the investigation?'

'DCI Alex Recht,' Efraim said. 'The officer you gave as a referee in your application.'

Peder swallowed hard. This was something new. A few years ago he wouldn't have been sitting here asking questions about an investigation that was being led by Alex. He would have been a part of the team.

He had lost so much.

'He's good,' he managed to say.

'That was our impression too.'

Silence followed, and Efraim gazed at Peder for a long time.

'I'll be completely honest with you,' he said eventually. 'We have another candidate who is perfect for the post of head of security, but he's not available until the summer, and the community can't leave the post vacant for that length of time, particularly in view of what has just happened.'

Peder waited for him to continue.

'If you would consider accepting the post on a temporary basis until July 15, it's yours. On two conditions.'

Efraim Kiel held up two fingers.

'Which are?'

'First of all, we would want you to start immediately, preferably tomorrow. And secondly, that you are able to maintain a good relationship with the police, regardless of your background.'

'No problem,' Peder stated firmly. 'I'm just finishing an

assignment with a large company, but I only need a few hours to clear that up. And as for the police . . . I don't foresee any difficulties there either.'

He had been surprised at Efraim's words: 'regardless of your background'. What did he know about that? Quite a lot, apparently. And yet they still wanted him in such a sensitive position.

As if he could read Peder's mind, Efraim said:

'We know you lost your job with the police, and we know why. Given the circumstances, we have no problem with that. Okay?'

Without realising how tense he had become, Peder suddenly relaxed.

'Okay.'

'We'll take up your references this evening, and if you don't hear anything to the contrary, I'll expect to see you here at eight o'clock tomorrow morning. There's a great deal to do, and you'll have a lot of new routines to get used to.'

An old feeling gradually came to life inside Peder. This was the closest he had been to police work for several years. The adrenalin started pumping, and his heart rate increased.

A murder had been committed at his new place of work, and his employers had no problem with the fact that he had shot dead his brother's killer.

That told him something about their expectations of him.

It told him a great deal, in fact.

Peder had found a place where he thought he could be happy.

If it hadn't been so icy, the cold and the snow would have made her start running. Home to Spencer, home to the children, with her violin case in her hand. But her brain knew better than her heart, and sensibly exhorted her to go carefully.

Her mobile rang when she was a hundred metres from home.

'Fredrika Bergman.'

'It's Alex – did you pick up my messages?'

She hadn't listened to her voicemail, but she had seen that he had called. She had been in too much of a hurry to get home to wonder what Alex wanted in her free time.

It's Spencer I'm married to. Not the job.

Spencer with his tall, lanky body and those eyes that could see straight through her.

'Was it something in particular?' she said, wanting him to know that she did care, even if it might not seem that way.

'You could say that. A pre-school teacher was shot dead outside the Solomon school in Östermalm a few hours ago.'

Fredrika came to an abrupt halt.

'Do you need me?'

'If you've got time, it would be very helpful if you could come with me to see her parents.'

'I'll be there. I just have to go home and drop off my violin first.'

'In that case I'll wait for you.'

Spencer was in the bathroom with the children when she got in; she could see them through the open door from the hallway, her son in the bath and her daughter perched on the toilet, fully dressed. It could have been a perfectly ordinary chair as far as Saga was concerned. Spencer was kneeling beside the bath with his back to Fredrika, his shirt creased and his sleeves rolled up.

So many people had told her it would never work, that she would have to do everything herself because Spencer was too old to be supportive; a man of his age didn't have enough energy to be the parent of small children.

And they had all been wrong. Fredrika had met people of her own age who seemed older than Spencer. It wasn't the number of years that mattered, but the general attitude towards life.

'Hi,' she said.

She dropped her bag and her violin case on the floor, kicked off her shoes and went into the bathroom. She sank to her knees behind her husband and wrapped her arms around him. Just a brief moment of closeness, then she would turn her attention to the murder Alex had told her about. A woman had been shot. In the middle of the city.

Spencer's body was like part of her own. After holding him for only a few seconds she knew that something was wrong. The feeling was so strong that she stiffened, didn't even reach out to the children.

'Hi,' he said.

Saga greeted her mother cheerily like an echo of her father, energetically waving the book she was holding. Isak splashed away happily in the bath, in a world of his own.

'Has something happened?'

She had lowered her voice without knowing why.

Spencer didn't reply; he just reached down into the water and fished out a bottle of shampoo that Isak had knocked down.

'What is it?'

'Fredrika, we need to talk. When the children are asleep. It's nothing serious.'

Her arms dropped. He still hadn't turned around. Fredrika was never more sensitive to the possibility of a setback than when she was happy. The sense of impending problems was so powerful that it bothered her as much as a foul smell would have done.

'Okay,' she said. 'Alex called – I have to go into work for an hour or so.'

'You're going into work? Tonight?'

'A teacher has been shot dead at the Solomon school in Östermalm.'

'I heard about that. What's it got to do with you?'

'Apparently we're investigating the case.'

'Since when have you been involved in hate crimes?'

He lifted his son's slippery body out of the bath and wrapped him in a towel. He still hadn't looked at her.

She made an instant decision.

'I'm not leaving here until you tell me what's happened.'

Isak tore himself free and scampered out of the bathroom, stark naked. Saga hopped down from the toilet and followed him, yelling at the top of her voice. Brother and sister. Created by Fredrika and Spencer. Yet another incomprehensible mystery: the fact that it was possible to make a new person. Biological magic.

Spencer was still on his knees, while Fredrika had got to her feet.

'For heaven's sake, what is it?'

She rarely snapped or raised her voice, but she was angry now. Or just scared?

Eventually he turned and looked at her as he had done so many times before. But only for a moment. Then he disappeared again.

'I was called to a meeting today,' he said.

'And?'

She still hadn't taken off her coat, and the sweat was trickling down her back.

Spencer stood up.

'I've had an offer, but we have to make up our minds right away. Ernst has had a stroke.'

Confusion made Fredrika take a step backwards. An offer? Ernst, Spencer's colleague at the university, had had a stroke. What did that have to do with anything?

'And?' she said again.

Spencer reached for a towel and dried his hands.

'Ernst was supposed to be going to Jerusalem. He was going to be one of the principal tutors on a course at the Hebrew University. But now he can't go.'

'And they've asked you to go instead?'

'Yes. It's a two-week course.'

Two weeks. That was a long time to be away, but even so Fredrika felt calmer. She had thought he must have terrible news of some kind.

I must stop getting so stressed.

'When would this be?'

'I'd be leaving on Sunday.'

'On Sunday? In four days?'

'Yes.'

'But Spencer, that's out of the question!'

'I know.'

But you want to go, don't you?

Of course he wanted to go. Was she being unreasonable if she said no?

She shook her head.

'We'll talk about it when I get home,' she said.

She went into the hallway and put her shoes back on, picked up her bag. Spencer was standing behind her as she moved to open the door.

'You know I love you?' he said.

She smiled, but didn't let him see.

You don't get away with it that easily, Professor.

'I thought so, but it's nice of you to remind me.'

She turned around, her hand still resting on the latch.

He smiled, and she went weak at the knees. There weren't many men over sixty who looked as good as Spencer. She hoped that she and the children would keep him young for many years to come.

Her mobile rang, and she fished it out of her pocket.

Alex. She rejected the call. She went over to Spencer and kissed him.

'See you later,' she said.

'I certainly hope so. Anything else would be a disaster.'

She left her family behind, closed the door of the apartment. When she was outside the building, she called Alex.

'I'll take a cab; I'll be at HQ in ten minutes.'

Cold and darkness.

And fear. Because it was too late; because he had done something stupid.

Simon and Abraham were sitting in a van. It was parked in the middle of a forest, and the man who had locked them in wouldn't be coming back until the next day. That meant they would be alone in the bitterly cold vehicle all night.

Both boys were crying with exhaustion. If only they hadn't got into the car. If only they'd caught the bus.

When Simon thought about the drive out of the city, for some reason it was the windscreen wipers he saw in his mind's eye, scraping back and forth, trying to clear the snow so that the driver could see where he was going. Simon could see the back of his neck.

He had felt the bonds around his wrists beginning to chafe. Once when they were younger, he and Abraham had played a war game. Abraham had hurled himself at Simon and tied his hands behind his back with a skipping rope. It hadn't been much fun, and they had never done it again. In the car it hadn't been a game. His hands were tied behind his back for real this time.

Simon was terrified.

Why hadn't he got on the bus and left Abraham behind?

The only thing he knew for sure was that they were in serious trouble. Abraham hadn't said a word when Simon got into the back seat. Not until the car stopped at the traffic lights. Then he had yelled:

'He's got a gun, Si!'

And Simon had thrown himself at the door, fumbling with the handle, trying to get it open so that he could jump out. But the door was locked, and he was going nowhere.

'Fasten your seatbelt and sit still!' the driver had bellowed, and Simon had done as he was told, trembling with fear.

'Sorry,' Abraham had whispered, turning to look at Simon.

'And you shut your mouth,' the man said.

Another apology, just as bizarre as the first.

Simon had wanted to say that everything was okay, that it didn't matter. That he forgave his friend. But he didn't dare say a word.

He didn't know what the man driving the car wanted; all he knew was that they weren't heading for the tennis centre. They had set off in a completely different direction. They had stopped once, when the man tied their hands and made Abraham move into the back seat.

It was like being in some horrible film, the kind Simon's mum and dad wouldn't let him watch. The mere thought of his parents gave him a burning pain in his belly. He wanted to go home. Right now.

The man hadn't driven particularly fast. He actually looked relaxed, which frightened Simon even more. After tying them up he had dug out their mobiles, switched them off and removed the batteries. Simon had no idea why, but he realised it wouldn't make any difference if he could reach his phone; it was useless anyway.

The car had driven up onto an impressive bridge, and all at once Simon recognised the location. They were heading out towards the big palace where the king and queen lived. Why?

They passed the palace without stopping. Eventually the man turned off the road and along a smaller track that led straight into the forest. Simon had travelled a great deal with his parents, and he had never seen as many forests as there were in Sweden. Especially not in Israel, where all his relatives lived. In Israel there were only towns and sand. And the sea. Wild and blue.

The car stopped and the man told them to get out on Abraham's side. It might have been warm sitting in the back with their coats on, but it was freezing cold standing in the snow. They couldn't see the palace.

'Come with me,' the man said.

Only then had Simon noticed the large van parked a short distance away. A black van, without any windows. The man led the way and opened the back doors.

'Get in.'

His voice was deep, and he spoke English. Simon wished he hadn't understood what the man was saying; it would have been easier to kick off. But not the way things were; they both did exactly as they were told. Not even Abraham was going to take on someone who had a gun.

Inside the van it was dark and cold. There were no seats, just a hard rubber mat on the floor. You couldn't see the driver's seat, because someone had put up a wall between the front and the back of the van.

When they were standing in the van, Simon realised the man wasn't coming with them. He was still outside in the snow. The two boys automatically backed away when he switched on a torch and shone it in their faces.

And then he said the words that made Simon lose all hope of getting home any time soon.

'You can sit down over there under those blankets.' He pointed towards the corner. 'You'll be staying here until daylight.'

Then the tears came, and Simon couldn't stop them.

Over an hour had passed since then, and he was still crying.

'I've been so stupid,' Abraham sobbed. 'I believed him when he said he wanted to talk to us about tennis.'

Simon didn't answer. What would he have thought if he'd got in the car first? He didn't know.

'He said it was a coincidence,' Abraham went on. 'He said he was going to email us tonight to ask if we wanted to meet up tomorrow, and then he was driving along and he just happened to see me. I swear that's what he said.'

Simon still didn't speak.

'I want to go home,' Abraham whispered.

'Me too.'

Then they both fell silent.

And outside it grew colder and colder.

The underground car park was both cold and dark as Alex Recht walked over to the car with Fredrika. She looked excited and pensive at the same time. Alex could almost always read Fredrika Bergman's body language; she was a mistress of non-verbal communication, and had the ability to project several different moods simultaneously.

Alex focused on the fatal shooting outside the Solomon school, and ran through the latest information. Many of his colleagues had been hard at work; witnesses had been interviewed, leads followed up. But so far there were still more questions than answers. A lot more.

A mantra kept on pounding in his brain.

The first few hours are the most important. Always and without exception.

'The perpetrator was lying on a roof on the other side of the street,' Alex said as they got in the car and fastened their seatbelts. 'It's difficult to interpret the evidence because of the wind and snow, but the indications are that he – or she – was lying on his or her stomach when the shot was fired. The killer then disappeared the same way he or she got in – through the attic. We've spoken to the residents' association, and apparently people sometimes forget to close the outside door behind them when they come in from the street, so the killer didn't necessarily need the entry code or a key to get in.'

'But surely the door leading to the attic must have been locked,' Fredrika said.

Alex drove out of the grubby car park.

'I'm afraid not. They're in the process of carrying out some renovations, and the workmen need access to all parts of the building. According to the chair of the association, the attic door is left open all day, and locked in the evening.'

'In that case there must be a pretty good chance that someone saw the perpetrator arriving or leaving. If there are workmen all over the place, I mean.'

Alex shook his head, his expression grim.

'Apparently not.'

They had found very few traces of the killer. No finger-prints or footprints inside the building, which was interesting given that his or her shoes must have been soaking wet from the snow.

'But we've got footprints on the roof?' Fredrika said.

'Nothing of any use. The weather more or less destroyed them before the police got up there. The only thing we have is an indentation in the snow, which as I said indicates that the perpetrator was probably lying on his or her stomach.'

The news that they hadn't managed to track down the dead woman's boyfriend worried Alex.

'He wasn't in the apartment when the police arrived; we've tried his registered mobile number, but there's no answer. As far as we know, he's unemployed at the moment.'

'But is he a suspect?' Fredrika asked. 'Do we think he shot his girlfriend?'

'To be honest, no. Admittedly he has a record as long as

your arm, but this shooting is too clean for someone like him. However, I still need to be able to eliminate him from our enquiries. We've shown a picture of him to the witnesses who were on Nybrogatan at the time of the incident and just beforehand; no one has seen him. On the other hand, we don't know how long the killer was waiting for Josephine to come out. We've issued an appeal asking anyone who was passing in the hours before the shooting to come forward, but that's going to mean interviewing a hell of a lot of people. I'm not sure it's going to be much help, to say the least.'

Fredrika thought for a moment.

'Are we even sure that Josephine was the target? He could have been aiming at someone else who was around at the time, and missed.'

'But in that case he would have tried again, wouldn't he?'

'I'm not so sure. The shot would have frightened people, made them start running around all over the place. He might not have got a second chance.'

Alex was doubtful. The woman had been shot in the back. Her death had been inevitable and instantaneous. He couldn't imagine the bullet had been meant for anyone else, and yet that didn't make sense either: why would someone think of firing from that distance in such terrible weather? It hadn't been quite so windy at the time, but it had been snowing heavily, with the storm already moving in.

'We'll speak to her parents,' he said. 'Then we'll know where we stand.'

The silence that followed was pleasant and comfortable. Many of his colleagues seemed unable to cope with an absence of noise, and would therefore ramble on about

nothing at all. But not Fredrika. Alex glanced at her profile; she was thinking something over. Alex was well aware
of what his male colleagues thought of her appearance,
and how many of them harboured inappropriate fantasies
about her.

Which was stupid of them, particularly in view of the
fact that she was taken. Married, actually. To a man who
was older than Alex, and who had been her professor and
lover when she was a student in Uppsala, according to the
rumours. He would probably never know the truth of the
matter; Fredrika shared a great deal, but not confidences of
that kind.

'How was the rehearsal?' he asked.

She gave a start.

'Good. Great, thanks.'

Alex made an attempt to comment on her pensive mood,
although he wasn't at all sure it was a good idea.

'You look as if you've got something on your mind.'

'It's nothing. It's just that Spencer's going away.'

'So you'll be on your own with the kids?'

Fredrika looked as if she didn't know whether to laugh
or cry.

'Exactly. If one parent goes away for a few weeks, that
leaves just one at home. But I'm sure it'll sort itself out.'

Alex's phone rang. It was a man speaking English, who introduced himself as the person responsible for human resources
at the Solomon Community. He wanted to know what Alex
could tell him about his former colleague, Peder Rydh.

Alex gave the same answer as always.

He spoke briefly about one of the most talented police
officers he had ever met.

The press just kept on calling. The journalists were drawn to the dead body in the snow just like those who happened to walk past the scene of the crime. It took them less than an hour to identify the victim, to find out where she lived and to expose her boyfriend's background. From then on the reports followed two separate strands: either they talked about the fatal shooting as an example of hate crime and anti-Semitism, or they suggested that the murder might have links to organised crime in the city. The police said nothing, and the Solomon Community tried to keep any comments as brief as possible.

Efraim Kiel left the room where the general secretary was dealing with one call after another from the press. It looked as if they finally had a satisfactory solution to the problem of the vacant post; Peder Rydh had made a good impression. Efraim would have liked to avoid making a temporary appointment, but Peder Rydh seemed more than capable of doing the job.

Efraim got in touch with the three referees in Rydh's application; the last call was to his former boss, Alex Recht.

He had no problem in eliciting the information he wanted. Just as Efraim had suspected, Peder Rydh had been an extremely conscientious and very popular police officer. A little hot-headed, perhaps, and there were one or two issues regarding his attitude towards female colleagues in the past, but otherwise Alex Recht had nothing negative to say.

'What's your personal view of the incident that led to his dismissal?' was Efraim's final question.

'What do you mean?'

'What's your assessment of the situation? Do you think that what he did – shooting the man who murdered his brother – is indefensible, or can you understand his actions?'

Alex was silent for a moment, then he said:

'I have no personal opinion on the matter; I do, however, have a professional view, which I am prepared to share only with my colleagues and superiors.'

'I understand,' Efraim said, and ended the call.

With considerable relief he handed over the relevant paperwork. He would spend his last evening in Stockholm checking on how the investigation into Josephine's murder was going. He really wanted to ask how someone with such poor judgement could have been appointed to a post at the Solomon school, but it was none of his business to allocate blame; the members themselves could do that.

Efraim's train of thought was interrupted by the general secretary who had come to find him, his eyes darting from side to side, his forehead shiny with perspiration.

'Has someone else been shot?' Efraim asked dryly.

'I do hope not, but we've had a call from one of the families within our community. Two ten-year-old boys appear to have gone missing. They were supposed to have a tennis coaching session after school, but they didn't turn up. And now no one knows where they are.'

A quick glance out of the window reminded Efraim of the cold and the heavy snowfall.

A tragedy was rarely an isolated event. But people never learned.

A grief so deep that it threatened to swallow up all sense and understanding. The interview was necessary, but it would be brief.

'What do you know about your daughter's boyfriend?' Fredrika asked the couple sitting opposite her.

Josephine's mother and father. They were rather older than Fredrika had expected.

They were still in shock, their grief fresh and raw. They had seen their daughter in the hospital morgue little more than an hour ago, and now they were back in their apartment, where life was expected to go on. Fredrika didn't have the words to explain how that was supposed to happen. Alex had more idea, having lost his wife a few years earlier. Sorrow had etched fine lines on his face.

Josephine's mother glanced at her husband, who answered:

'Not much, and we're not interested either. We just assumed she would eventually realise what a waste of space he was, and leave him.'

'In what way do you regard him as a waste of space?' Alex said, making an effort to sound as neutral as possible.

'A man with a criminal record longer than the Torah is hardly likely to have made very many good choices in life.'

'So how come you knew about his background?'

Josephine's father sighed and folded his arms.

'Contacts,' he said tersely.

In the police, no doubt, Fredrika thought, and decided not

to pursue the matter. Alex seemed to be of the same opinion, and changed tack.

'Were you aware that they were living together?'

'Yes.'

'Were they happy?'

A sound that was somewhere between a sob and a snort escaped Josephine's mother.

'*Happy?* I'm sorry, is that supposed to be a serious question?'

She shook her head, angry and upset at the same time.

'Am I to understand that your daughter was dissatisfied with the relationship?' Fredrika asked gently.

Or was it just you and your husband who felt that way?

'Interpret it however you want. I'm not saying that happiness is always the same thing, but the relationship between my daughter – *our* daughter – and that man was rotten.'

'Rotten to the core,' Josephine's father said, as if he felt that his wife's words needed further clarification. 'His only contributions were expensive parties and problems.'

'He didn't have a job or an income?'

'As far as we know he had certain resources, shall we say, but no job.'

'Was he violent towards her?' Alex asked.

The question made both parents drop their guard. They looked genuinely stunned.

'No. No, I don't believe he was. She would have told us.'

Fredrika didn't think that was something that could necessarily be taken for granted, but it was probably best to leave Josephine's parents with that delusion.

'Did you see your daughter often?' she asked.

'Yes, but less so after she moved in with that man.'

'Was she involved in his criminal activities?'

As Alex spoke Fredrika could see that he might just as well have punched the parents in the face.

'What the hell are you insinuating?' the father said. 'Of course she wasn't!'

'Had she had similar boyfriends in the past?' Fredrika asked, trying to draw attention away from Alex's question.

'Never.'

Parents were always parents. They rarely said anything about their children in a way that reflected how things actually were, rather than how they wished they were. The distance between these two realities could be significant.

Fredrika looked at her watch, then at Alex. There was no reason to continue interviewing the parents. Their answers were mechanical, their tragedy incomprehensible. It was Fredrika and Alex's duty to leave them alone.

Fredrika had been spared the loss of those who were near and dear to her. Once she had almost lost Spencer in a car accident; she didn't even want to think about what it would have cost her mentally if he had died. She had been expecting their first child at the time, and at long last he had been ready to give up his marriage in order to live with Fredrika.

And now he wanted to go off to Jerusalem for two weeks. What a brilliant idea. Fredrika didn't know what bothered her most: the fact that he seemed to think it ought to be achievable in spite of the short notice, or that she herself would never have considered such a thing.

'One last question,' Alex said. 'What did Josephine do before she qualified as a teacher and started working at the pre-school?'

A pale smile shimmered across her mother's face.

'She was lost back then, our Josephine. She tried just about every job you could think of.'

'And a few you wouldn't think of,' her father muttered. 'But nothing illegal,' he added quickly.

'I presume she liked children?'

'I'm not so sure about that,' her mother said. 'But she loved her job, so I suppose she did.'

Fredrika and Alex got to their feet, both feeling relieved at the thought of leaving the apartment. No one wants to visit the province of grief with a one-way ticket.

'Did she have any enemies?' Fredrika said as they stood in the doorway.

'Not that we knew of.'

'No conflicts or arguments? Not necessarily in the recent past?'

Both parents shook their heads. They looked so abandoned standing there, so desperately lonely.

'Is there anyone we can call for you?'

'Thank you, but some close friends are on their way.'

'In that case, thank you for your time, and once again, our condolences on your incomprehensible loss.'

She felt Alex stiffen as she uttered the last three words.

Your incomprehensible loss.

It sounded so artificial, like something out of a bad play.

'We'll be in touch,' Alex said, opening the door. 'Please don't hesitate to call us at any time if anything occurs to you, or if there's anything we can do.'

Seconds later they were out in the street, and Fredrika thought that Josephine's last day had been an unusually cold one.

An unusually long day. An unusual start to the new year, in fact. Alex Recht was exhausted; he just wanted the day to end so that he could go home. His mobile rang as soon as he dropped Fredrika off outside her door.

Diana.

The second great love of his life, the fresh start he hadn't believed was possible after the death of his wife Lena.

He longed to hear her voice.

But it wasn't Diana. It was his boss.

'How did it go with the parents?'

'I don't really know what to say, except that we're none the wiser.'

His boss starting coughing, a rattling, smoker's cough. As far as Alex knew, smoking was his only vice, but it was remarkable to think that one wrong choice could bring a person so much closer to the end of their life.

'We've had another call from the Solomon Community.'

Alex waited, hoping this wasn't more bad news. But it was. First of all came something that he already knew.

'Have you heard that Peder Rydh has just been appointed as their new head of security?'

'I found out when they called and asked me for a reference earlier this evening.'

'What did you say to them?'

'The same as I always say. That he was a very talented police officer with certain issues regarding his temperament, and one or two problems when it came to his attitude towards women in the past.'

His boss was coughing again.

'Issues regarding his temperament? I suppose you could put it that way.'

Alex had no interest in discussing the matter any further. A lot of things would have to change before he stopped supporting Peder Rydh.

'It's most unfortunate that he's been appointed to the post at this particular moment. Don't you agree?'

'Perhaps.'

'I mean, you're going to have to work with him – have you thought about that?'

'I've worked with Peder before, and we've never had any problems.'

Untrue. And he knew it. His boss wasn't slow to pick him up on his mistake.

'I'm sorry – you've never had any problems?'

Alex couldn't listen to this; he didn't have the energy to get involved in a discussion. His current boss had never actually worked with Peder, but knew his history like everyone else.

'I know, I know.'

He thought back to the beginning of their conversation.

'So did the Solomon Community call to ask you for a reference too?'

'No, they just happened to mention Rydh in connection with the real reason for their call.'

'Which was?'

'Two boys who belong to the community didn't arrive at their tennis coaching session. The parents have reported them missing to the police, and the case should end up on your desk. You're the person who's most familiar with this kind of thing.'

Of course. Shit.

'There's absolutely no way that Fredrika and I can deal with two major investigations – the fatal shooting and two missing kids. Forget it.'

'I realise that; we'll sort it out tomorrow. Unless of course there's a connection, in which case it would probably be better to expand your team. Fast.'

Why would there be a connection? Because all three were Jews? Because the boys had gone missing on the day the teacher was shot? Were they actually missing? Kids got the most peculiar ideas; they could be back home in a couple of hours.

'Have the parents been interviewed?' he asked, sincerely hoping that he wouldn't have to speak to them as well.

'Yes, you don't need to think about that for the time being. And the Stockholm City Police and the National Crime Unit are helping to search for the boys. You won't have to deal with any of this until tomorrow.'

Good. Tomorrow was another day.

A busy day, by the sound of it.

'The Solomon Community is also organising a search. They've gathered in the centre in Östermalm and they're ringing everyone in the boys' classes to see if anyone has heard from them. You could drop in on your way home, if you feel like it.'

Why would he want to do that? They'd be in touch if the boys turned up.

It was eight o'clock. Alex wanted to go home. Listen to Diana telling him about her day. Have something to eat. Ring his children. If necessary he could come back in later, leave his mobile switched on all night.

But to his surprise he heard himself say:

'I'll drop by and call you afterwards.'

'Good. And Fredrika Bergman? Is she still playing the violin?'

'She's with her family.'

Alex's response was curt and angry. To protect Fredrika. He thought about her frown, how pensive she had been. He hoped she wasn't having problems at home. The way she had looked today, she wouldn't have the energy to fight a war on two fronts.

The weather was atrocious, and it seemed to be getting worse all the time. Stockholm looked deserted as he drove towards the Solomon Community for the second time today. Cars covered in snow lined the streets like white sculptures, silent and motionless.

Nothing evoked stronger feelings than children at risk; Alex was well aware of that, so he wasn't surprised when he walked in and saw how many people had gathered to support the parents in their search for the two boys.

The general secretary recognised him.

'Any news?' he said, his tone almost pleading. He adjusted his glasses which had slipped down his nose. The yarmulke perched on the back of his head was black and crooked. It was interesting to observe the effects of a divergence from normality.

'I'm afraid not,' Alex said. 'I was about to ask you the same question.'

The general secretary shook his head gloomily.

'Not a trace.'

'And there's no reason to suspect that the boys might have gone off somewhere of their own accord?'

'No. Where would they go? They're ten years old, there's a blizzard and it's minus five out there.'

Just as Alex opened his mouth to say something about children who went missing and where they usually went, he caught sight of someone he hadn't seen for a long time.

Peder Rydh.

A tsunami of emotions surged through his body. Peder had been there when Alex's career reached its zenith, when he was asked to lead his own freestanding team. He had selected Peder himself, and Fredrika had joined immediately afterwards. As time went by they had become one of the best teams Alex had ever worked with.

The pain of loss seared his soul like salt on an open wound. He was leading a similar team now, with a small core and a wide periphery. But without Peder Rydh.

When had he last seen Peder? They had bumped into one another in town about a year ago, but that was all.

Peder was sitting at one of the tables, deep in thought. He was holding a sheet of paper in his hand, frowning as he read. The years had left a clear impression on his face. He looked hardened. Hardened but balanced.

'Excuse me,' Alex said to the general secretary, and walked over towards Peder.

When he was only a metre or so away, Peder looked up and saw Alex. His face broke into such a broad grin that

Alex had to take several deep breaths to stop the tears from coming.

They hugged each other tightly, without saying a word.

'You're looking well,' Alex said when they had let go.

'I'm fine,' Peder said. 'I don't actually start until tomorrow, but they asked if I'd come in tonight.'

A shadow passed across his face, and a flicker of the defiance that had been so typical of him was visible for a split second.

'What can you tell me?' Alex said.

They sat down at the table. This was neither the time nor the place to discuss private matters.

'Not much. The boys didn't turn up for their tennis coaching session, and they hadn't said anything to their friends about other plans.'

'Have you met the parents?'

'The mothers are over there; the fathers are out searching.'

'Out searching.' As if that was a feasible option. A search party in Stockholm city centre. In a blizzard. Senseless and pointless.

'They seem, at least at first glance, to be harmonious families. One of the fathers is perhaps a little unstable, but I can't decide whether that's because of what's happened, or whether he's always like that.'

Of course not – how could he possibly know when the investigation had been going on for less than an hour? And a person could be unstable for all kinds of different reasons.

Peder lowered his voice.

'The community has a lot of contacts within the police.'

'So I've realised,' Alex said.

'One name in particular has been mentioned several times

over the last hour: Eden Lundell. I've never heard of him or her – have you?'

He certainly had.

Eden Lundell. A woman so strong that she could declare war on any country, all by herself. They had worked together only once, but that was enough. Alex had the greatest respect for Eden Lundell.

'I know who she is,' he said. 'She's a very special woman.'

'Special enough to find two missing boys and clear up a premeditated murder?'

'I'd be very surprised if she got involved in all this,' Alex said.

'Why?'

'Because she's Säpo's head of counter-terrorism.'

He was so damned good.

Like most other men, her beloved husband wasn't perfect, but he was a bloody good lover. Which was fortunate, because otherwise he would never have won Eden Lundell's heart.

She buried her face in his shoulder to smother her cries as she came. Pulled him closer, wrapped her legs more tightly around him. Her heart was pounding like a hunted animal, and she could feel his sweaty upper body pressing down on hers. Then he stopped moving and her pulse rate dropped.

Eden was satisfied. Obviously a successful encounter.

Mikael withdrew and lay down by her side. The sheet stuck to her skin as he laid his arm across her breasts and breathed against her neck. Closeness was important to him, and she let him be. For a while, anyway.

'Do you mind if I have a cigarette?' she said.

'Eden, for fuck's sake!'

'You can't blame me for asking. One day you might say yes.'

'No bloody chance.'

'Goodness me, all this swearing. Are priests really allowed to swear?'

'This one is.'

She caressed his arm distractedly. The bedroom still smelled of fresh paint. From the street came the muted sound of traffic. Quieter than usual; the bad weather must have persuaded people to stay at home.

It had been Eden's idea to sell their boring house and move into the city. Mikael had taken some convincing, but when Eden made the point that she would have more time for the family if she had a shorter commute, he gave in.

'Was it my mobile or yours that rang just now?' she said.

'Bound to be yours. The rest of us switch off our phones when we're making love.'

Making love – was that really what they had just been doing? Eden would have said they were screwing, and that they knew exactly what they were doing.

'You can't be serious,' Mikael said, raising his head as she slipped out of bed.

'I'm just going to check,' Eden said as she walked across the room to pick up her bag.

She sat down on the edge of the bed and took out her mobile. Mikael grabbed it.

'Give it back!'

Sometimes she sounded like her daughters, barking out staccato orders and expecting instant compliance. However, she was far superior to the girls when it came to getting her own way. Mikael maintained that he and the children lived in the shadow of Eden's whims and caprices, but she thought that was unfair.

It wasn't her fault that others were so weak.

Mikael gave her the phone and she listened to the message that came from a withheld number. It was the general secretary of the Solomon Community.

'Eden, I don't know if you're in Sweden or if you've been following the news, but we've had two terrible incidents today. A member of staff at the Solomon school was shot dead this afternoon, and this evening two boys have been reported missing by their parents. Give me a call if you can.'

She put the phone back in her bag. Mikael looked pleased as she lay back, resting on his outstretched arm.

'Anything important?'

'Nothing that can't wait until tomorrow.'

She had already heard about the shooting, but not the missing boys.

Do I need to get involved? No.

For some obscure reason the Solomon Community had got the idea that they could count on her support and resources in various situations. This was, to put it mildly, a misapprehension. She felt no loyalty whatsoever towards what were somewhat inaccurately referred to as 'her people'.

'I thought we might go away in March,' Mikael said.

Did you indeed?

'Where?'

'Somewhere hot. Just you and me and the girls.'

As if they usually went away with a whole crowd of other people.

'I don't know if I can get away from work.'

'I'm sure you can, if you book the time early enough.'

'We've talked about this before; you have to realise there's a difference between what you do and what I do.'

Mikael was a priest, and Eden loved him for that. Everything was possible in Mikael's world. The sky was the limit as far as he was concerned, but his naive attitude towards time, and above all to obligations outside the family, drove her crazy. It created conflict and all too often led to arguments.

Things had been calm for a while now; Christmas had been enjoyable, and January hadn't sprung any surprises. Eden had even managed to drop the girls off at day care and pick them up, just like an ordinary mum.

A *normal* mum. One who didn't feel like screaming 'For God's sake will you hurry up!' as soon as she saw the twins ambling towards her, eager to show and tell what they had been doing at day care. As if they had all the time in the world. As if it was the most obvious thing in the world, they would hand her drawings and trolls made of stones and all kinds of crap that Eden realised other people took into work and placed on their desks; personally, she just wanted to chuck the whole lot in a box in the garage. She understood that the children thought they had made something wonderful, but she felt as if she would be doing them a disservice if she lied. Ugly was ugly, end of.

'How long do you think you'll stay with Säpo?' Mikael asked.

Excellent, he had already dropped his holiday plans.

'Why do you ask? I've only been there just over six months.'

'I'm asking because I know you, Eden. You're a restless soul.'

She stared up at the ceiling. Was that true? Was she restless? Maybe, maybe not.

'I'll stay for a while. There's a lot to do within their organisation before I'm satisfied.'

'Their organisation? Not yours?'

No. She would never again make the same mistake as she had in London, becoming as one with an organisation that wasn't hers after all.

The desire for a cigarette grew too strong.

'Back in a minute,' she said, getting out of bed again.

'Say what you like, nobody could accuse you of being a romantic,' Mikael said, and for a moment it bothered her that he didn't sound in the least ironic.

She let the comment pass. In the bathroom she unzipped her toilet bag and took out the packet of cigarettes and the lighter she always kept in the side pocket. She ran water into the hand basin, then opened the window and lit up. She closed her eyes as she blew out the smoke, the cold air cooling her body. Just a few drags, then she was satisfied. The odd snowflake found its way into the bathroom, melting on her bare skin.

As usual she doused the cigarette under the running water and flushed the stub down the loo. She was brushing her teeth when her mobile rang again.

She went back into the bedroom. Why couldn't the Solomon Community understand that she was neither willing nor able to help them?

But it wasn't the Solomon Community. It was her boss, Buster Hansson, the General Director of Säpo, usually known as GD.

'We have a problem,' he said. 'Efraim Kiel is back in Sweden.'

The telephone slipped out of Eden's hand and landed on the floor.

'What's happened?' Mikael asked, sitting up in bed.

'Nothing,' she said, picking up the phone.

But inside she was in turmoil.

Efraim Kiel. She could think of several reasons why he might turn up in Stockholm.

None of them was good news.

It was almost nine thirty, and Fredrika Bergman was sitting alone in the kitchen with a cup of tea. Spencer was in their bedroom, and she had asked him to stay there. They had had an unexpectedly bitter argument about how he thought he could possibly go off to Jerusalem, because it turned out they had completely different perceptions of what was achievable, and what they could demand of one another.

'How would you react if I suddenly said I was going off to play the violin for two weeks?' Fredrika had snapped.

'The fact is you don't actually do everything at home while I just watch,' Spencer had replied, as if that had anything to do with Fredrika's question.

'What's that got to do with anything? Am I supposed to go around feeling grateful because I don't have to look after the kids and run the house on my own? Is that what you're saying?'

Spencer had made the mistake of sounding more than a little condescending in his response.

'If I travel to Jerusalem to work for two weeks, it's hardly the same as you going off to China to play the guitar.'

At that point Fredrika had hit the roof.

'I don't play the fucking guitar! And China? Are you going senile?'

That had been the starting pistol for an extremely undignified row.

So now she was sitting alone in the kitchen. The guitar. In China. She couldn't help it, she just burst out laughing. Half her girlfriends would have advised her to file for divorce. Right now.

For God's sake, Spencer, sort yourself out.

The strength in their relationship had always – *always* – been the unconditional trust, and the fact that they were able to communicate with one another. During all those years when Spencer was still married, they had still known exactly where they were; he had never disappointed her by giving her false expectations or making promises he couldn't keep. Not once. Their situation was complicated enough; there was no need to make it even more complex with a whole load of lies.

Fredrika wearily ran her hand across the surface of the table. A table on which Spencer had actually taken her just a couple of nights ago, when the children were staying over with their grandparents. She hoped her parents liked babysitting, because if she was going to be on her own for two weeks, she wouldn't be able to cope without them.

If only everything wasn't so fragile.

She had never thought she would have everything she had dreamt of.

Spencer.

The children.

The violin.

Now that she had all of those things and was happy for once, why did Spencer have to make such a fuss about something so trivial? Or was she the one who was kicking off? Because she was so afraid of losing everything?

She heard footsteps behind her.

'I'm sorry if I upset you,' Spencer said. 'You're right and I'm wrong. Two weeks is too long.'

He sat down at the table. He even looked good in pyjamas. Fredrika tilted her head on one side, wondering what she would have wanted him to say if she had been offered the chance to go to Israel.

That's terrific!

'Go to Jerusalem,' she said. 'You have to go.'

'That means you'll be on your own with the kids for two weeks.'

Or for the rest of my life, if I suffocate you.

'It'll be fine. I'll ask Mum to help out.'

His face broke into a smile.

'Thank you,' he said.

'Don't thank me,' Fredrika said. 'You can return the favour some time.'

He got up and moved around the table. Placed a hand on her shoulder.

'Are you coming to bed soon?'

'I'm just going to check my phone first.'

Spencer wasn't the only one who worked at strange times. *The job.*

She yawned and picked up her phone to see if Alex had called about the murdered teacher. Perhaps something new had come up during the evening that she ought to know about before she went into work tomorrow.

God, it was cold outside. The winter chill seemed to find its way in through the walls and the floor, making her shiver.

The snow was falling heavily now, covering everything in its path. Fredrika curled up on the kitchen chair and read a message from Alex.

Two ten-year-old boys had gone missing. Alex's team would probably be working on the case tomorrow if the boys hadn't turned up by then.

As she read the message she was transported back four and a half years. She had been the new recruit, and for several terrible days that summer they had worked against the clock to find a little girl who had disappeared from a train. Fredrika still remembered her name.

Lilian Sebastiansson.

Fredrika's first difficult case with Alex's team.

Back then she had been the enigmatic single woman approaching thirty-five who never said a word about her private life. The woman who was sleeping with her former university professor, pretending that he wasn't the man in her life. The only member of the team who had a civilian background rather than police training.

Resolutely she got to her feet. She hoped the missing boys were at least somewhere indoors, in the warmth. If they were outside they wouldn't survive the bitterly cold night.

CONCLUSION

FRAGMENT II

The detective inspector who thought he had seen everything is standing in the bedroom, frozen to the spot. He cannot take his eyes off the man lying on the bed with his two children. Around them a handful of people are trying to work a miracle. Anything else would be of no use. The inspector has seen enough dead bodies during his career to know that no one on that bed is alive.

There are paper bags on the floor. Without saying it out loud, he knows that someone has drawn on them.

He hears a commotion, shouting from the stairwell.

'She got away! Stop her!'

But the inspector knows that it is not possible to stop the woman who is on her way up the stairs. Standing in her way would constitute attempted suicide.

Let her come, he thinks. After all, this moment is unavoidable.

And then she is standing in the doorway, and he turns to face her.

Snow in her hair, snow on her clothes, a violin case in her hand.

No one moves, apart from those who are trying to bring the dead back to life. The woman doesn't move either. At first it looks as if she is about to take a step towards the bed, but then she changes her mind. Stays exactly where she is. Slowly she puts down the violin.

Someone pulls out a chair, asks if she would like to sit down.

She doesn't answer; she simply stands there. She doesn't scream, doesn't shed a tear. Perhaps because it is impossible to take in what she sees before her? A future without her family. A life without the man the inspector believes she regarded as the love of her life. Probably a life without children, because how long does a woman remain fertile? Not long enough for her to have more children than those she has already given birth to, the children who are now lying dead in her bed.

'Do you know her?' a colleague says, nodding towards the woman in the doorway.

Oh yes, they know one another. Well enough for the inspector to realise that it is best not to approach her.

'Is there anyone we can call?'

He can't answer that. Is there?

Then one of the paramedics by the bed says:

'I've found a pulse! She's alive!'

A miracle has happened.

One of the children is alive.

EARLIER

The Second Day

THURSDAY, 26 JANUARY 2012

The snowstorm was over.

Simon blinked into the light as the man told him to get out of the van. Frozen stiff. He was enclosed in a bubble of fear, and he couldn't make a hole in it. He didn't think he had ever been so cold in his whole life. The night had felt like an eternity. He and Abraham had lain very close to one another, covered by a blanket that was far too thin. Neither of them had slept. They had both wept, shaking with cold.

All night.

'Where's Abraham?' Simon asked.

His legs could hardly hold him up, and his voice was so thin, destroyed by tears and exhaustion.

There wasn't a sound to be heard. No wind whispering in the tree tops, no animals moving around.

Simon didn't know where he was. A little while ago someone had got in the van and started the engine. The vehicle had begun to move, and the two boys had looked at one another in a panic.

After just a few minutes, the van had stopped.

The man had come for Abraham first. Simon had heard the snow crunching beneath their feet as they walked past the side of the van, then everything had gone quiet. He had remained motionless for a long time, his body rigid with fear.

Until a loud gunshot made him leap to his feet as quickly as if it had been fired inside the van. Warm piss trickled down his legs. Simon had gone hunting with his father several times, and knew the sounds that went with such expeditions. But the shot he had just heard had nothing to do with the hunt. He could feel it in every fibre of his ten-year-old body.

He waited and waited.

Exhausted and even more terrified, he sank to the floor. At long last the man came back.

Without Abraham.

The man didn't answer his question.

'Tell me where he is!'

Simon's voice was weak as he tried to shout.

He couldn't control himself any longer. Tears poured down his grubby cheeks.

'I want to go home,' he sobbed. 'Please let me go home.'

The man just looked at him. Then he took a cigarette out of his pocket and lit it. He gazed around in the way that people do when they don't really have anything to look at. His eyes roamed across the bare trees without alighting anywhere.

By the time he eventually spoke, Simon had dropped to his knees in the snow, his arms wrapped around his body. Where had Abraham gone?

He gave a start when he heard the man's voice.

'Has your father told you about the Paper Boy?' the man said, staring at him.

Simon nodded.

'Answer me!'

Simon wiped the snot and tears from his face with the back of his hand.

'Yes, he has.'

The man took a long drag of his cigarette.

'Good. In that case you know why you're here.'

Did he?

Simon didn't understand a thing.

The cigarette smoke smelled strong, making him cough. The piss in his pants made them feel stiff.

'Get up.'

Automatically he did as he was told. His legs were so cold they hurt.

The man threw his cigarette down on the snow and slowly turned to face him.

Simon took a step backwards.

It looked as if smoke was coming out of the man's mouth as he breathed. He ran a hand over his chin.

'Your father had the greatest respect for the Paper Boy when he was little. As you know, the Paper Boy is happiest in the warmth and the darkness. He sleeps during the day, and comes to the children at night. But this time he has made an exception, and has come in the cold and the daylight instead.'

Simon couldn't think clearly.

The Paper Boy.

'Why does he come to the children at night?'

His voice was no more than a whisper.

The man grew serious.

'He steals them. Takes them from their parents and tears them to pieces.'

Suddenly the man was angry. He hissed:

'And you know what? Your father became just like him.'

Simon realised two things simultaneously:

He was in a very dangerous situation. And he had no idea how to get out of it.

The man took a step towards him, and Simon fell backwards in the snow as he tried to move away.

'Get up and take off your shoes and socks.'

Simon blinked.

'You heard me. Take off your shoes and socks and I'll give you a chance.'

Without waiting for Simon to obey, he walked past him and opened the driver's door of the van. Simon stood there as if he had turned to stone, and saw the man reach inside for something. When he turned around he was holding a rifle.

Simon started crying again.

'There's no need to be afraid. If you just do as I say, I'll give you a chance.'

He lowered the gun as if to show that he meant what he said.

'Do as I say and I'll let you go.'

With trembling hands Simon slowly began to undo his shoelaces.

His feet were freezing cold.

And he was weary.

Bone weary.

As he stood barefoot in front of the man, he almost didn't care what was going to happen.

The man stared at him for a long time.

'Okay, Simon. Listen carefully. I want you to run as fast as you can. Do you understand?'

Not really.

Run?

Run where?

'Run! Run like the wind, and you might get away from him.'

Simon blinked again, still numb with cold and shock.

'Who?' he whispered. 'Who's after me?'

The man raised his gun.

'I am after you. I am the Paper Boy.'

It was such a beautiful day that you just wanted to get in the car and head out of the city. Drive out into the country and let the children go crazy in the snow.

But a conscientious person like Fredrika Bergman couldn't do that. Not with a murder and two missing boys to think about. The morning passed in silence as she and Spencer moved around the apartment like two restless souls, getting the children ready for day care.

'So you'll pick them up this afternoon?' she said eventually as she stood in the doorway with her son and daughter in the double buggy.

'Of course.'

Of course.

Now Fredrika had agreed that he could go away for two weeks, there was nothing he wouldn't do for her.

Very wise.

Fredrika had hardly slept. The missing boys and memories of the past had kept her awake. In the middle of the night, at God knows what time, she had glanced over at Spencer and realised that he too was wide awake, lying on his side and watching her in the darkness. He couldn't settle either.

'I don't know what I'd do if you left me,' he had whispered. 'Are you sure it's okay if I go?'

He had reached out and touched her chin.

The desire came from nowhere, and she had leaned over and kissed his forehead. His cheeks. His chin. And his mouth.

'Of course it is,' she had whispered in return.

The clear air and open sky made life seem even more tranquil as she left the apartment block and ploughed through the fresh snow with the buggy. She was taking the children to day care, then she was going to work. One foot in front of the other. Always moving forwards, never backwards.

Soon she would be there. Get to grips with the case of the missing boys.

She offered up a silent prayer that it wouldn't be too late by the time they found them.

It was as if Stockholm had become a different city overnight. Someone had shot a teacher, standing on the pavement surrounded by children. And the two boys who had disappeared on their way to a tennis lesson were still missing.

'I can't lead both investigations,' Alex Recht said to his boss first thing in the morning.

'I've asked for the murder to be handed over to the National Crime Unit. I'd like you to focus on the boys.'

Alex was frustrated.

'But I've already made a start on the murder!'

'Yes, but we didn't know these boys were going to disappear. I've spoken to a colleague in the NCU; they're very familiar with Josephine's boyfriend, and would like to take over the case as part of their own work in mapping serious organised crime.'

But what if Josephine had been shot for some other reason? What if her death had nothing to do with her boyfriend?

In that case they would have to pick it up later. They had the capacity to run only one of the two investigations. Alex's team was still incomplete.

'We can't have a team that consists of just two people,' he had said when it had first been suggested that he should lead a special investigative unit once more.

'Absolutely not. You'll have a core team of three, as before. Recruitment will be down to you. If you need additional resources, all you have to do is ask and I'll allocate colleagues on a temporary basis to assist with any ongoing preliminary investigations.'

But recruitment took time, and at the moment the team consisted of Alex and Fredrika. They had put together an advertisement for the third member, and had started to go through the applications as they came trickling in, but so far none of them had been particularly impressive.

Fredrika sailed into the office, her cheeks rosy after walking to work in the cold; her eyes were brighter than they had been the previous day. Playing the violin was clearly doing her good.

'Forget the teacher,' Alex said. 'We're working on the boys.'

Fredrika leaned against the wall.

'Missing kids,' she said. 'The perfect first case for our little team, wouldn't you say?'

She pulled a face.

'You're thinking about the little girl who disappeared from the train?' Alex said. 'Lilian Sebastiansson?'

As if we could ever forget her.

'Aren't you?'

'Only because it was the first serious case we investigated; otherwise I can't see any similarities.'

Fredrika shrugged. 'Maybe not, but children are children, after all.'

Alex knew she was right. He really didn't like this business of the two missing Jewish boys. The media had gone crazy overnight, wanting more information, more details, but Alex refused to feed them at such an early stage.

'Is it just you and me?' Fredrika asked.

'We can request any additional resources we need, but we'll be leading the case.'

That wasn't strictly true. Alex was the boss, not Fredrika, but as there were only two of them that seemed like an unnecessary distinction.

The media had been given pictures of the boys as evening turned into night and the snowstorm reached its peak. Public reaction was instant. Everyone thought they could help. Every single person who had been in inner city Stockholm and seen a child with a rucksack and a woolly hat trudging along unaccompanied by an adult decided it was their duty to get in touch with the police.

'Have we had any calls that might be useful?' Fredrika asked.

'Not yet.'

'So where do we start?'

'We'll go over to the Solomon Community; you interview one set of parents and I'll take the other. If they're there, of course. Yesterday the fathers were out searching.'

As he got up and reached for his coat, there was a loud knock on the door and an assistant came in.

'An elderly lady called and said she's sure she saw one of the boys at a bus stop on Karlavägen yesterday afternoon.'

'And what makes her any more reliable than all the rest

of the people who've called and said more or less the same thing?' Alex wanted to know as he pulled on his coat.

'Because it's the stop from which the boys always catch the bus to the tennis centre, according to their parents. And because she says the boy had the kind of bag that's used to carry a tennis racquet.'

His first day at work was actually his second.

Peder Rydh slithered along on the fresh snow that hadn't yet been cleared from the pavements. His sons had cheered when he dropped them off at day care and they saw the thick white blanket of virgin snow waiting for them in the playground.

'We'll be able to get the toboggans out!' one of the boys had roared with delight.

There were days when Peder wished he was five years old, wanting nothing more from life than good weather and time to play freely. His brother Jimmy's life had been a bit like that; he had remained a child after falling from a swing and injuring his head.

On that occasion they had been playing a bit too freely.

Peder walked faster. It was never a good idea to start the day by thinking about Jimmy. The memory still hurt; the sense of loss was still immense.

But I avenged your death, little brother. And it was worth the cost.

The smell of coffee greeted him as he arrived at the Solomon Community. The air felt thin, as if too many people were all trying to breathe it in at the same time. The noise level was muted; some people had been there all night, ringing around to ask about the boys.

No one had seen anything.

No one had heard anything.

The general secretary took Peder to one side and went over everything that had happened since Peder went home at just after two o'clock in the morning to grab a few hours' sleep. The general secretary hadn't slept at all, which made Peder feel a little unsure of himself. Should he have stayed all night too, then worked all day as well?

'Still no sign of them,' his boss said. 'The police have no information either. The parents have kept their phones switched on, of course, but no one has contacted them to demand a ransom or anything like that. So it doesn't seem to be a kidnapping.'

'I think perhaps it's a little early to draw that kind of conclusion,' Peder said. 'There are different kinds of kidnapping.'

The general secretary went on as if Peder hadn't spoken:

'The parents aren't rich; they wouldn't be able to pay a large ransom. My guess is that some lunatic has taken them, and that it's exceptionally important that they are found as quickly as possible.'

The police officer in Peder, the one who had been sacked in disgrace, suddenly came to life.

First of all, people were sometimes kidnapped in spite of the fact that their relatives weren't rich.

Secondly, the possibility that the boys had disappeared voluntarily couldn't be ruled out.

And thirdly, it didn't matter whether they had gone off on their own or been abducted by someone else – finding them was still a matter of urgency.

'What about their phones?' he said. 'I'm assuming both

boys have their mobiles with them – do they ring when you call the numbers?'

'They seem to be switched off.'

'We'll check with the police, see if they've managed to pinpoint their position. There's no guarantee that the boys and the phones will be in the same place, but at least it would be a start.'

A shadow passed across the general secretary's face.

'If the person who's taken them is thinking far enough ahead to realise he can be tracked using their phones, and has dumped them . . .' he began.

'Then he's a man with a plan,' Peder finished the sentence for him.

Silently he added: And in that case we're in trouble, because even the weather is on his side.

The boys would have had no chance of surviving the night if they had managed to get away from their abductor. They would have frozen to death within an hour.

The police officer inside Peder refused to go away.

Two children and a pre-school teacher.

All members of the Solomon Community.

All with a clear link to the Solomon school.

It was obvious that this couldn't possibly be a coincidence.

The only question was what was going to happen next?

One of the boys had definitely been seen at the bus stop on Karlavägen. The elderly lady confirmed this when Fredrika Bergman showed her some pictures of the children.

'He's the one I saw,' she said, pointing to the photograph of the one called Simon. 'I spoke to him.'

'What about?'

'I asked him what time it was, and he answered very politely.'

Fredrika looked at the photographs provided by the parents. Both boys looked so serious; Simon in particular wore a melancholy expression that affected his whole appearance. The other boy, Abraham, looked more insolent. Cocky. The kind of kid who might get hold of a boy like Simon and shove his head down the toilet, just because it was fun.

Fredrika stopped her train of thought. It was wrong to think badly of children. They deserved more protection than adults in that respect; they weren't yet fully formed individuals. It wasn't right for Fredrika to come up with aspects of Abraham's character when she didn't even know him.

'Have you remembered anything else?' she said to the woman, keen to bring the conversation to an end as quickly as possible so that she and Alex could get over to Östermalm.

'I have, actually. He looked so angry.'

'Angry?'

'Yes, really upset. Almost as if he was standing there getting quite worked up about something. And I was surprised when he didn't get on the bus.'

'Why?'

'Because he was obviously waiting for it. Lots of different routes use that stop, but I saw his face change when we spotted the bus. And then he didn't move a muscle. It was as if he was standing there debating with himself, deciding whether to get on or not.'

Fredrika could clearly see the boy at the bus stop in the snow. It had been just after four o'clock, and the tennis lesson was due to begin at four thirty. Even if he'd already changed, which his parents said was usually the case, he didn't have much time. She presumed he hadn't caught the bus because Abraham wasn't there – but why was Abraham late? He was due at the tennis centre at four thirty as well.

Fredrika thanked the woman for taking the time to come in, and showed her how to find her way out.

The last sighting of Simon was at the bus stop, which meant that at least they had a geographical location to start from.

'We need to go over what we know,' she said to Alex a little while later when they were in the car on the way to Östermalm.

'Haven't we already done that?'

'No. We've had too much to think about – first the fatal shooting, then the missing boys. I'm not saying that everyone isn't doing what they're supposed to be doing – they are. But we haven't yet sat down and worked out a clear picture. For example, do we have the slightest idea where the boys went missing?'

'On their way to their tennis lesson,' Alex said. 'Both of them were in school, then they went off to do some home-work with different friends. They always met at the bus stop at four o'clock.'

'Exactly. But we don't think they got on the bus?'

'We've spoken to the bus company and all the drivers who might have picked them up, but no one remembers seeing them.'

'So where does that take us? Do we think that they decided to go and do something else, for some unknown reason? Or that they started walking instead of catching the bus? The woman who saw Simon at the stop said she thought he looked as if he wanted to get on the bus when it arrived, but then stayed where he was.'

Alex pulled up at a pedestrian crossing and waited for a man pushing a buggy to cross.

'In that case I suppose we can assume he was waiting for Abraham,' he said. 'And when he turned up . . .'

'Yes?'

'No idea. The trail ends at the bus stop. That's where they were last seen.'

'Wrong,' Fredrika said. 'That's where Simon was last seen. It would be very useful if we could say the same about Abraham. Where are we up to with the analysis of their tele-phone traffic? Have we been able to pinpoint their mobiles?'

They had arrived, and Alex was looking for a parking space. The car glided slowly along, the snow crunching beneath its tyres.

'I checked while you were talking to the woman from the bus stop; both mobiles are switched off. No signal whatsoever. I've asked for lists of their calls over the last few months, and we should have those in an hour or so.'

'Do we know who each of them called last?' Fredrika said as she pointed. 'There's a space.'

'Simon's mother spoke to him after he left school; she said he sounded just the same as usual. He said he wanted meatballs for tea.'

He reversed into the space.

'If he was talking about tea, then it definitely sounds as if he was intending to go straight home after tennis. What about Abraham?'

'He spoke to his father before he went to meet Simon. He'd been doing some homework at a friend's house. But I don't know if that was the last call he made or received.'

They left the car and set off towards the Solomon Community. The police cordon outside the school had been removed, and the snow had done a good job of covering the blood. The street looked perfectly normal.

'They're ten years old, Alex. We have to gain access to the family's computers, see what they've been doing on the internet. That's where children communicate these days, however sad that might sound.'

'We'll sort it out with their parents now. To be honest I'd be more worried about that if we were dealing with young girls.'

'Because of the risk that they might have arranged to meet someone they've got to know online?' Fredrika said.

'Yes. Unfortunately we live in an age where it's more common for girls to be picked up by perverts.'

'But that doesn't mean boys are safe. These two are young enough to attract all kinds of perpetrators.'

Paedophiles. That was the word she had meant to say, but she couldn't quite bring herself to do so. The involvement of a paedophile was always the last thing they wanted, and the worst case scenario.

She pushed aside the unwanted images in her mind and decided to think of something else. They knew where Simon had last been seen. Now she wanted to know where Abraham's trail ended.

The heat inside the centre was overwhelming. Alex automatically unbuttoned his coat and noticed that Fredrika had done the same. The situation seemed almost unchanged from the previous evening, with several people working hard to find out where the boys had gone. However, the energy level had dropped. He could hear it in their voices, see it in their body language. They had already phoned everyone they could think of; everyone who might be able to help was already here.

Peder Rydh met them at the door. He and Alex shook hands, but Fredrika reacted as Alex had done the previous day and gave him a hug. The memory of a time Alex could never recapture flared up once more. He, Fredrika and Peder had been a super-troika, and those years had corresponded with the most difficult time in his private life. The loss of Lena to cancer had damaged him in so many ways. Diana only had to mention a word like mammogram or biopsy for him to panic.

'Darling, you can't go around being scared of life itself,' she would say.

As if it were life and not death he feared. He had no problem with the idea that we have a limited time on this earth; however, he did struggle to accept that death was forever. That people don't come back. Ever.

When had Fredrika and Peder last met? He had no idea, but they both looked quite emotional as they broke apart.

'I heard you got married,' Peder said. 'Congratulations!'

So it must be quite a while ago. Fredrika had been married for over a year.

'Thanks. We tied the knot while we were living in New York,' she said with a smile. A big smile. It was obvious that she and Spencer were very much in love. Alex still hadn't had the pleasure of meeting Spencer, but he had heard a lot about him. Bloody stupid name, but he sounded like one of the good guys.

'So you're working here now,' Fredrika said, changing the subject.

'It's my first day.'

'Not a good start, what with the murder and the boys going missing.'

Peder nodded.

Alex looked around. 'I see you've done part of our job for us,' he said, referring to the barrage of telephone calls that had been made by volunteers.

'It's an impressive turnout,' Peder said. 'I had no idea the Solomon Community was so tight.'

Alex was in the same boat, and he wondered what the implications might be if the police found any leads that pointed towards the community itself.

'Anything you can tell us?' he asked.

Peder grew serious.

'How far have you got? Are you leading the case now?'

Alex was surprised. Was Peder trying to trade information?

'Yes, I'm leading the case, and I'll be happy to tell the families what we know so far. Are they here?'

Peder relaxed.

'The boys' mothers are here; the fathers are still out looking.'

Still. Where were they looking, and what were they looking for? The families lived in Östermalm, the tennis centre
where the boys played was no more than a kilometre away
on Lidingövägen. If someone had taken them, they could be
anywhere.

People are never more irrational than when they are afraid,
Alex knew that. He also knew that hope was the last thing
to go. You only had to ask Peder. He could tell you what
happened when hope disappeared and hell became a reality.

'I know what you're thinking,' Peder said quietly so that
no one else could hear. 'About the parents. But they're just
incapable of sitting at home and waiting. Do you want me
to call the fathers?'

'Leave them for the time being,' Alex said. 'We'll start with
the boys' mothers. It would be helpful if we could speak to
them separately.'

Peder indicated that they should follow him.

'There's someone I'd like you to meet before you do anything else. He's a friend of Abraham's, and I think he has
something important to tell you.'

The boy was sitting in the general secretary's room, where
Peder had asked him to wait for Alex and Fredrika to arrive.
Peder introduced him to his former colleagues.

'Tell them what you told me,' he said.

The boy shuffled uncomfortably, obviously overwhelmed
by the gravity of the situation. Alex sat down opposite him.

'There's no need to be scared,' he said. 'No one thinks
you've done anything wrong.'

'But you think something terrible has happened to Abraham and Simon!'

His eyes were huge with anxiety. Peder knew that his parents had been heavily involved in the search.

'We don't know that yet,' Alex said. 'But we are worried that they might come to some harm if we don't find them soon. It's bitterly cold out there.'

The boy automatically glanced over at the window, as if to confirm what Alex had said. He nodded, gazing at the snow.

'I spoke to Abraham yesterday.'

'And when was that?'

Fredrika stayed in the background, next to Peder. They had both silently reached the same conclusion; it was best if Alex handled this on his own.

Peder looked at her profile. Motherhood had made her even more attractive. Her face was more relaxed, not as stressed as it used to be. However that worked – having small children wasn't exactly a piece of cake. At least, not at Peder's house.

'I called just before he left for tennis; I'd forgotten he had a lesson.'

'Do you play too?'

'No, my dad wants me to play football instead.'

Alex smiled, but said nothing. Peder and Fredrika made no comment either; what kind of father forces his kid to play football?

'And what did Abraham say?'

'He was walking to the bus stop when I rang.'

Abraham didn't live far from Karlavägen, where he was supposed to be meeting Simon. No more than two hundred metres in the direction of Djurgården.

The boy went on:

'I was going to ask if he wanted to play computer games later, but he told me to ring back after his tennis lesson. I asked him if he knew whether we were going skating with the school today, because if so I needed to ask my mum to get my ice skates down from the loft.'

He paused, and Peder noticed that Fredrika was moving her feet up and down impatiently. It took an eternity for children to get to the point; interviewing them required an enormous amount of patience.

'Abraham said he thought we were going to the ice rink, but then he said he had to go. He said that really, really quickly.'

'Because he'd reached the bus stop where Simon was waiting?' Alex asked.

'No, because someone in a car had pulled up and offered him a lift. At least that's what he said before he rang off.'

Alex turned to Peder and Fredrika, stunned into silence. Peder could see that they were all thinking the same thing.

The boys had accepted a lift and been abducted by someone known to them.

Two mothers on a journey through hell that Fredrika Bergman could not and would not begin to imagine. Their sons had been missing for just over eighteen hours. During those hours the silence had been deafening; they hadn't heard a word from or about their ten-year-old children.

I wouldn't be able to cope, Fredrika thought. Without Isak and Saga I am nothing.

Before she had children, she had sometimes doubted whether she was capable of a mother's love, a mother's strength; of those qualities that seemed to make women capable of moving mountains for the sake of their children. Fredrika had thought she was too egotistical, too self-centred to stand being needed all the time. She had been wrong. On the contrary, it suited her perfectly to be so loved, so much in demand.

She looked at the woman in front of her.

Her name was Carmen Eisenberg, and her son was missing.

It seemed to be a very conservative arrangement: the men were out in their cars searching for the boys, while the women remained in the centre, engaged in a different aspect of the search. Abraham's mother was in the room next door, talking to Alex.

'Have you been here all night?' Fredrika asked.

'Of course – where else would I be?'

'I thought perhaps you might have other children at home.'

'Some good friends are looking after our daughter. We have two children. Simon is the eldest.'

Fredrika already knew how many children they had. She also knew how old they were and where they had been born: Simon in Jerusalem, the year the family moved to Stockholm, and the girl in Sweden. She thought about the elderly lady who had seen Simon at the bus stop, and said he looked angry.

'What kind of person is Simon?'

'Quiet. Conscientious. Popular. Maybe too nice.'

Maybe too nice? Was that possible when you were ten years old?

'What do you mean?'

Don't evaluate what is said, just listen and ask for clarification if you don't understand.

'He's always keen to fit in with everyone else, always ready to compromise. Sometimes others take advantage.'

'His friends, you mean?'

'Yes.'

'Abraham?'

'Especially Abraham.'

Her tone was neutral, she didn't look upset. Fredrika had watched the interaction between the two mothers for a little while; they seemed to know each other well, and worked together with no friction. However, she hadn't got the impression that they were close friends.

'Tell me.'

Carmen crossed her legs and tilted her head on one side. She spoke with a noticeable accent, a legacy from Israel.

Fredrika didn't understand a word of Hebrew, but she recognised the language.

Israel. The country to which Spencer would be travelling on Sunday.

Without her.

'How can I explain?' Carmen said. 'On the whole, Abraham is a good kid; he's tough and confident, and nobody can tell me that those aren't important qualities in life. But the negative side is that he's incredibly competitive. Every single thing is a competition. Reaching the front door first when you get out of the car; scoring the highest marks in the maths test. Simon's not like that at all. He won't take on Abraham's constant challenges; instead he just lies down, so to speak. In school he runs his own race. If Abraham wants to make comparisons, he's welcome to do so, but as far as Simon is concerned, thinking of every test or piece of homework as a competition does nothing to improve his motivation.'

'And of course Abraham is aware of this?'

'Absolutely. So if they're playing football or computer games or whatever, he's very good at getting his own way. Whatever the cost. Simon can't cope with all that.'

Fredrika thought about Simon standing at the bus stop, annoyed and probably cold.

'Does Simon often end up waiting for Abraham?'

'Far too often. My husband sometimes tells him off about it; he thinks Simon should make it clear to Abraham that you can't behave like that.'

Very wise. As long as Dad's criticism didn't turn into yet another problem.

'I realise this might sound stupid, but I have to ask,' Fredrika said. 'Do you think there's the slightest chance that the boys might have gone off somewhere on their own?'

'No.'

Neither do I.

'Abraham wouldn't be able to persuade Simon to do something like that?'

'The point is, if Simon ever got the idea of doing something as ridiculous as running away from home, Abraham would be the last person he would choose as his accomplice.'

Why did it have to be so hot in here? Alex thought about taking off his jacket as well, but would that look too informal? Probably.

So he kept it on as he interviewed Abraham's mother.

Daphne Goldmann. A tall, dark woman with a steely expression. Just like Simon's parents, Abraham's mother and father had relocated to Sweden ten years ago. Alex wondered if this was a coincidence, or whether the move had been a joint enterprise.

'I understand that you're under immense strain,' he began. 'Is someone helping out with your other children while you and your husband are here?'

'Abraham is our only child.'

So if something happens to him, you have no one left.

'Do you work outside the home?'

'My husband and I run a company offering various kinds of security solutions for organisations involved in activities in need of protection.'

Alex had no idea what any of that meant, but didn't really want to dig any deeper.

'When and how did you discover that Abraham was missing?'

He already knew the answer, but he had to start somewhere.

'We realised something had happened when he didn't come home after tennis. We called his coach, who said that neither Abraham nor Simon had turned up for their session. He had assumed they'd had problems because of the weather; apparently several of the children weren't there yesterday.'

'And what was your initial reaction?'

'That something was wrong. That something had happened to them. If they'd got stuck somewhere because of the snow, they would have called.'

'Why? Couldn't they just have decided to skip tennis and do something that was more fun?'

Daphne folded her arms.

'Definitely not.'

'Because?'

'Because as far as Abraham is concerned, nothing is more fun than playing tennis.'

'Is he good?'

'He's good at everything he does. Tennis is no exception.'

Alex ran a hand over his chin, remembering the photographs he had seen of the boys.

'What's his temperament like?'

'He's very similar to his father. He can be hot-headed, but he can also be very considerate. Above all, he's totally loyal.'

'To his family? His friends?'

'To everyone he cares about.'

'Does he have a lot of friends?'

'Absolutely.'

Alex thought about Simon, waiting in the cold at the bus stop.

'We think Abraham was late getting to the bus stop where he was due to meet Simon. Have you any idea what could have delayed him?'

'No. Abraham always has a thousand things to do, which means he sometimes finds it difficult to keep an eye on the clock.'

She shrugged and reached up to touch a pendant hanging around her neck.

A silver Star of David.

'My husband and I don't regard it as a problem. People don't usually mind waiting for someone who has a reasonable excuse.'

Alex thought this wasn't necessarily true, but he didn't say anything. It wasn't his job to correct a grown woman.

'It sounds as if Abraham is very driven. Qualities like that can sometimes lead to conflict.'

'Really?'

Not a hint of irony in her voice. She really didn't get it.

'I'm just thinking about other people, who either regard a competitive instinct as provocative, or who are equally competitive themselves. Does Abraham have any enemies?'

'Not as far as I know.'

Why did he dislike her so much? Alex looked searchingly at the woman sitting opposite him. A woman whose son had been missing for far too long in a bitterly cold Stockholm. Why didn't he feel any empathy for her situation?

Because her whole attitude rejected empathy and understanding. She was like a predator on the hunt, completely focused on the mission to find her son.

Dead or alive.

'Is there anywhere Abraham particularly liked to go?'

He disregarded the fact that she had just said that she didn't believe her son would have gone off of his own accord. Children sometimes got the strangest ideas, and Alex was sure that Abraham was no exception to that rule. Alex also guessed that if he was as driven as he sounded, he could probably carry through quite advanced projects behind his parents' backs.

'You mean in Sweden?'

Alex was surprised.

'Well yes – that's where we are.'

'I'm only asking because he loves visiting my parents in Israel,' Daphne explained. 'I'm not sure if he has any favourite places here in Sweden. We have a summer cottage that he loves, but he never mentions it in the winter when we're not there.'

Alex made a mental note of the summer cottage, but he didn't really think it would get them anywhere.

He was just about to end the interview when his mobile rang. The call came from one of his colleagues at HQ.

They thought they had found the boys.

If Eden Lundell had the choice, she thought she would like to die on a cold winter's day just like this one. But not until she was old or worthless, of course, whichever came first.

The call had come in just under an hour ago. Someone had reported hearing shooting out at Drottningholm. Two shots at an interval of approximately twenty minutes. Not in the immediate vicinity of the palace, but security had decided to contact Säpo's personal protection unit anyway. A group of bodyguards accompanied by members of the National Task Force had searched the park and surrounding area, but found nothing out of the ordinary.

They were just about to call off the operation when they found the bodies on the edge of the Royal Drottningholm Golf Club. They were lying on their backs, approximately fifty metres apart.

Eden was informed about the original call only because she was spending a few weeks as acting head of the personal protection unit, while carrying out her duties as head of counter-terrorism at the same time.

'I know you're not exactly short of something to do,' GD had said. 'But I'd really appreciate it if you could support our bodyguards while their chief is on sick leave for two days a week.'

Eden always had time. Time was something you created, not something you were given. She also felt that the work of the personal protection unit had many links to the activities of her own team.

The discovery of the two bodies was reported directly to Eden and the head of the protection unit. Five minutes later they were in a car heading towards Drottningholm, at Eden's suggestion.

'I hope it's not those boys who went missing in Östermalm yesterday,' her colleague said.

Who else would it be? Eden thought.

It did her good to get away from Kungsholmen for a while. There had been just one thing on her mind ever since GD called her the previous evening:

Efraim Kiel.

The biggest fuck-up in her entire life.

What the hell was he doing back in Stockholm?

She had had a brief meeting with GD first thing in the morning. Efraim had checked into the same hotel as last time, and was already under surveillance. No doubt he felt safe there. He wouldn't be able to go anywhere without them knowing exactly what he was up to. Whatever that was supposed to achieve.

They stopped in the avenue leading to Lovö church, where several vehicles were already parked. Eden slammed the car door and greeted the colleague who came over to meet them, a young man she hadn't seen before.

'You were the one who ran the investigation into the plane hijacking last year, weren't you?' he said.

'Yes,' she said. 'I was.'

She had been relatively new to the job back then. A

plane carrying four hundred passengers had taken off from Arlanda, and was hijacked high above the clouds. The only person who had so far been held responsible for his actions was the captain, who had been sentenced to life imprisonment in the USA. The chances of his being allowed to serve his sentence in a Swedish prison were negligible, and the prospect of a pardon was even less likely.

They ploughed through the snow, sinking up to their knees.

From a distance they could see only two paper bags, sticking up out of the snow and breaking the line of the landscape. Brown and hard. Both bodies had sunk down, and were difficult to see from a distance.

Two children. Like snuffed-out snow angels with paper bags on their heads.

Two boys. With bare, frozen feet.

Eden crouched down.

'Fuck,' the head of the protection unit said behind her.

The forensic pathologist would be able to provide more information about what had happened to the boys, but at first sight there didn't appear to be any major injuries, apart from the bullet wounds that had presumably killed them.

'Is this where they died?' Eden asked one of the CSIs standing a short distance away.

'We haven't got that far yet, but yes, I think that seems to be the case. If you look at the tracks in the snow, it looks as if the boys walked or ran to the spot where they are now. They appear to have been shot in the chest.'

Eden looked around.

Children's footprints in the snow. Bigger prints alongside the small ones. The killer's. He, or she, had walked up to the victims to check that they really were dead.

And put paper bags over their heads.

Why?

Someone had drawn faces on the paper bags. Big eyes, wide open as if in terror. And big mouths that looked as if they were calling out to someone or something.

'This isn't our case,' her colleague said. 'I've spoken to the police, and they're on their way.'

Eden gazed at the boys for a moment before she got to her feet. She knew instinctively that the paper bags were important to the killer. They carried a message, directed to someone other than the police.

The only question was – to whom?

But someone else could work that out. Eden had enough problems of her own.

If Efraim Kiel dared to take as much as one single step in her direction, he would pay a higher price than he could ever have imagined.

Three murders in less than twenty-four hours. Something like that would send shock waves through any community, particularly in a country like Sweden. Sheltered and protected, a kingdom of safety and security.

A discovery had been made on the edge of a golf course not far from Drottningholm Palace. No further details had been released, but that was enough for Efraim Kiel. He realised they must have found the boys. He listened attentively to the news bulletin on the radio.

He packed his case, his movements slow and hesitant. He hated the constant travelling, the endless series of anonymous hotel rooms that served as his home. The apartment in Jerusalem was just one of many places where he stayed; it had never been his real base.

He missed having a proper home.

Sometimes he thought he had no roots at all.

He flipped his case shut. The Solomon Community in Stockholm had a new head of security. Two, if you counted Peder Rydh, who would fill the post until the summer. Poor sod. He had no idea of what was waiting for him.

Efraim gazed out at all the snow. The summer seemed so far away. How could people live in a place like this? Cold and dark. That was his overall impression of the past few days.

He had been in Stockholm before, of course. As recently as last October. His employer had decided it was time for a fresh approach. One final attempt to recruit Eden Lundell. At the time she had only just started her job as head of counter-terrorism with Säpo; by now she must be well established.

She had said no. Very clearly. Only two weeks after Efraim had made his move, Mossad's liaison officer for Scandinavia had been called in to see the general director of Säpo, and had been castigated for the fact that his organisation had the gall to try to infiltrate Sweden's security police. It pained him to admit it, but Säpo's handling of the issue had been impressive. Mossad had also been surprised by Eden's reaction; it seemed she had gone straight to her boss and put all her cards on the table.

'There is nothing I don't know,' Buster Hansson had said. 'I know that you got one of your operators to seduce Eden in London, and made her look like an idiot in front of MI5, her British employer. I know that she's only human, and that she made a terrible mistake. But now she has finished paying for that mistake.'

Unexpected. So Eden had told her boss whom she had had a relationship with. That was a brave thing to do. It must have really hurt.

Unfortunately Buster Hansson was wrong. He had said there was nothing he didn't know. That wasn't true.

Efraim sat down on the bed. His plane was due to take off in less than two hours. Back to Israel. Home to Jerusalem. He thought about Eden and took a deep breath. He had been borrowing an apartment from a friend in Tel Aviv back then, when he seduced her. When they had had a relationship.

A very unfair relationship, because she had actually fallen in love, while he had just screwed her in the interests of national security.

But he had said that he loved her, and she had believed him – until she realised who he was, and what his agenda must be. The humiliation had driven her crazy; the fact that she had walked straight into his simple trap had made her lose all self-respect. For a while he had thought that she wouldn't settle for an outburst of rage, that she would come after him, determined never to give up until she had killed him. But that wasn't what happened. Instead her fury had been followed by total silence, and then she had left London.

Resolutely he got to his feet. He had no reason to remain in Stockholm. It was time to go home, to wait for his next assignment. This had been a turbulent ending to his stay in the Swedish capital; it would be interesting to follow the progress of the police investigation.

He had made a point of staying away from the members of the Solomon Community, visiting the centre only to do his job. Distance was important; he didn't want to be recognised and remembered.

But that damned feeling kept on coming over him. The same feeling that had stressed him out when it looked as if they weren't going to find a suitable candidate for the post of head of security. It hovered in the air, hanging over him like an omen of impending doom, an Armageddon that was being held at bay only by the beautiful winter weather that had blessed the city today.

He tried to shake off the sense of unease as he picked up his suitcase and left the room. He went down to the lobby to check out.

The receptionist smiled.

'There's a message for you,' she said, handing him an envelope.

Slowly he put down the case. He stood there holding the letter. Who knew he was here? A few people from the Solomon Community, but they wouldn't contact him in writing. They would phone him.

Efraim moved away from the desk. With his back to the receptionist, he opened the sealed envelope.

It held only a simple white card. He read the brief message.

What the hell?

This wasn't happening. It *couldn't* be happening.

He read the message over and over again.

'Excuse me, did you want to check out?'

He turned around in a daze.

'No,' he said. 'No, I'm staying.'

He slipped the card into his pocket, knowing that he wouldn't need to look at it again to remember what it said.

I heard you were in town.

So am I.

The Paper Boy

Children's bodies, laid to rest in the cold snow. Fredrika Bergman was standing a short distance away with Alex, trying yet again to understand how someone could believe they had the right to harm other people. Take on the role of the supreme judge, presiding over life and death.

The life and death of *children*.

She could hardly remember how she and Alex had managed to get from the interviews with the boys' mothers in Östermalm to the deserted golf course at Drottningholm.

'I don't understand this,' Alex said.

'Who does?'

'What the hell are these paper bags supposed to mean?'

When the bags had been removed, there was no longer any doubt. They had found Simon Eisenberg and Abraham Goldmann.

'They must have some significance for the murderer,' Fredrika said. 'But I have no idea what it might be.'

Sometimes a murderer would try to distance himself from his crime by covering the victim's face, depersonalising him or her. Could it be something along those lines?

She looked at the bags. Brown, sturdy. With big faces drawn on the front.

'It seems as if whoever shot the boys wanted to tell us

something,' Alex said. 'With the bags, I mean. Have you checked if there's anything written on them?' he asked one of the CSIs.

'Yes,' she said. 'There's nothing. The only thing of interest is the face on each one. I'll take them back to the lab and check them over.'

They could always hope, of course. With a bit of luck the killer would have suffered an attack of megalomania, and would have left his or her fingerprints all over the thick paper. Or used a very rare pen that would be easy to trace. Somehow.

Fredrika was very downhearted. They wouldn't find a single thing on those bags; she felt it in every fibre of her body.

'Is there anything else you can tell us?' she said. 'For example, how did the boys get here?'

'Good question. You can see the boys' footprints,' the CSI said, pointing. 'They ran quite a distance through the forest over there; we've been able to follow them all the way to a narrow track that branches off Lovövägen. The most likely scenario is that they managed to escape from their abductor, but I've no idea how that happened. Hopefully the forensic pathologist will be able to tell us more on the basis of their injuries.'

Fredrika shuddered. She couldn't take her eyes off the children's bare feet in the sparkling snow. Who knew what they had been forced to endure before they managed to get away? And in the end they had both been shot dead.

They must have been terrified.

'You said you were able to follow their footprints,' Alex said. 'That must mean they didn't get away until it had stopped snowing.'

'Exactly. The tracks are very clear and well preserved. I think they were running in daylight, with the weather on their side. And the shots were fired less than an hour ago.'

They had been given that information in the car on the way over, along with the news that Säpo had been called out first, because the shots had been heard by the guards in the palace gardens.

'How much time elapsed between the two shots?' Fredrika asked.

The CSI frowned and thought for a moment.

'You'll have to double-check the witness statements, but I think it was about twenty minutes.'

Alex didn't say anything, and Fredrika saw his jaw tense as it so often did when he was thinking. Twenty minutes between the shots, yet the boys had gone down fifty metres apart. How was that possible?

'I can't make any sense of this,' Fredrika said.

'Me neither.' Alex shook his head. 'So let's imagine they managed to get away from whoever abducted them. That they ran off together. Obviously the perpetrator went after them, and . . .'

He was interrupted by the CSI.

'They didn't run together. There's a whole tangle of foot-prints among the trees over there. It's clear that they ran in different directions, but it seems likely that they both spotted the golf course and decided to get out of the forest and head for open ground.'

Fredrika could understand that. A golf course would make them think of some kind of civilisation, the hope of meeting a saviour even though it was the middle of winter. Then again, could you actually tell it was a golf course? She looked around and decided you couldn't. The flags that normally marked the holes had been removed, and the course resembled nothing more than a gigantic white field.

'Children act on instinct,' Alex said. They don't like dark forests. If they see an alternative, they'll go for it.'

'But they would have had more protection in the forest,' Fredrika objected.

'I'm not sure they were thinking logically.'

Fredrika thought he was probably right.

'What can you tell us about the perpetrator's tracks?' she said. 'Or was there more than one?'

She hadn't really thought about that possibility before she spoke. There could have been more than one person hunting children out on the island.

She and Alex exchanged a look of mutual understanding. The boys might not even have chosen to leave the cover of the trees; they might just as well have been driven out.

But the CSI shook her head.

'We've found prints made by only one pair of shoes. Either we have two killers wearing shoes that are exactly the same size and make, or the children were shot by the same person, which seems more likely.'

The golf course was cold and desolate. Fredrika adjusted her scarf and pulled on her gloves. She wanted to get back in the car, gather her thoughts and digest what she had seen.

The forensic technicians came forward with stretchers. Gently they freed the boys from their icy bed, ready to be transferred to the forensic laboratory in Solna.

'We need to inform the parents,' Fredrika said.

She glanced at the police tape that cordoned off the entire area. The first journalists had already appeared. So far all they knew was that shots had been heard in the vicinity of Drottningholm Palace, and that the police had discovered something, but Fredrika was well aware that it was only a matter of time before they learned that the boys had been found.

'Already in hand,' Alex said. 'The mothers are still in the centre, and the fathers have been asked to join them there.'

There were routine procedures for everything, even for the cruellest, most unthinkable news.

Fredrika couldn't imagine anything worse than being taken aside in the middle of searching for her missing child, and being told that the child was dead.

'Come on, let's get back,' Alex said.

As they turned away, Fredrika couldn't stop thinking about the paper bags with the faces drawn on them. There must be a message, but she couldn't see it. Perhaps she wasn't supposed to; the message could be meant for someone else. In which case the question was whether that person would come forward, or whether he or she would have to be tracked down.

The triumph of good over evil was a recurring theme in the stories Peder Rydh read to his children. It was also a principle that meant a great deal to him.

We get what we deserve.

Past sins may grow old, but they should never be forgotten; there is always time for vengeance.

Just once he had taken on the role of executioner. It had cost him his job, but had probably saved his sanity. He had no idea of what might save Simon and Abraham's parents.

The boys had been found shot dead, not far from Drottningholm Palace.

In the Solomon Community centre the news was received with shock and sorrow. The silence that followed was so dense that Peder could almost touch it. One by one, the members left. Went home to their families. Back to their lives. Eternally grateful that tragedy had struck someone else and not them.

Peder stayed behind. It was a devastating start to a job that only yesterday had seemed challenging and exciting.

For the second time in as many days, parents from the Solomon Community were being taken to a forensic laboratory to formally identify their dead children. It was incomprehensible.

He found a quiet corner and called Ylva. He wanted to hear her voice, know that she was okay.

'What's going on?' she said.

Anxious.

There was no way she was going to let him drag more crap into their lives. That was what she really wanted to say.

'I don't know,' he said.

'Is there a connection? Between what happened yesterday, and this?'

Was there?

The police didn't seem to think so.

Peder was trying to stay out of the police investigation; he knew he didn't belong there any more. But if he had still been a serving officer, if he had been a part of Alex's new team . . . He would have slammed his fist down on the table.

Because he was convinced the cases were linked.

When he had finished talking to Ylva, he went into the room that had been designated as his office. The security team at the Solomon Community had conducted a parallel interview of their own with everyone who had witnessed the murder of the pre-school teacher after the police had spoken to them. Interview was probably the wrong word; the community didn't have that kind of authority. But they had talked to the three parents who had been standing next to Josephine, and to the people who had been passing by at the time. They hadn't spoken to the children.

Peder read through their notes, but found nothing useful.

Frustrated, he went through the material the team had put together, but couldn't find what he was looking for. How could the community find out what the murder weapon was? Or any details about distance and the trajectory of the bullet? Or if there were any suspects among the victim's circle of acquaintances?

Actually the media had answered the last question; as usual they had been fed by leaks from within the police. Josephine's boyfriend had a string of convictions for serious crimes. Peder guessed that the police would conclude that she had been dragged into some kind of transaction, either willingly or under duress, and had ended up as a victim of organised crime.

Peder didn't agree.

This crime was spectacular. Cocky. As daring as picking up two boys in a car and driving off with them.

What was the best way to proceed? Would he be able to persuade Alex that it was essential for him to sit in on some of their briefings? He needed access to their investigation if he was going to get anywhere.

He broke off his train of thought.

What the fuck was he doing?

He wasn't going to 'get anywhere'. He was no longer an investigator, he was head of security. It was time to get to grips with his new job, familiarise himself with his team. The general secretary had had a long conversation with him, explained how the community viewed Peder's role. He had also explained how the security team worked and what their working routine was.

There was a knock on his door. The sound made him jump and shout 'Come in' rather too loudly.

The general secretary came in.

'I'm extremely concerned,' he said, closing the door behind him.

Peder listened.

'Tell me honestly, do you think either of the dreadful crimes that have shaken our community over the past twenty-four hours could be motivated by anti-Semitism? Or could there really be completely different reasons behind them?'

It was a straight question, and it deserved a straight answer. Had Josephine or the two boys been killed because they were Jewish, or not?

'I can't tell you that,' Peder said. 'I don't know enough.'

'What do you think about the police's main line of enquiry with regard to Josephine? The idea that the murder is linked to her boyfriend?'

Peder didn't hesitate.

'I think there's a different explanation. But once again – I have too little information to draw any conclusions.'

The general secretary gazed at him.

'In that case I hope you will come up with a way of acquiring more information, because many members of our community are terrified.'

Terrified?

'Of what?'

'They are terrified that they or their children are next in line to be executed. Because Josephine, Simon and Abraham were killed by a murderer who will return to our community to seek out further victims.'

So the boys were dead. Hunted down and shot. Alex Recht knew that he couldn't do anything useful until he had the preliminary report from the forensic pathologist.

Which should tell him how the boys had been killed. And what they had been subjected to before they died.

He thought about the impressions their feet had left in the snow. How far could you run if you were ten years old, barefoot, frozen, and had been awake for hours on end? If you could trust the tracks in the snow, they had got quite a long way.

Alex tried to set aside his own emotional reaction to the case that had landed on his desk. Fredrika had mentioned Lilian Sebastiansson, a little girl who had gone missing from a train one summer's day a few years ago. Several children had disappeared, and only one had survived, with severe burns. Alex would never forget, because he had been there. Seen the flames burst into life, raced towards the child to save him. His hands still bore the scars.

Was this something similar? Another bloody lunatic going after the youngest, the most vulnerable? Alex looked at the photographs from the edge of the golf course. A fractured pattern of footprints in the snow. Two boys lying on their backs, with paper bags on their heads.

Those fucking bags.

What did they mean?

If it hadn't been for the faces drawn on them, Alex might have thought the bags were there simply to alleviate the murderer's sense of regret, or whatever the hell you felt when you had killed two children.

But the faces.

Eyes, nose, mouth. A large mouth. Impossible to tell if it was laughing or screaming.

The paper bags worried him, because they made the whole thing even more sick. And if it was sick, then it was also irrational, which meant there was no way of knowing what to expect.

A ghostly voice whispered in Alex's ear.

Serial killer.

Were they dealing with a serial killer? If so, there would be more victims. With paper bags pulled over their heads.

But serial killers were unusual. Not even unusual, to be honest. They were virtually non-existent. Not in real life, anyway.

Alex stared at the material in front of him. What did they know, and what could they rule out? To begin with, the gun put paid to the idea that the whole thing could have been a game that had gone wrong. So did the fact that the boys had been missing for a whole night before they died. Nor did it seem like a kidnapping that had gone wrong; the parents hadn't been contacted. Unless of course they had been contacted, but hadn't informed the police.

But why would that happen?

Which left two alternatives.

Perhaps the whole thing was a terrible coincidence. The

boys had somehow bumped into a killer who had selected his victims on a whim, which meant that any child could have been abducted.

Or those two boys had been deliberately chosen. This seemed more likely to Alex; there was some kind of personal motivation, either directed at the boys themselves, or with the aim of punishing someone else. Their parents, for example.

He dug out his notes from the conversation with Abraham's friend; Abraham had told him he was getting a lift to his tennis lesson. They were assuming that the killer had picked Abraham up on the street, but it was possible that something had gone wrong, and that Abraham and Simon had been dropped off somewhere else altogether, not outside the tennis centre. And that the person who killed them had picked them up from wherever that might be.

They had so little concrete information.

Alex glanced at his watch. By now the parents would have been informed; he and Fredrika weren't due to see them until the following day. This would give them more time to formulate the right questions.

He went back to the issue of how well Abraham must have known the driver to jump into that car. It would simplify matters considerably if the boys had been picked up by an acquaintance, because that would almost guarantee that their parents also knew that person.

A teacher, perhaps, or a family friend.

Or one of the parents.

That was another key piece of the puzzle: they needed to check whether all the parents had an alibi for the time when the boys went missing.

Alex's phone rang, and he felt something akin to relief. He was in danger of getting lost in the labyrinth of his thoughts.

It was Peder Rydh.

'Am I disturbing you? Have you got five minutes?'

He sounded hesitant, as if he wasn't sure whether this was a good idea or not.

'Sure,' Alex said.

'Are you still investigating the murder of the teacher at the Solomon school?'

So Peder wanted information.

'No, it's been passed on to the National Crime Unit.'

'Right. To the team dealing with hate crime?'

'To Organised Crime.'

Silence.

'You don't think you're jumping to conclusions, just because her partner has a criminal record?' Peder said eventually.

'What are you trying to say?'

'In the light of the fact that the boys have now been found dead, I'm just wondering if we can rule out the idea that there might be a connection.'

Had they ruled it out? Alex wasn't sure. They knew too little; they hadn't even got details of the murder weapons yet.

'We're not ruling anything out,' he said. 'But we need more concrete evidence before we can link the two. Both the MO and the choice of victim are very different; there doesn't have to be a connection.'

'It depends on your point of view,' Peder said. 'You could say there are several similarities between the two incidents. The boys were abducted on the day Josephine was shot. All three were members of the Solomon Community. They were all part of the Solomon school. And all three were shot dead.'

Alex was all too familiar with the energy in Peder's voice. The hunger, the desire to be right.

'So you think we're looking at a hate crime in both cases?' he asked, sounding angrier than he had intended. 'I think that's one hell of a long shot.'

'That's not what I'm saying. I just think there's a connection. And I don't believe it's a coincidence that all the victims were Jewish.'

Alex didn't say anything. He didn't want to tell Peder that the boys had been found barefoot, with paper bags over their heads. These were clear differences from Josephine's murder; she had been shot in the street, in broad daylight.

'One more thing,' Peder went on. 'Are you really sure that the right person was shot dead yesterday afternoon?'

'What do you mean?'

'There were three small children standing next to Josephine when she was shot. The killer might have missed the person he actually intended to kill.'

'You're suggesting that one of the children was meant to die?' Alex said dubiously.

'Why not? It was two children who were abducted just over an hour later, not adults.'

Alex thought for a moment. Fredrika had said something similar the previous day, wondering whether someone other than Josephine had been the intended victim.

'I don't think so,' he said to Peder. 'Unless I see some evidence pointing in that direction. Keep in touch; we'll swap notes if we hear anything new.'

Trying to link the children who had been standing on Nybrogatan with the boys who had been shot near Drottningholm was a dodgy enterprise. On the other hand, they would soon have details of the murder weapons that had extinguished three lives.

If the victims had been shot with the same gun, it would be impossible to deny that the cases were linked.

The gym in the basement of Police HQ was a cavern characterised by too much sweat and adrenalin, and too little brainpower; hard, muscular bodies that happened to bump into one another. Skin against skin, a wry grin over the shoulder, accompanied by a 'sorry'. Which was all too frequently followed by 'Haven't I seen you somewhere before?' or 'What are you doing this evening?'

Eden Lundell trained as often as she could, but preferably not among her colleagues. Unfortunately, today she didn't have time to go anywhere else. Holding herself erect, she walked into the cattle market, saw the male police officers checking her out. Someone had tried to chat her up just once; it hadn't ended well. Eden didn't appreciate uninvited attention.

Her feet thudded against the hard surface of the treadmill. She couldn't forget the boys she had seen lying in the snow, even though it wasn't Säpo's case. She had heard Alex Recht's name mentioned just before they left, and had considered staying around to see him. They had been in touch several times during the autumn, above all when Alex had needed help to bring his son home from the USA after the hijacking of Flight 573. She was happy to do whatever she could; Alex was an excellent police officer, and would have been invaluable if Säpo had been able to recruit him. However, he wasn't interested, and that was that. Not everyone loved the world of secrets.

The sweat was trickling down her back.

Step by step she whipped the stress out of her body.

Efraim was back in Stockholm.

There was no end to it.

Eden's hatred burned with undiminished strength. She couldn't bear to hear his name, to know that he was anywhere near her. She had too many memories. Too many – and too good, unfortunately. It had started out as an affair, and grown into something else, something that began to seem serious, leaving her in despair.

And she had forced herself to answer the biggest question of all:

Was she prepared to leave Mikael for Efraim?

Eden increased her pace on the treadmill. Faster, faster. She refused to remember her answer. Refused to remember what she had been ready to pay for something that had turned out to be nothing more than thin air.

I could have left. I could have lost everything and gained nothing.

She had taken another call from the Solomon Community just before she came down to the gym.

The situation was desperate, the person on the other end of the line had said. They could be looking at a serial killer, handpicking his victims among the members of the community.

Eden thought that was unlikely. Admittedly she knew only what she had read in the newspapers and what she had seen with her own eyes out on the island, but that was enough. At the moment there was no evidence to suggest that it was the same murderer. The fact that the crimes had been committed within such a short space of time looked like no more than an unfortunate coincidence.

But what if it wasn't?

Eden ran faster.

If it wasn't, if someone really was selecting members of the Solomon Community as his targets, then it could only end in an even greater disaster.

Efraim popped into her head again.

Fuck, this had to stop.

She was going out of her mind.

Eden had confessed everything to Buster Hansson, the general director of Säpo, that autumn night when the situation became critical. She had almost lost her job, because it looked as if she was working as an agent for Mossad, the Israeli intelligence service. That was bad. It didn't get much worse.

And it had happened before.

She had been working for MI5, the British intelligence service, and had been regarded as one of the organisation's top operatives. She had met Mikael in London, where he had been working as a priest in the Swedish church. Eden had fallen fast and hard for his charisma and his unshakeable belief that he could make her whole. Their first year together had been good. Then Efraim Kiel came into the picture, and everything changed.

So many lies.

So many secret trysts in cheap hotel rooms, and eventually a trip all the way to Israel.

Just to be with Efraim.

Because she had fallen for him too. She had believed they

had met by chance, brought together by an invisible, magical hand. But that wasn't the case. Everything had been planned in advance, down to the smallest detail. Eden had been no more than a counter in a game so meticulously worked out that the very thought of it made her shudder.

Efraim had tried to deny everything. Sworn that he had meant everything he said, everything he did, that she was important to him, that they still had the chance of a future together.

Bullshit.

She had told Buster Hansson all this – more than she had told Mikael, in fact. A lot more.

However, she had kept one thing to herself. The grubbiest truth of all, the one that could still make her hate herself. These days she thought about it less and less often, but she didn't believe she would ever have real peace of mind.

Never.

Because she didn't deserve it.

She stepped off the treadmill. Saw two well-built men helping each other on the bench press. Men did stuff together. That's the way it had always been.

She picked up her bag and slipped out of the gym. Went into the changing room and took out her phone. One missed call, from Mikael. If he had rung to discuss the trip he had mentioned, she would go crazy. She had a job to do, terrorists to keep in check. And incoming agents to deal with.

Unfortunately it wasn't possible to refer to Efraim in any other way.

And she wanted the bastard out of the country. Out of her life.

Once and for all.

A clear blue sky, cold air. Efraim Kiel was strolling along Strandvägen, wondering whether he could be bothered to get annoyed with the Säpo agents who insisted on shadowing him. They didn't seem very bright. He had been in Sweden for several days before they realised he had entered the country, and decided that perhaps they ought to keep an eye on him.

Being followed was a bit of a nuisance, but not unmanageable. Efraim would have no problem in shaking them off. He had already done it twice, and could do so again if necessary. But not too often; it was important to give them the impression that they were on top of things.

He was more worried about the fact that the person who had left the envelope at reception had tracked him down.

He had asked the receptionist who had brought it in, demanded a description, but he had been unable to get anything out of her. She just couldn't remember, nor could any other member of staff. The lobby was covered by CCTV, but they refused to let him look at the film. If that was how they wanted it, Efraim was happy to play along. He knew how to get hold of information without first asking permission; when evening came he would take what he wanted.

Unconsciously he was heading towards the Solomon Community. They would be surprised to see him; they thought he had gone home.

The short lines on the card inside the envelope were still reverberating in his brain. The message was written in Hebrew, and was clearly meant for Efraim's eyes only.

Feeling frustrated, he increased his speed. His Säpo followers kept pace like nonchalant shadows, naively convinced that he hadn't noticed them.

What the hell did this person who called himself the Paper Boy want?

Efraim had several problems that he wasn't yet sure how to solve. He had to find out more about the murders that had shaken the Solomon Community. See how far the police had got, what they knew about the three deaths. But he had no sources within the Swedish police. Eden was a last resort, of course, but she was with Säpo, and had nothing to do with these investigations.

The very thought of Eden stressed him out.

The Paper Boy; was he a mutual acquaintance? He didn't think so.

Efraim rarely felt uneasy. Years of training and experience had prepared him for most of what life had to offer, but not the sort of challenges the Paper Boy posed.

He would have to make sure that he didn't lose his grip. The mere fact that he was actually thinking of the Paper Boy as a real person was ominous.

You don't exist, he thought, clutching the note in his pocket.

Although he couldn't be certain.

He knew of two Paper Boys; it depended which of them

had contacted him. The one who was a myth, or the one who had once existed.

He had reached the community centre on Nybrogatan. He stopped in the street and stared at the door of the Solomon school, where the teacher had been killed. There were no traces of yesterday's drama to be seen; last night's storm had very efficiently swept away all the bloodstained snow. He moved closer to the building, examining the facade.

It didn't take him long to find the spot where the bullet had penetrated the wall. It wasn't there now, of course; the police had removed it and taken it away. But the hole was still there, and it was lower down than Efraim had expected.

If the killer had been lying on the roof on the opposite side of the street, he would have had a pretty good chance of being able to see what he was doing and to hit his target – assuming that he was a good shot, which Efraim took as read. Otherwise no one would attempt this kind of attack. Not in the middle of a snowstorm.

He squatted down, ran his hand over the wall. Josephine had been surrounded by children when she was killed. Shot in the back. Had she been standing upright, or bending down? Perhaps she had been about to kneel down to help one of the children with something? The newspapers hadn't given any details, but nor could they be expected to.

Was the bullet really meant for Josephine?

Or for one of the children?

Reluctantly his thoughts returned to the Paper Boy.

Was it you who did this?

He was overwhelmed by a sense of impotence. Had he misunderstood who the message was from?

Efraim had no specialist knowledge of the Paper Boy, but two things he did know:

First of all, he always left a calling card when he had taken a victim.

And secondly, he took only children.

Concentrating on the pattern of footprints and impressions left by shoes in the snow quickly became confusing. It was possible to track two sets of children's bare feet, and one set of adult boots. Size 43, so probably a man's. CSI thought they had found the place where the boys had managed to escape from their abductor, but how the children had got there remained a mystery.

Fredrika Bergman frowned as she looked at the documents in front of her: a map, photographs and scribbled notes.

A theory was beginning to take shape. The boys had been taken to Lovön by car. At the moment it wasn't clear whether the perpetrator had a specific link to the island; nor did they know where he and the children had spent the night. CSI had found evidence to suggest that a larger vehicle had been in the area where they thought the boys had escaped. The width of the tyre tracks and the size of the wheelbase indicated that this was some kind of van.

So the boys had been driven to the spot.

But how had they managed to escape?

Fredrika just couldn't work it out, but it must have happened somehow. The boys had fled and sought refuge among the trees; it looked as if they had run around in circles. In certain places they appeared to have knelt down, or even lain on the snow beneath the trees. They had presumably hidden behind the tree trunks, watching out for whoever was chasing them. But why had neither of them got away? If only they had set off in different directions, then the killer wouldn't have been able to go after both of them at the same time.

Fredrika reminded herself that they were children. And that they had been barefoot, frozen, exhausted and terrified.

They must have been so cold.

She looked at her watch. Their first team meeting was due to begin shortly.

Reluctantly she had begun to take an interest in the boys' fathers, the men who had driven around and around the city searching for their sons while the mothers stayed in the community centre, calling friends and acquaintances.

Both men worked in security. Simon's father was a specialist in IT security, Abraham's in personal protection. Fredrika rapidly came to the conclusion that she was in the wrong job. Abraham's father had successfully built up a company with something in the region of fifteen employees, offering security packages to everyone from embassies to small and medium-sized enterprises. Fredrika glanced at the homepage and wondered what kind of background you needed to start a business like that. She must remember to ask.

Simon's mother was an architect, while Abraham's mother worked for her husband. That was all Fredrika managed to find out.

Both families had a fascinating background. They had moved to Sweden in 2002; again, this was something worth asking about. Why would someone move from Israel to Stockholm?

She found the pictures the parents had given to the police

while they still believed that the children were alive; she gazed at the boys with their serious expressions for a long time.

Now they were gone.

She felt as if the photographs were burning her fingers. Who would target children, hunt them down and shoot them?

A thought came and went, and disappeared so quickly that she didn't have time to catch it. She put down the pictures of the boys and dug out the photos of the place where they had been found.

They were missing something vital. Something the tracks in the snow were telling them.

Alex opened her door. 'We're about to make a start,' he said.

She got up and followed him down the corridor, still thinking about those footprints in the snow. Eventually she had to try to put her thoughts into words.

'Alex, the boys' footprints in the snow.'

He looked at her.

'Yes?'

They stopped outside the meeting room – no longer the Lions' Den. They were one floor higher up these days, and the room was known as the Snakes' Nest. Fredrika presumed someone had come up with the name in connection with a Christmas party or some similar occasion; she much preferred the Lions' Den.

'I think we're on the wrong track – no pun intended.'

'In what way?'

'We're assuming that Simon and Abraham managed to escape from their abductor, and that he chased them through the forest and out towards the golf course, where

he shot them dead. But why was there a gap of twenty minutes between the two shots? And why did the one who was
shot last leave the forest, if he had seen his friend go down?'

'Because they're children,' Alex said, then immediately
corrected himself. 'They *were* children. The one who was
still alive could have run over to the one who was shot first,
thinking that something could be done.'

'But twenty minutes is a long time.'

'The second one might have stayed in the forest for a
while before he broke cover. We did see indentations behind
several trees, remember.'

Fredrika shook her head.

'Even if the snowstorm had eased by the time they took
off, it was still minus five out there. And they were barefoot.
That means it would be impossible to lie still in the snow for
twenty minutes, then start running.'

Why had no one seen anything?

It was hard to believe that two boys could have been running for their lives so close to Sweden's head of state, and no
one had seen or heard a thing.

Alex opened the door of the Snakes' Nest.

'They ran away and they were shot down,' he said. 'What
else is there to say?'

It was obvious that he wanted to bring the discussion to
an end, and Fredrika had to admit he was right; what else
was there to say?

There was only one alternative to Alex's brief summary of
events, and it was totally improbable.

What if the boys hadn't managed to escape, but had been
released?

If that was the case, then why?

The Snakes' Nest was a really bad name for a meeting room. It carried overtones of a sex club rather than an appropriate venue for a collection of highly skilled investigators. Apart from that, Alex Recht felt entirely at home in the room, because it looked exactly the same as the Lions' Den.

He recognised everyone, but hadn't worked with all of them in the past. Everyone introduced themselves briefly, and once again Alex thought back to his former team. There had never been any problem when it came to bringing in additional resources for high-priority cases, and the same applied this time.

'Okay,' he said. 'Two young boys, Simon Eisenberg and Abraham Goldmann, were abducted in Östermalm yesterday afternoon when they were on their way to a tennis coaching session. Today they were found shot dead in the vicinity of Drottningholm Golf Club. We know that Simon was waiting for Abraham at a bus stop on Karlavägen, and we know that when Abraham was speaking to another friend on the phone, he said he had to end the call because he'd been offered a lift to the tennis centre. The weather was terrible yesterday, so I don't think either of the boys would need to be asked more than once if they would like a lift rather than waiting for the bus – with the proviso that they knew the driver, which we believe they did.'

'Do we know anything about the car that picked them up?' a colleague on loan from the National Crime Unit asked.

'No.'

'Any thoughts about who might have been driving?'

'No, again. We might have a better idea when we've spoken to the parents.'

'But we think the person who picked them up is the same person who shot them?'

'That's our working hypothesis at the moment,' Alex said.

He looked around the room: representatives from CSI and several investigators.

'We're expecting the post mortem report later, but the forensic pathologist has provided us with some key information that we need to take into account at this stage. First of all, there is no sign of sexual interference with either of the boys.'

A collective sigh of relief, as if such a crime wouldn't have been eclipsed by the fact that they had been murdered. But in principle Alex felt the same; it was good to know that the children had been spared that ordeal.

'Secondly, there are no defensive injuries whatsoever. There are no indications that they have been fighting, or that they have been hit. No bruises. However, they do have cuts and scratches on their feet and ankles from running through the forest.'

'But how did they manage to get away from their abductor?' asked a woman who hadn't managed to get a place at the table, but was sitting in a corner.

'We don't know,' Alex replied. 'On the other hand, I'm

sure none of us seriously believes that two ten-year-old boys managed to knock down an adult male who wears size 43 shoes.'

The room fell silent.

'Have we heard anything about the murder weapon?' someone asked.

'Later this afternoon.'

'Are we ruling out a link between this case and the shooting of the pre-school teacher?'

'We're not ruling out anything until we know for certain,' Alex said. 'The priority is to compare the murder weapons as soon as the information comes through.'

And then, he thought, we have to rule out the possibility that the shot fired from the roof the previous day might have been meant for one of the children standing next to Josephine. Or their parents.

The pressure was mounting. They had a lot to do.

'I need hardly point out that we have major gaps in our knowledge at the moment,' Alex said. 'We know when the boys went missing and when they were found, but we have no idea where they were in the interim period, or what they were subjected to. Nor do we know if it's pure chance that they were shot on the golf course, or if the location was chosen deliberately.'

'So we're sure they were shot there and not somewhere else, then moved to the spot where the bodies were found?' a colleague asked.

Alex nodded to one of the CSIs to take over.

'Based on their footprints in the snow, we have been able to conclude that they were shot where they lay. The bullets were fired from the front, and hit them in the chest. We found them lying on their backs, and there is nothing to suggest that they were moved even a millimetre. Then there are the larger prints in the snow. Shoes – men's size and style. They show that the killer went over to the victims after he had shot them, probably to check that they were actually dead, and to put the paper bags over their heads.'

Fredrika raised her hand.

'What else can you tell us about these larger prints? The pattern of movement in relation to the boys' footprints?'

The question made the CSI lean over and confer with a colleague before he answered.

'Actually, when it comes to the adult's tracks we have come across a number of things we're finding puzzling. It's clear that the boys ran back and forth and around in circles in the forest; the man seems to have followed them at a distance, never getting very close. It doesn't look as if he was moving as fast as the boys. The footprints are very distinct; the snow hasn't been kicked up and scuffed, which is what happens when you run fast.'

A murmur spread around the room, but Alex didn't take his eyes off Fredrika. He had seen her looking exactly like this on so many occasions: on full alert, right down to her fingertips. She was formulating a new theory. Alex realised he was smiling. She obviously hadn't lost her edge while she'd been away.

'Exactly how did he move around the bodies? Can you explain?' she said.

'What do you mean?'

'I mean, can you tell how he acted after he'd shot the first child? Did he go up to the body at that point, or did he wait until he'd shot them both?'

The CSI nodded to show he'd understood.

'That's another anomaly,' he said. 'It looks as if the killer went up to the children separately. There are no tracks linking the bodies, nothing to indicate that he walked from one to the other. One could therefore conclude that he shot one of the boys, went over to the body, then went all the way back to the track, where we think his vehicle was parked. This may have been to reload his gun, but that's just a theory. Then it looks as if he came back out of the forest.'

'Drove out the second child, and shot him when he was fifty metres from his friend,' Fredrika said.

'That is a possible scenario.'

Alex tried to process what he was hearing. A man walking purposefully among snow-covered trees. A man who didn't appear to be in any hurry. Who didn't leave until he had finished what he had set out to achieve.

What he had set out to achieve.

Bloody hell.

The realisation struck Alex like a punch in the face.

Fredrika put his thoughts into words:

'I don't think the boys escaped. I think he let them go. One at a time. Then he pursued his prey, like a hunter. The paper bags over their heads aren't necessarily a hidden message meant for a particular recipient; they could just as easily be his calling card.'

The meeting had lasted no longer than fifteen minutes, but it had stirred things up for Peder Rydh. Efraim Kiel had come to see him. In spite of the fact that he had appeared calm and collected, Peder had sensed an air of frustration, a degree of stress that he couldn't quite figure out.

Kiel asked questions about the murdered teacher and the boys; wondered if there was any information about whether the killer had marked his victims, or left some kind of calling card at the scenes of the crimes. He was particularly interested in the murder of Josephine.

Peder was surprised and confused.

A calling card?

Not that he'd heard of, no.

But if that was the case, he was certain the police would keep quiet about that particular detail. It could jeopardise the entire investigation if there was a leak about what made this killer unique.

'I do realise that,' Efraim Kiel said. 'But I'm not asking you what you've read in the online press, but what you've found out from your former colleagues.'

'Next to nothing,' Peder replied.

Truthfully.

'Well, I suggest you contact someone you can trust and find out how far they've got. Because we need that information.'

Do we?

Peder didn't like Kiel's tone of voice, and nor did he understand what 'we' meant. Wasn't Kiel supposed to have gone home by now?

Then Kiel asked what Peder thought about the two cases.

'Are they connected?' he said.

Peder hesitated. How much did he dare say?

'I'm not sure,' he said. 'We can't rule out the possibility that the bullet was meant for someone else.'

Efraim Kiel looked pleased.

Satisfied.

'I agree. It would be unfortunate if any other members of the community died just because we ignored the obvious, wouldn't you say?'

It wasn't a question.

It felt more like a threat.

'Of course,' Peder agreed, trying to sound as if he was on top of things, as if he understood the background to their conversation. Which he didn't. Not at all.

'I'll be staying in town for a while,' Efraim Kiel said finally. 'And while I'm here we'll be working together. Understood?'

Peder understood. He nodded, got to his feet and shook hands.

He understood that he didn't understand people like Kiel, that he had never been a part of that world. And when he was alone in his office with a cup of coffee a little while later, he couldn't help wondering: Why was someone like Efraim Kiel interested in the murder of a teacher and two boys in Stockholm?

Peder thought about going home. The working day was over; the phone had stopped ringing. There was a high level of anxiety among the members of the community; people had started asking whether they ought to keep their children off school. Peder didn't think that was necessary.

There were two inquisitive journalists for every anxious parent. In the police service such calls went straight to the information unit, but at the Solomon Community Peder was expected to deal with them personally. When it came to that particular aspect of his job, he felt weak and inadequate. And he had absolutely no patience.

And then there was Efraim Kiel, asking questions about calling cards at the scene of the crime. Why hadn't he gone back to Israel as planned? Peder didn't like the feeling that someone was keeping an eye on him, questioning his actions. However, was it advisable to fall out with a man like Efraim Kiel over the issue?

He thought not.

It was almost six o'clock, and Eden Lundell was already on the way home to her family. She was feeling better since she had been to see GD and demanded to know what they were going to do about Efraim Kiel.

'We have to be patient,' GD had said. 'Wait for him to make a mistake. So far all he's done is move between his hotel and the Solomon Community in Östermalm. We can hardly deport him for that.'

From a logical point of view Eden knew that GD was absolutely right, but on a more emotional level, it wasn't enough. She knew both Efraim and his employer, Mossad. Something was going on, otherwise he wouldn't have stayed for so long.

She was a little calmer after speaking to a former colleague in the National Crime Unit; he had been in touch with the Solomon Community because of the murdered teacher, and told her that the community was in the process of appointing a new head of security. That sounded like something Efraim might be involved in.

But guesses weren't enough for Eden. She wanted to know exactly what she was talking about. The simplest method would be to confront him, of course, demand an answer. But could she really do that? Did she have the strength to see him?

I don't think so.

It took her less than fifteen minutes to walk from Police HQ at Polhemsgatan 30 to their apartment on Sankt Eriksplan.

'Perfect,' Mikael had said when they first went to see it. We'll be able to walk to Vasa Park with the girls.'

Eden had been taken aback, then she had burst out laughing.

'Of course we will, darling,' she had said, squeezing his hand.

In spite of the fact that they both knew that the only person who would be taking the girls to the park was Mikael.

A wonderful aroma filled her nostrils as she opened the front door.

Her daughters were drawn to the sound of her key in the lock like iron filings to a magnet. They raced into the hallway and hurled themselves at her. Eden opened her arms and gave them a big hug.

You do know I love you, even though I rarely say it out loud?

Twin girls. Non-identical in appearance, and even more different when it came to their personality. Saba was like Eden, spirited and straight-backed, stubborn and uncompromising. She even looked like a copy of her mother. Dani, on the other hand . . . Sometimes it actually hurt when Eden looked at the child who had been born fourteen minutes after her sister.

Because Dani was a carbon copy of the twins' father.

But Eden was the only one who could see it.

The apartment was almost completely silent when Fredrika Bergman got home. The only sound came from the TV in the living room. For a moment she was gripped by an illogical fear that something had happened.

'Hello?' she said, when she had hung up her coat and taken off her boots.

She walked quickly down the hallway, glanced into the kitchen, which was empty.

Her son came rushing towards her out of nowhere. He was grinning from ear to ear and babbling at the top of his voice. He was a clever boy, but unfortunately he couldn't talk yet.

She picked him up and held him tight. Inhaled the smell of him, stroked his hair. Tried not to think about the boys she had seen lying in the snow that morning. Tomorrow the parents would be interviewed again. A colleague had asked a few brief questions when they were informed of the deaths; neither family had been able to think of a single person who would have any reason to do this to them. And both couples had alibis for the time when the boys went missing. That was enough to begin with.

Saga came racing after her little brother.

'Daddy's reading us a story,' she said.

Fredrika bent down, put an arm around her and kissed her cheek.

'Lovely,' she said.

Saga took her hand, pulling Fredrika towards her bedroom.

Spencer was sitting on his daughter's bed with a book of fairy tales on his knee. He looked abandoned. His silver-grey hair was sticking up, and his shirt was creased.

A mature parent of two small children.

'Hi,' she said.

'Hi yourself,' he said, looking up.

They smiled at one another.

She moved towards the bed, and Saga immediately scrambled up and onto Spencer's lap. Fredrika put down her son, who crawled under his daddy's arm. Fredrika joined them on the edge of the bed.

If I wasn't around, would he be able to bring them up himself?

'Sorry I'm late,' she said. 'Have you eaten?'

It was only six thirty, but the children ate early.

'We had macaroni and sausage an hour ago. There's some left if you want it.'

She did. She got up and went into the kitchen, took out a plate and filled it with food from the pans on the hob. As she warmed it in the microwave, she allowed herself to reflect on the small things that they had lost since having children. There had been a time when they ate only delicacies and drank obscenely expensive wines when they got together. On the other hand, back then they had had nothing else apart from the food and wine.

If she was forced to lose her current life . . .

If someone took her children away . . .

Would she be able to replace them with a good cheese and a glass of fine wine?

She swallowed hard. Some things couldn't be changed; it went against nature. These days she couldn't care less what she ate, just as long as her family was alive and healthy.

She tried to make sense of all the images that had come crowding in during the day. The boys who had died, their grieving parents. And she still couldn't shake off the feeling that they had overlooked something, that the material they had to work on was somehow too much and yet at the same time, too little.

We're missing something, she thought again. Something fundamental and important. Something to do with the Eisenberg and Goldmann families. And the paper bags. The killer's calling card. Suddenly Fredrika was convinced that there would be more victims. She just didn't know when.

Alex wasn't really a fan of unwritten rules, particularly as they usually passed him by and made him appear clumsy and insensitive. Which he wasn't. But there was one rule that he always observed to the letter: the one that said he wasn't allowed to talk about work at home if the case involved children or young people who had died or been mistreated.

The background to this rule was both simple and painful. That was how he and Diana had met; he had been investigating her daughter's disappearance. He had promised Diana that he would never stop looking, that he would make sure she got her daughter back. Which she did. But it took three years before he found the place where her killer had laid her to rest.

So Alex didn't mention the two boys when he got home.

'Have you had a good day?' Diana said as they stood in the kitchen with a glass of wine.

'Absolutely,' Alex said, taking a sip.

She stroked his arm.

'Could you make a salad?'

'Of course.'

If his children could see him now . . . Over all the years he had been married to their mother, they had never seen him make a salad. Or anything else, for that matter. Lena had taken care of all the cooking, along with everything else in the household.

At an early stage Diana had made it clear that she didn't want things to be that way. She wanted them to build and look after their home together. They had never argued about it; he had simply fallen in with her wishes. He was still embarrassed to think about how he had let Lena fight to keep the home and family running smoothly while he worked.

'It doesn't matter whether you get home at six o'clock or ten o'clock,' Diana had said. 'I'll wait for you, and we'll eat when you get in. And it will be a meal that we have prepared together.'

Simple and fair. A routine he had grown to love.

But the boys with the paper bags over their heads refused to leave him in peace. They were in his thoughts as he washed rocket leaves and sliced tomatoes.

Just before he left work he had received the news he had been dreading. The news he didn't want to hear.

The boys had been shot with the same gun as the preschool teacher. Therefore there was an undeniable connection between the two cases.

And outside the snow began to fall once more.

CONCLUSION

FRAGMENT III

It is time to remove the bodies. The child who is still alive has already been taken to Karolinska Hospital in Solna, but her mother refused to go with her.

'She won't need me until she comes round,' was all she said when someone pointed out that there was room for her in the ambulance if she wanted to go with her daughter.

The inspector is in hell.

The air in the apartment is thin, lacking in oxygen, and he has to fight for every breath.

Eventually he goes over and opens the bedroom window.

The dead are placed on trolleys, ready to be wheeled out of the room.

Then at last the woman moves; until now she has remained standing by the doorway as if she has been turned to stone.

Slowly she walks over to her husband and looks at his lifeless body.

'He will never come back,' she says.

It is impossible to tell whether this is a question or a statement. The inspector decides to act as if it is the former.

'No, he won't.'

The inspector watches as the woman processes what he has just said. But what can he see in her face?

Relief?

Of course not. Why would she be relieved because her husband is dead?

Then she turns to the child.

'I will miss you until the day I die,' she says.

She bends down and kisses the child's forehead, then she straightens up and moves back a step.

The scene is so upsetting that the inspector doesn't know what to do with himself.

And he cannot take his eyes off the violin. Music can have a healing power, but the inspector isn't sure it will be enough in this case. Particularly if the child who has been taken to hospital dies.

If that happens, it will all be over.

When the trolleys have been wheeled out, he goes over to the woman who has been robbed of her family. He doesn't touch her, but stands close.

'How can I help you?' he says. 'If there's anything at all . . . I'll do whatever you ask.'

Her gaze is fixed on something outside the bedroom window.

'Thank you, but I don't need anything.'

And so they stand there. All around them the CSIs work silently and with total concentration. You get the feeling that if they interrupted their task for just one second, they would burst into tears. The inspector feels as if he is walking on brittle glass. One false move and the ground will collapse beneath his feet.

During his entire career, he has never known a greater tragedy. Never.

But that is not the worst thing.

The worst thing is that he doesn't understand what has

happened. Why the Paper Boy came to this particular address and took fresh victims.

He daren't ask. Not right now.

He doesn't need to; she tells him anyway.

'You're wondering why he came here,' she says.

'Yes.'

'It's my fault.'

'None of this is your fault.'

She nods slowly, and then he sees them. The tears. Welling up in her eyes and spilling over.

'It's my fault,' she says again. 'I have always known that I wouldn't get away with what I did.'

He feels a spurt of anger, shakes his head.

'What on earth do you think you've done, for God's sake?'

But she doesn't answer. She is not yet ready to share her secret.

EARLIER

The Third Day

FRIDAY, 27 JANUARY 2012

More fucking snow. A punishment from God for a crime he wasn't even aware of. Efraim Kiel was sitting in his hotel room, staring at the grainy images on his computer. He couldn't see a fucking thing. If he hadn't stolen the tape from the CCTV camera, he would have gone down to reception and asked what kind of useless fucking camera they were using.

It had been laughably simple to get hold of the film. He had installed similar cameras elsewhere; it had taken him less than an hour to locate the computer where the sequences were saved. Bizarrely, it was in the luggage storage room. It wasn't clear if this was a temporary arrangement, but he hoped so, otherwise he felt sorry for the hotel management; they must have had terrible advice when they installed their security system.

However, it had made it much easier for Efraim to get hold of the images that would show him who had left the message at the desk. He had his suspicions, but was praying to every higher power he could think of that he would be proved wrong.

And now he was sitting in his room trying to make sense of what he was looking at.

A blizzard.

A chimney sweep in a darkroom.

And that bothered him, because he wouldn't have expected images from this kind of camera to look like that.

Irritation and a feeling that was entirely unfamiliar to him – anxiety – spread through his body like an itch. Could someone have sabotaged the camera? Put something over the lens?

But how was that possible when reception was always staffed?

He told himself to calm down. There were a thousand ways to get into buildings and areas where you weren't supposed to be. You dressed up as a tradesman. Someone who had come to install cable TV. A cleaner. Anyone at all who opened doors that were otherwise locked.

The Paper Boy could have easily got into the hotel lobby and done what he wanted to do.

Efraim clenched his fist and pressed it against his forehead. He had to stop thinking about the Paper Boy as an individual, as someone who actually existed.

It's only a story, a myth. He doesn't exist.

But in that case, who had sent him the message?

He was starting to think that it must be the Paper Boy who had once lived. Who had not been a myth. But if that was the case, then Efraim had a difficult task ahead, because that Paper Boy couldn't be left to his own devices; he would need help, someone to bring him to his senses.

Efraim's heart rate was normally forty-seven beats per minute, but at the moment it was significantly higher. And it was pounding, as if it was having difficulty in pumping the blood around his body. He got up and went into the bathroom. Washed his face and dried it with a hand towel.

He had to pull himself together.

Focus.

The Paper Boy had issued an invitation to the dance, but Efraim wasn't interested in meeting him halfway. He couldn't really understand why he didn't just pack his bag and go home, why he was still here.

Because I know I can't get away, wherever I hide.

Resolutely he left his hotel room.

As he closed the door, he saw the note.

It was lying on the floor outside his room. Out in the open, so that anyone passing by could read what it said. Then again, they probably wouldn't understand it, because once again the message was written in Hebrew.

A piece of white paper with black characters.

I can see you
all the time
but you can't see me.
Strange, don't you think?

His coffee had gone cold. Peder Rydh didn't really want it anyway. Perhaps he needed a glass of wine, or a whisky. Although it was too early in the day. Even when he had been at his lowest, he had never drunk alcohol for breakfast.

He was sitting at his desk, frowning. How the hell was he supposed to find the answer Efraim had demanded? He wanted to know whether the person – or persons – who had shot the teacher and the two boys had left behind any kind of calling card. He would never be able to get that kind of detail out of the police, and Alex certainly wouldn't tell him something like that.

But perhaps he could try someone he knew in the National Crime Unit.

Because hadn't Alex said that the case of the murdered teacher had been passed over to the team specialising in organised crime? Peder knew at least one of the investigators on that team – not very well, but he didn't think that was necessary. Not when it came to that particular person.

His colleague answered almost straight away. He sounded stressed at first, then surprised when he realised who was calling.

'Peder, it's been a long time!'

You could say that.

'How are you?' his colleague said.

'Fine, thanks.'

After one or two more polite exchanges, Peder explained what he was after. He rarely answered honestly when someone asked 'How are you?' or 'How are things?' Nobody really wanted to know the truth.

'Are you involved in the investigation into the fatal shooting outside the Solomon school?' he said.

His colleague sounded extremely dubious when he replied.

'The teacher, you mean? Yes, I am.'

'Listen, I know I'm not part of the job any more,' Peder said, although it still pained him to say the words out loud. 'But I'm working as head of security with the Solomon Community, and as I'm sure you understand, what's happened has given rise to a hell of a lot of questions.'

'Sorry, but the whole thing is proscribed. I can't . . .'

'I'm not asking you to. I'm just wondering whether you found anything, some object the killer might have left behind. A calling card.'

'Where?'

That was a good question. *Where?* What had Efraim meant?

'Where he was lying when he fired the shot,' Peder said eventually. 'Or anywhere else inside the building.'

'Not a thing. He seems to have been an ice-cold bastard. He just went up there, did what he'd come to do, and left.'

'Okay. Thanks very much, and I'm sorry to have disturbed you.'

'No problem, sorry I couldn't help.'

Peder ended the call, then got to his feet, put on his coat and left the building. The weather had deteriorated; soft clouds filled the sky, making him shiver.

He went across the street to the Solomon school, nodding to the guards outside as he went inside. He recognised the secretary on reception; she had shown him round the previous day. Her greeting was a little subdued; Peder knew there was to be a service for Josephine and the boys in the synagogue later that morning. He wondered if he was expected to attend, or stay away.

'How can I help?' she said.

He hardly knew himself. He supposed he was still looking for calling cards, but how could the secretary help him with that?

'I just wanted to check that everything is okay,' he said. 'You haven't had any strange phone calls, anything like that?'

He sounded like a police officer, but she didn't appear to react. She shook her head.

'No, nothing.'

'Good, that's excellent. And no unexpected packages or messages?'

'No.'

Of course not. What had he expected? That the killer would have sent a calling card over by courier?

'But we have had a huge amount of flowers,' the secretary said, smiling for the first time. 'Look.'

She pointed to a table at the other end of the room; it was almost completely covered in flowers and pot plants.

'We're going to display them in the hall later so that the children can see how many people care.'

'That's lovely,' Peder said. 'Are they from community members?'

'Mostly, but some have come from outside.'

She got up and went over to the table.

'For example, this one arrived yesterday,' she said, showing Peder a large red flower; he had no idea what it was called.

'Lovely,' he said again.

He noticed that the waste bin under the secretary's desk was overflowing with the discarded paper the flowers had been wrapped in; some had spilled over onto the floor.

'Goodness, look at the mess,' she said apologetically when she noticed Peder looking at the bin. 'I'll tidy it up in a minute.'

He could see a number of paper bags on the floor, and assumed they had been used for delivery. He crouched down automatically to take a closer look. Ordinary paper bags, some bearing address labels giving details of both the sender and the recipient.

One of the bags caught his attention. A brown, medium-sized bag with no label – but someone had drawn on it.

'That was one of the first to arrive,' the secretary said. 'A beautiful chrysanthemum.'

She pointed and Peder picked up the plant, which was in a plain white pot.

'No card,' he said.

'No,' the secretary said unhappily. 'Some of the cards must have fallen off, which is annoying. Or they were attached to the bags, and I just didn't notice them.'

Peder looked at the bag once again. No name anywhere.

But there was a drawing.

'Don't throw this one away,' he said. 'Show it to the police.'
'But why?'
'Because I think it might be important.'

The morning after yet another night of very little sleep. The dead boys haunted her, mixed up with other cases that Fredrika Bergman had investigated in the past. Cases where children had fared badly.

Life was fragile. Small mistakes could have disastrous consequences. Fredrika had seen it happen more times than she could remember, and yet she was always equally surprised.

She didn't know whether Carmen and Gideon Eisenberg had made any mistakes that might explain why they had lost their son. There wasn't a sound when she and Alex walked into their house the morning after they had been told that their son had been shot dead out on the island of Lovön. It had been a long night; that was clear from their exhausted faces.

Did grief have a different shape and colour in a foreign land? Perhaps people dealt differently with heavy losses if they had grown up in a place where peace never seemed to last, where there was always unrest and no one could ever be sure how tomorrow would turn out.

Fredrika realised she felt completely at a loss with the Eisenbergs. Carmen, to whom Fredrika had spoken the previous day, was sitting at the table with her husband. He had reached across the polished surface and placed his hand on hers, and was just gazing at her.

No tears, no screaming.

Not then.

Not in front of Fredrika and Alex.

But she could see that they had been crying, and no doubt there would be more tears once she and Alex had left.

The parents had been given answers to the most important questions at the hospital.

No, it didn't look as if their son had been subjected to violence or physical abuse before his death.

No, he wouldn't have suffered when he died; death would have been instantaneous.

However, they had not been told that the boys had had bags on their heads, or that they appeared to have been hunted down by their killer. There would be a time for that kind of information, but this wasn't it.

There would be a short interview today, nothing more. Not on the first day.

It was less than forty-eight hours since Fredrika and Alex had been talking to Josephine's parents about the loss of their daughter. Fredrika thought about the three deaths, trying to digest the news that they now had proof that there was a connection.

Her own words still echoed in her brain: the paper bags could be a calling card. A serial killer's calling card. In which case they could expect more victims.

But that kind of thing just doesn't happen. The worst nightmares never become reality. And serial killers don't exist. Not in real life.

Fredrika and Alex were sitting side by side. The table seemed too small for two grieving parents and two stressed-out investigators. The whole kitchen was too small. And the silence was too huge.

It was Alex who broke it.

'At the moment we don't know why this has happened,' he said, speaking slowly as if he were choosing every single word with the greatest care. 'But I can promise you that we will spare no effort in this case. We will do everything, and I mean *everything*, to find the person or persons behind the murders of Simon and Abraham.'

He stopped speaking, allowing what he had just said to sink in. That was how he built trust, by focusing on clarity and pledging only what was reasonable. He had said they would do everything they could to find the perpetrator, and that was true. He had not, however, promised that they would succeed, which was also true, unfortunately. Sometimes they failed. It had happened as recently as last autumn, when the person responsible for hijacking Flight 573 had got away.

But they knew who the guilty party was, and they were still looking.

They would never stop.

Sometimes that was as far as they got, even if it was incredibly frustrating.

'What's your take on all this?' Alex said. 'Do you have any enemies or unresolved disputes?'

They had been asked the question before, and they would be asked again. Sooner or later they would remember something that was key to the inquiry.

Carmen and Gideon Eisenberg looked at one another, and Fredrika knew what they were thinking. Unresolved disputes? Of such magnitude that they had cost their son his life?

They both shook their head.

'No,' Gideon said. 'No, we haven't.'

At first glance they were a harmonious couple. Same sense of humour, same character. But Fredrika thought she could sense something else beneath the surface. There was a fragility about Gideon that she couldn't see in Carmen. She was the stronger one, although Fredrika couldn't imagine how much strength she would need to get through what lay ahead: burying her son, and learning to live with his absence.

'And what about Simon?' she said. 'Did he have any enemies?'

Gideon stared at her as if she had lost her mind.

'He was a child.'

Fredrika swallowed hard. Children could be cruel; they could do the most unforgivable things. And behind every humiliated child was a frustrated parent, determined to stand up for their offspring.

Alex understood what she was asking.

'We believe Simon and Abraham were picked up in a car by an adult they knew. Would they have got in the car if they didn't know that person well?'

'No,' Carmen said firmly. 'Neither of them would have done that, particularly not Abraham.'

Which was interesting, because Abraham wasn't her son.

'How can you be so sure?' Fredrika asked.

'His parents were very strict about that,' Gideon said. 'And we were the same with Simon, although Abraham was more receptive to rules.'

Another peculiar turn of phrase.

'More receptive to rules.'

'Both his parents have a military background,' Carmen

explained quietly. 'Abraham is . . . was . . . very impressed by that. Discipline appealed to him, clear guidelines. It went hand in hand with his arrogance. As you know, being late didn't bother him at all. Simon was a more normal child; he usually did as we said, but occasionally he went his own way.'

'But he would never have got into a stranger's car,' Gideon said, sounding decisive for the first time.

Fredrika allowed her curiosity to take over.

'Could I ask about your background?'

The couple exchanged glances.

'I studied engineering at university in Jerusalem, and I now work in IT security,' Gideon said. 'Carmen is an architect.'

Fredrika and Alex already knew that; she had asked about their background.

'What did you do when you lived in Israel?'

'The same.'

The answer was curt and evasive.

'So you don't have a military background like Abraham's parents?'

Gideon's expression was dark as he looked at Fredrika.

'Everyone in Israel has a "military background". Like eighty-five per cent of the male population, I did three years' military service.'

'Why did you move to Sweden?' Alex asked.

Carmen sighed.

'We had family here, and Gideon had been over several times through work. Israel can be . . . trying. If it's not the heat, it's the political situation. We were tired of all the tension. I don't know if you remember, but 2002 was a terrible year in Israel. That was when the violence reached its absolute peak following the second Intifada. And when we found out we were having a baby . . .'

She broke off, unable to go on.

And Fredrika, who had carried and given birth to two babies, felt the tears well up.

Get a grip. Get a grip.

Alex looked from Gideon to Carmen, his gaze steady but sympathetic.

'You can ring me at any time,' he said, giving them his card. 'About anything you think could be of interest in the investigation, or if you have questions.'

He got to his feet.

'We'll leave you in peace.'

The four of them walked from the kitchen to the hallway. Fredrika thought back to what Carmen had said about their reasons for leaving Israel. It was a cruel irony that they had come to Sweden to escape terror and violence, only to see their firstborn murdered.

She realised she had one more question.

'Did Simon spend a lot of time on the internet?'

Gideon put his arm around Carmen's shoulders.

'No more than other children, I imagine.'

Fredrika had no idea what that meant. Her own children were too young for computers, and if their father had his way, they would never go anywhere near one. They would learn to use a typewriter, and if they wanted to play games, they could play chess.

Carmen leaned against her husband.

'He discovered a new forum only a month or so ago,' she said. 'On the internet, I mean. Abraham showed him, although we didn't really like it. Super Troopers, it's called.'

A forum. A place for people to meet. Possibly a place for a killer to find his victims.

'Why didn't you like it?' Alex asked.

'I got the impression that nobody was being themselves,' Carmen said. 'Everyone had an alias, and it was nothing but a place to boast and show off. It seemed to attract young boys so that they could tell each other how to excel at various activities.'

They would have to check this out. It might be a dead end, but it could be important.

'Did Abraham and Simon also have aliases?' Fredrika said.

A single tear ran down Carmen's cheek.

'Both boys used their real names for some aspects, but they wanted an alias as well. Abraham was keen to make a bold impression as usual, and called himself the Warrior. But not Simon.'

'No?'

'No, he called himself the Paper Boy.'

There was no such thing as a lie-in in Eden Lundell's world. She got up at six and liked to go for a run before she woke the rest of the family. Then she would make breakfast and eat in silence. Her daughters did the same.

Eden loathed noise. Some people seemed to think that kids couldn't help being loud, but Eden didn't agree. She had walked out of a restaurant halfway through dinner more than once because children at nearby tables didn't know how to behave. How hard could it be to turn small people into decent human beings?

Mikael didn't necessarily agree; he thought she was too harsh, and said that kids have to be allowed to be kids. No one was denying that, but Eden couldn't see any contradiction between being a child and understanding the importance of not acting like a monster.

She dropped the girls off at day care and walked to work.

Mikael had a meeting with a youth group, and had left home early. He was always keen to get to work, and that gave Eden peace of mind. He was needed out in the real world, beyond the home that he and Eden had built for themselves and their children.

Eden loved her job too. The first thing she did when she got in to the office was to make sure she was up to speed with the counter-terrorism unit's latest initiative. Meeting after meeting. Why did they have to spend so much time stuck in a room with other people, talking? Talking and talking, as if that was what would bring peace on earth. She remembered the previous day's sad excursion to Drottningholm; the children lying in the snow. How much would it help them if the grown-ups in the world shut themselves in a room with crap air conditioning and talked?

Not one fucking jot.

The Solomon Community seemed to have abandoned its attempts to get her involved in the case. Just as well, because she didn't want to know. Her parents would have been bitterly disappointed if they had known that she was turning her back on her people. Since they had left London for Israel, the relationship had been strained. Mikael had actually wanted to go with them, and had put the idea to Eden as a serious suggestion.

She had wondered if he had lost his mind. He wasn't even Jewish – he was a priest in the Swedish church – so why the hell would he want to emigrate to Israel? A country smaller than the province of Småland, surrounded by countries that in the best case scenario might possibly accept its existence, but would never make the effort to develop good relations. She had said the same thing to her parents, wondering why her British mother and Swedish father wanted to become Israeli citizens.

But no one knew the real reason why she could never consider going to live in Israel.

Efraim Kiel.

The man who had almost cost her everything, the man she sometimes still dreamed of at night, damn him. The man who was now wandering the streets of Stockholm. Much too close for comfort.

When the cavalcade of meetings was finally over, she hurried back to the glass box that served as her office. She closed the door and found the latest surveillance reports. What had Efraim been up to overnight and during the morning?

Not much, as it turned out.

He had left the hotel and gone to the Solomon Community. Just as on the day before, he had stood outside inspecting the bullet hole in the wall. He had also spoken to the security guards before going inside.

Was he a part of the community's security set-up? She didn't think so.

But he was obviously interested in the deaths that had shaken the group over the last couple of days. There was nothing strange about that; he had an impressive background in intelligence, and would no doubt be able to make a significant contribution to the investigation.

Eden tapped her pen impatiently on the desk.

The case was being investigated by the Swedish police. There was no way they would let Efraim or anyone else from the community into their work. She opened up the homepages of the major newspapers, glanced through the articles that had already been written about the murders. Alex Recht was quoted in several instances.

Eden knew she could call him; that wouldn't be a problem. She reached for the phone, then put it down. What would she say? What was it she wanted to know?

Säpo had nothing to do with the cases, and Eden didn't know any of the victims. She could of course pretend that she was just generally concerned; play the Jewish card. But bearing in mind that she had turned her back on the Solomon Community, that went against the grain.

You see, I do have scruples.

She looked up from the screen, glanced out of the glass walls of her office. It was as if Säpo had been lifted out of the world around it, cut off from the universe. In a way it was a universe of its own, enclosed and turned away from everything else. When she saw the heavy snow coming down, she felt even more isolated.

She had to pull herself together; it was no good sitting here getting miserable.

She had one last surveillance report on Efraim to look through, and that was where she found her first concrete lead on what he was up to.

The guys tailing Efraim had been quite creative. One of them had gone into Efraim's hotel, up to the floor where he was staying, and stood outside his door, ready to pretend that he was lost, if anyone asked what he was doing. He had wanted to know if Efraim was alone in the room. According to the report, he hadn't heard a sound from inside. He had, however, made a discovery. Someone had left Efraim a message. It was lying on the floor outside his door, out in the open so that anyone could read it. The agent had taken a photograph with his mobile.

It wasn't actually correct to say that anyone could read it; the message was written in Hebrew, and as far as Eden knew, there weren't many Hebrew speakers in Sweden.

She, however, was an exception. It was an easy language; she had needed less than a year to master it. She read the short lines.

I can see you
all the time
but you can't see me.
Strange, don't you think?

Indeed it was strange. Could it be a joke? Was it meant to be funny? She didn't think so.

She read the message again.

This had nothing to do with any kind of intelligence work, she knew that. Agents and spies didn't leave each other such indiscreet notes. So it must be related to a private matter.

I can see you.

But you can't see me.

Eden didn't understand, and it was clear that she wasn't meant to. But she did understand one thing, and it bothered her.

Säpo weren't the only ones watching Efraim.

Someone else was following every step he took.

Alex and Fredrika didn't waste any time, but went straight from the Eisenbergs to the Goldmanns. They left the car where it was; the very thought of starting it up and driving through the narrow streets of Östermalm in the heavy snowfall raised Alex's blood pressure.

The Warrior and the Paper Boy.

From what they had learned about both boys so far, these seemed like pretty good descriptions. What bothered Alex was the fact that they had chosen the names themselves. The Warrior he could understand, but what ten-year-old kid would come up with the Paper Boy? Paper was weak, fragile. Easily torn apart. And Boy? Ten-year-olds weren't usually keen on that word either.

'Their aliases,' he said to Fredrika.

'I was thinking about the same thing. Especially the Paper Boy. Why would he call himself that?'

'I've no idea. We must remember to mention it to his parents, ask if it really should be taken literally, or if there's some reference we've missed.'

They walked in silence through the snow. Why did it have to be so cold? All the time? Alex increased his speed. Perhaps it wasn't just the Paper Boy they should be puzzling over; the Warrior wasn't necessarily the obvious choice for a boy in Year Four.

When Alex's children were little they had played football. Climbed trees. Played hide and seek and hopscotch. Built snow caves. Did kids still do that kind of thing? Or did they spend every waking hour in front of the computer?

Alex hated it when men of his age started to sound like old farts. Nobody listened to old farts, not even Alex himself. But sometimes he caught himself thinking that certain things actually had been better in the past. He and Lena hadn't even wanted to buy a video player for their children, because they had thought it would make them stupid if they filled their heads with too much crap.

But nowadays children seemed to spend at least half their lives on the computer. Where were their parents during all those hours? Alex had no idea, but they certainly weren't with their kids. It was hardly surprising that so many young people went astray and came into contact with the wrong people online. You might as well drive them to a sex club and chuck them out of the car with the words: 'You're okay to get home on your own, aren't you?'

The previous day the police had taken the computers the two boys normally used from the Eisenberg and Goldmann households. Alex had spoken to the IT technicians, but had been told that they needed more time; there was too much material to get through in an afternoon. As he and Fredrika left the Eisenbergs he had called the technicians again:

'There's a forum called Super Troopers, some sort of elitist crap for kids who want to be winners. Check it out, will you?'

The apartment lay a short distance from Karlaplan, and it was enormous. The Goldmann family business had been very successful, but otherwise their lives were in ruins.

Daphne and Saul Goldmann had lost their only child. Alex just couldn't imagine what that must do to a person.

How many ways are there to offer condolences? Many, he decided. For the third time this week he was sitting with grieving parents, trying to tell them that he understood that what had happened to them was the most horrific thing imaginable, and that he would do all he could to see that justice was done.

'It was very strange,' Daphne said in the same icy tone Alex had heard the last time they met. 'We saw a counsellor at the hospital. Do you know what she said?'

It was a rhetorical question. She didn't seem to expect an answer.

'No,' Alex said anyway.

'She said we were still parents. Parents without a child.'

She looked at her husband.

'Parents without a child? What kind of parents are those? Is that supposed to make me feel better?'

Alex and Fredrika exchanged a glance. They were in deep waters here. They could say that the counsellor was only doing her job, but it was probably best not to get involved.

'I agree,' Alex said instead. 'That was a very peculiar thing to say.'

'Wasn't it just?' Daphne said.

Silence fell in the library where they were sitting. Between the tall bookcases they could see framed enlargements of black and white photographs. A young Saul and Daphne in uniform. With and without guns in their hands. Or on their backs. Alone or with others. Alex recognised Gideon Eisenberg in one of the pictures.

'You know the Eisenbergs?' he said.

Daphne and Saul nodded.

'Is that how Simon and Abraham became friends?'

The parents without a child looked as if they didn't know how to answer.

'Yes and no,' Saul said eventually. 'Gideon and I knew each other well in Israel, and then we moved to Stockholm at the same time. Had children at the same time. But we grew apart, as they say.'

Daphne joined in.

'We got to know different people here, worked in different places. After a while we didn't seem to have that much in common. But the boys ended up in the same class at the Solomon school, and carried on spending time together.'

Alex could see that Fredrika had also noticed the picture of Gideon.

She pointed: 'Did you and Gideon do your military service together?'

'Yes.'

'Was that where you got to know one another?'

He shook his head.

'We grew up on the same kibbutz. We're the same age, and we were in the same class until we finished high school.'

So they had known each other since they were born, and had eventually decided to emigrate together, yet they were no longer close friends. There must have been some kind of disagreement, otherwise that wouldn't have happened.

'Did you stay in the army, or did you have a civilian career in Israel?' Fredrika asked.

Saul stiffened.

'I went to university in Tel Aviv,' he said curtly. 'I did another two years in the army, and that was it.'

Alex looked at the picture again. Admittedly it was always difficult to gauge how old someone else was, but he thought both Gideon and Saul looked older than the usual age for military service.

'And you were also in the army?' Fredrika asked Daphne.

'Yes, but only for a few years, like Saul.'

That didn't match what Gideon and Carmen had said; they had implied that the Goldmanns' military career had been longer.

Alex looked away from the photographs.

'Abraham must have been impressed by your background,' he said.

He smiled as he spoke, hoping to convey warmth.

'Absolutely – he was fascinated,' Daphne said.

'Did he have any thoughts of going into the army?' Alex asked, thinking that Israelis in particular were likely to react more strongly than others to the fact that Sweden had abolished military service, and had virtually no defence left to speak of.

'He was too young for that kind of talk,' Saul said harshly.

But he called himself the Warrior.

'There's an online forum called Super Troopers,' Fredrika said. 'It's for young people; are you aware of it?'

'Of course,' Daphne replied. 'Abraham was often on there chatting to others his own age.'

'It was a good site,' Saul said, sitting up even straighter. 'It encouraged competitiveness; it was character-building, good for morale.'

'So you monitored Abraham's online activities?'

'What do you think? He was ten years old – of course we did,' Daphne said.

And Alex believed her. These were no ordinary parents. They were coaches who had seen it as their duty to prepare their son for adult life, and to do so with a firm hand.

'Why did he call himself the Warrior?' Fredrika asked.

Daphne smiled for the first time. It was a brittle smile, painful to see.

'Because that was his grandfather's nickname, and Abraham really looked up to him.'

Her face crumpled, and Alex thought he was going to see her cry for the first time. It didn't happen.

'Did you or Abraham have any enemies?' he said.

'You asked the same question yesterday,' Daphne said.

'And now I'm asking it again.'

'No.'

'No past disputes or injuries festering away?'

'No.'

So what had happened? Had the boys been picked up by someone who had taken them just because he was crazy? The fact that they had probably known the driver made that unlikely, and suggested that the crime had some personal motive.

It could of course be a combination of the two. The killer could be driven by both insanity and the desire for revenge.

But if someone felt such hatred that it could lead to murder, the people involved usually had an idea of the reason behind it. Daphne and Saul Goldmann didn't seem to have a clue.

Alex felt as if the ground beneath his feet was giving way. His thoughts went back to the case he had investigated with Fredrika and Peder during that summer when it wouldn't stop raining. When Lilian Sebastiansson had disappeared. On that occasion they had been hunting a true psychopath, someone to whom rituals were of great importance. A killer hell bent on avenging past wrongs so diffuse that the parents of the children who went missing had no idea what they were supposed to be guilty of.

Were they back in that same place now? In the hands of a mentally ill person whose motives were unclear?

He hoped to God that wasn't the case, and that this was something different.

'I'm going to be honest with you,' he said. 'I don't think Abraham and Simon were taken at random. The perpetrator was after one or both of them. Probably both, as they were killed in the same way. I also think they were murdered by the person who picked them up on the way to their tennis session. What I need from you and Simon's parents are more leads. Who has done this to you?'

His words settled over Saul and Daphne like a wet cloud. He hadn't sounded angry, hadn't accused them of anything. He had spoken clearly and to the point: he and Fredrika needed their help. That was all there was to it.

'What about your business? Can you think of any disputes or arguments you've been involved in?'

Daphne and Saul looked at one another.

'No,' Daphne said, her voice weaker now. 'No, nothing like that.'

'Think carefully,' Fredrika said. 'It could be something that didn't seem all that serious at the time, but had major consequences for someone else.'

The Goldmanns thought hard, digging in their past for an explanation for what had happened.

Alex didn't think they were lying, but he was concerned that they might be withholding information for private reasons, making their own decisions as to what may or may not be relevant to the investigation. Few things were more dangerous.

He directed the conversation back to the Eisenberg family.

'So you all moved to Sweden at the same time.'

'It was pure coincidence.'

Saul's comment came quickly. Too quickly. It was very clear that he realised he had made a mistake.

'So the move wasn't a joint project?'

'No.'

Once again a response that wasn't a lie, but wasn't the whole truth either. There was something there, Alex could feel it. In the past. Hidden away, buried in Israel. The question was how they were going to get at it if nobody was prepared to talk.

Fredrika moved on to what was intended to be the final key question.

'Can you tell me who the Paper Boy is?'

Daphne didn't move a muscle.

But Saul . . . He opened his mouth to say something, then closed it again. Every scrap of colour drained from his face.

Then he pulled himself together. The colour returned, his breathing slowed down. But it was too late. Both Alex and Fredrika had seen his reaction.

'Why do you ask?' he said.

Alex leaned back in his chair.

'Answer our question first, then I'll answer yours.'

Saul's body language was defensive now.

'He's a fairy-tale character. An Israeli myth. He doesn't exist.'

His jaws were clamped together as he ground out the words.

'Good,' Alex said.

'Why do you ask?' Saul said again, louder this time.

'Because that's what Simon called himself on the Super Troopers forum,' Fredrika said. 'That's all.'

Her answer calmed Saul, but not Alex. Because now he had two leads to follow. First of all he wanted to know why the Eisenberg and Goldmann families had moved to Sweden, and secondly he wanted to know more about the so-called Paper Boy.

Both questions led to Israel.

Food from Thailand and lingonberry juice from Kivik. An extremely late lunch. It was two o'clock before they found time to eat, and Fredrika Bergman was practically screaming with hunger. She and Alex shut themselves in the Snakes' Nest with a takeaway from one of the many Thai restaurants that had opened in the streets around Police HQ. She had no idea who Alex had stolen the juice from, nor did she care.

The aroma of curry spread around the room as soon as they opened the plastic boxes.

'This isn't exactly environmentally friendly,' Fredrika said as she put down the messy lid.

'You're not wrong,' Alex agreed.

Then they settled down to their lunch and forgot about the environment. They had two murders to solve; someone else could worry about the greenhouse effect, dead zones in the Baltic and a whole load of other stuff that Fredrika vaguely felt she cared too little about.

They now had food in their bellies and silence in the room. Silence, but an absence of calm. They had too much to do, too many questions to answer.

Two murders.

Or three, if they included the teacher.

Their efforts to track down the person who had killed the boys out on Lovön had produced sparse results. CSI thought they had an idea of what kind of vehicle had been parked in the spot where they were assuming the boys had been released: a van. A vehicle of that type had been reported stolen the day before the boys were abducted, but it appeared to have vanished into thin air; the number plate hadn't been picked up at any of the pay stations on the city's toll roads. They had tried to find potential witnesses on Lovön, but no one had noticed a van around the time the boys went missing, or when they were shot. It had taken a while to find the bodies in the snow and set up roadblocks on the island, so the killer had had plenty of time to get away.

'Are we working on Josephine's murder as well, now we know the same weapon was used?' Fredrika asked.

'That remains to be seen.'

'It would be the logical move. If we're not running both cases, then we could end up duplicating the work but missing information at the same time.'

'We can't cope with two investigations. There aren't enough of us.'

'But why are we referring to two investigations? It's the same case. Three deaths, one killer.'

Alex pushed away the empty box. Fredrika was always amazed at the speed with which he ate; it was as if he simply inhaled the food.

'How do we know there's only one killer? There could easily be two people working together,' Alex objected.

'The footprints in the snow suggest one perpetrator.'

'And how do you know that the person who hunted down

the boys is the same person who lay on the roof and shot Josephine?'

'You mean someone shot her, then gave the gun to someone else, who took care of the boys?'

Alex shrugged.

'We know nothing, Fredrika. Not a bloody thing.'

She didn't agree.

'We don't know anything for sure, but we have to come up with hypotheses, otherwise we'll get nowhere.'

She put down her fork. She would eat later.

'Alex, I don't believe the boys escaped from their abductor. I think he let them go, one at a time, hunted them down and shot them. I have no idea why. Nor do I know why he made them take off their shoes and socks, or why he put paper bags over their heads.'

'I agree. I don't believe they escaped either, but I'm not sure the fact that they were barefoot is so strange; the killer could have done that just to make sure they wouldn't be able to run very far.'

'Which makes the hunt itself even more interesting. Why was that so important to him?'

Alex's face was distorted with anger when he replied.

'It's more than interesting, it's downright sadistic. The boys must have set off thinking they had a chance of escape. Which they never had. The murders are ritualistic, for fuck's sake. Don't ask me how, I just know that there was nothing random about what we saw out there. The hunt, the bare feet, the paper bags – they're all connected.'

Fredrika had to agree.

Alex rested his elbows on the table and leaned forward.

'So can we assume that the murder of the teacher was also

ritualistic, even though we haven't found any evidence to suggest that?'

'That's what I'm wondering,' Fredrika said. 'The differences in the MO could be down to the fact that the perpetrator wanted it to look as if the murders were unconnected, but then surely he wouldn't have been so careless as to use the same gun.'

'Exactly. Which makes the whole thing so bloody cocky. He doesn't care if we realise he's involved in both crimes. He doesn't even try to hide it.'

'Perhaps that was the idea: the murders were carried out in such different ways so that we'd end up sitting here scratching our heads and wondering who we're looking for.'

Alex stared at her for a long time.

'You're a wise woman,' he said eventually.

Fredrika blushed.

'I just mean . . .'

'I know what you mean, and you're right. Even if you're wrong. We're wasting time, trying to find an explanation for two such different murders, when in fact we only need to solve one in order to find the person responsible for both.'

Fredrika nodded slowly.

'So you think we should leave Josephine's murder with the National Crime Unit after all?'

'For the time being, we carry on working separately; we'll probably meet in the middle at some point anyway.'

That sounded logical.

'Do you seriously believe the only reason behind Josephine's murder was to confuse us?' Fredrika said.

She could hear the doubt in her voice, and did nothing to hide it.

'No. But I do think that we shouldn't ignore leads just because they don't match both cases. Do you have a third hypothesis, or would you like to hear mine?'

Fredrika thought for a moment. The smell of the food was less than pleasant, and she wished it wasn't too cold to open a window, get some fresh air and a shot of energy.

'I do have one more theory,' she said. 'The victims weren't taken by chance. He knew exactly who he was after.'

'Good. I agree. I think our killer is driven by personal motives. The Solomon Community's fear that we're dealing with a crazy serial killer hell bent on murdering Jews is groundless. He doesn't give a toss if they're Jews or Arabs or Chinese. This is personal.'

'In which case there must be a link between the boys and the teacher.'

'Absolutely, but we're not going to start there. We're going to start with what we have.'

'Which is?'

'I have a feeling that the Goldmann and Eisenberg families are being a little circumspect about why they left Israel. It may be of no relevance to the inquiry, but I still want to know what they're not telling us. And there's something else.'

Fredrika's stomach contracted.

'The Paper Boy,' she said.

'Exactly. The boy who called himself the Paper Boy online is found dead with a paper bag over his head. Is that supposed to be a coincidence?'

'Maybe not. The only problem there is that his friend, who called himself the Warrior, was also found dead with a paper bag over his head. We have to be able to explain both deaths, not just one.'

'True. The Paper Boy is supposed to refer to some Israeli myth that I've never heard of,' Alex said. 'It could be that this myth has nothing whatsoever to do with the case, but I still want to know more.'

He looked up with a wry smile.

'Didn't you say Spencer was going to Israel? We might have to give him a little job to do while he's there.'

Fredrika managed a smile in return.

Spencer on a mission in the Promised Land. It was an entertaining but unimaginable concept.

'Just joking,' Alex said.

As if that wasn't obvious. At that moment his mobile rang. Fredrika ate a little more while he was on the phone, but she had lost her appetite. Inside she was in chaos after everything that had happened, while outside heavy snow was falling once more. And somewhere in between, in a no-man's-land that she couldn't even begin to define, she and Alex were supposed to take a murder investigation in the right direction.

She chewed, swallowed.

Alex ended the call.

'That was the secretary at the Solomon school. She rang to tell me about a pot plant that was sent to them anonymously following Josephine's death.'

'And?'

'It arrived in a paper bag with a face drawn on it.'

The stairwell was in darkness. A door opened a couple of floors above, then the light came on. Footsteps on the stairs. Muted crying from one of the apartments. Efraim Kiel thought the child responsible was probably very young; the sound lacked any real strength. It was a long time since Efraim had been a parent, but the memory lingered.

It had taken a while to shake off his Säpo shadows. This time it had been essential to ensure that they didn't follow him; if they had, it would have caused big problems.

Even bigger than the problems he already had.

Efraim's frustration was bordering on intolerable. Whoever had decided to start leaving him messages was starting to get careless. The note outside his hotel room had been nothing short of stupid. It wasn't just that the person could easily have been spotted – it was almost as if he or she *wanted* to be caught.

The tone of the messages was playful, but Efraim knew what they really meant. Someone was following him, and that wasn't good. Particularly in view of the fact that the individual in question was calling himself the Paper Boy.

He had gone to see Peder Rydh again, and that had got him thinking.

Rydh had done his job at long last, and looked for

something that could be a calling card. He didn't seem to understand the importance of what he had found.

A paper bag with a face drawn on it.

The discovery terrified Efraim.

The plant and the bag had been sent to the Solomon Community after the schoolteacher had been shot, but before the boys were found on the golf course. And that told Efraim everything he needed to know.

Now he was almost sure he knew who had contacted him.

Someone passed him on the stairs and carried on down to the ground floor. He couldn't stay here. He was running the risk of being noticed if he didn't move soon.

Why had he actually come here? So that he would know where she lived in case he ever needed to get hold of her in a hurry. He read the nameplate on the door one last time.

'E & M Lundell'.

Good. So this was where Eden had settled down with her husband and children. He looked at the lock; he would be surprised if it was easy to force, but on the other hand he didn't think it would be impossible.

He turned away and went back down the stairs. Personally he would have preferred to live a couple of floors higher up. Distance was good – in all directions. He left the building and cut across Sankt Eriksplan, heading towards Vasa Park.

He never saw the woman standing at the bus stop on Torsgatan as he crossed the road. Nor did he notice when she set off after him.

A paper bag with a face drawn on it.

Three victims shot with the same gun, but on two different occasions.

Fredrika Bergman couldn't take her eyes off the bag in which the chrysanthemum had been delivered to the Solomon Community. It had been picked up from Östermalm by a patrol car and brought to HQ before being sent on to the National Forensics Lab for analysis.

Alex had asked to see it first, and now they were standing in his office, staring at it.

'What the hell are we missing here?' he said, his voice suffused with annoyance. 'A paper bag. With eyes, a nose and a mouth. What's the message, and who is it meant for?'

Fredrika thought about the boys lying in the snow and the paper bags someone had pulled over their heads. At the time she had believed the bags were a nod to an as yet unidentified recipient, then she had wondered if they could be the killer's calling card. This new discovery strengthened that view.

But there was something that didn't fit.

'Tell me what you're thinking,' Alex said, his tone brusque, challenging.

Fredrika took her time before she spoke. She looked

closely at the bag: the large eyes, the pointed nose, the gaping mouth.

She found the photographs of the bags that had been over the boys' heads.

She studied them in detail, then passed them to Alex.

'Look,' she said.

Alex stared at the photographs.

'And now look at this,' she said, pointing to the bag from the school.

Alex made the same comparison. He didn't speak for a moment.

'They're different,' he said eventually.

'I agree. The bags from Lovön are similar, but not identical. The bag the plant was in . . .'

She paused.

'Look at the face. It's much more aggressive. And drawn in different colours.'

The eyes on this bag were coloured blue. The noses were different too: short lines on the original bags, considerably bigger on this one.

'You think we're looking for different perpetrators?' Alex said.

The doubt in his voice told Fredrika that he didn't share her point of view, if that was the case.

'I don't think we can rule it out,' she said.

She sat down and went on:

'First of all our perpetrator shoots a woman outside the Solomon school. He does so while lying on his stomach on a rooftop on the opposite side of the street. By the time the police arrive, he has managed to get off the roof and leave the building without anyone seeing him. But he doesn't stop there. Instead he gets in a car an hour later and picks up Simon and Abraham. Keeps them overnight, and shoots them the following morning.'

Alex was still holding the paper bag. The gloves he was wearing covered the scars on his hands from the time when he saved a child from burning to death.

Fredrika looked away. She didn't want to think about children being burned or hurt in any other way.

'Does that sound reasonable to you?' she said. 'The idea that the same person did all that?'

'What evidence do we have to suggest that there's more than one perpetrator? Concrete evidence, I mean?'

Fredrika took a deep breath.

'None at all.'

'We need to inform the National Crime Unit,' Alex said. 'As I said before, we'll continue to investigate the two crimes separately, but I'm afraid we have to accept what the evidence is telling us: there is only one perpetrator.'

He put down the bag. 'Okay?'

Fredrika nodded. The days when she and Alex stood in opposite corners fighting over which direction the investigation should take were long gone. The team was too small now; she couldn't afford to fly solo any more.

The soloist.

That was what Spencer had called her when they first got to know one another almost twenty years ago. When their love was secret, her desire overwhelming. She had loved him so much back then. She still did. They had both been worried about how they would cope with ordinary everyday life together, but on the whole it had gone unexpectedly well.

The weekend loomed before her like an iceberg. In only

two days' time Spencer would be leaving for Jerusalem. Fredrika had spoken to her mother, who had promised to help out with the children.

She straightened up. Wished she was somewhere else, perhaps with the orchestra. The violin made her feel safe; her job didn't. Not the way things were right now.

Playing the violin was pure enjoyment.

Dead children were about as far from enjoyment as you could possibly get.

As Fredrika was on her way out of Alex's office, a thought suddenly struck him.

'Why did the secretary react to the way the bag looked?' he said.

Fredrika turned back.

'What do you mean?'

'We haven't said a word to the press about the bags we found over the boys' heads. So why did she think it was worth mentioning that someone had drawn on this bag?'

'I've no idea,' Fredrika said. 'You were the one who spoke to her.'

Alex picked up his phone and called the school.

'What was it about that paper bag that made you call the police?' he said. 'Why did you think it would be of interest in our inquiries?'

The secretary sounded surprised.

'I didn't, to be honest.'

Now it was Alex's turn to be surprised.

'So why did you call?'

'It wasn't my idea. Our new head of security suggested it. Peder Rydh.'

Alex thought fast, trying to understand.

'You showed the bag to Peder first?'

'No, he found it himself. He came and asked me if we'd received anything odd after Josephine and the boys were murdered, and then he started looking at the wrapping that the plants and flowers had come in. Why he thought a paper bag would be of interest to the police, I have no idea.'

Nor had Alex. And that bothered him.

Had Peder known what he was looking for among the wrapping? And if so, who was feeding him the information?

The discovery should have pleased him. He had found a significant clue; both Efraim Kiel and the police had confirmed that. If Alex hadn't thought the paper bag was interesting, he wouldn't have had it picked up so quickly.

The only problem was that no one had told Peder Rydh why the bag was so bloody important. In fact, he felt really stupid. He had reacted when he saw the bag in reception, thought it looked different from all the rest and wondered why. But would he have noticed it if Efraim Kiel hadn't talked about calling cards? He wasn't so sure.

The question now was how much he should tell Alex and Fredrika. Without anyone actually putting it into words, he had realised that Efraim Kiel was no ordinary security expert. Apparently he had travelled all the way from Israel to assist the Solomon Community to recruit a new head of security; that said something about his background, and even more about the importance the community attached to appointing the right man.

Therefore, Peder was anxious not to disappoint them; he didn't want to go behind their backs.

Alex and Fredrika took him by surprise; they turned up in his office without warning, wanting to talk about the paper bag with the face on it.

For some reason this made Peder nervous, which annoyed him. He offered them coffee, and when they said yes, he felt like some kind of lackey who was obliged to serve them. He didn't have an assistant.

'I spoke to the secretary who called about the bag,' Alex said, taking a sip of his coffee. 'She said you were the one who found it.'

Peder stiffened.

'I didn't "find" it. It was lying on the floor under her desk, along with a load of other bags and wrapping paper.'

'But it was you who said she ought to show it to the police, wasn't it?'

There was nothing aggressive in Alex's tone; he was just asking. And yet Peder couldn't help feeling slightly uncomfortable. Where was Alex going with this?

'It stood out, made me wonder if it might be significant. And there was no card to say who had sent the chrysanthemum.'

'Was that the only anonymous delivery?' Fredrika asked.

'No, there were several, but the vast majority came with a card.'

Alex put down his cup.

'But this one came after Josephine was shot? Before it became known that the boys had also been murdered?'

'If I've understood correctly; that's what the secretary said.'

Alex leaned back in his chair; Peder unconsciously did the same. An air of tension was building in the room, and he didn't like it.

He didn't like it at all.

'Peder, how did you know that this bag would be of interest to us?'

The question came from Fredrika. Simple and direct, as her questions usually were. Impossible to misunderstand, but sometimes difficult to answer.

'I didn't know.'

Which was true.

'But I thought it might be, because it was different from all the other bags. Because there was something about that face . . .'

He broke off.

Alex looked curious.

'Yes?'

'I don't bloody know. I mean, it wasn't exactly an attractive face. If it had looked as if a child had drawn it, I might have thought the plant had come from one of Josephine's pupils, but that face seemed so . . . adult, somehow. As if an adult had drawn it, I mean. Combined with the fact that there was no card . . . well, that's why I reacted as I did.'

Alex drank a little more coffee, then he looked Peder straight in the eye.

'I sincerely hope that you're absolutely clear about why we're here,' he said, stressing every word. 'You guessed correctly. That bag *is* extremely important to us. That's why we're wondering if you really did come across it by pure chance.'

Peder's pulse rate increased. He couldn't stop himself, he had to ask more questions.

'Have there been more anonymous deliveries in bags with faces drawn on them?' he said.

Alex looked surprised for a second.

'No. No, not as far as we know.'

'So why is it interesting?'

Neither Alex nor Fredrika answered, and there was an uncomfortable silence.

'It's too early to talk about it right now,' Alex said eventually. 'But I promise I'll tell you as soon as I can.'

Peder couldn't help feeling put out. He knew that Alex was right; he couldn't tell Peder why the bag was significant at this stage. But it still hurt to know that he was an outsider, that he couldn't be a part of police work any more. Of Alex's work.

His thoughts turned to Efraim Kiel. The man who hadn't gone back to Israel, in spite of the fact that his job was done. The man who had come to see Peder, talking of calling cards.

Peder's brain was working overtime. Alex said there had been no other deliveries in similar bags, and yet the bag was important. Very important, in fact. In which case Efraim must have been right. There had been other calling cards.

But how had Efraim known that?

Did he have his own contacts within the police?

'I can see you're mulling something over,' Alex said in a pleasant tone of voice.

Fredrika crossed her legs.

'You're not suspected of any crime, Peder. We're just very curious about what made you go to see the school secretary and ask her those particular questions.'

When Peder didn't reply, Alex took over.

'Another reason for our curiosity is that you also called a former colleague in the National Crime Unit and asked if they had found some object the killer might have left behind after Josephine was shot. I think you referred to it as a calling card.'

Peder felt himself blushing.

Fuck.

So his colleague had contacted Alex and told him that Peder had been in touch. Marvellous.

Alex realised what he was thinking.

'He mentioned it to me when I called to tell him about the paper bag you found. Since the NCU are still technically leading the investigation into Josephine's death, we have to pass on any information that could be relevant.'

Peder felt a spurt of anger.

'That's bloody ridiculous,' he said. 'Splitting the investigations. Surely it's obvious it's the same killer! All the victims are Jewish, they all belong to the same community, they all have links to the same school.'

He fell silent.

'And they were shot with the same gun,' Alex said.

Peder blinked.

'Really?'

'Yes, but keep it to yourself. It seems to have been leaked to the press already, because they're asking questions, but we haven't confirmed it yet.'

'But it's definitely true? They were shot with the same gun?'

'Yes.'

So he'd been right.

'Now tell us what you know,' Alex said, and this time his tone had changed. 'Why did you think the person who shot Josephine might have deliberately left something behind?'

Peder swallowed; he couldn't help feeling that he shouldn't mention Efraim Kiel to the police, but at the same time he kept wondering what Efraim was hiding. He was the one who had started talking about calling cards; had he just been fishing, or did he know something?

Hesitantly he began to speak.

'There's a man in the Solomon Community – well, not really in the community; he's come over from Israel to help with the appointment of the head of security. His name is Efraim Kiel.'

'I've spoken to him,' Alex said. 'He rang me to ask for a reference.'

Good – in that case Alex already knew who he was.

'Exactly,' Peder went on. 'He came to see me yesterday, and asked if I had any information about the police investigation into the murders. He was very keen to know what was going on, and he was particularly interested in whether the killer had left some kind of calling card at either of the crime scenes.'

Alex and Fredrika looked at one another.

'Did he say why he wanted to know?' Fredrika asked.

'No.'

'Where can we reach him?' Alex said.

'I think he's staying at the Diplomat. Hang on, I'll find his phone number.'

As Peder searched among the papers on his desk, Alex asked:

'What's his background, this Efraim Kiel?'

'I've no idea. I assume he's some kind of security expert.'

'Has he mentioned anyone called the Paper Boy?'

Peder found the phone number.

'The Paper Boy? No – who's that?'

'Just a story that's come up. If you see Efraim again, you might like to ask him about it.'

Peder jotted down the number and gave it to Alex. 'Are you going to contact him?'

'We'll see,' Alex replied. 'But I'd appreciate it if you didn't tell him about this conversation.'

Peder knew he would do as Alex said. His job as head of security was to provide the community and its members with the highest level of protection, and Peder was no longer convinced that Efraim Kiel had the same goal.

'There's something going on here, Buster. And we're missing the whole damned thing.'

Eden Lundell had gone to see Säpo's general director, Buster Hansson, armed with the surveillance reports. A Mossad agent whom Säpo had specifically warned off had entered the country for reasons unknown. He was a hunted man. Someone who was cocky enough to leave messages out in the open was after him.

Eden had warned their own surveillance team about what was in the message they had found, explained that they must keep an eye open for someone who, like them, was following Efraim Kiel's every move.

But so far they hadn't picked up a thing.

GD, who was used to Eden's temperament and out-bursts, listened to what she had to say with an expression of concern.

'So you think there's some kind of transaction between agents going on here?'

The scepticism in his voice was palpable.

'No, that's not what I think.'

Transaction between agents? What the hell was that? Not something that was part of real life.

'An acquaintance in the National Crime Unit told me the

Solomon Community has just appointed a new head of security,' she said. 'That could well be why Efraim came over in the first place; he's dealt with that kind of thing before. But the head of security is now in post, and Efraim is still here.'

'Is that so strange? Given his background, I mean,' GD said. 'The Solomon Community has had a terrible couple of days.'

'Absolutely, but I don't believe he told the community about his background, or what he does and who his real employer is.'

'So who's creeping around outside his hotel room leaving him cryptic messages?' GD said.

'That's what we don't know. But since the message is written in Hebrew, and Efraim belongs to Mossad, I can't help worrying. Either someone has followed him all the way from Israel, or someone here in Stockholm is monitoring his activities. Which means that person must be part of the Solomon Community, because he hasn't met anyone else. According to the surveillance reports, that is.'

She took a deep breath, knowing that what she was about to say could be perceived as controversial.

'Which brings me to my next point. I'm not convinced that surveillance is one hundred per cent effective in this case.'

Buster raised his eyebrows.

'You're not?'

'No.'

She placed the latest reports in front of GD.

'Don't you think he seems to be spending rather too much time in his hotel room?'

She spoke softly, taking care not to sound supercilious.

Efraim Kiel had had a completely different training from the agents who worked for the Swedish security service; it was only to be expected that he would be able to get away.

'You mean he's leaving the hotel without our guys knowing?'

'Yes.'

'What else?' GD said, folding his arms.

Eden drummed her long fingers on the desk.

'I don't think it's pure chance that these anomalies co-incide with the murders of the past few days.'

GD was taken aback.

'And how exactly do you believe all this hangs together?'

Eden sat back and pushed her hands into her trouser pockets.

'I don't know. But I intend to find out, because I'm convinced that there's a link between the murders and Efraim's stay in Stockholm.'

GD looked away, focusing on a point behind Eden.

'And how exactly are you going to do that?'

Eden gave him the only possible answer:

'I'll do you the courtesy of not telling you what I've done until afterwards.'

There was no one by the name of Efraim Kiel staying at the Diplomat. Alex Recht wasn't exactly surprised, but it did bother him. The case was already complicated and wide-ranging enough; now they had an Israeli citizen who had officially entered Sweden in order to recruit a head of security for the Solomon Community, but who seemed far too knowledgeable when asking questions about an ongoing police investigation.

'I don't like this,' he said to Fredrika.

They were back at HQ, sitting opposite one another in the Snakes' Nest. Alex had just finished a brief conversation with the hotel manager.

'Could there be a simple explanation? Perhaps the Solomon Community has much closer links with the police that Peder realises? And that's why Efraim Kiel knew that he should be looking for something the perpetrator had left behind?'

'You mean someone tipped him off about the paper bags on Lovön? In that case, shouldn't someone else have approached Peder? Efraim Kiel isn't even a member of the Solomon Community. Why would he get involved in the murder of a teacher and two boys?'

Diana called, wondering when he'd be home.

It was almost six o'clock. Alex had told everyone else that he wouldn't be calling another briefing before the weekend, but there was one more thing he wanted to discuss with Fredrika before he left for the day.

'I should be there in an hour,' he said.

Fredrika looked away as he dealt with the personal call. She stared as if hypnotised at the snowflakes landing on the windows, leaving tiny white dots behind for a split second.

Alex apologised for the interruption and put down his phone.

'So you think it all boils down to the fact that Efraim just happens to be well-informed because he's been given confidential details through the community's own contacts within the police? I'm afraid I don't agree,' he said.

'So what do we do? Do we try the phone number Peder gave us?'

Alex laughed dryly. 'And say what?'

Fredrika ran a hand over her dark hair, making sure that no strands had escaped the thick plait hanging down her back.

'We say we're contacting him with regard to an ongoing police investigation, and that we believe he could be of assistance. We don't have to confront him with a whole load of accusations; we don't have anything concrete anyway.'

'You mean we make it sound as if we're impressed by how astute he is? That it was very perceptive of him to realise that the killer would leave or send some kind of calling card?'

'Something along those lines.'

It wasn't a bad idea. They couldn't rule out the possibility that Efraim Kiel just happened to have an instinct for what might be important in an investigation. Peder knew nothing about his background; perhaps Kiel was a former police officer, or had something to do with intelligence? In either case he would be well placed to be able to put two and two together and to draw conclusions which appeared to be unexpected.

'There isn't necessarily anything odd about the fact that he realised the killer might have left something behind,' Fredrika said to underline her point. 'I say realised, but he might just have guessed.'

Alex agreed with her in principle, but in that case why had Kiel checked into the hotel using a false ID? Or had he given Peder the wrong hotel so that no one would be able to find him? Either scenario didn't sound like normal behaviour to Alex.

His thoughts turned to Eden Lundell. She would have a much better understanding of why someone would be travelling on a false ID. Perhaps Efraim Kiel wasn't even his real name. If he had a sensitive job back home, there could be other reasons why he wanted to keep a low profile.

'I'll call him,' Alex decided. There was no reason not to. He dug out the number Peder had given him, picked up his phone and keyed it in. He waited for Efraim Kiel to answer, but that didn't happen. Instead a metallic voice informed Alex that this number was not in use.

He tried again.

And again.

He put down the phone.

'No subscriber on that number,' he said.

Fredrika frowned. Peder had once said that she looked pompous when she was thinking, but Alex didn't agree; he thought she was a classic beauty.

'But hadn't Peder called Efraim on that number?'

'Possibly, but it's no longer in use.'

'Maybe he's left the country?' Fredrika suggested. 'If he's not at the hotel, and he's no longer using a Swedish mobile?'

Alex knew that could be the explanation. It had taken a few days to sort out the appointment of a new head of security, so it wasn't surprising if Efraim had decided to get himself a Swedish phone number temporarily. If he had completed his mission, then it was logical to assume that he had gone back home.

But he had told Peder he was staying on.

So where the hell was he?

'Eden Lundell,' Alex said.

Fredrika went from pensive to surprised.

'What about her?'

'I want to ask her about Efraim Kiel. She might be able to throw some light on all these elements that seem so inexplicable at the moment. Tell us what kind of background a man like Efraim might have, why he's behaving this way. And whether she thinks it's worth contacting him.'

'I didn't realise you were still in touch with Eden.'

For the first time all day, Alex saw a hint of a smile on her face. It was a refreshing sight.

'Oh yes, Eden and I are like this,' he said with exaggerated enthusiasm, holding up two crossed fingers.

Fredrika burst out laughing.

'Alex, *no one* is that close to Eden Lundell!'

That was probably true, but he still wanted to speak to her.

At that moment his mobile rang again. It was one of the IT technicians, finally ready to report on their examination of the boys' computers.

'Can you come over right away? We've found something that might be important.'

Any progress in the investigation into the deaths of the two boys was welcome. Because of a leak in the roof, the IT technicians had had to move down into the basement; entering their office felt like visiting another universe.

Lasse, the technician who had called, showed them into a dingy room that smelled of dust. He switched on a desk lamp, then closed the door behind them.

'Look at this,' he said, handing them a pile of computer printouts.

They looked like extracts from an exchange of emails.

'That Super Troopers forum is interesting, to say the least. It was originally created by a man who'd made a name for himself as a so-called sports parent – you know, one of those idiots who'll do anything to make sure his kids are going to be world-beaters at tennis or golf or chess or some other crap.'

Fredrika caught herself nodding. Oh yes, she had met parents like that.

'As you already know, the boys were members and called themselves the Warrior and the Paper Boy. They rarely participated in the same discussion, and judging by their input they seem to have been very different individuals. The Warrior wants to win at all costs, while the Paper Boy seems more interested in having fun.'

That fitted in with what they had been told by the boys' parents. Once again Fredrika thought of the pictures she had seen of Simon and Abraham: serious and focused.

'Did they make any friends on the forum?' she asked.

'Not many, but there was one exception. Both boys were contacted by someone calling himself the Lion. At first they communicated briefly in the open chat room, then they moved over to email. And that's where it gets interesting. Because if we're interpreting their correspondence correctly, the Lion wanted to meet them.'

Lasse pointed to one of the pages he had given them. Fredrika quickly skimmed through the text; all the messages were signed Zalman, which she assumed was a forename.

According to the Lion, he was able to give excellent advice on how to achieve success. He said he was planning to set up a new tennis academy in Stockholm, and had therefore started to look around for fresh talent in Sweden. He had heard from his Swedish contacts that Simon and Abraham had won a number of minor competitions and tournaments, and he was curious to know more. To Simon, who had slightly less drive to win than Abraham, he wrote that it was possible to win without being nasty. The tone was playful, the messages brief. All communication had taken place in English; the boys seemed to be pretty good at the language. On one occasion the Lion apologised for his lack of expertise in Swedish: 'but I'm going to learn as soon as I move to Sweden', he wrote.

Fredrika's heart beat faster when she saw the date on which the Lion had suggested meeting up. Some time between January 23 and 27. Now, in fact. The week they went missing. This was something they would have to discuss with the boys' parents, as soon as possible. They had to find out whether this meeting had taken place.

'Have you managed to find out who the Lion is?' she asked.

Lasse spread his hands wide.

'I've been working on it all day, but I'm getting nowhere. I even became a member of Super Troopers so that I could get closer, but the Lion isn't on there any more. I've contacted the administrator, but it's impossible to trace the Lion.'

'Why?' Alex said.

'Because he or she has used different public computers every single time the Lion has been active.'

'Where, for example?'

'Places like the 7-Eleven convenience stores, or smaller internet cafés.'

'Give us a list and we'll contact them. With a bit of luck one or two will have CCTV, and we'll be able to get a picture.'

Lasse's expression was grim.

'I can give you a list, but it won't do you any good.'

'Why not?'

'Because all the places are in Jerusalem.'

All roads lead to Rome. But not this time. In this case all roads appeared to lead to Israel. Alex Recht was alone in his office; Eden Lundell was on her way over from Säpo to talk about Efraim Kiel, although Alex had chosen not to mention his name on the phone. He had simply said that a certain individual had come up in his investigation, and he thought Eden might be able to tell him more about that person.

Fredrika had gone home. Alex had said he would call her later, because he still hadn't had time to discuss his plan with her. He sincerely hoped she would think it was as good as he did; if all roads led to Israel, there was no point in the team setting off in a different direction.

Just before Eden arrived, he called Diana.

'Sorry, I'm going to be really late tonight as well.'

A laugh at the other end of the phone.

'In that case I'll have a glass of wine in the meantime. Come home as soon as you can.'

'I will.'

And then, just as he was about to end the call, he said: 'I love you.'

'I know.'

And then she was gone.

'I know.' What a way to answer, but a warm feeling spread through Alex's chest, because he knew that Diana loved him too.

The sound of rapid footsteps in the corridor interrupted his train of thought, and then there she was, standing in the doorway. Taller than he remembered, glasses perched on the end of her nose. Messy blonde hair and a thin smile on her lips.

'Alex.'

'It's been a while.'

He got up and shook Eden's hand. He had never seen a woman wearing so many bracelets, fine and chunky, on both wrists.

She sat down, crossed her legs and looked around.

'You should do what we've done – knock down the walls and go open plan.'

Alex suppressed a snort of laughter. Several of his colleagues would rather sell their own children than work in an open plan office.

'I don't think that would be a very good idea.'

'People get used to it. Can I smoke if I open a window?'

Alex was so taken aback that he didn't know what to say. Smoke? Indoors? She took his silence for assent.

'Thanks!'

In a single fluid movement she rose and pushed open a window, letting in cold air and snow.

'Bloody awful weather,' Eden said, lighting her cigarette before she sat down again.

'It's supposed to get better next week.'

'Really?'

She raised an eyebrow.

'I think that's what they said. The experts. But what the hell do I know – it might carry on snowing until midsummer.'

Why was he rambling on about the weather? There weren't many people who had that effect on him, but Eden certainly did.

The smoke from her cigarette was making his eyes sting. Alex blinked and wondered what she did in her own workplace; surely she couldn't smoke in an open plan office? He suspected the answer was that she probably could. Eden did as she pleased.

'You asked for my help,' she said.

She was in a hurry to get home, of course. Her family were waiting, and the weekend was approaching. Alex felt slightly stressed, unsure where to begin.

'You've heard about the murders in the Solomon Community?' he said eventually.

'Indeed.'

He saw a flash of surprise on her face.

'I've already told the community that I don't want to get involved,' she said.

It was Alex's turn to be surprised.

'The community?'

Eden nodded and reached for an empty coffee cup on his desk.

'Okay if I use this as an ashtray?'

Not really, no.

'No problem.'

Grey ash landed in the bottom of the cup.

'Are you saying the community rang you?'

'They think they can count on my support, my resources. But they can't. I work for Säpo and no one else.'

'And exactly what did they want your support and your resources for?'

'You might well ask.' She sighed and rolled her neck from side to side. 'It's not that I don't sympathise with their situation, because I do. It would be stupid to deny that there's a increased threat level against Jews and Jewish interests, but dealing with security issues of that kind is not part of my job.'

She stubbed out her cigarette in the china cup and pushed it away.

'But I don't imagine I'm here to talk about the Solomon Community's security issues.'

'No. You're here because a certain individual has come up in our inquiry, and to be honest I have no idea how to approach him. I contacted you because I suspect you have a similar background, and I thought it would be interesting to hear if you have any advice.'

'I'm listening.'

Alex took a document out of his secure filing cabinet.

'There are certain things that link the three murders – the teacher and the two boys.'

'Really?' Eden said. 'My guess was that they were unconnected.'

'Mine too, but it seems we were wrong. For example, all three victims were shot with the same gun.'

Eden let out a whistle.

'That makes it rather difficult to claim there's no link,' she said.

'Quite.' Alex took out a photograph of the paper bag in which the plant had been delivered to the Solomon Community. 'And then there's this.'

He passed her the picture, and she looked at it closely.

'It's identical to the bags the boys had over their heads,' she said.

Alex knew she had been out to Drottningholm before he and Fredrika arrived; he had heard her name mentioned among his colleagues.

'Not identical, but almost,' he corrected her.

He told her about the delivery, and how the bag had ended up in the hands of the police. When he had finished, Eden sat there motionless, staring at him.

'Can I just check if I've got this right?' she said slowly. 'An Israeli is currently helping the community, and he seems worryingly well-informed about what the police are doing?'

'Yes.'

'And you want to get hold of him?'

'Yes.'

'And you think I can help you?'

He felt utterly stupid. What had he been thinking? He spread his hands wide.

'I realise I'm skating on thin ice here,' he said apologetically. 'It's just that I don't like the way this guy is behaving. He's not at the hotel where he said he was staying, at least not under what he claims is his real name. And the phone number he gave is no longer in use.'

Eden held up a hand.

'You misunderstand me, Alex. I'm not saying he's not suspect, or that he might have a background in intelligence. The problem is that I don't know how I can help.'

Nor do I, Alex thought.

'By giving me some good advice?'

Eden burst out laughing.

'Good advice costs nothing. If he has an intelligence background, he might well have several passports, and good reasons to use different names in different circumstances. There's nothing strange about that. But let me ask you a question: is this man a suspect in some way? Why are you surprised that he thought the killer might have left some kind of calling card?'

'Well, that's just it,' Alex said. 'I'm not necessarily saying there's anything suspicious about his behaviour, but as he guessed correctly, it would be interesting to talk to him. There's no more to it than that, really.'

Eden looked pensive as she fiddled with her bracelets.

'If you can't get hold of him, you might just have to wait until he gets in touch with your former colleague at the Solomon Community,' she said.

'You could be right. I'd just like to find out if he's conducting his own investigation running parallel to ours. And if so, is it on the instructions of his employer in Israel?'

Eden looked dubious.

'I find it very difficult to imagine that the Israeli authorities would have any interest in a case like this.'

She tilted her head on one side.

'But I can ask around, if you like. What's the name of this man?'

'Efraim Kiel. Would you like me to spell it for you?'

'That won't be necessary, thank you. But you didn't answer my question: is he a suspect? Do you think he's involved in the murders?'

Her face changed from open to closed so fast that Alex didn't have time to react.

He needed to think.

Did he believe Kiel was involved?

No.

Besides which, he had an alibi for both murders; he had been at the community centre finishing off the appointment of Peder Rydh. Hadn't he?

'No,' Alex said. 'But as I said, we'd still like to speak to him.'

'I'll do what I can.'

Alex felt a wave of relief.

Eden looked as if she was about to leave.

'One more thing before you go,' he said.

She waited patiently.

'There are several loose ends in the case that all lead to Israel. Do you think it would be possible to set up some kind of collaboration with the local police if I sent over someone from our team?'

'That depends,' Eden said. 'Who were you thinking of sending?'

'Fredrika Bergman. The thing is, her husband is going out there anyway on Sunday.'

At first she had thought he was joking, but apparently he wasn't. Fredrika Bergman couldn't believe her ears when Alex outlined his so-called plan. A plan that involved her travelling to Israel to follow up on various leads over there.

If she wanted to. As Spencer was going anyway.

Otherwise Alex would go himself.

But there wasn't much time if she was to leave on Sunday. It was only in films that the police hopped on a plane and started conducting an investigation in another country. In reality that kind of thing was extremely rare, and it never happened without a preliminary discussion with the local police authorities. Alex didn't really know how it worked.

A collaboration with the Israeli police.

Had they ever done anything like that before? Alex's boss could recall a few occasions, but there were no established channels to fall back on. Eden Lundell had made it very clear that she couldn't provide any contacts in Israel, but she had promised to check out Efraim Kiel for them. Fredrika thought that sounded very useful.

But travelling to Israel with Spencer . . . How was she going to manage that, even if she wanted to?

'You wouldn't have to stay long,' Alex had said. 'Just a couple of days.'

'I don't see how I could do it,' Fredrika had replied. 'Who'd look after the children?'

Alex didn't have an answer to that.

Nonetheless, Fredrika had called her parents as soon as she finished talking to Alex, just to ask if they could possibly have the children.

Her mother sounded worried.

'But why do you have to go to Israel as well?'

'It's work, Mum. Otherwise of course I would have taken the kids.'

Spencer overheard the conversation, and was staring at her when she put down the phone.

'Pardon me for asking,' he said. 'But am I to understand that you're coming with me on Sunday?'

'It looks that way. If Mum and Dad will have the kids.'

Spencer smiled, and she knew that he remembered too. The time they had gone to Israel together. Locked themselves in their hotel room and said that Spencer was too ill to attend some of his conference sessions. When darkness fell they had crept out into the city, away from the prying eyes of his colleagues.

Those were the days.

The decision-making process would take care of itself. If the practical issues could be solved, she was prepared to go.

Her mother rang a little while later; they were happy to look after the children, who at that moment were whirling around the apartment like two small tornadoes, heartily sick of their mother's lack of attention. Spencer had spent a great deal of time alone with them over the past few days. She hoped they would be okay; she hardly ever went away and left them.

She grabbed her son as he shot past.

'Yes, I am coming with you,' she said firmly to Spencer, 'but only for a couple of days.'

'What will you be doing there?'

'Working on the case. We can't find all the answers we need here in Stockholm.'

Alex could sort out all the practicalities. It was Friday evening, the beginning of the Jewish Sabbath. On Saturday everything would be closed, and it would be impossible to get hold of anyone, or at least anyone in authority. And then it would be Sunday, the day they were supposed to be travelling. Alex would have to get things moving so that Fredrika could set to work straight away; she didn't have time to sit around waiting when she got there.

With her son balanced on one hip, she made a start on dinner. Spencer worked beside her in silence, preparing a salad as she fried the meat. The potatoes were already in the oven, and the wine was breathing.

Isak chortled as the meat began to sizzle. Fredrika kissed his forehead, thinking that he was like his daddy, and that he ought to be proud of that.

Thoughts of the investigation were threatening to overwhelm her. Alex had unrealistic expectations of what she was going to be able to achieve. He wanted a more detailed description of who the Paper Boy was. Fredrika had searched online for the mysterious boy, but had found nothing. She had even asked Spencer, since he was a professor of literature, but he had had nothing to contribute.

Alex also wanted to know more about why the Eisenberg

and Goldmann families had left Israel. Success depended on whether Fredrika managed to track down any relatives, and she felt as if the project was doomed from the start. Why should they agree to speak to her, even if she did find them?

The last thing Alex wanted her to follow up was the only one that seemed achievable: to visit the places from which the Lion had emailed, and to ask if she could look at any customer records they might have.

If they could just find out who the Lion was, Fredrika thought they would have made significant progress.

When he fired her, Eden Lundell's British boss had mentioned what he regarded as her finest quality: an uncanny ability to spot connections that anyone else would have missed.

'Don't imagine that I believe for one second that you didn't realise who Efraim Kiel was,' he had roared, slamming his fist down on the desk. 'You knew perfectly well that you were fucking Mossad and taking a huge risk.'

He had been both right and wrong. Eden certainly had a unique talent when it came to drawing conclusions far beyond the obvious, but on one occasion it had let her down, and that was when she embarked upon a relationship with Efraim Kiel. A man who was once again haunting her and turning her life upside down.

Eden was a gifted strategist, but she was also a very good poker player. She hadn't even blinked when Alex mentioned Efraim Kiel's name. He had unconsciously confirmed what she had suspected – that there was a link between Efraim's stay in Stockholm and the murders in the Solomon Community. Alex had said that he didn't suspect Efraim, and nor did Eden. But somehow Efraim knew more than seemed reasonable about what had happened, and Eden wanted to know how and why.

As expected, Mikael was furious when Eden walked in and announced that she was off to London the following morning.

'*Tomorrow*? It's the weekend, Eden. That means you spend time with your family; we do stuff together.'

Eden looked at her daughters, who were watching wide-eyed as their parents argued. They saw this kind of thing far too often, which wasn't good. The knowledge that she was damaging them was painful, and it made her feel sad. And exhausted.

It's for your sake I'm doing this, she wanted to say.

Because as long as Efraim Kiel was on her mind, she would have no peace.

There were times when she wondered if she had been right to tell Mikael what had happened. It wasn't the fact that she had told him per se; she had had no choice. However, she wasn't sure she had told him enough.

She had told Mikael only that she had met someone else. That it had to do with work, which was why they had to leave London.

She had admitted that she had fallen for this other man, started a relationship with him.

And ended it after a very short time.

Which wasn't true. Her affair with Efraim had lasted, on and off, for two years, which told her two things she found very difficult to cope with: that she had really wanted him, and that Mossad had really wanted her.

Two years was a long time to run a recruitment operation. They had got nothing from her. She had no idea how frustrated that made them, but she could hazard a guess.

Dani crept over to Eden and wrapped her arms around

one leg. Eden stroked her curly hair, which had surprised so many members of both her family and Mikael's. A trick of nature, Eden always said if anyone mentioned it.

'Are you going away?' Dani said.

'I'll be back on Sunday.'

'Is that a long time?'

'It's hardly any time at all, sweetheart.'

Dani smiled. She was much easier to cheer up than Mikael; easier to talk round.

Eden freed herself from her daughter's iron grip and went into the kitchen.

'This is important, Mikael,' she said. 'I can't tell you any more than that, but I'm asking you to trust me. I wouldn't do this if there was any alternative.'

He stared at her, his eyes burning with anger. His hair was loose for once, long and dark, falling to his shoulders. His hair had been utterly fantastic when Eden first met him: a priest, over six feet tall, with long hair and a beard. His confirmation students called him Jesus, which Eden thought was a very appropriate nickname.

'Please, Mikael,' she said, reaching out and placing a hand on his chest, pleading for understanding in a way that was unusual for her.

'Is there really no one else who can go?' he said.

He was beginning to crumble; he hated arguments.

'Not on this particular trip, no. I'm the only one who can do what needs to be done.'

All of a sudden she felt fragile. She couldn't cope with a row, not right now. It was too hard, too exhausting. What bothered her most was the fact that he was right, of course. It wasn't fair to mess up a weekend with a trip to London. So

Eden did something that was even more rare than pleading. She offered a compromise.

'I've been thinking about that holiday you mentioned. In March?'

A spark appeared in Mikael's eyes, but was immediately extinguished by doubt. Justifiably so. She tried again.

'You were right and I was wrong. If we settle on a date now, of course I can prioritise and book some time off.'

'Seriously? You've thought about the holiday, and you can take some time off?'

The first part was a lie – she hadn't thought about the holiday at all. But the second part was true; of course she could take some time off, if she wanted to.

'Yep. Where would you like to go?'

Mikael didn't react as she had expected at all. Instead he placed his big hands on her cheeks, and in his eyes she could see nothing but fear.

'Eden, you have to tell me what's happened.'

Shaken by his reaction, she backed away. He stepped forward.

'Nothing,' she whispered. 'Nothing's happened.'

That was one of the reasons why she was so keen to go. Because the fact that nothing had happened was not enough. It was equally important to ensure that nothing was going to happen.

She knew who she was going to see: a man who had been involved in the sensitive operation which MI5 must have carried out against her when they realised she was in an intimate relationship with a Mossad agent. A man who had to tell her everything he knew, so that she would have sufficient knowledge to free herself from Efraim Kiel once and for all.

If she didn't win this final battle against Efraim, she would pay the highest price of all.

The film was called *Katinka's Party*; images of something that Efraim Kiel assumed was supposed to be a Swedish idyll flickered on the cinema screen. All the actors were speaking Swedish. Efraim didn't understand a word, which amused him.

He had made a point of leaving the hotel by the main entrance so that his Säpo shadows couldn't possibly miss him. They had caught a tram to Sergels torg, then walked to Hötorget. Efraim grinned to himself, wondering what the Swedish security service would make of the fact that he had gone to the cinema to watch a Swedish film.

He sank down in the soft seat and allowed his thoughts to run free. It was still early; he would call Peder Rydh as soon as the film was over. He wanted to know if anything new had come up; something that might explain how that paper bag had turned up at the Solomon school.

He hadn't received any more messages, but that gave him no peace of mind. There was something frantic about his pursuer, something that suggested a lack of patience, and for that reason Efraim had been expecting further attempts to contact him. The silence frightened him. It would be unfortunate if this was the preliminary to an escalation; as long as Efraim didn't know who was after him, he was at a disadvantage. And that was never a good thing.

His superiors in Israel had raised no objections when he said he was staying on in Sweden for a few more days. Complications with the recruitment process, he had told them. Peder Rydh needed to be supervised for a little while, assessed. They bought his explanation lock, stock and barrel back in Jerusalem; Efraim was a trusted colleague who was allowed to plan his own overseas trips as he saw fit.

He was shaken by the turn his visit to Stockholm had taken. It had sounded so simple, so uncomplicated. It had seemed like a welcome break from the usual intensity of his work, which mainly consisted of recruiting new sources and double agents for the Israeli military security service.

Eden had been a failure. The project had taken two years, and had produced nothing. Two years, two attempts. The first had been broken off for the simple reason that Eden had told him she was pregnant when Efraim first seduced her. He had made sure that she was well and truly hooked before he brought the first attempt to an end. And then, when she was back at work after her maternity leave, he had reappeared. It had gone well. Very well, in fact. But not well enough.

No one within the organisation had blamed him. Sometimes you succeeded, sometimes you didn't. Efraim had many assets, and was still regarded as one of their most skilful agents. Eden Lundell had been a high risk project, they had known that from the start. And they had lost.

Eden most of all.

The film was indescribably boring. Efraim didn't think he would have liked it even if he had been able to understand what they were saying. When it came to an end at long last, he had to make a real effort to stop himself running out of the cinema.

It had finally stopped snowing as he set off back to the hotel. The sky was dark and clear, studded with stars. It was a quarter to nine, and the inner city had a pulse that Efraim hadn't noticed before. A Friday night phenomenon, no doubt. There were people everywhere, even though it was so cold. In a country where it was apparently impossible to motivate men and women to train to bear arms, people were clearly happy to freeze to death for a couple of beers.

It would have been easy to dump his Säpo shadows in the crowd, but Efraim let them stay with him. They were between fifteen and twenty metres behind him, all wearing black boots and woolly hats. If he had been their boss he would have turned around and asked them what the hell they were doing.

The soles of his shoes were too thin to keep out the cold, so he increased his speed and went past the theatre and the attractive little shops along the first section of Strandvägen. By the time he reached the warmth of the hotel, his cheeks and ears were glowing.

He went up to his room, using the stairs rather than the lift. There were no messages outside his door. Or inside. He opened up his laptop and plugged in the micro-camera that he had installed above the bathroom door in order to check whether anyone was coming into his room. No one had been there since he left.

He took off his coat and picked up his mobile. He had got rid of the first pay-as-you-go card he had bought when he came to Sweden; he was trying to make himself as invisible as possible. Traceability equalled vulnerability.

Peder Rydh answered almost immediately. When he realised who was calling, there was a brief silence.

'I hope I'm not disturbing you,' Efraim said.

'No, not at all. How can I help?'

You would have needed only half of Efraim's experience to hear that Peder's tone of voice had changed since they last spoke. It was strained, almost stressed. Possibly with a hint of fear and nervous anxiety. A clear indication that he wasn't comfortable speaking to Efraim.

'Have you spoken to the police?' Efraim said.

'What? No, absolutely not, of course not, why would I do that?'

The words came pouring out. With a certain amount of surprise Efraim realised that he had been given more information than he had expected: Peder had definitely spoken to the police.

About Efraim.

'Why would you do that,' Efraim said rhetorically. 'Perhaps because I asked you to?'

Silence.

Efraim pictured Peder, cursing his own stupidity.

'Oh right, yes, of course,' he said, his voice a little steadier. 'Yes, I have.'

'In that case, let's try again. Have you or have you not spoken to the police?'

'I have spoken to the police.'

'Okay. What about?'

Efraim wished Peder had been sitting in front of him; that would have made things so much easier, both in terms of frightening him and reading his reactions.

'About . . . about what you said.'

'Which was?'

What kind of fucking amateur had they appointed as head

of security? Efraim had met children who were better liars than Peder Rydh.

'The bag. You wanted to know more about the bag. So I asked.'

'Who did you speak to?'

'Alex Recht.'

'Good. And what did you find out?'

'He didn't say anything about the paper bag.'

'Nothing at all?'

'He wouldn't tell me whether it was of any significance in the investigation; he said it was too early.'

'But the police came and collected the bag, didn't they?'

Peder hesitated.

'They did, yes.'

'So Alex Recht wouldn't tell you anything about the paper bag; did he say anything else that might be of interest to me?'

A longer hesitation this time.

'Only what's already in the news.'

Efraim frowned. He hadn't checked the news since he got back from the cinema, and to be honest it was a fairly pointless exercise; he didn't have a decent translation program to work with.

'For obvious reasons I find it difficult to follow the Swedish news,' he said. 'What exactly are you referring to?'

'This business about the gun.'

Efraim froze.

'The gun?'

There was a rushing noise inside his head, and his pulse rate had increased to an alarming level.

'The boys were shot with the same gun as the teacher,' Peder said.

Impossible.

Impossible, impossible, impossible.

He forced himself to answer Peder.

'Oh yes, I knew about that.'

Then he ended the conversation with a promise to call Peder again over the weekend.

He stood there with his mobile in his hand. This was worse than he had thought. If the children had been shot with the same gun as the teacher, then that ought to mean that they had been killed by the same perpetrator.

But they hadn't.

Because Efraim Kiel knew who had shot the boys, and that person had had nothing whatsoever to do with the murder of the teacher.

CONCLUSION

FRAGMENT IV

The snow is falling heavily, desperate to bury all evil beneath its blanket of white. The inspector leaves the apartment with the woman who has lost the love of her life and one of her children.

'I was never meant to have it all,' she says when they are standing on the pavement.

He has no idea what to say. He knows nothing about her past and her personal life apart from what he has heard from others.

He does know that her story contains elements of darkness that she does not wish to share with anyone else. Soon she will have to be interviewed about what has happened, fill in the gaps for the investigators. Because somewhere in Stockholm, there is a killer on the loose.

'I thought we'd got him,' the inspector says eventually.

The snow chills his face, and he feels like crying out there in the street.

Because he doesn't understand what went wrong.

When she doesn't respond, he says:

'I can't make any sense of this. When you feel up to telling us what you know . . .'

He breaks off as she turns her back on him and walks away.

'Hang on a minute!'

He hurries to catch up with her, places a hand on her shoulder and almost slips in the snow.

'Let go of me.'

Her voice is calm, but there is no misunderstanding the steel in her tone. He has the feeling that if he doesn't let go, he will die.

'Listen to me,' he says.

Begs.

Pleads.

Because in a world where all is chaos, only pleading remains.

'You must realise that I can't simply let you walk away.'

He glances back at his colleagues, waiting by the door. Like him, they are in shock at what they have seen and experienced. If necessary, he will not hesitate to ask for their help.

Because the woman who has lost almost everything cannot be left alone.

The risk that she will declare war on her opponent is too great. She will not rest until she has her revenge.

'Who has done this?' the inspector says, his voice betraying a higher level of frustration than he would wish. 'Who was it?'

'Me,' she says, beginning to weep. 'I did this.'

EARLIER

The Fourth Day

SATURDAY, 28 JANUARY 2012

So many loose ends, so many roads that led nowhere. Alex Recht couldn't settle. Not at night, not during the day.

'Are you going in to work?' Diana had said when he slipped out of bed and started to get dressed.

Alex had always worn pyjamas during his marriage to Lena; with Diana he slept naked, except when the grand-children stayed over. Then he dug out an old pair of ugly PJs, as his son put it.

'I've got a few things to sort out,' Alex had replied.

Diana had looked disappointed. She had thought they could take their cross-country skis and drive up to Nacka, which wasn't a bad idea. The weather had once again changed from foul to fantastic; the sun was shining with every scrap of its winter strength, and the snow looked like stiffly whipped meringue.

But Alex couldn't bring himself to take the day off and go skiing, because in that same stiffly whipped meringue they had found two murdered children just days earlier. So work had to come first, particularly as Fredrika Bergman was flying out to Israel the very next day. Alex had to get in touch with his Israeli colleagues and set up a collaborative process that Fredrika could tap into.

He had spoken to the National Crime Unit the previous

evening; they already had a network of contacts with Israel, and had set the ball rolling. The prosecutor liked the direction the investigation was taking. He had great confidence in what he referred to as 'the Israeli lead', and thought Fredrika would solve the whole thing in just a couple of days. Alex was rather more doubtful. The case had started to look like a jigsaw, with far too many of those involved claiming too great a share of the pieces available.

For example, Abraham and Simon's parents were withholding information that Alex needed, which was why Fredrika was going all the way to Israel. But Alex had no intention of giving in so easily. He called Gideon and Carmen Eisenberg and asked them to stay at home for the next few hours.

'I'm coming over; I need answers to one or two additional questions.'

'Have you made a breakthrough in the case?' Gideon wanted to know.

His voice was strained and weary; it belonged to a man going through hell, and Alex's call had clearly ignited a spark of hope.

'We'll talk about that when I see you,' Alex said.

He wasn't prepared to have that kind of conversation over the phone. When he had finished speaking to Gideon Eisenberg, he called Fredrika.

'I'm going to show the parents the pictures of the boys when we found them,' he said.

'Why?'

'We have to find out the significance of those paper bags over their heads.'

'Are you going to tell them about the bag that was sent to the school as well?'

'No. They might hear about it anyway, through the Solomon Community, but as far as I'm concerned the most important thing is to see if those damned bags mean something to the parents.'

'Do you want me to come with you?' Fredrika asked.

'Thanks, but no – there's no need.'

Then he changed his mind.

'Actually, yes, if you've got time. It might be useful for you to talk to the Eisenbergs before you go off tomorrow.'

He could hear the sound of children's voices in the background, and felt guilty; why hadn't he told her to stay at home? However, he needed her – more than ever. The team must be expanded as soon as possible, with permanent members; they couldn't carry on like this.

'No problem,' Fredrika said. 'I'll meet you in the car park.'

Alex threw down his mobile. They had three key questions for the parents: did they know who the Lion was, had their sons met him, and could they explain the background to the paper bags?

He hoped to come away with at least an embryonic lead.

As far as the Lion was concerned, Alex was surprised they had found so little to go on. The boys' email accounts and their conversations on Super Troopers had been checked, and it appeared that Simon and Abraham had never communicated with one another about the Lion, not once. That didn't mean they hadn't spoken about him in school or over the phone, of course, but there was nothing at all in their online messages.

To be on the safe side, he went through the material one more time. The Lion had contacted the boys about three weeks ago. He wanted to meet them to discuss their sporting ambitions and his tennis academy. Grants for short training courses at international schools had also been mentioned.

Surely the boys' parents must have known about that?

He went through the latest material, and established that the analysis of the traffic on the boys' mobiles had also failed to generate anything useful. There wasn't a single call to or from an unknown individual. Every person on the list was a friend from school or the tennis centre, a parent, or another relative.

Fuck.

He made a note to pass on a list of Simon and Abraham's school friends to the technicians who were analysing the telephone traffic; it was worth checking whether the Lion had contacted anyone else. Maybe they could track his communication, if that was possible. Now that he was no longer active on the forum, perhaps that information was no longer available.

The phone on his desk rang just as he was about to go down to the car park. It was a colleague from the National Crime Unit.

'I thought you'd be in today, somehow.'

'Hard to avoid it under the circumstances,' Alex said, thinking briefly of Diana. He pictured her gliding along on her skis, and wished he was by her side. With a bit of luck the snow would linger, and they would be able to go another day.

'I'm calling about the murder of the schoolteacher,' his colleague said.

'Yes?'

'It's about the tracks on the roof where we think the sniper was lying.'

'You mean the tracks that had almost been blown away or covered in snow by the time we got there?'

The weather had definitely not been on their side.

'Exactly. The footprints were useless; the weather had more or less destroyed them. The only thing CSI would say with any certainty was that the large imprint must have been left by the perpetrator's body. Indentations in the snow showed where the knees and elbows had been placed.'

Alex already knew this, but he assumed there was more to come.

'You found some footprints out at Drottningholm as well, I believe? Size 43 shoes, if my information is correct.'

'That's right.'

'And this is where things get weird,' his colleague said. 'Because even taking into account the fact that the imprint on the roof had been affected by the wind and the fresh fall of snow, we have been able to establish that the person in question can't possibly have been any taller than one metre seventy.'

This was unexpected.

'You mean that someone of that height wouldn't be wearing size 43 shoes?'

'I mean it seems highly unlikely,' his colleague said. 'And the footprints we found support that view.'

'I thought you said they were no use?'

'It was impossible to secure a cast of the sole, for example. However, CSI were able to get a rough idea of the size.'

Alex pressed the receiver to his ear.

'And?'

The tension in his voice was clear.

'There is no possibility whatsoever that those prints were

made by someone wearing a size 43. According to CSI's cal-
culations, the maximum length of the shoe was twenty-five
centimetres. Which means that the perpetrator's feet were
a centimetre or so shorter than that. Which means that the
person who lay on the roof and fired the gun was wearing
shoes somewhere between size 36 and 38.'

Alex sat motionless in his chair.

He thought about the killer who had settled down on the
roof and shot his victim through the falling snow. A killer
who was no more than one metre seventy tall, and whose
feet were small enough to fit into a pair of size 38 shoes.

A killer who could be a woman.

The toboggans crunched in the snow as they walked through Vasa Park, heading for the hill behind the playground. Eden Lundell was towing one toboggan, her husband the other, a little girl riding on each one. Mikael was holding her hand, and she hadn't pulled it away. It was his day today. The weather had been kind to him, and he deserved to play happy families.

In Stockholm the sun was shining, but in London they had sleet and high winds. All flights had been postponed, and Eden wouldn't be able to get away before evening at the earliest.

'There you go,' Mikael had said when she told him. 'Sometimes things just sort themselves out.'

Eden had no idea what he thought had sorted itself out; she wasn't going to be home any sooner just because her flight was delayed.

However, it was too nice a day to argue, so she didn't object when Mikael suggested an outing to the park. Instead she packed sausages and rolls and drinks in a rucksack and pulled on her thermal tights. The food was Mikael's idea; he claimed there were big outdoor barbecues in the park for public use. Eden knew nothing about that kind of stuff.

The rucksack bounced against her back as they walked

along. So at last the day had come: Eden was going to Vasa Park. She almost thought it might be fun.

Her daughters were thrilled when they realised where they were going, and their laughter warmed Eden's heart. Sometimes she did the right thing. It was important to remember that.

From time to time Mikael said hello to people they met. People Eden didn't recognise. When he spoke to a tall dark woman who gave him a big smile, Eden felt something she hadn't experienced for a very long time. Jealousy.

'Who the hell was that?' she said.

The tone of voice and choice of words gave her away. Mikael couldn't help smiling.

'Jealous?'

'Of course not. I just wondered who she was.'

'A colleague.'

Eden forced herself to keep on walking.

'A colleague?'

'Yes.'

'You mean she plays the organ or something?'

Mikael's laughter rang out across the park.

'For fuck's sake, pull yourself together,' Eden said, punching him on the arm.

'You pull yourself together! Plays the organ – what the hell are you talking about?'

'Well, answer me then – and stop swearing!'

'*Me* stop swearing?!'

'Don't change the subject.'

Mikael let go of her hand, and for a fraction of a second Eden felt the ground give way beneath her feet.

You're not going to leave me, are you?

But Mikael wasn't the kind of man to leave the woman he loved. Instead he put his arm around her shoulders and gave her a big hug. Bigger than she deserved.

Eden slipped her arm around his waist.

'So who is she?'

'She's a priest.'

'In your church?'

'No.'

'Do you find her attractive?'

Mikael laughed again, quietly this time.

'Do you?'

'What do you want me to say?' he said.

'How about: "No, she's the ugliest woman I've ever seen".'

He kissed her cheek.

'I think she's gorgeous,' he said.

Eden couldn't believe how much energy was contained in a child's body. She lost count of the number of times the girls ran up the hill to slide down again. At one metre eighty, she felt like a giant among all the children.

'Again!'

Dani grabbed Eden's hand and dragged her along. Her hat had slipped to one side and she had taken off her gloves, which dangled from the sleeves of her snowsuit. Eden picked her up and carried her off to the side.

'Put me down!'

The child kicked out at Eden, who was determined to have her way.

'Quiet! We'll go back up as soon as you put on your gloves, okay?'

She put her daughter down on one of the wooden picnic

tables. Eden's stomach rumbled as she thought about grilled sausages; she was getting hungry.

As she was helping Dani with her gloves, she detected a movement in her peripheral vision. Or rather a lack of movement. Someone was standing in the snow, watching her.

Slowly she turned her head.

And there he was.

Efraim.

Less than ten metres away.

No, no, no.

She could do nothing about her reaction. She stood there as if she was frozen to the spot, in front of her daughter with one glove in her hand.

They stood in silence staring at one another, Efraim and Eden. If she hadn't had Dani with her, she would have done what she didn't do the last time she saw him. She would have hurled herself at him, knocked him to the ground.

'Mummy?'

Dani's voice sounded so far away.

Oh God, Dani.

With a start Eden woke from her trance and looked away from Efraim.

Got to get away got to get away got to get away.

He mustn't see her.

Please, please, please God, don't let him see her.

She picked up her daughter and began to back away. She had to get out of here.

But it was too late. That was obvious when she glanced in his direction. His expression had changed from indifference to something that resembled a mixture of shock and horror.

He was looking at Dani.

Staring at Dani.

He couldn't take his eyes off the face that revealed so much, if you knew what you were looking for.

Dani noticed Efraim over her mother's shoulder as Eden turned her back on him and set off towards Mikael.

'Who's that man?' she whispered in Eden's ear.

'Nobody. Just someone who's lost his way.'

But inside she was in total panic. The words she knew she would never say out loud to her daughter echoed in her heart and her head.

That, Dani, is your daddy and your sister's daddy.

It had been a long, restless night. Time and time again he had woken up with all his senses on full alert. Dreams he couldn't remember made his heart race. Eventually he gave up, and went for a shower.

'Are you okay?' Ylva asked when he came back to bed.

'Absolutely,' Peder said.

Morning came and the curse was broken. Peder got up at seven when he heard noises from his sons' bedroom. He found them sitting on the floor, playing with their Lego, still in their pyjamas and with their hair standing on end. They hardly noticed him; they were completely absorbed in what they were doing.

For a while everything seemed fine.

Calm.

Peaceful.

Without Ylva and the boys, I would never have got back up again.

'Do you want some breakfast?'

'Not yet.'

Peder left them and went into the kitchen, put the coffee on and went to fetch the paper. Ylva came to join him; they enjoyed a leisurely breakfast and made plans for the day.

'I need to put in a few hours' work.'

'Oh, Peder . . .'

'I won't be long.'

'But we said we'd go somewhere – it's such a beautiful day.'

In a previous life Peder would have reacted with fury, felt as if Ylva was accusing him of something, putting him under pressure. But not any more, because now he knew that she was right. It was wrong to prioritise work over family; it always had been and it always would be.

Although that didn't mean there was no room for compromise.

'I've got a new job,' he said. 'And some terrible things have happened over the past few days.'

'You're not a police officer any more.'

'I know that. But I am head of security. And I was a police officer for several years. It's my duty to be around for a few hours over the weekend.'

Ylva stroked his arm.

'I just want you to be careful.'

He knew she meant well. What she really wanted to say was that she was afraid, he thought. Afraid that he would lose control once again, make himself unhappy. But she didn't need to worry about that. The Solomon Community murders weren't personal, and therefore his duties were only professional. Otherwise he would never have walked into such a hornets' nest.

An hour later he left the house and drove into the city. There were two things he wanted to check out.

The hole in the facade was small, but not difficult to find. After Alex and Fredrika's visit, Peder had spoken to the security guards who were taking it in turns to monitor the entrance to the Solomon school. He had asked if they had seen Efraim Kiel; they had. One of the female guards said she had seen Efraim outside the school on at least two occasions.

Both times he had been interested in just one thing.

The bullet hole in the wall.

But why?

Peder leaned closer and peered at the hole. He had no idea what CSI had to say about the matter, and he couldn't see anything odd about it. He turned around and looked up at the roof where the sniper had been lying.

It had been a bold enterprise, shooting someone from that distance in such terrible weather.

Peder gazed up at the roof. Then back at the hole. Then back at the roof.

Wasn't the hole a hell of a long way down?

The teacher had been shot in the back. The bullet had gone straight through her body. Even if you took into account the sharp angle of the shot, Peder still couldn't make sense of it. If you drew a straight line from the roof to the wall, it looked as if the bullet should have hit Josephine in the leg.

If she had been standing up, that is.

By this time, Peder knew the witness statements off by heart – the statements that had been taken by the community's security guards, who had conducted their own interviews with those who had been out in the street and seen what had happened.

The second before the shot was fired, Josephine had crouched down to help a child with a shoelace that had come undone. Either Josephine had been incredibly unlucky – if she had remained standing, the bullet would have caused nothing more serious than a leg injury – or she had taken a bullet that was meant for someone else.

Peder breathed in the cold air.

That had been one of his very first thoughts: that the bullet wasn't meant for her. That it was supposed to have hit one of the children instead. The discovery of the paper bag strengthened his suspicions. Alex and Fredrika hadn't been willing to tell him why the bag was important, but Peder thought he knew anyway: they must have found similar bags where the two boys had died.

And still they were letting the National Crime Unit run the investigation into Josephine's death.

It made no sense at all.

Peder went back to his office and pulled out the file containing all the information he had gathered so far. Which children had been standing outside when Josephine was shot?

He read the names out loud, but they meant nothing to him. That wasn't necessarily significant; if the killer chose his victims at random, then he might not have been aiming at one particular child. But if the choice wasn't random, which child might he have been aiming at?

Peder read through the list again. He didn't know the children, had no idea who they were. However, none of them was over four years old. The boys who had been shot out on Lovön were ten.

There was one more thing he wanted to follow up. No doubt the police had already done the same thing, but that didn't matter, because Peder didn't have access to their material. When reading through the witness statements, he had noticed something which one of the parents who witnessed the shooting had said:

Josephine turned around to call to the child who was still inside. At the same time, one of the other children came up to her to ask for help with a shoelace that had come undone. As she crouched down, the shot was fired.

Peder thought the phrase 'the child who was still inside' was odd. Surely there must have been several children inside, so why would Josephine call one particular child? It didn't look as if any of the witnesses had said that the child was theirs. Peder pictured the scene: it was after three o'clock, and parents had started arriving to pick up their children from day care and pre-school. Josephine hadn't been wearing a coat when she died; had she just popped out to speak to a parent?

She was due to finish work at five that afternoon. She was shot just after three, when she happened to step outside.

But how could the killer have known that he would get the chance to shoot her two hours before she was due to go home?

The answer was simple. He couldn't.

Peder slammed his hand down on the desk. He had known it all along: the killer on the roof hadn't been aiming at the schoolteacher. He had been aiming at the children. Or possibly at one of the parents, but he thought that was less likely.

The children were the common denominator in both

crimes, apart from the fact that they had been shot with the same gun. And now Peder wanted to know whether the killer had been after one specific child, or whether any child would have done.

'I've got a terrible sore throat.'

Spencer was standing behind her in the hallway as she put on her boots.

'I'll be back in less than two hours.'

She pulled up one zip, then the other. Scarf, gloves. Woolly hat. It was so bloody cold. The fact that the sun was shining didn't help at all when you lived in one of the most northerly countries in the world.

'The thing is,' Spencer said, 'I'm worried about the trip to Israel.'

His shoulders were slumped, his posture poor. His eyes were dull and exhausted. For a moment Fredrika was afraid, as she always was when he felt ill or showed signs of tiredness. She stood up and placed a hand on his forehead. He pressed against it, wanting to get close to her.

'You've got a temperature.'

Damn. All at once leaving him at home with the girls didn't seem like such a good idea.

And what about the trip to Israel? Would she still go if she had to travel alone?

'Go and lie down,' she said. 'I'll stay at home.'

'Nonsense, I can manage two hours. Go on – Alex is waiting.'

Fredrika could hear the sound of shrieking from her daughter's room; it sounded as if Saga and Isak were about to start demolishing the apartment.

'I won't be long,' she said, slipping out through the front door. She ran down the stairs; she didn't even have time to say hello to a neighbour in passing.

Quick, quick.

She would have loved to go back to Israel with Spencer. If she had to go alone, the adventure was much less appealing. But she would still go.

Her mobile beeped; it was a text from the orchestra. Would she be coming to their rehearsal tomorrow evening?

In just a couple of days, the violin had disappeared from her universe. She was going to Israel; there was no chance that she would be able to make the rehearsal.

'No time, will be there later in the week' she replied.

She dashed through Tegnérlunden and over Barnhus Bridge. Crossed Fleminggatan and turned into Scheelegatan, heading for Police HQ.

Her mobile rang; it was Alex, wondering where she was. He was already in the car. He sounded tense; Fredrika sensed bad news.

'Pick me up outside Spisa hos Helena,' she said, stopping in front of the restaurant. Three minutes later she was sitting in the car.

'The National Crime Unit called,' he said. 'They think the person who was lying on the roof could be a woman. The footprints indicate smallish feet, and the indentation left by the body in the snow shows that the person in question was no taller than one metre seventy.'

Fredrika was totally bewildered.

'A woman? But whoever hunted down the boys on Lovön was wearing size 43 shoes.'

'It could still be a woman,' Alex said. 'A smartarse who knows how to confuse the police.'

Fredrika's mind was whirling.

It was possible that someone with small feet could have put on shoes that were too big . . .

However, it was less likely that someone with big feet could have put on shoes that were too small.

'What do we do now?' she said.

'We carry on as before.'

'With NCU investigating the murder of the teacher, while we concentrate on the boys?'

'Yes.'

'What if there's more than one killer, Alex? Working as a team?'

'In that case we've got twice the chance of catching them, if we carry on as we started.'

Fredrika tried to bring together the evidence to form a coherent picture. It was impossible. Different killers, same gun. Different kinds of victim, different crime scenes. Same community, same ethnicity.

One of her earliest thoughts came back to her.

'I'm still not sure that the bullet that killed Josephine was meant for her rather than one of the children.'

'To be honest, we can't be sure of anything right now,' Alex said.

'In that case let me raise the stakes and say that this is something we are particularly unsure about.'

'What's that got to do with anything?'

'What's that got to do with anything? Don't you think it's

important to find out whether that lunatic actually meant to shoot a child?'

'Because?'

Because in that case we could be dealing with the one thing we don't want to say out loud.

A serial killer.

'Because then we'd have three children who belong to the same school and the same community, who have been attacked with the same gun, and a killer who has marked each death with a paper bag with a face drawn on it,' Fredrika said.

'Would the killer have sent the bag to the school if the wrong victim had died?'

'Maybe. If he or she wanted us to believe that the teacher really was meant to die. To stop us looking for other possible victims.'

Another thought occurred to her.

'What if the chrysanthemum was sent before the murder took place?'

Her voice was quiet, her tone almost submissive.

'But we know that wasn't the case,' Alex said. 'It was delivered the following morning. The boys were missing but their bodies hadn't been discovered, and Josephine was dead.'

Fredrika felt an all too familiar surge of obstinacy. The same obstinacy that had once driven Alex crazy, and alienated her from the rest of the team.

'That's got nothing to do with when it was ordered, or when the delivery was arranged.'

Alex sighed.

'Well no, but . . .'

Fredrika interrupted him.

'Do we know anything about those details? Have we been in touch with the firm responsible for the delivery?'

'No, we haven't, because as you might recall, this is not our investigation.'

'In that case I'll call NCU and check.'

Fredrika got out her mobile. 'Who's your contact?'

They had almost arrived; Alex started looking for somewhere to park.

'Please, Fredrika, don't waste your time on this.'

But Fredrika had no intention of giving up now.

'Tell me who I need to speak to.'

Another sigh, then he gave her a name.

The call was answered almost immediately. Fredrika explained her question as Alex reversed into a space that felt at least half a metre too small.

'We thought about that, of course,' their colleague said, 'but we got nowhere. The name of the delivery firm wasn't on the bag, and the secretary couldn't remember whether the person who handed it over was wearing any kind of logo.'

'Shit,' Fredrika said.

Her colleague laughed.

'We said much the same thing.'

'Have you tried ringing around different firms?' Fredrika said. 'They ought to remember if they were asked to deliver a plant in a bag with a big face drawn on it.'

'We called a dozen or so, but it was no good. The only thing we had to go on was that according to the secretary, the girl who brought the plant in didn't speak Swedish.'

Fredrika froze. Alex was already out of the car.

'She didn't speak Swedish?'

'No, but why would she need to? She only had to hand over a plant.'

But Fredrika didn't agree.

'Send a sketch artist over to the secretary,' she said. 'Right now.'

'But why?' Her colleague was taken aback.

'Because I think the girl who delivered the plant was the one who lay on the roof and shot Josephine.'

The feeling that he had hit upon something vital was intoxicating. Peder Rydh had known he was right all along, but now he thought he could prove it.

I need to speak to Alex about this.

He just wanted to check one more thing.

His hands were shaking slightly as he dug out a list of contact details for the witnesses the security team had interviewed. He called one of the parents, the father of a three-year-old boy.

The man sounded wary when Peder had explained who he was and why he was calling.

'I've already spoken to the police and the community's security team. What's this about?'

'I wonder if you could help me understand a couple of things,' Peder said. 'For example, what was Josephine doing outside? Why did she leave the school building?'

The man didn't say anything for a moment, presumably because he was trying to recall.

'There was nothing strange about it,' he said eventually. 'Three parents had arrived at the same time; everything was just the way it always was. We went inside and collected our children, helped them to put on their outdoor clothes and said goodbye to the staff and the children who were still there. Just as we got outside Josephine came after us. She said that one of the children, a little girl called Lova, was wearing the wrong hat. That caused a bit of a discussion, because Lova flatly refused to give it back. Josephine came out to retrieve the hat, that's all there was to it.'

So chance had brought Josephine outside, and led to her death.

'I believe the last thing Josephine did was to call a child who was still inside,' Peder said.

'That's right. She wanted the little girl who owned the hat to come to the door and bring Lova's hat, because of course it was still sitting on the shelf.'

Peder's brain was working overtime, desperate for more details. Every scrap of the instinct that had once made him a skilled investigator was screaming at him to keep digging. Because there was more to come.

'Was there something special about this particular hat? Why did it cause such a fuss?'

God knows, small children didn't need a sensible reason to start squabbling, but Peder still felt he had to ask.

'Actually, it wasn't just any old hat,' the parent said. 'It was a big, red, hand-knitted hat.'

Peder found it difficult to understand why a big red hand-knitted hat would be so popular.

'One of those that looks like a berry?'

'Not at all – it was more like a big red ball. Several of the parents laughed when Polly turned up in it; none of us could have produced anything like it, but Carmen is very talented.'

Carmen?

'I'm sorry? Carmen?' Peder said. 'Carmen Eisenberg? Simon's mother?'

'That's right – Polly is Simon's little sister. Or rather she was . . . Well, you know what I mean.'

The man's voice broke with emotion.

And suddenly Peder understood.

He was so agitated that it was all he could do to stop himself shouting down the phone.

'So what you're saying is that when Josephine was shot, there was a child standing next to her wearing a big red hat? A hat that actually belonged to Polly Eisenberg?'

'Yes.'

'But Polly wasn't picked up at the same time?'

'She should have been, but Carmen was obviously running late.'

She should have been.

Polly Eisenberg, Simon's little sister, should have been going home at the time when her teacher was shot. She should have been outside the school just after three o'clock, wearing her big red hat.

Peder closed his eyes, thought about the snow that had fallen that day, and the fact that it was already starting to get dark. He thought about the distance from the roof to the school entrance.

And he thought that a big red hat would have been the perfect target.

The investigation was beginning to resemble the tracks in the snow out on Lovön: the leads appeared to be going around in circles, taking the team in all directions. However, as Alex Recht had already established, most led in the same direction.

To Israel.

'We have a man who's travelled from Israel to Stockholm to recruit a head of security for the Solomon Community,' he said to Fredrika, as they walked from the car to the Eisenbergs' apartment. 'A man who is either a bloody good investigator, or who is disturbingly well informed about our inquiries. At the same time, we have someone calling himself the Lion who has been exchanging messages with Simon and Abraham. From Israel. He claims his name is Zalman.'

'Efraim Kiel could have sent those messages, if we're looking at him as a possible suspect,' Fredrika said. 'The correspondence took place before he came to Sweden.'

They had reached the apartment block.

'The Lion, whoever he is, could be the person who picked up the boys,' Fredrika said.

'I know.'

'In which case he – or she – must have rented or borrowed

a car. Or driven here from Jerusalem, which seems highly unlikely, wouldn't you say?'

She attempted a wan smile, which Alex returned.

'I think that sounds like great fun,' he said. 'Driving to Jerusalem. Perhaps Diana and I should give it a go some time.'

'Have you heard anything from Eden yet?'

Alex's expression grew serious.

'No, she said she'd be in touch when she had something to tell me. *If* she had something to tell me.'

He held the door open for Fredrika. If his daughter had seen him, she would have given him a long lecture about why opening a door for a woman constituted oppression. Alex couldn't give a damn. Opening the door for a woman was just like closing the door when you went to the toilet; it was just something you did.

'There are several things we need to ask Carmen and Gideon about,' he said as they went up the stairs. 'The Paper Boy and the paper bags are our number one priority. The Lion, and why they left Israel ten years ago, are also important. I can't shake off the feeling that's where the answer lies – or part of it, at least.'

'We also need to ask them about Efraim Kiel,' Fredrika pointed out.

Once again they were standing outside the Eisenberg family's door. Alex was just about to press the doorbell when his mobile rang. It was Peder Rydh. After listening to him for less than a minute, Alex signalled to Fredrika to follow him back down the stairs.

The visit to the Eisenbergs would have to be postponed.

*   *   *

A big red hat on a little girl's head.

Without it, Peder's argument was nothing.

They met in a café on Östermalm Square; Alex had already forgotten the name of it. Alex, Peder and Fredrika: just like the old days. But they had never met in a café; it was a new environment for the old team.

'Thanks for this – I thought it was best if you didn't come to the community centre.'

Alex agreed.

What Peder had done was far beyond the remit of his role as head of security; he had done the police's job for them, and he had done it well.

'You have to take back Josephine's case from the National Crime Unit,' Peder said. 'I'm sure they've given up any attempt to link the murder to organised crime by now; it could just be lying there, with no one making much of an effort.'

He took a sip of his coffee, then bit into a cinnamon bun the size of a saucer.

Fredrika was drinking tea and eating a marzipan cake.

'I thought you didn't eat crap like that,' Peder said.

'Well, there you go.' She took a big bite. 'What made you think that?'

Peder looked down, picking sugar crystals off the table-cloth.

'I thought you were too much of a gourmet for that kind of thing.'

Alex was about to interrupt the discussion before Fredrika made mincemeat of Peder, but discovered that he no longer needed to act as playgroup leader. Those days were gone. The years that had passed had tempered both of them, in different ways.

Fredrika looked as if she was about to burst out laughing. No doubt she realised that she was partly to blame; she had been quite difficult in the past.

Obviously Peder still didn't quite know where to draw the line, because when he realised that he had got away with his comment about the cake, he decided to carry on:

'Since you've started eating like a cop, maybe you could try dressing like one too,' he said, glancing at her smart blouse and jacket, which looked more like something a banker or stockbroker might wear.

At that point Alex decided he had had enough; they didn't have time for this.

'A red hat,' he said. 'Worn by the wrong child. You think that's enough to jump to the conclusion that the Eisenbergs' daughter was the target, not the teacher.'

Peder bristled.

'You wouldn't be sitting here if you didn't think the same.'

Always difficult when people knew you . . .

'Besides,' Peder went on, 'this doesn't just come down to a red hat.'

'Convince me.'

'First of all: the timing. The killer was lying high up on a roof. It was snowing and several degrees below freezing. So he or she wouldn't want to stay there for too long. Therefore, I believe we can assume he was intending to carry out his mission at about three o'clock, which was when Polly was due to be picked up. Secondly . . .'

'How did the killer know she was due to be collected then?' Fredrika asked.

'I don't know. But we can assume he checked it out; if he knew what school she attended, it seems likely that he would have found out when her parents usually came for her. Polly is collected at three o'clock every day; her parents take it in turns. The killer could easily have watched the family for a few days, and very quickly got a handle on their routines.'

'But why shoot the child outside the school?' Alex said. 'There must be a hundred other opportunities to choose from.'

'In inner-city Stockholm?' Peder said. 'Think about it. You found the two boys out on Lovön. In broad daylight. Not far from Sweden's head of state. Not a particularly discreet crime. You have to admit the person you're dealing with here is seriously disturbed.'

The three of them fell silent.

'Or someone who likes the attention,' Peder added so quietly that Alex had to lean forward to hear what he said.

'Okay, I'll stop interrupting,' he said. 'Carry on. You were talking about the timing.'

Alex Recht gave his former colleague one more chance to prove his point.

Peder felt a fresh surge of energy.

'Secondly, as I said, it was very cold on Wednesday, and it was windy too. And it was snowing. Our friend on the roof can't have wanted to stay there any longer than absolutely necessary. Polly Eisenberg was supposed to go home at three o'clock, not Josephine. There was no reason whatsoever why the sniper would have expected to see Josephine out there before five o'clock, when she finished work. And another thing – the angle of the shot is wrong. If Josephine hadn't crouched down to help a child do up his shoelace, the bullet would have hit her in the leg, not the back.'

'Which suggests that he was aiming at someone shorter than Josephine,' Fredrika said.

'Exactly.'

'In which case he missed,' Alex said.

'It was snowing,' Peder said. 'Visibility was very poor. And just as the shot was fired, the little girl who was wearing Polly's hat moved. Josephine turned around to call to Polly, who was still inside, and the girl who had taken Polly's hat got cross and pulled away from her father. Then the gun went off.'

'You mean if she had stayed where she was, she would have been hit?'

'I only have second-hand accounts to go on, but yes, it looks that way.'

Alex sipped his coffee. He had decided against a pastry; Diana had suggested that both of them ought to be eating less rubbish. Reluctantly he had accepted that it was a good idea, particularly on days like this.

He caught Fredrika's eye.

'What do you think? This is what you said right from the start: that there was a chance the bullet wasn't meant for Josephine.'

Fredrika finished off her cake.

'That was just a guess, but at the time I didn't know there was a link to the Eisenberg and Goldmann families.'

'And now?'

The door of the café opened and closed as a customer came in. Cold air sliced across the floor.

Fredrika hesitated.

'I don't think we can rule it out. But regardless of what I think, Peder has managed to reinforce one key point.'

'Which is?'

'That Josephine died by pure chance. There is absolutely no reason to believe that someone would have stayed up there on the roof for hours, just waiting for her to appear. It's out of the question.'

'So where does that leave us?' Peder said.

'Either things really are as bad as in some TV drama, and we're looking at serial killers who specialise in Jewish victims – but in that case, why haven't we seen more victims, given how quickly things happened that first day? Or the bullet actually did hit the right victim, but she was chosen at random – the killer was prepared to shoot whoever was outside the school at that particular moment.'

Alex prayed that Peder wouldn't pick up the additional information Fredrika had just revealed – information that was most definitely not intended for anyone outside the team.

His prayer was in vain, of course.

'Serial killers?' Peder said.

'That's just one theory we're considering,' Fredrika said.

'I understand that, but you're talking as if there's more than one killer.'

Fredrika blinked.

'Sorry, I made a mistake.'

'No, you didn't. It was the same murder weapon; are you still saying there was more than one killer?'

A man and a woman, Alex wanted to say. We think there could be two of the bastards working together.

But it was too soon to share information like that with an outsider.

'It's just one of a number of theories we're considering

at the moment,' he said, placing a calming hand on Peder's shoulder. 'I'd be grateful if you'd keep it to yourself.'

Peder reluctantly agreed.

Alex knew exactly what he was thinking. He had taken the trouble to call them, placed all his cards on the table, and now Fredrika and Alex wouldn't let him in.

Fredrika tried to move the discussion forward.

'To be honest, I think Peder's idea is the closest to the truth.'

'You believe Polly Eisenberg was the intended victim?' Alex said.

She nodded. Peder looked pleased.

'In that case, we have a problem,' Alex said.

'We do.'

'But isn't it a good thing if Polly was the target?' Peder said. 'It means this is personal, so you're not looking at a serial killer. In other words, we don't need to worry about more victims.'

Alex raised his eyebrows; he could see that Fredrika shared his unease.

'Unfortunately I don't think we can make that assumption,' he said.

'Because?'

'Because if Polly was the target, then the killer has failed to achieve his goal. Which means we have a five-year-old girl who won't be safe for a second until we have caught whoever is after her.'

The sunshine made Stockholm look even more stunning than usual. The most beautiful capital city in the world, Eden had once said. Efraim Kiel had contradicted her, said he couldn't imagine a lovelier city than Jerusalem. They had spent a day driving from Tel Aviv to Jerusalem. Taken tea on the magnificent terrace of the King David Hotel. Strolled through the Old City and visited the Western Wall. Eden had slipped her hand into his and he had let it happen. He had sensed, believed, that her love for him would eventually be so strong that he would be able to win her over to their side.

He had failed. Failed, but he had been convinced that she was the only one who would have to pay.

How wrong he had been.

How very wrong.

Efraim Kiel was sitting motionless on the edge of his bed in his hotel room. He had left the glorious winter weather behind; he wanted no part of that particular idyll. He had waited for Eden outside the door of her apartment block, thinking that she and her family wouldn't want to stay indoors on a day like this.

Right so far.

Her carefree attitude had surprised him; at no point had he thought she might spot him. That was one of the main reasons why he had been tempted to creep up on her as he had done; he had wanted to put her in her place, make her realise that it didn't matter how many of her Säpo goons she put on his tail.

He would always win.

That's how he had felt when he walked up to her.

Before he saw the child who was obviously her daughter.

He couldn't believe his eyes.

It was like staring at a carbon copy of his younger sister. She had died in a car crash as a child, and he still carried a picture of her in his wallet. Eden had seen that picture, which had been a big mistake; he should never have let her touch any of his personal possessions. Everything he had shown her had been a facade, an invention, a stage set. The small amount that was not a part of this facade was in his wallet, but the only thing Eden had been interested in on that one occasion when she unconsciously got too close to the truth was the photograph of his sister.

She had thought it was his daughter.

'You're so alike,' she had said.

'We were,' he had said. 'But she's not around any more.'

And he had immediately come up with a story of how his sister had been blown up in a terrorist attack, and how his parents had never got over it. The last part was true, in a way; his parents were still grieving for their lost little girl. But there had been no terrorist attack, just an unnecessary car accident.

Efraim closed his eyes, conjuring up once again the image of Eden's daughter.

Their daughter.

But how was that possible?

They had used protection. Every single time. Or had they? Efraim recalled just one time when he hadn't used anything, but Eden had stroked his cheek – *how fucking stupid had he been?* – and said:

'It's okay. I'm already pregnant.'

Why had she said that?

Efraim had had no reason to doubt her, because after a while the pregnancy had begun to show, and Mossad's leaders had decided to put the project on the back burner. If motherhood meant that she was likely to move back to Sweden and leave MI5, then she would no longer be of interest to them. But Eden had given birth to her children and remained in London. Six months later, Efraim had made another attempt. It took a few weeks, but then she was his once more.

That was when he had realised that she was in love.

Deeply in love.

During the first phase of their relationship she had been driven by lust, but in this second phase it was all about love. He had been surprised when he saw the change in her, and he hadn't been slow to capitalise on it. Recruiting an MI5 agent was invaluable.

Thank God she had fallen for him.

She must have known he was the father of her children. The only question was what he should do with that information now.

Efraim felt as if the challenges were beginning to pile up, but the fact that he had unexpectedly become the father of two little girls didn't necessarily need to be one of them. Eden clearly had no intention of causing him any problems, and if he had interpreted the situation correctly, she hadn't told her husband what she had done. Hadn't mentioned that he wasn't the father of the children he loved and supported.

How the hell could she live with such a huge lie?

Efraim wondered if he was supposed to feel something for the kids. He didn't think so. He hadn't been there at the birth, hadn't been a part of their lives. He hadn't even known they existed, so he hadn't missed them either.

Not the way he had missed Benjamin over the past ten years.

As always his heart swelled with sorrow when he thought of the boy he hadn't been allowed to keep. To think that grief could hurt so much for so long. The things we are prepared to do for those we love . . . He hadn't understood until he himself suffered the greatest loss of all.

If it hadn't been for what had happened to Benjamin, Efraim would have been less inclined to appoint a man like Peder Rydh as head of security. But when he learned about Peder's past, the terrible choice he had been forced to make, Efraim had felt nothing but respect. Seeking vengeance for those who have died at someone else's hand was a duty and a curse.

Efraim knew why Simon Eisenberg and Abraham Goldmann had had to die.

It was as obvious as any law of nature.

But the second murder, the teacher outside the Solomon school . . .

Efraim didn't understand that at all. When he heard that the same murder weapon had killed all three victims, he knew who had murdered Josephine.

But he didn't know why.

What the hell was going on? It must have been a mistake. The bullet must have been meant for someone else.

There had been another message waiting when he got back from the park. This time it had been pushed under the door of his room. When he read it, he realised that the game was over, and that the person going by the name of the Paper Boy was seeking peace. And his support.

I will finish what you cannot bring yourself to do.
Try to understand.

Two hours, Fredrika Bergman had said to Spencer. She would be gone for two hours, no more. But with the new development in the case, she wasn't at all sure she could get home by then.

'Can you cope?' she said on the phone.

Spencer sounded hoarse when he replied.

'Of course.'

'Are you going to be well enough to travel tomorrow?' she said.

She really didn't like the idea of going on her own; it just felt wrong in every way.

'I don't think so, Fredrika.'

Her heart sank.

'Okay, but . . .'

'Maybe we should talk about this when you get home?'

He was right. He usually was, unfortunately.

'I'll be as quick as I can.'

He laughed.

'I know you will. You said that before you left.'

As she slipped her phone back into her bag, she felt a pang of guilt. She had left her children the day before she was due to go to Israel. She had left Spencer with both of them, in spite of the fact that he wasn't well. They stuck rigidly to certain unwritten rules, one of which was that they didn't go in for punishment. Leaving someone who was ill home alone with two small children definitely sounded like some kind of penalty.

But the intention was key; she couldn't possibly have known how the day would turn out.

Once again she and Alex were standing outside Gideon and Carmen Eisenberg's apartment, and this time they weren't going to walk away.

'We won't start with the possibility that Polly might be in danger,' Alex decided. 'We'll go for the other stuff first.'

Fredrika agreed; it sounded like a sensible approach.

If only they could get the parents to talk.

It was Gideon who opened the door, and at first Fredrika didn't think it was the same man. Sorrow had eaten away at his soul, leaving him a damaged and broken individual.

'Sorry to disturb you again,' Alex began, 'but we'd like to ask you a few more questions.'

'Come in.'

Carmen was waiting in the living room. She was sitting in a large armchair, gazing towards one of the windows. The apartment was silent; Fredrika wondered where Polly was.

They sat down, and Alex got straight to the point.

'The Paper Boy.'

Both parents looked at him, their expressions weary but attentive.

'You said that was the name Simon used on the Super Troopers forum.'

Gideon cleared his throat. 'That's right.'

'Could you explain why?'

'What do you mean, why?'

'Why did he choose that particular name?'

Gideon and Carmen exchanged glances which Fredrika was unable to interpret.

'It's just a name,' Carmen said.

Her tone was neither evasive nor annoyed, but empty of emotion.

'But he must have got it from somewhere,' Fredrika said. 'The Paper Boy. It doesn't sound like something a ten-year-old boy would choose to be called.'

Carmen looked away.

'It's a story,' Gideon said. 'A legend, if you like.'

'It's not a story I'm familiar with,' Alex said. 'What's it about?'

Gideon sighed. His entire being radiated exhaustion. And something else. Fear.

'It's just an Israeli story. Simon heard us talking about it once. I didn't want to tell him the real story, so I changed it a bit to make it more child-friendly. If I had known he was going to use it as his online alias, I would have asked him to choose something else.'

'What do you mean, you changed the story?' Alex said.

Gideon shuffled uncomfortably.

'People used to talk about the Paper Boy when I was growing up. They said he used to abduct children and do them harm. The story was told so that children would respect the political situation in Israel, and not go rambling around the streets late in the evening or at night. But I didn't feel it was necessary to give Simon all the details, so I said that when I was little, the Paper Boy was the name we gave to a boy everyone looked up to.'

Simon's choice of the name immediately sounded more logical.

'The problem was that Daphne and Saul had chosen to tell Abraham the real version,' Carmen said. 'So when Simon started to call himself the Paper Boy on that forum, Abraham reacted quite strongly, wanting to know what he thought he was doing. Simon was upset and tried to change the name, but apparently that wasn't possible unless he gave up his membership of the forum and reapplied, and he didn't want to do that.'

'So he stuck with the Paper Boy,' Fredrika said.

'Yes.'

Hesitantly Alex reached into his inside pocket and took out a photograph. Fredrika was only too well aware of its subject.

'There's something we have to show you,' Alex said.

Alex placed the photograph on the table in front of Gideon and Carmen. They stared at the image as if they couldn't work out what it was.

Carmen was the first to realise.

'Oh God,' she said, covering her mouth with her hand.

Her eyes widened and filled with tears.

'Is that Simon?' Gideon whispered. He couldn't take his eyes off the picture of the boy with a paper bag over his head. Barefoot in the snow.

'I'm afraid so. That's how we found both Simon and Abraham: barefoot, and with paper bags over their heads.'

Carmen was weeping openly by now.

'I'm so very sorry we have to show you this,' Alex said. 'But we need to know whether you can explain it to us. Why do the boys look like this?'

Fredrika was watching Gideon. He looked as if someone had cast a spell on him. He was staring at his son, his breathing irregular, his face chalk-white.

'Would you like a glass of water?' she said.

'Please.'

She was back in no time. Gideon drank greedily, then pushed the photograph away.

'That's how they were supposed to look,' he said.

Quietly, as if he didn't want anyone to hear what he was saying.

'Sorry, who are you talking about?' Alex asked.

'The Paper Boy's victims. He tore off their clothes and left a paper bag as his calling card.'

The atmosphere in the room was oppressive.

'So we can conclude that whoever killed the boys was familiar with the story of the Paper Boy,' Alex said. 'How widespread is this tale? Is it known outside Israel?'

'I have no idea,' Gideon said.

'What about within the Solomon Community?' Fredrika said. 'Is anyone else familiar with it, apart from the two of you and Abraham's parents?'

Carmen shook her head.

'I don't think so. I'm not even sure it's all that widespread in Israel. I'd never heard of it until Gideon told me.'

Fredrika thought that was interesting.

'But where you grew up, children were told about the Paper Boy?' she said to Gideon.

'Yes, but I've no idea how many other people knew about him. It's years since that story was a part of my life.'

'But you said you and Carmen talked about it,' Alex said. 'That was how Simon chose the name as his alias.'

They didn't get any further. Fredrika couldn't decide whether she was satisfied or not. It was obvious that whoever had murdered Simon had done so for deeply personal reasons; she just couldn't work out what those reasons were, and it seemed that Gideon and Carmen were in the same position.

'On our last visit you mentioned that you left Israel in 2002,' Alex said. 'Could you tell us a little more about that decision?'

Carmen shrugged.

'I'm afraid there's nothing more to tell.'

'It's going to be difficult for us to move this investigation forward if we don't have access to relevant information,' Alex said.

Gideon looked distressed.

'What do you want us to say? We told you last time why we left Israel. The political situation was so volatile that we wanted to make a fresh start somewhere else.'

Fredrika was trying to work out if he was lying, but it was difficult.

'We've looked at Simon and Abraham's activities on Super Troopers,' she said, hoping that Alex would forgive her for changing the subject. 'In the weeks leading up to their deaths, they were both in contact with a person calling himself the Lion. Were you aware of this?'

Alex picked up the photograph and slipped it back in his pocket. No one needed to look at the face of evil any longer. Carmen and Gideon's silence suggested that Fredrika's question had touched a nerve.

'Simon mentioned the Lion,' Carmen said eventually. 'He seemed to be one of the people who had joined the forum in order to coach children and young people in how to improve at various sports, for example. Teach them how to be courageous and go for it.'

'The desire to win is so controversial here in Sweden,' Gideon said. 'Parents who provide elite training for their children often acquire a bad reputation. It's quite different in other countries, and several contributors to the Super Troopers forum belonged to overseas sports clubs or academies for children. The Lion said he was planning to set up a new tennis academy in Stockholm, but it's difficult to know how much of that was just talk and how much was true.'

'Do you know his real name?'

'Only his first name – Zalman. He'd just moved to Stockholm, or maybe he was about to move here, I don't remember. He had emigrated to Israel from Russia a few years ago, so he didn't write to the boys in Hebrew or Swedish, just English.'

'Did he ever meet Simon and Abraham?' Fredrika asked.

'No, definitely not. We would never have agreed to that unless we were there too,' Carmen said.

Silence. Fredrika could hear the faint sound of traffic, and she thought about all the people who had to work on a Saturday. The silence also allowed other thoughts to rise to the surface: they had no idea who the Lion was. He could be anyone, anyone at all.

It was as if time was standing still in the apartment, which rarely happened in a home with children. Simon was gone, but Polly was still alive. Fredrika wondered where she was, because she obviously wasn't at home.

'Do you think he's involved?' Carmen said. 'The Lion, I mean. Zalman.'

'We'd certainly like to speak to him,' Alex replied.

Carmen was crying softly again, but Gideon remained motionless and mute.

'Efraim Kiel,' Alex said. 'Do you know anyone by that name?'

There was no mistaking the astonishment on Carmen and Gideon's faces. Carmen stopped crying immediately.

'What's he got to do with anything?'

That's exactly what we're wondering, Fredrika thought. Had it been a mistake to mention his name?

'Possibly nothing at all,' Alex went on. 'We've discovered that he's in Stockholm at the moment, helping with security issues at the Solomon Community, but he's proving rather difficult to get hold of.'

'Efraim Kiel is in Stockholm?' Gideon said slowly.

'How do you know one another?' Fredrika said, unable to hide the surprise in her voice.

Gideon made a dismissive gesture.

'We don't. Not any more. But we did our military service together. Unless of course you're talking about a different Efraim Kiel.'

'You don't have a picture of him?' Alex said.

'I don't think so.'

Fredrika was fascinated by the links that had emerged. They had lived on a kibbutz together, done their military service together. A different context; a different philosophy. Did the fact that Efraim had once known Gideon and Carmen make him more or less interesting? She had no idea.

She spotted a doll lying in a corner. Definitely Polly's.

But where was she?

Alex had also noticed the doll. He glanced at Fredrika. They had one more thing to discuss with Gideon and Carmen; the most difficult thing of all.

'Unfortunately there's another matter we need to bring to your attention,' he said.

He looked at the doll.

'Where is your daughter at the moment?'

'With a friend,' Carmen replied. 'Her mother called to ask if it would help if they took Polly out for a few hours. We said yes. She doesn't understand what's happened, and she's finding it difficult to see us so upset.'

Fredrika sympathised completely.

However, there was something in what Carmen had just said that started alarm bells ringing in her head.

Her mother called to ask if it would help if they took Polly out for a few hours.

Out where?

'Where are they now?' she asked.

Her pulse rate was rising, her heart pounding.

'I think they said they were going to Tessin Park,' Gideon said. 'There's a little toboggan run that the kids love.'

'When are you expecting her home?' Alex said.

Fredrika could see how serious his expression was.

He's just as worried as I am.

Carmen glanced at her watch. 'In an hour. Why do you ask? What's going on?'

The sound of a telephone sliced through the apartment. Gideon got up so quickly that he knocked over his glass of water.

'Hello?'

Carmen stood up and followed her husband into the hallway. Gideon came back into the living room, still holding the phone.

'Has something happened?' Carmen asked from behind him.

The telephone fell out of Gideon's hand and crashed to the floor.

'They can't find Polly.'

The afternoon sky lay dark and heavy over Stockholm. The sun had made its guest appearance, and didn't seem to have any plans to return. At least not according to the weather forecast.

'It looks as if you'll be able to get away to England tonight, but who knows when you'll be home,' Mikael said.

He was lying on his stomach on the bed, checking the weather on his laptop. Eden was busy packing.

'I always manage to get home,' she said.

Her hands wouldn't stop shaking. The tremor was only slight, but she was afraid Mikael might notice. She would rather say she had developed an acute form of Parkinson's disease than tell him the real reason for her anxiety.

I met the biological father of my children today. I've met him before, of course. But never with the girls.

She knew he had realised. It had been written all over his face. Ironically, that was what it took for the brilliant Mossad agent to lose his composure.

The children's voices filled the entire apartment. They were playing with an old dolls' house their grandmother had given them. Fear squeezed Eden's heart. Was it safe to leave them with Mikael? Who knew what Efraim Kiel might do now he knew what she had never meant him to find out.

Eden realised she was more frightened of how Efraim would react than of what Mikael would do if he ever found out that he wasn't the father of the girls he had brought up.

No words would suffice if Mikael learned the truth. Right at the beginning, when she was pregnant and then when the girls had just been born, she had thought about telling him. Saying those terrible words.

I deceived and betrayed you. And I got pregnant. But he doesn't exist any more, the other man. For me there is only you.

But not one syllable had passed her lips.

She remembered so clearly why she had first fallen for Efraim. Her whole life had been nothing but crap. She had just had a miscarriage, and Mikael had blamed her, saying that if she hadn't been working so hard, if she had taken better care of herself, she would never have lost the baby.

His words had devastated her, because the doctor told her something different. She would have lost the child anyway. It was a miracle that she had fallen pregnant in the first place; medically speaking, she was virtually sterile.

That afternoon she went home to Mikael and said that she couldn't see a future for them as a couple. He had pleaded with her, begged for forgiveness. Eden had turned her back on him, left him in limbo. Two days later she met Efraim at a conference organised by the London School of Economics. He had introduced himself as a researcher from the University of Tel Aviv, and she had believed that their meeting was pure chance, just like a fairy tale. At the end of the second day she went back to his hotel room, and stayed there until well after midnight.

That was the start of their affair.

It was cheap and passionate. And just a bit of fun. She stayed with Mikael, but their relationship was broken, and she didn't know how they were ever going to be able to fix it.

As a researcher it was easy for Efraim to find reasons to visit London on a regular basis, and eventually he was there more or less all the time. With hindsight Eden realised that she had never once visited him at his place of work. Of course not – he didn't have one.

The most important thing about the affair as far as Eden was concerned was that every time she went to bed with Efraim, it felt like a kind of revenge for the fact that Mikael had blamed her for the miscarriage.

So unbelievably petty.

The memory made her want to throw up. Just once she and Efraim had failed to use protection; Eden couldn't have cared less. The only thing she was afraid of was an unwanted pregnancy, and according to the doctors, that was the last thing she needed to worry about. She had told Efraim she was already pregnant. She didn't know why, but afterwards it had been impossible to retract her words.

And Efraim had said that the fact she was pregnant was irrelevant, because after all, their relationship was just a bit of fun.

I hope you feel the same, Eden?

Both Mikael and the doctor had been wrong. She could get pregnant, and she could carry the child to full term. When she realised she was expecting, it had struck her that she couldn't actually be sure who the father was, but she had convinced herself that it wouldn't matter. Efraim obviously didn't care about her, and becoming a father was what Mikael wanted most in the world. Infidelity was the catalyst Eden needed to fix her marriage. When her relationship with Efraim ebbed away, she tried to tell herself that she didn't miss him; Efraim had fulfilled his role in her life.

Until the day the girls were born.

Seeing them for the first time had been utterly terrifying.

Because Eden had known immediately.

She had given birth not to Mikael's children, but to Efraim's.

'Are you okay?'

Mikael sounded worried.

'I'm fine.'

She forced herself to smile. Finished off her packing and closed her suitcase.

She had survived for this long; she wasn't about to let Efraim win, just by standing in silence in a snow-covered park on a winter's day.

If only he hadn't come back. If only he'd left things the way they were.

Because it was in the second round that he had knocked her out.

The realisation of what she had done – gone through an entire pregnancy imagining that it didn't matter who the father of her children was – had eaten away at her soul. For a while the idea of leaving Mikael to be with Efraim had seemed like the ideal solution.

It had been close.

So very close.

Eden had often thanked her lucky stars that she had never

told him that the twins were his. He knew of their existence, and she let him believe they were Mikael's. That was the only thing that saved her when everything went to hell in a handcart.

She still had a place to retreat to. A place where she had remained ever since; a place where she loved to be.

With Mikael and the girls.

She dropped the case on the floor with a thud, then climbed onto the bed and lay down next to Mikael. He closed the laptop and put his arm around her. Stroked her back.

Efraim could go to hell. Compared to Mikael, he was a big, fat, ice-cold zero.

'I was thinking,' Mikael said. 'As you're going to be in London anyway, would you have time to call in at that music shop where I always used to go?'

'You mean the one you used to go to back in the good old days, when you thought you could play the guitar?'

'That's the one. I thought maybe you could get Dani a violin for her birthday.'

Eden stiffened involuntarily. Mikael had got it into his head that Dani was a gifted musician, and he wanted her to learn to play an instrument using the Suzuki method. The violin was Dani's own idea.

'I'll have to see,' she said. 'I don't think I'll have much time for shopping.'

At that moment Alex Recht called, and saved her from a much longer discussion.

'Another child has gone missing,' he said.

'You know I can't help you with that.'

Another child? But why?

'I realise that. I wanted to check if you've found out any more about Efraim Kiel.'

'Not yet. Why do you ask?'

'Because I'm beginning to suspect that he's somehow involved in all this.'

Emotions and vague assumptions had no place in a serious police inquiry. Alex Recht had learned that the hard way. His early years on the force had been marked by the odd case of misjudgement, errors that had eventually made him the skilled investigator he was today.

Efraim Kiel.

He wasn't at the hotel where he had said he was staying; he couldn't be reached on the number he had given. Most importantly, he knew the parents of one of the murdered boys. That was one step too far.

He had called Peder Rydh the previous day, asking questions and digging for information.

Strange guy.

Alex had asked Peder to check whether Efraim still had obligations to fulfil within the Solomon Community, which might explain why he hadn't left the country. But according to Peder, the general secretary had been very surprised to hear that Kiel was still in Sweden. He had done what he came to do, and the general secretary hadn't spoken to him since Peder took up his post.

So there was definitely something odd going on.

Alex was at Police HQ. Fredrika had gone home to pack for her trip to Israel; they had decided that she would be away for only two days. She was needed in Stockholm. The corridor outside his office had been silent and deserted in the morning, but since it became clear that another child had gone missing, there had been a constant flurry of activity.

Polly Eisenberg.

Alex looked at the photograph supplied by her parents. Would she meet the same fate as her brother?

Carmen and Gideon Eisenberg seemed to have no idea why this was happening to them. However hard Alex pushed, they were unable to supply him with any useful information.

He had lost his patience. Seen through their shock and despair, and the fear at the thought of losing their youngest child too.

'You're lying,' he had roared in a voice he very rarely used. 'There isn't a cat in hell's chance that you don't know why someone is abducting and killing your children!'

His words had produced sheer hysteria. Polly wasn't dead yet – or was she?

Was she?

Alex thought about the sun shining on freshly fallen snow earlier in the day, and wondered if Polly, like her brother, was lying in a cold grave somewhere. The thought was unbearable. No more children must be allowed to die. It was out of the question.

Polly's disappearance had led to a change of plan. The Goldmanns were on their way to Police HQ to answer the same questions Alex and Fredrika had put to the Eisenbergs. Alex intended to show them the photographs of the boys with paper bags over their heads, find out what they knew about the Lion. If they had any sense, they wouldn't choose to remain silent as their friends had done.

But they weren't friends, were they? Just four people whose paths had crossed more times than Alex could count. In their childhood and their youth. In the army. At university. Through the move to Sweden, and through their sons.

And now through the fact that their sons had been murdered by the same killer.

An investigator, temporarily assigned to Alex's team, tapped on his door.

'The Goldmanns are here. Do you want anyone to sit in on the interview?'

'No, but I would like to question them separately. Could you take care of Daphne if I start with Saul?'

'No problem.' His colleague's expression darkened. 'How long has Polly Eisenberg been missing now?'

'Just under two hours.'

When she was formally reported missing, she had been gone for less than thirty minutes. Under normal circumstances the police would have first checked to make sure that she hadn't wandered off to the nearest sweet shop or something along those lines, but not this time. Not when her brother had been murdered so recently, and there was reason to believe that Polly might also be at risk.

The police had thrown a ring of steel around Stockholm, and roadblocks were also set up outside the city. The media quickly ran the story as headline news, and the switchboard was inundated with calls from journalists demanding answers that Alex just didn't have.

'The parents,' his colleague said. 'Do they have an alibi?'

'Obviously the Eisenbergs do, because they were talking to me and Fredrika when Polly disappeared. I don't know about the Goldmanns yet.'

It was always the same when the situation was serious: they knew too little, had too many unanswered questions. Alex thought about the different impressions in the snow, on the roof and on Lovön. Small shoes and big shoes. On the same feet? The same gun had been used both times, after all.

He picked up his notes, took the lift down to the basement and walked into the interview room where Saul Goldmann was waiting. Daphne would be questioned up on the ground floor in a room with both curtains and a view, but not Saul. Alex wanted him to realise the gravity of the situation. Saul had given the impression of being quite cocky the last time they met; on this occasion, Alex was determined to make sure he had the upper hand.

'Thank you for taking the time to come in.'

Saul Goldmann looked exhausted. A man who had lost too much in such a short period of time.

'No problem,' he said. 'Needless to say we will do all we can to help you.'

But his eyes told a different story. His expression was wary, bordering on hostile.

Alex understood, to a certain extent. The last time they met, Saul had been on home turf, secure in his role as a victim. After the meeting with Carmen and Gideon, Alex was determined not to make the same mistake again. It wasn't that he didn't feel sorry for the parents, because he did. Immensely sorry. But as long as he was convinced they were withholding information, he had to be hard on them. He was the one who decided what the police needed to know in order to do their job – not the Eisenbergs or the Goldmanns.

He began with the most important question.

'Where were you between one and two p.m. today?'

For a moment Alex thought he had misjudged the situation, and that Saul Goldmann was about to attack him. The other man was far more disturbed by the question than Alex had expected him to be.

'What the hell do you mean by that?'

'I mean exactly what I say, and nothing else. Please answer the question.'

'Am I suspected of some crime? Do you think I've taken Polly? Is that why I'm here?'

Alex slowly put down his pen.

'In less than a week, three children have gone missing from the Solomon Community here in Stockholm. Two of them have been found dead. One of them was your son. It's my duty to find out what their close family and friends were doing when those children disappeared. Because however much I wish it wasn't the case, the perpetrator is usually someone known to the child. *So answer the bloody question!*'

Adults who feel under pressure often start to behave like children. Alex had seen the phenomenon many times, yet he was still surprised when he saw Saul's reaction. The man's eyes shone with defiance.

What was it that he found so infuriating?

'I was out for a walk. A circuit around Djurgården.'

The most classic of all walks in Stockholm.

'With Daphne?'

'Alone.'

'Did you meet anyone you knew while you were out walking?'

'No.'

'Did you make or receive any phone calls?'

'No.'

So he had no alibi.

That was why he was so angry. Because he was afraid. Afraid of looking like a suspect.

'I've just lost my only child. I needed to be alone. Okay?'

'Okay.'

Alex moved on; he didn't want to waste time on the issue of Saul's alibi at this stage, so he pretended to let it go. It was clear that Saul was surprised. Alex sat calmly opposite him, waiting.

Eventually Saul broke the silence.

'So was there anything else?'

Alex glanced at his watch. Wished the time wasn't going so fast. Not just for his own sake, but mainly for Polly Eisenberg's. Because in spite of all the roadblocks, all the officers who had been called in to work overtime, in spite of the fact that every media outlet in the country was following Polly's disappearance, Alex had the horrible feeling that he was in the middle of a chain of events over which he had no influence whatsoever.

The chances of finding Polly alive weren't just small, they were infinitesimal.

And sitting opposite Alex was a man who, like certain others, had chosen not to tell the police everything he knew.

A man who didn't have an alibi.

That wasn't enough to make him a suspect, of course. They had to understand the motive in order to find the perpetrator.

'Yes,' he said to Saul. 'There was something else. I have

several more questions. Let's start with something that should be comparatively simple. Do you know a man by the name of Efraim Kiel?'

In the world of fairy tales, limitations were set only by the bounds of imagination, which appealed to Fredrika Bergman. The impossible became possible; the happy ending was obligatory. And as a reader she always had the option of setting the book aside if the story got too unpleasant.

Which was what her daughter did when Fredrika tried to read to her.

'Yuck,' she said, knocking the book out of her mother's hands.

Fredrika picked it up, looked at the dark images. Saga was right. It was a dark and scary story, not the kind of thing she should be reading to a child who was only three.

Her thoughts turned to the tale of the Paper Boy. The story Gideon had grown up with, told with the aim of keeping the children at home in the evenings. In a country like Israel, there was probably good reason to frighten a child in that way. The problem was that the Paper Boy seemed to have come to life – but not in Israel, in Stockholm.

Fredrika had searched online, but no one seemed to have heard of him. Nothing had been written about him. Perhaps her lack of success was due to her inability to read Hebrew; her searches in English and Swedish got her nowhere.

But something told Fredrika that even if she had been

able to speak Hebrew, she wouldn't have found many hits. Carmen had heard of the Paper Boy through Gideon, when she was an adult; he hadn't featured in her childhood.

The Paper Boy.

Fredrika shuddered. The very concept was too abstract to stimulate the imagination. Why boy and not man? The Paper Man would be more logical. Using a child to frighten a child was tasteless, and surely ineffective: who would be scared of someone called the Paper Boy?

Me. I was scared of everything when I was little.

Fredrika gazed at her daughter, who had already forgotten about the story and was playing with a car instead. A blue car that Spencer had bought for their son. In his rather conservative view of the world, little girls couldn't possibly be interested in such things. She laughed quietly to herself. Spencer was a good man, in spite of his shortcomings. Almost perfect. And he was perfectly capable of backing down when he was wrong. If his daughter wanted to play with cars, that was fine.

Beyond the fairy stories and the fun lay her trip to Israel. Without Spencer. He wasn't up to it, that was obvious. She hated the thought of travelling alone, even though it was only for a couple of days.

She tried to shake off her feeling of unease. What could go wrong in such a short time?

Everything. The cataclysmic changes don't happen over a long period, but from one second to the next.

The sound of her mobile interrupted her thoughts.

'Could we meet up before you go?' Alex said.

Fredrika didn't like the idea at all; she really didn't want to leave her family again at this stage.

Alex picked up on her reluctance.

'I can come to you, if that's easier.'

Fredrika was taken aback.

'Come here? To the apartment?'

'It was just a suggestion.'

Why not?

'Of course,' she heard herself saying. 'Good idea.'

Spencer opened the door to Alex a little while later. Fredrika heard them say hello, saw them shake hands. She had to smile as she watched Alex trying to hide his surprise. Just like everyone else, he knew that she lived with a man who was twenty-five years older than her, but he still seemed bemused by how old Spencer actually was. Which was the way most people reacted when they first met him.

Alex glanced over at her, seemingly at a loss. He was acting as if someone had forced him across the threshold at gunpoint, rather than as if the whole thing had been his idea in the first place.

The children realised someone had arrived, and came running. Like eager little puppies. They certainly weren't shy.

'Coffee?'

Alex declined. Fredrika led him into the library and closed the door.

'Right you two, shall we make a start on tea?' she heard Spencer say to the children. His voice was hoarse; he definitely wasn't well.

'He seems nice,' Alex said, mainly for the sake of having something to say.

'He is,' Fredrika said. 'And good-looking.'

Nothing was as liberating as humour.

Alex laughed uncertainly.

'Are you on the same flight tomorrow?' he asked.

Fredrika looked downcast.

'Spencer's not coming,' she said. 'He isn't well enough.'

'But you're still going?' Alex asked anxiously.

'I am.'

He looked relieved.

'We've questioned Saul and Daphne Goldmann,' he said with an air of resignation. 'I wish I had some useful information to pass on, but unfortunately that's not the case. To start with, they had nothing to add to the story of the Paper Boy; they merely confirmed what Gideon and Carmen had told us, that it was used to frighten children.'

'Saul grew up on the same kibbutz as Gideon,' Fredrika said, 'so it's hardly surprising that he's heard of the Paper Boy too. But what about Daphne? Was she already familiar with the story?'

'She was, but that's not surprising either – she grew up on the neighbouring kibbutz.'

Fredrika made a mental note of that snippet.

'Do we have the names of these kibbutzim? I'm just wondering whether I ought to try and visit them.'

'I think you should – if they're still there, that is. Quite a lot have gone bankrupt or closed down for other reasons.'

Time had moved on from the basic premise of the kibbutz, an idealistic society where everything was owned collectively and no one earned more than anyone else, even though some carried more responsibility than others.

Alex went on:

'Then they were asked about the Lion. Same again – they

had nothing to add to what we had already heard from Gideon and Carmen.'

Fredrika thought about the prospects of finding the Lion in Israel; after all, it was from Jerusalem that his emails had been sent.

'Have you spoken to the Israeli police?' she asked.

Alex nodded. 'We've given them everything our tech guys have found out about the Lion, and they're going to help us search for him. They should have done a fair amount by the time you get there.'

'So we've made a formal request for assistance?'

'Sweden doesn't actually have an international agreement with Israel, but as the victims belonged to the Solomon Community, it wasn't particularly difficult to persuade them to co-operate with us. I don't think we'd be able to secure an extradition to Sweden, but we'll cross that bridge when we come to it.'

'How did Daphne and Saul react to the photograph of Abraham with the paper bag over his head?'

'Like the Eisenbergs, but even more strongly. Particularly Saul – he was very vocal.'

There was nothing strange about that; the pictures were terrible. Fredrika could still see the boys lying there on their backs in the snow, barefoot and with a bullet wound in their chests. And a paper bag on their heads.

'And still the parents seem unable to help us move forward,' she said.

'They insist they have no idea why this is happening to them, but I'm not sure they're telling the truth. Now that Polly Eisenberg has gone missing too, I'm more convinced than ever that chance has nothing to do with any of this.'

'Of course not. It's obvious that there's a personal motive behind the murders and Polly's disappearance; the only question is what that motive might be.'

Fredrika thought about the Paper Boy once more, wondering who the perpetrator was. The Paper Boy seemed like a suspect, an evil fairy-tale figure who didn't exist.

Except that he did exist, because the children who had died on Lovön had been marked in the way that the Paper Boy marked his victims, according to the legend.

'I've spoken to the tech guys about whether it would be possible to trace the Lion's other contacts,' Alex said. 'They've spoken to the administrators of Super Troopers, and it turns out that the information was still on the system, in spite of the fact that the Lion had deleted his profile.'

Fredrika felt a flicker of hope.

'And you're only telling me this now?'

Alex pulled a face.

'It was another dead end, I'm afraid. The Lion had no contact with any of the other members.'

Fredrika's mind was whirling. She didn't regard that as a dead end at all.

'Which means he was only interested in Simon and Abraham. But how did he know he would find them on Super Troopers?'

'That's a bloody good question. Maybe someone tipped him off?'

Maybe, maybe not. So many questions, so few answers. What a mess. Fredrika tried another tack.

'We wondered if the Lion could be the person who picked up the boys; did we follow up the car rental idea?'

'As we don't have a name to go on, I haven't set the ball rolling yet,' Alex said.

'Didn't the Lion say his first name was Zalman?'

'Yes, but that's not necessarily true. But you're right; we'll check it out. He could have two sets of ID papers.'

Could he? Fredrika thought about Efraim Kiel, an Israeli security expert who had entered Sweden and now couldn't be found. Alex had probably been wise to contact Eden; the police lacked the tools to identify their suspects, which said something about their background. Something very unpleasant.

'Did the Goldmanns know who Efraim Kiel was?'

'They knew him from their military service, but that's all.'

Alex ran a hand over his chin. 'I have a feeling the parents are hiding a lot of things from us, but I don't understand why. It's so bloody frustrating.'

People lied for the strangest reasons, Fredrika knew that. A groundless fear of becoming a suspect was often the main motivation; they got themselves entangled in all kinds of unnecessary lies in order to make life simpler, which had the opposite effect. Always and without exception.

Alex met Fredrika's gaze.

'I'm not saying that I expect you to achieve miracles during your trip, but almost . . . Are you sure you can cope with all this?'

'I can cope.'

She looked at her watch, working out how long Polly had been missing. Her heart sank as she thought the unthinkable: they weren't going to find her in time. Not if she had been taken by the same person who had abducted her brother.

Arlanda was a quiet place on a Saturday evening. Eden Lundell loved airports. She was fascinated by the stream of people who had something in common: they were all heading to or from somewhere.

And the sense of being in the midst of that stream usually brought her a feeling of peace.

However, peace was sadly lacking as Eden sat waiting for her flight to London. Stress crawled under her skin, making it impossible for her to sit still.

I shouldn't have left Mikael and the children alone.

In many families it was the man who was the hunter-gatherer, who protected his family, took on the physical responsibility. But not in Eden's case. From a purely physical point of view, Mikael was the perfect warrior; Eden had no doubt that he would give up his life for her and their daughters. The only problem was that death was rarely a particularly productive option. It was noble, but not very sensible. If Mikael chose that option, both he and the children would be gone in two seconds.

The thought made her feel sick. She dug out her phone and called home.

'Has something happened?' Mikael said anxiously, highlighting the fact that Eden didn't usually do that kind of thing.

'I just wanted to check on you,' she said.

'You left forty minutes ago.'

'Speak soon.'

She ended the call, cursing herself. She never got nervous. There was no room for weakness. And fear was the greatest weakness of all.

Eden realised she was watching the people around her, scanning her surroundings like radar, alert for the slightest deviation from the norm.

Efraim. What would she do if he sought her out again?

Because his appearance in the park had been anything but a chance encounter. He wanted something.

He's deliberately stressing me out. Provoking me. I just don't understand why.

Alex Recht thought that Efraim might have something to do with the murder of the two boys, and that he had taken another child.

But Alex didn't know that Säpo had been watching Efraim, shadowing his movements outside the hotel; at least insofar as he was willing to be be shadowed.

Where the hell had Säpo been when he turned up in the park?

Eden had realised something then: she would never be free of Efraim. Not unless that was what he wanted. She thought about the gaps in the surveillance reports, the fact that Efraim appeared to be spending far too many hours in his hotel room. They had changed their approach after Eden had pointed out the failings in their routine; they had located alternative exits from the hotel, which were now covered.

But Eden knew that wasn't enough. His appearance in the park proved her point.

A catastrophic incident. Thinking about it caused her physical pain.

Her mobile rang; it was GD.

'I'm afraid I have some bad news,' he said.

'So have I.'

She hadn't got round to telling her boss about what had happened earlier. She felt a surge of pure rage. If the surveillance operatives hadn't been such amateurs, Efraim would never have been able to get so close to her. God only knew what he had been up to during all those missing hours.

She thought about the two boys, lying in the snow with paper bags over their heads.

She pushed the suspicion aside; it was impossible.

Surely the man who was the father of her children couldn't have murdered someone else's sons?

'You first,' Buster said.

Eden gave a brief outline of Efraim's appearance in the park, but she omitted the worst part of all: the fact that Efraim had seen Dani, and realised what she hadn't told him before they broke up. Eden's silent revenge, her darkest secret.

Buster didn't say a word.

'Are you still there?' Eden said.

'I am. So the bastard came and found you? In the park, when you were with your family?'

Technically, some of them are his family.

'Yes. So it's obvious that the surveillance just isn't working.'

Don't sound angry, don't flare up. It was so easy to ignore people who flew off the handle.

'Which is exactly why I called,' Buster said. 'Because something has gone terribly wrong with our surveillance. I rang to warn you Eden. I'm very sorry that it was too late.'

'What do you mean?'

'They haven't seen him since yesterday. Eventually they went into the hotel and spoke to the receptionist; he'd checked out.'

'So now we have no idea where he is?'

'Correct.'

She forced herself to breathe calmly.

'Have they seen anything of the person who's leaving him messages?'

'Not yet.'

Not yet. As if they had all the time in the world.

'Alex Recht has been in touch again,' she said. 'They seem to think that Efraim might be involved in the murders of those two children from the Solomon Community.'

'Shit.'

Buster's voice was a stress-filled exhalation.

'The question is whether we can provide him with an alibi,' Eden said. 'Although that seems unlikely, under the circumstances.'

'But why are they interested in Kiel?' Buster wanted to know.

Eden passed on what Alex had told her. The police had nothing concrete to go on, but their suspicions were growing, and the fact that he was so difficult to get hold of didn't exactly help his case.

'It definitely sounds as if we ought to tell them that we're following him too,' Buster said. 'Where are you, by the way?'

'Arlanda.'

'Eden, please don't do anything stupid. Where are you going?'

'I'll tell you when it's over.'

'No you bloody won't. You'll tell me right . . .'

'I'll be away on Monday, but I should be back on Tuesday.'

'Just so you know – I can't support you if you're running your own race. I want to make that perfectly clear.'

Behind Eden, on the other side of the huge windows, the illuminated runways sparkled with frost and snow. She would soon be on her way.

'You can't help me with this, Buster.'

'How do you know? You won't even let me try.'

'You have tried. Efraim ended up following me and my children to the toboggan run.'

'I can't tell you how sorry I am about that.'

'I know. But it's not enough. Säpo can't access the information we need. Only I can do that, on my own.'

A plane taxied past the window, its white metallic bulk moving slowly towards the runway.

Eden's flight was called; it was time to board.

'I have to go.'

'Will you call Alex Recht, or shall I ask someone else to do it?'

Eden thought for a second.

'I'll speak to him when I land.'

She was about to end the call, but Buster hadn't finished.

'Be honest with me, Eden. Just between the two of us. Do you think Efraim Kiel is involved in the murders?'

She stopped.

Pictured him. Tall, dark and tanned. Hand in hand at a market in Jerusalem. Whispering in her ear, telling her how much he loved her.

The most treacherous, lying bastard she had ever met in her entire life.

'I don't know,' she said.

And realised to her horror that she meant what she said.

She didn't know what she thought about the question of Efraim Kiel's guilt.

As long as she had any doubt on that issue, she couldn't be sure that her family was safe.

Up on deck the air was cold and damp. The wind seared his cheeks, brought tears to his eyes. Efraim Kiel stood alone at the rail, watching the dark water foam against the metal hull. It was ten o'clock at night. The following morning they would be in Helsinki; he would fly back to Stockholm before lunch. Good.

He thought about the latest message from the Paper Boy and realised someone had been watching him. And he hadn't noticed.

Although it wasn't the fact of being followed that bothered him the most. Much more critical was the question of what would happen when the Paper Boy discovered that the next victim had disappeared. Would he choose someone else, or let it lie?

Efraim knew better than to count on the latter.

The Paper Boy never gives up; he always comes back.

Efraim was aware that his options were limited. The Paper Boy was impatient, and with good reason. However, Efraim must engender a meeting with him, explain why the hunt must end. Justice had been done, vengeance served. So the game must stop. Immediately.

It won't get any better than this. You have to accept that.

The water carrying the ship billowed beneath the hull.

Anyone with a tendency towards seasickness had chosen the wrong night to sail. The northerly climate was merciless. Only the darkness was worse. Efraim couldn't remember when he had last felt so tired.

The cold made him shiver, reminding him of why he had gone up on deck in the first place. He wasn't dressed for the biting wind that had come with nightfall. Soon he would have to go back inside.

He looked around, to the right and to the left. There was no one there, no one to see him. Quickly he bent down, unzipped his bag with gloved hands. Felt for the object he had wrapped in towels and items of clothing. It was right at the bottom.

Efraim's hands closed around the black metal with practised ease.

He stood up, leaned over the rail.

Not a living soul saw him as he dropped the gun that had killed three people into the sea.

CONCLUSION

FRAGMENT V

The inspector who is standing in the street outside the apartment block where a man and his children have been murdered is wishing that the weather was different. Because right now everything is so horrific that a fresh snowstorm is the last thing he needs.

But the weather is not his biggest worry.

It is the woman who has lost her family; he doesn't know what to do with her.

Resolutely she turns her back on him and walks away. He calls her name, once, twice. She doesn't answer, doesn't turn around. She just walks. And he lets her go. Decisively he signals to his colleagues to follow her, on foot or by car. They do both. He watches her disappear in the snow, sensing the thoughts whirling around in her head.

Feeling frustrated, he goes back to the apartment. He cannot stay out here in the street.

The CSIs look up when he walks in.

'Worst I've ever seen,' one of them says.

The inspector does not respond. He thinks that he has probably seen worse, but nothing more incomprehensible. He even thinks that he will never be able to learn to live with this. They lowered their guard for just a few hours, and this is what happened.

There is a wedding photograph on the chest of drawers. It hurts the inspector's eyes to look at it, and he moves away.

He wonders if the deceased knew the killer. If so, it shouldn't be too difficult to work out who he or she is.

But there are no guarantees. If the perpetrator has got away with it up to now, there is a risk that they will never find the person in question.

'Where did they die?' he asks.

'We think the man died instantaneously when he was shot in the hallway. It seems likely that the children were attacked in here; they were probably already in bed.'

The words go round and round inside the inspector's head. He cannot process what he is hearing, cannot take it in.

His mobile rings.

'We've lost her,' says his colleague. 'She was walking along the pavement, and then she was gone. It was as if the snow just swallowed her up.'

EARLIER

The Fifth Day

SUNDAY, 29 JANUARY 2012

The last day of the week. Peder Rydh was moving restlessly around the house. One of his sons had woken up with a temperature, the other with far too much energy.

'I'll take him out,' Peder said to Ylva.

She looked grateful as he dressed the boy in several layers of warm clothing.

'Where will you go?' she asked.

'I've just got to call in at the office.'

Gratitude was replaced by annoyance, but he got in before she had time to say anything:

'I have to show my face. I'm head of security, and another child has gone missing. I have to show that I care, because I do. And it's good for our kids to be in town occasionally.'

It had been Ylva's idea to move out of the city, and Peder had taken a great deal of persuasion. Reluctantly he admitted that there were many advantages to living in a house rather than an apartment. The garden was a blessing when the weather was good enough for the boys to play outside; their parents could watch their every move from the kitchen window, without having to go out themselves. Ylva had commented that their garden looked more like a prison exercise yard by the time Peder had finished reinforcing the boundary with impenetrable shrubs and a high fence.

'It's important to make sure they can't get out into the street,' was his justification.

But deep down he knew it was more about making sure that no one could get in. Following the death of his brother, he had become dependent on setting boundaries, both mental and physical. As far as his home was concerned, the fence was critical. Inside there was security, outside everything that fed his many fears.

Peder parked outside the main entrance of the community centre. He got his son out of the car, and as they stood hand in hand on the pavement, he wondered whether it had been such a good idea to bring the boy.

Another child was missing.

Polly Eisenberg.

The very thought made Peder furious.

How the hell had they let her slip through their fingers?

The only thing that calmed him slightly was the fact that Polly had disappeared just hours after they had begun to suspect that she could be at risk. Her disappearance also seemed to have had the effect of reassuring the members of the community; they no longer thought there was a serial killer out there, picking off victims because they were Jewish. Everyone now believed this was a private vendetta against the Goldmann and Eisenberg families, who were now paying an unacceptably high price for what must be an old transgression.

But what justified the loss of your children?

Peder couldn't understand it at all.

Nor did he understand the logic of punishing a person by hurting someone else, someone who had done nothing wrong.

He thought about the boys, hunted down like animals out on Lovön. The feeling of his son's hand in his gave the illusion of security. If the children stayed close to him or Ylva, everything would be fine.

The community centre was much quieter than it had been when Simon and Abraham went missing. Peder thought gloomily that this was probably to be expected; people had learned something since the last time. They weren't going to find the perpetrator by sitting around making phone calls, working their way through class lists.

One of the assistants came towards them, smiling at his son.

'Do you like chocolate cake? And how about a glass of juice?'

Peder left his son with her and went into his office, leaving the door open. Trust was good, but control was better.

He hadn't heard any more from Efraim Kiel. He had no idea whether that was a good thing or a bad thing, but he realised that the police were interested in Kiel, which worried him.

It couldn't do any harm if Peder checked out the man who had recruited him. He would begin by finding out whether Kiel could possibly be in the frame for the shooting of the teacher and the kidnapping of the two boys. If the Solomon Community could provide an alibi, then he could be eliminated as a suspect.

The police officer within Peder was still there, occupying his body like a restless soul. He couldn't escape, couldn't get away. Not that he wanted to. The desire to know more drove Peder from his desk and down the corridor to the general secretary's office.

He looked up when Peder tapped on the door and walked in.

'I'm glad you're here,' he said. 'Have you heard anything from the police about Polly Eisenberg?'

'No, but that's not why I'm here.'

'*Bevakasha*, please sit down.'

The general secretary glanced over Peder's shoulder.

'Would you mind closing the door?'

'I'd rather not. My son is out there.'

Peder sat down. He had planned his strategy.

'Efraim Kiel, the man who was here when I was appointed,' he began. 'Do you know how I can get hold of him?'

'Efraim? No, the only contact details I have are the ones I've already given you. Why do you want to speak to him?'

It was clear that the general secretary was shaken. He was the leader of a community that had suffered terrible losses over the past few days. Evil had placed its cold hand on their lives, terrified them all beyond rhyme and reason.

If only they knew how to stop all this.

'The police are looking for him.'

The words just came out, but he felt no regret. It was true.

'Efraim? What on earth for?'

That was the most difficult question to answer; Peder didn't want it to look as if he was trying to do the police's job for them.

'It seems he's cropped up in their investigation. Somehow. But that's just between you and me.'

The general secretary went pale, then he burst out angrily:

'That's the most ridiculous thing I've ever heard! Why would someone like Efraim be mixed up in all the terrible things that have happened here? If that's the way the police are working, I'm not surprised that another child has gone missing!'

Peder made an effort to retain control of the conversation.

'I'm not saying he's a suspect; I think he's important for other reasons. Given his background and so on.'

Meaningless words, meaningless sentences. Time was running out for Peder, and he was getting nowhere. The general secretary's eyes narrowed, and Peder realised that his anger was about to be directed at Peder instead.

He changed tack.

'Besides, Efraim is automatically ruled out as a suspect, isn't he? He was working here when Josephine was shot and the boys went missing, wasn't he?'

'Exactly,' the general secretary said. 'Efraim was here. With me. So unless I'm a suspect too, the police can cross him off their list. You can tell them that from me.'

Peder thought about Alex and Fredrika, wondered what they were doing.

I'd give anything to be a part of this investigation.

'Absolutely,' he said.

When he left the centre a little while later with his son, he took out his mobile and called Alex.

'It's Peder. I think I have some information that might interest you.'

The silent protests were the worst. The ones that were not uttered out loud, but settled in the air like a thin filter. Diana's body language told him all he needed to know. She didn't like the fact that he was working on a Sunday. 'Unhealthy' was the word she would have used if she had said anything about it, but she didn't, and that was even worse than an open confrontation.

'Do you know how boring it is to ski alone?' she said when she called Alex.

It was morning, and he felt worn out. He had slept badly because of all the thoughts crowding his brain, most of them about Polly, who still hadn't been found. Alex was afraid that she was already dead.

But if that was the case, we would have found her.

Diana wasn't indifferent to his job, but it worried her that he sometimes let himself be swallowed up by it, that he withdrew from what other people referred to as everyday life. When work occupied every single waking hour, things had gone too far.

'When this is over, I'll take some time off,' he said.

'I should think the snow will be long gone by then.'

He laughed, then fell silent, overcome by sadness. He was convinced that with the speed the case was moving, it wouldn't be many days before they were sitting there with the answers. The snow would be the least of his problems.

He ended the call and focused on the matter in hand.

A missing five-year-old girl.

A teacher who had been shot dead.

Two ten-year-old boys, hunted down and shot.

And a series of strange elements that he didn't understand at all. The paper bags with faces drawn on them. The story of the Paper Boy, who attacked other children. Two families who seemed to be at the centre of the investigation, but who were unwilling or unable to explain why. Two families who had left Israel and moved to Sweden, for reasons which were unclear. Plus two Israelis who had entered Sweden and now could not be found.

Eden Lundell had called Alex the previous evening. Unfortunately his phone had been switched off by mistake; the battery had run out. She had left a message, but it wasn't clear what she wanted; she had just said she had something to tell him, and would call again later.

Alex couldn't work Eden out. She was frighteningly sharp, but incredibly difficult to reach on a personal level. He thought – or rather knew – that they would have made a good team and worked well together. She was neither emotional nor confrontational. Above all, she didn't take things personally. Alex often found himself analysing what he had said to Fredrika about this or that, checking to see whether some comment could have been taken the wrong way, but that never happened in his dealings with Eden.

But apart from that . . . Leaving aside the fact that they could talk to one another, what a special person she seemed to be.

Curiosity got the better of him: why had she called? Perhaps she had information that was vital to the case. There was no harm in trying to reach her; if she was busy, she would say so.

Before Alex had time to call, his phone rang. It was Peder Rydh.

'I've been checking up on Efraim Kiel,' he said. 'Well, I say checking up . . . I spoke to the general secretary of the Solomon Community.'

Alex had a bad feeling about this. Peder was driven, full of energy; nothing ever moved fast enough for him.

'I hope you didn't tell him that we have our suspicions about Kiel?'

It sounded as if Peder was out and about; the sound of the traffic was noticeable, making it difficult to hear him.

'No, of course not. But I had to give him something, otherwise he would have wondered why I was asking questions. I said you were trying to get hold of him because it would be interesting to discuss the investigation with someone with his background.'

That sounded like an acceptable lie to Alex, and to be fair it wasn't entirely untrue. Without knowing the details of Kiel's background, Alex thought he might well be able to make a valuable contribution.

If only he hadn't been behaving so strangely.

His task within the Solomon Community was obviously not a secret; Peder had met him, and Alex had spoken to him on the phone. His voice had been deep and rough, leaving very little margin for compromise.

So why had he checked into the hotel under a false name? If he had stayed there at all. And why had he got rid of his mobile, even though he was still in the country?

Something occurred to him.

'Sorry Peder, before you go on: you didn't get Kiel's new number the last time he called you?'

'No, I didn't. If I had, I would have passed it on to you.'

Alex heard what Peder really wanted to say:

I'm on your side, don't you get it?

Once again he was conscious of how much he missed working with Peder.

When this is over, before or after the snow has melted, I will do whatever I can to get you back in the police.

'Anyway, I called to tell you that Efraim can't have shot Josephine or kidnapped the two boys.'

'And how do you know this?'

'He was in a meeting with the general secretary all afternoon. They were working on staffing issues. When they heard someone had been shot, Efraim went outside with the security guards. He was still on the premises when the boys were abducted on their way to their tennis coaching session.'

That was a classic watertight alibi. It didn't mean that Efraim wasn't involved in some other way, of course, but it definitely made him less interesting. Alex felt a stab of disappointment. This was one of the few leads they had.

Fredrika's plane would soon be landing. Israeli colleagues were meeting her at the airport. Alex was trying to keep his expectations about her visit in check, but it was hopeless. Without a miracle they were lost.

'I'm glad you called,' he said to Peder. 'Thanks for your help – I won't forget this.'

Peder said something that Alex didn't hear.

'Sorry, there's a lot of noise at your end,' he said. 'Can you say that again?'

After a pause, Peder said: 'It was nothing important. I'll speak to you again soon.'

'Good,' Alex said.

He meant what he said. Peder's help had been invaluable in many ways, and Alex would make sure his superiors knew that.

After the conversation came the emptiness. Efraim Kiel was out of the frame; he was no longer a viable suspect. Coincidences could be significant, or they could be nonsense, and in this case they appeared to be nonsense. There was probably no exciting explanation as to why Kiel had asked Peder about calling cards left at the crime scenes; he was just a particularly skilled investigator.

His mobile rang again; number withheld.

Eden's husky voice came down the line.

'I missed your call yesterday,' Alex said.

Which was a stupid thing to say – why waste time stating the obvious?

'My fault, it was very late when I called. Are you free to talk now?'

'Absolutely. If you'd rather meet face to face and you happen to be at work, you're welcome to come over.'

It was no problem for Eden to come to Alex's office, whereas his chances of dropping in to see her at Säpo were non-existent.

'That would have been nice, but unfortunately I'm not in today.'

Did he think everyone else worked Sundays as well? Even someone like Eden Lundell was entitled to some time off to breathe in the fresh winter air, spend time with her family. She was married with children, wasn't she? Or was that just a figment of his imagination?

'Alex, I haven't been completely honest with you.'

Her tone was serious.

'I lied when I said I didn't know who Efraim Kiel was. I'm very sorry, but given the situation, I couldn't tell you what I knew until I'd spoken to my boss.'

Eden was the head of the counter-terrorism unit, and she had had to speak to her boss. Who was the General Director of Säpo.

'Okay,' Alex said. Warily, because he had no idea what he was supposed to say.

'You absolutely must not pass this on, but I can tell you that Säpo has had reason to monitor Efraim Kiel's activities here in Sweden. I can't tell you why, but I promise you it has nothing to do with the murders you're investigating.'

'Hang on a minute,' Alex said, but Eden interrupted him.

'You'll just have to take my word for it. Säpo is not investigating the murders of individual members of the Solomon Community, but if we had information that could benefit your work, then needless to say we would have passed it on.'

Unless of course national security was at risk, Alex thought.

Less than five minutes ago, he had received information that virtually ruled out Efraim Kiel as a suspect, but of course Eden didn't know that. He appreciated the fact that she had called, and he couldn't care less why Säpo was following Efraim, as long as it had nothing to do with the murders.

His thoughts turned to Polly Eisenberg. To her brother's body, lying on the dazzling white snow. To the paper bag over his head.

This has to end.

He heard a rustling noise, then Eden was back.

'Has Fredrika left?'

'Yes, she should be there by now.'

He wished they could have gone together, that it hadn't been so urgent.

And he hoped Fredrika would take care of herself, all alone in the land of the Paper Boy.

ISRAEL

One of the smallest countries in the world, from a purely geographical point of view. The desert meeting the sea. Heat and aridity. Two nations laying claim to the same narrow piece of land. Almost two decades ago there had been a peace process, but there was nothing left of that initiative now. The country where the Paper Boy had once been given life was a strange place.

'Have you been here before?' asked the man who met Fredrika at the airport.

'Once, but it was a long time ago.'

She had been twenty-four years old, and she had just fallen in love.

This would have been so much more fun if Spencer was here.

They were in a car on the way to Jerusalem from Ben Gurion airport. The hills forming the landscape were a fascinating sight, a mixture of barrenness dotted with patches of vegetation and settlements.

Her companion was called Isak Ben-Zwi. He was roughly the same age as Alex, and as far as Fredrika could make out, worked for the Israeli equivalent of the National Crime Unit.

'You have a terrible situation in Stockholm,' he said.

Fredrika could only agree.

'Have you found the little girl who went missing yesterday?'

'I'm afraid not.'

She took out her mobile; a new message she hadn't had time to listen to yet. She was about to put her phone away when Isak said: 'Please – we're not here to make small talk, we're here because we have a job to do. Don't mind me.'

She gave him a grateful look and clicked on her voicemail.

Alex's voice in her ear was a reminder of why she was there.

'Peder called. Efraim Kiel can't have abducted the boys or shot Josephine, because he was in a meeting with the general secretary of the Solomon Community at the time. Speak to you later.'

So. That considerably reduced the possibility that Efraim was involved. Of course it could be that one person had abducted the boys and another had shot them, but that seemed unlikely. As a general rule, if there was more than one perpetrator, they were usually responsible for different victims.

'Problems?' Isak said.

Fredrika didn't want to share what she had just heard. She and Alex had agreed before she left that it was best to leave Efraim Kiel out of their collaboration with the Israeli police.

'Yes, but nothing new.'

She forced a smile and gazed out of the window.

'Is the weather always this good in January?'

The sun was shining, and it was eighteen degrees. The contrast with Stockholm was depressing.

'Not always, but sometimes – if we're lucky. Jerusalem is a

little cooler; the city is higher up than Tel Aviv. We even have snow there occasionally, but it's very rare.'

They drove in silence towards the Israeli capital, which was still not recognised internationally.

'We've started going through the material you sent over,' Isak said eventually. 'The various addresses where the individual calling himself the Lion logged into Super Troopers.'

Fredrika's spirits rose.

'Any luck?'

'Not so far, but as I said, we've only just started. I've got some of my team visiting these places to see whether they keep customer records, or whether any of them have CCTV.'

If so, they might be able to get a picture, which would be invaluable. A picture and personal details. Fredrika tried not to be over-optimistic.

'We're very grateful for your co-operation,' she said.

Isak kept his sharp eyes fixed on the road.

'We're happy to help,' he said. 'The Jewish people have the right to feel safe. Wherever they may be.'

Fredrika knew what he meant, but felt no empathy. She didn't really know who her own people were. A small political elite in Europe was trying to create a European identity for the members of the European Union, but Fredrika couldn't see them succeeding. Such constructs didn't usually have a long-term future.

'I believe you have some other matters to look into during your stay,' Isak said.

It was hard to tell whether there was a question in there, but Fredrika thought so. She and Alex had carefully planned their strategy for her visit. It would be inappropriate to reveal that they distrusted the boys' parents. They had nothing concrete against them, but Fredrika thought that was irrelevant; the parents must be left out of the whole thing.

But she had to respond to Isak's question – or statement.

'An old Israeli legend has come up in our investigation,' she said. 'Have you ever heard of the Paper Boy?'

Isak frowned.

'The Paper Boy? No, never. Who is he?'

Fredrika told him, trying to put into words a story so unpleasant that she couldn't understand why anyone would ever have told it to their children. She omitted specific details relating to the inquiry, such as the fact that Simon and Abraham had been found with paper bags over their heads.

'What a strange story,' Isak said. 'I'll get someone to do an online search in Hebrew, but don't expect miracles; it sounds as if you've stumbled across a local urban myth.'

His words gave her the perfect opening.

'That's exactly what we thought, which is why I'd really like to visit two kibbutzim where the story was told, according to our sources. Just to see if I can find out any more about where it comes from.'

'I understand. If you give me the names of the kibbutzim I can help you with transport. If they're still in existence, of course.'

Fredrika hoped that at least one of them was still in operation. She had come a long way to track down the Paper Boy. The boy who came in the darkness and attacked small children. The boy who had now made his way to Sweden to seek out new victims.

Abraham, Simon, Josephine.

And Polly.

The yellow express train sliced through a snowy landscape so white and beautiful that it looked as if it belonged in a fairy tale.

So much space for such a small population.

Efraim Kiel couldn't stop staring out of the window.

The Swedes had no idea how privileged they were. Over two hundred years of uninterrupted peace. A population where no one who was alive today had experienced the horrors of war on home territory. For a man like Efraim, that was incomprehensible.

Conditions in Israel were so different that it hurt to think about his own country. Efraim had sacrificed more than most Israelis for the common good, for safety and security. He was well aware of the damage this had done to his heart and soul, dulling his senses and making him capable of doing harm to others in order to achieve a higher goal. But he thought it had been worth it, on the whole. Not everyone could enjoy a life spent barbecuing sausages in the back garden. Some people had to take responsibility.

At least that was what Efraim told himself as he sat on the train, his thoughts once again turning to Eden and the child he had seen in her arms as she walked away.

Responsibility.

Efraim had taken responsibility when he had deliberately made her fall in love with him, even though he felt nothing in return. Perhaps things would have been different under other circumstances. If he hadn't already met the woman in his life – the woman who had been his secret for so long. Both for his sake and hers, so that neither of them would come to any harm, and be punished for their reckless love.

He had told her that the very first time he kissed her.

'This is doomed.'

She had responded by getting even closer to him. Then the boy came along, and everything else lost its value.

Almost everything else.

The only thing that could rival his love for his son was his love for Israel, and for that, fate had punished him severely.

The train raced towards its final destination. Signs inside the carriage boasted that it took only twenty minutes to travel from Arlanda airport into the city centre. Efraim couldn't have cared less whether it took twenty minutes or thirty. He was better prepared now and felt that he had regained control of the situation.

The gun was gone.

So was the child called Polly.

The child whose screams still echoed in his head.

Efraim didn't speak Swedish, but there was one word he thought he would understand in any language.

Mummy.

A word with a unique tone and melody that a father could only dream of coming close to.

Ima in Hebrew. *Umi* in Arabic.

The train pulled in; Efraim got off and walked calmly out of the station. He had shaken off Säpo some time ago, and he had no intention of renewing his acquaintance with them. Not until he needed their help. If that day should ever come.

He thought it unlikely.

He felt strong. Confident.

He headed north along Vasagatan, up towards the congress building that hid his new hotel. It was nowhere near as luxurious as the Diplomat, but it served its purpose. The receptionist didn't appear to react as he walked in; there was no reason why she should be aware that he had been away overnight.

Up in his room he took a shower, changed his clothes, and went back out into the cold. He had to visit the Diplomat just once more. A final visit before war broke out.

He caught the bus this time. Got on and showed the strip of tickets he had bought. The driver stamped it and the bus moved off towards Djurgården. A green space right in the middle of Stockholm. An outpost by the sea. Efraim thought it was much more beautiful in the summer.

He got off at Nybroplan and took a circuitous route to the hotel.

There was a risk that Säpo might be waiting for him, hoping he'd come back, because by this stage even they must have realised they'd lost him.

He saw them from some distance away, sitting in a car parked much closer to the hotel than he would have done. He turned off Strandvägen, disappeared up a side street. He would have to use the entrance at the back of the hotel, the one he had located on his very first day there. It was easier to use when darkness had fallen, but not impossible in daylight.

That was the only advantage of this insane winter darkness:

it was easy to become invisible. Efraim couldn't think of anything else remotely positive about the fact that the sun disappeared at three o'clock in the afternoon.

He walked straight into a cleaner as he opened the fire door and slipped into the corridor. Shit. She looked surprised and said something he didn't understand. He smiled apologetically, explained briefly that he had taken a wrong turning.

She stared after him for far too long.

Foolish of her. Very foolish.

Time would tell whether he could leave the matter, or whether he would need to deal with it.

The receptionist recognised him. He could see that she was confused because he hadn't come in through the main door, which was less troublesome, but still irritating. He would have avoided the visit if he could, but it was impossible. He had no doubt about that.

'I was in such a hurry when I checked out yesterday,' Efraim said, his most charming smile firmly in place. 'I just wanted to make sure I hadn't forgotten to pick up any messages.'

The receptionist began to go through the file in front of her.

'Something did come for you; we were talking about it this morning, wondering what to do with it. We didn't know how to get hold of you.'

'Well, I'm here now.'

Still smiling, and the message was in his hand.

He moved away from the desk and the windows, where he was far too visible.

He opened the envelope and read the brief communication. The declaration of war he had been expecting. To think that so few words could cause such pain.

I will never forgive you for this.

LONDON

There were two things that Eden Lundell had found particularly difficult during her years in London: the ingrained conservatism, and the terrible weather. Instinctively she felt that the latter would be easier to come to terms with than the former.

The sleet had turned into a classic autumn rain, lashing her face as she left the hotel, on her way to the man she had come here to see. The man who would tell her what she needed to know in order to get rid of her problem. To crush Efraim.

Her thoughts were constantly with Mikael and the children she had left behind. The anxiety she couldn't shake off had grown into a monster that was threatening to drive her insane. She had to end this, and soon. She didn't know why, she just knew that time was short.

The rain hammered against her waterproof jacket, the drops turning to transparent beads that almost looked like pearls. Eden had always hated pearls, mainly because her mother thought they were the last word in elegance. Eden wondered if she still felt the same. It was a long time since they had seen one another. Israel wasn't all that far away, but after the affair with Efraim, Eden had been unable to bring herself to go there. She didn't think she would get through passport control anyway – not without being taken to one side and questioned.

The water on the pavement softened the sound of her heels. There was hardly anyone else around, which wasn't surprising; it was Sunday, and it was pouring down. Why would anyone be out and about? She had chosen a hotel less than five blocks from where he lived. The most unexpected plan was often the best strategy. Her visit would lead to discussions, and might also have certain practical consequences in the long term. She was under no illusion that he would be pleased to see her; those days were gone forever.

But that's irrelevant; this is a matter of life and death, and that takes precedence over all the crap that's behind us.

She had arrived.

She stood outside the house she had visited more times than she could count. The house where Fred and Angela Banks lived. They had been her and Mikael's best friends when they lived in London. The most treacherous friends she had ever had.

At least as far as Fred was concerned.

He had been her colleague as well as her friend. And the first person her boss had chosen to involve in the investigation into her affair with Efraim.

A natural choice. He was closest to Eden, and would easily be able to keep himself informed about her private life without arousing any suspicions.

The memories flooded her mind.

Memories of the holidays she and Mikael had spent with Fred and Angela. Dinner parties and celebrations. Fred with a cigar in the corner of his mouth ('I only smoke when I'm drunk, you know'), and Angela with a décolletage so deep you could practically see her navel ('Without these boobs I would never have been such a successful broker!'). On the surface they didn't seem to have anything whatsoever in common with Eden and Mikael, but in reality they had shared everything.

Interests.

Values.

Humour.

And sorrow.

Because Fred and Angela were unable to have children, which led to a painful friction that Eden and Mikael not only witnessed, but helped to heal.

Eden swallowed hard. She went up the steps, her finger trembling as she was about to ring the bell. Because they hadn't made any friends in Stockholm who were as close as Fred and Angela had been.

We don't let anyone get close any more.

Eventually she had to do what she had come for. Prick a hole in the bubble in which she had been floating around ever since she left England. Not every aspect of her relationship with Fred had been false. They had established a friendship in her very first week with MI5, years before she met Efraim.

The sound of the doorbell was so loud that Eden thought the entire neighbourhood had probably heard it.

She rang it again, hoping to hear some movement on the other side of the door. However, she had to press the bell several times before she heard footsteps approaching. Then came the usual silence as someone peered through the peep hole. Which was normally followed by the sound of the latch being turned, the door opening.

But not this time.

After a while she realised that the person who had looked out had recognised her, and crept away. Left her to her fate.

I refuse to be let down yet again by anyone at this fucking address.

She banged on the door with all her might, ringing the bell over and over again.

The footsteps returned, heavier and quicker this time.

Angry.

The door flew open so fast it almost hit her in the face.

Fred Banks, who had once been her very best friend, filled the entire doorway with his furious bulk. In spite of the fact that she had promised herself she wouldn't react when they met for the first time in several years, she couldn't help taking a deep breath when she saw him. And Fred, who had no doubt intended to start by bawling at her for daring to darken his door, froze in mid-movement and stood there with his mouth open.

When he eventually broke the silence, he was brief and to the point:

'I have no interest in speaking to you, Eden. Go away, please.'

She had hated him when she left London, because he had done what his boss told him to do – spied on her. Because he had turned his back on her, betrayed her. Because through his involvement he had complicated the break-up, making her lie to her husband even more; Mikael had never understood why Fred and Angela suddenly went from being friends to enemies. Mikael had been told about the affair with Efraim, but not about her secret lover's background and the difficulties that created.

The years had moderated her anger more than she had realised. When she saw Fred she felt nothing but a bottomless sorrow.

'I'm going nowhere,' she said. 'Either let me in, or come with me to a place nearby where we can talk.'

'No chance. I've nothing to say to someone like you.'

'On the contrary. You have a great deal to say to me.'

He was still staring at her, clearly shocked at her unexpected reappearance in his life. Who knew what stories they had told about her to make her seem like a worse person than she actually was.

Fred shook his head slowly.

'If you think I'm going to help you in any way, you're wrong. I want nothing whatsoever to do with your sort.'

'My sort?'

'*You betrayed everything we worked for! Every fucking ideal I thought we shared!*'

He was shouting now, his cheeks red, the veins in his neck standing out. As they always used to do when he got really angry.

Her face wet with icy rain and something that might be tears, Eden said firmly:

'You're right, there was a betrayal. But not of you, and not of our organisation. The only person I ever betrayed was Mikael, and that's between him and me.'

She moved a step closer, making it impossible for him to close the door without squashing her.

'You don't know the whole story,' she went on. 'You think you do, but you're wrong. And you have to listen to me now, because I'm afraid I've ended up in a very dangerous situation. And I don't know anyone else who can help me.'

She could feel the fear spreading from her chest and through her entire body as she spoke. Because she knew she was telling the truth. She *was* afraid. Afraid of the motives and powers that she didn't understand, but which had brought Efraim to Stockholm. Afraid of Alex Recht's hints that Efraim might have something to do with his murder inquiry. But most of all she was afraid that everything that was happening hung together in a way she couldn't yet see, which meant she was unable to protect herself.

Fred hesitated. Eden knew why; it was because she was asking for help. Eden, who had made a point of needing no one's help.

'What's this about?' he said.

He was still clutching the door handle, wanting nothing more than to shove her down the steps and forget that she had ever come calling.

'My family,' she whispered.

And saw him slowly begin to soften.

According to the reports he was getting from Fredrika, the weather in Jerusalem was mild and summery. Difficult to imagine how that felt when you were sitting in Alex Recht's office in Stockholm.

His plans to go home had been postponed.

Time was passing. Hour followed hour with inexorable inevitability, and there was no trace of Polly Eisenberg. It was only a matter of time before she was found. Dead, and with a paper bag over her head. With a face drawn on it.

Eyes, nose, mouth.

They still didn't understand what the paper bags meant, nor whether they had anything to do with the so-called Paper Boy. Alex offered up a silent prayer that Fredrika would be able to solve that puzzle during her stay in Israel.

And the rest.

Alex was more stressed than he liked to admit. He hated failures that cost lives. They caused too much suffering, too much pain. But with the amount of unanswered questions facing him right now, he found it difficult to see how he could turn this tragedy into success.

The evidence suggested that there were two perpetrators, yet there was only one murder weapon. Therefore, they must know one another. And at least one of them must know who the Paper Boy was.

Certain circumstances pointed in the direction of Efraim Kiel, who appeared to have gone to ground. But he had an alibi.

And then there was the Lion, who had actively sought out the boys online and arranged to meet them. Who could be the person who had picked them up. But that meant he couldn't be Efraim, who had an alibi for that period of time.

But he could still be involved.

There was no getting away from it: Efraim had an alibi for Josephine's murder and the point at which the boys disappeared, but not for the morning when they were shot. Not as far as the police were aware, anyway. If Efraim Kiel and the Lion were the two people they were looking for, then the Lion was presumably a woman. But in that case why had she called herself Zalman, which was a man's name? Had she never intended to meet the boys face to face?

Everything would be so much simpler if they just knew who the Lion was, or if they could eliminate the person in question from their inquiries.

Alex couldn't work out how the perpetrators had been thinking. If it hadn't been for the gun, the police probably wouldn't have been able to confirm the link between the murders at such an early stage. They would have had nothing more than circumstantial evidence, supposition.

Which admittedly would have been confirmed when Polly Eisenberg subsequently disappeared.

He tried to distance himself from the material, identify the key issues.

If he assumed that Efraim Kiel and the Lion were working together: why had two Israelis travelled to Stockholm to kill three children?

Because they had some kind of dispute with the children's parents, who had left Israel for reasons that were unclear ten years ago, when their sons were born? Revenge was a classic motive for murder, but revenge for what? As long as the parents kept quiet, the investigation would remain at a standstill, unless Fredrika could save it from a distance. She was capable of a great deal, but miracles?

Alex had his doubts.

He felt very much alone. Without Fredrika he lacked a sounding board, someone to cast a critical eye over his thoughts and suggestions. The team must be expanded by another permanent member, and fast. As soon as he had time, he would go through the applications again.

They must be able to find someone. Someone who was worthy of a place on the team.

Alex knew exactly who he wanted: Peder Rydh. He shouldn't be grubbing around in the private sector, moving from one contract to the next. Perhaps the matter could be resolved through the Labour Court; Peder hadn't even been charged, he had simply packed up and left.

That wasn't the right thing to do. You had to fight for your successes in order to cope with setbacks.

But that could wait; right now his priority was the children from the Solomon Community. He had to find a way to get their parents to talk so that the move the investigation forward.

The National Crime Unit had been in touch: a sketch artist had visited the Solomon Community and spoken to the secretary who had taken delivery of the chrysanthemum in the paper bag with a face on it. He had produced a drawing, which was faxed over to Alex.

He looked at it with a feeling of deep scepticism. The woman in the picture could be just about anybody.

Alex wondered if Fredrika had guessed correctly: did this woman have something to do with the murders, and if so, was she the Lion?

With a mounting sense of irritation he realised that a growing number of people were of interest purely because they couldn't be identified or reached. Therefore, he decided to focus on those they did know and could contact.

Did he have suspicions about any of these individuals?

Yes.

Someone who had appeared unnecessarily defensive and aggressive; someone who was close to the children who had died.

Saul Goldmann.

He had clearly found it difficult to co-operate with the police, and he had no alibi for the time when Polly went missing. But why would he have shot his own son? Alex had to work that out before he could move on.

Unless of course it had been a mistake.

Perhaps Abraham Goldmann was never meant to die. Perhaps he had been picked up in the car purely so that it would be easier to get Simon to come along.

Although that seemed unlikely.

Nevertheless, Alex decided to double-check Saul Goldmann's alibi for the time when the boys disappeared. If there was one thing he had learned during his years as a police officer, it was that whatever seemed most unlikely at first

glance would probably turn out to be the only logical explanation in the end.

Saul Goldmann had said he was in a meeting when his
son went missing. The meeting had taken place in Kungsholmen, not far from where Alex was now. Saul had met an
associate at her business premises on Hantverkargatan. This
associate, Mona Samson, had confirmed that the meeting
had taken place.

Alex read carefully through what Mona Samson had said.

Saul Goldmann had arrived as agreed at one o'clock, and
had left just after five. By that time both Abraham and Simon
were missing, and Josephine had been shot dead.

One till five.

That was a bloody long meeting.

Not that it was illegal in any way, but he couldn't see
any indication of what had been discussed. The feeling that
something wasn't right grew stronger; he couldn't settle.
Something was grating – something he couldn't quite put
his finger on.

Without hesitation he picked up the phone and called
Mona Samson. He wanted to hear her voice, try to sense
whether she might be lying. He thought about the indentation in the snow on the roof; the person lying there had
probably been a woman. One metre seventy. Size 36 to 38
shoes.

There was no reply. Alex didn't leave a message; instead
he got up and pulled on his jacket. It would take only a few
minutes to walk to her office, check things out, ring the bell,
see if she was there. Then again, why would she be there on
a Sunday?

He made a mental note of the address and the name of the

firm: Samson Security AB. A security firm which, according to its website, specialised in various alarm systems. Alex couldn't tell how big it was; Mona Samson could well be the sole employee.

The lift made its way laboriously down to the ground floor. He went out onto Stråket, which linked the buildings that made up Kronoberg, Stockholm's Police HQ. How many times had he walked along here? Back and forth, never wanting to be anywhere else. He was very different from Fredrika Bergman, who had taken half a lifetime to work out what she wanted to do.

How hard could it be?

You just had to live.

He emerged via the old building leading onto Scheelegatan. The air was raw and damp. The sun that had shone so brightly the day before was gone. On days like this it was hard to imagine that it would be back later in the year. Stockholm's weather was hard on those who were tough, and even harder on those who were already weak.

Hantverkargatan was a long street running all the way from Sankt Eriksgatan down to the City Hall. Diana had been to dinner there once, and she still talked about it. Candelabras and linen napkins, an orchestra playing, male guests who danced like gods. Listening to her made Alex break out in a sweat. If she wanted candelabras and linen napkins, she could find another man. Although he could dance. Very well, in fact.

'That'll do,' she had said when he mentioned it.

Samson Security AB lay only three blocks from Police HQ, in a very attractive building on the left hand side. Alex stopped outside the main door.

He felt at something of a loss.

What had he actually thought was going to happen here?

He tried the door. Locked, of course. But there was an intercom with a list of names. He glanced through them: several private individuals, a small number of businesses. Samson Security AB was not one of them.

There was, however, a Mona Samson. Strange – why wasn't the name of the company listed? Did no one ever come here on business?

But Saul Goldmann had been here.

Alex rang the bell. No response. He tried again. Not a sound from Mona Samson.

So he tried someone else, with more success. A deep male voice answered. When Alex explained who he was and asked if he could come in, the door buzzed and he was soon standing in the foyer. People with nothing to hide rarely refused to co-operate when the police asked for help.

Mona Samson lived on the third floor. The lift was broken, so Alex had to walk. That didn't bother him; it enabled him to get a better idea of the property.

There were four doors on the level where Mona Samson lived. Alex tried her doorbell, heard the sound reverberating through the apartment. As he had expected, no one came.

With a certain amount of hesitation he rang her neighbour's bell. The man who answered the door was wearing shorts, in spite of the cold. Alex recognised his voice; it was the man who had let him in off the street.

Alex introduced himself again and showed his police ID.

'I'm looking for Mona Samson. I don't suppose you know where I can get hold of her?'

'Has something happened?'

A legitimate question when the police turned up on a Sunday afternoon.

'No, nothing serious, but I do need to speak to her.'

The man thought for a moment.

'Hang on, I'll ask my partner. He has a better idea than I do of what the neighbours get up to.'

He turned away and called out:

'Andreas, do you know where Mona is? The police are looking for her.'

Excellent, now the entire building knew what was going on.

A red-haired man ambled into the hallway. He nodded to Alex, and like his partner, asked whether something had happened. Alex repeated his answer.

'I've no idea where she is,' Andreas said. 'I bumped into her in the laundry room on Tuesday, but I haven't seen her since.'

Alex couldn't help feeling disappointed. His resigned expression made Andreas keep talking. 'She might have gone home,' he said. 'She does that sometimes.'

'Home?'

'To Israel. That's where she's from.'

ISRAEL

The American Colony Hotel: an oasis consisting of beautiful stone buildings and a lush, green garden, situated only ten minutes' walk from the so-called Damascus Gate in the wall around the Old City. Originally built by a group of Americans and Swedes, the same Swedes that Selma Lagerlöf later wrote about in her book *Jerusalem*.

Fredrika Bergman was given a room in the building known as the East House. It was a small, minimalist but charming room, with a high ceiling. Lovely double aspect windows. A bathroom so stunning that Spencer would have insisted they sleep in the shower.

Darling, you should be here with me.

Isak Ben-Zwi had dropped her off about an hour ago. She had stayed in the hotel, had lunch in the magnificent restaurant. If the background to her trip hadn't been so horrific, she would have felt privileged; as it was, she just felt burdened.

She sat in the restaurant for a while and worked. To Spencer's surprise and delight, she had taken her violin with her.

'I thought you were going there to work,' he had said.

'I am, but there's always time for meditation.'

Meditation. That was how she referred to the time she spent playing the violin, so that people would understand what it meant to her. An essential breathing space.

But now she was actually here, that was the last thing on her mind. She was sitting with her back to the wall, eyes fixed on her laptop. She liked to have people around her, the noise and bustle reminding her that the reality with which she was confronted in her work was not her own life. She was not the one who had lost her children. It was someone else.

And for that she was deeply grateful.

Daphne and Saul Goldmann.

Carmen and Gideon Eisenberg.

Alex wanted her to find out more about their past, try to understand why they had left Israel and moved to Sweden, because neither he nor Fredrika believed that the move had been motivated only by the feeble reasons the families themselves had put forward – although Fredrika did sympathise when it came to the issue of security. It was doomed to be a fragile commodity in Israel; conflict followed conflict, and the people never had any peace. Perhaps eventually some had had enough, and simply upped sticks and left. Particularly if they had children.

In the car on the way from the airport, Isak had said that security had improved. The first years after the outbreak of the second Intifada had been extremely difficult. Fredrika realised that he was speaking from an Israeli perspective. The calm surrounding her in Jerusalem seemed deceptive, like a bubble that could burst at any moment, because presumably the Palestinians didn't share the Israeli view that things had got better.

She was ashamed as she shook off thoughts of the Israeli-Palestine conflict as if it were an unwelcome insect, but she just didn't have room for that kind of thing alongside the immediate crisis she was here to try and solve. A crisis involving two murdered children.

The same questions that had haunted her over the past few days were still going round and round in her head. She wrote them down. Read through them. Again. There was nothing new to add. She must have patience, wait for the results of the Israeli efforts to identify the Lion, so that they could either eliminate him or establish what role he had played.

And then there were the kibbutzim, where she hoped to find out more about the Paper Boy, and about the past history of the Eisenberg and Goldmann families.

Her phone rang, making her jump.

'We need to take a closer look at Saul Goldmann,' Alex said.

Fredrika listened attentively as he went through what he had found out.

Another trail leading to Israel. Another Israeli citizen.

'Why would Saul Goldmann kill his own son?' she said. 'Or be involved in his murder?'

'That's what we need to find out,' Alex said.

'Do you think the Goldmann lead is more promising than Efraim Kiel and the Lion?'

'As I always say, I don't think anything at this stage. Anyway, how do you know we're looking at two different leads? We know next to nothing, Fredrika. We think we're looking for two perpetrators, but it could just as easily be three. Or four. Or just one. We think one of them might be a woman, but we don't know that either.'

'If you give me Mona Samson's details I can find out if she's entered Israel over the past few days.'

'Good idea. Because I'm wondering why I can't get hold of her either.'

It wasn't an irrelevant question, but nor was it the most important. One of their colleagues had spoken to her, and she had confirmed Saul Goldmann's alibi. There wasn't necessarily anything suspicious about the fact that they couldn't get in touch with her at the moment, but if she was in Israel, it became more difficult to regard her as a person of no interest. She might have been there all the time, in which case Saul didn't have an alibi.

'Israel again,' Alex said. 'Don't tell me it's just a coincidence.'

He was quite right; whichever way they turned, they ended up in Israel.

'Then again, is that so surprising?' Fredrika said. 'After all, we are investigating the murders of members of the Solomon Community, and the victims come from Israel. So it's not so strange if the case has a geographical bias.'

Alex said something she didn't hear.

'Sorry?'

'I don't agree. You have a point, but the murder of the two boys and Polly's abduction have something to do with events that took place in Israel. I'm sure of it. And there are people who obviously know what's going on, but refuse to talk. Which is annoying the hell out of me.'

They were in agreement on that point.

The sounds around Alex grew quieter, and she assumed he had gone inside.

'Where are you?'

'At work. I'm going to stay for a few more hours, then go home. Call me any time if something comes up. And I mean that literally – any time.'

'Thanks.'

She liked people who made her feel safe, and Alex was one of those people. His voice could bring her down to earth in seconds, blowing away the threatening clouds she thought she could see gathering on the horizon. When he had ended the call, she felt unexpectedly lonely.

Until Isak rang her.

'I'm on my way to the hotel,' he said. 'Wait for me in the restaurant.'

'I'm already there. What's happened?'

'We think we've got a name for the Lion.'

LONDON

Wood panelling on the walls and 80s music coming through the speakers. They were in a pub five minutes away from Fred Banks's house. They had been sitting there for three hours. At first the words had come slowly. Eden had done all the talking. She hadn't thought through what she was going to say, how she would say it. To begin with she had felt inhibited by the fact that she wasn't sure how much Fred knew, then she had decided that it didn't matter.

More important assets than her own integrity were at risk.

She had to make her peace with the past, move on. Ultimately she also had to forgive herself, but neither Fred nor anyone else could help her there. She would have to manage that on her own.

She had practically dragged Fred out onto the street and down to the pub, appealing to the warm heart she knew he had.

He had said he would give her half an hour. If she hadn't said anything that caught his attention by then, he would walk out. She noted with relief that he was still there, and he had started talking. Tentatively, hesitantly, but he was talking.

Eden was surprised to hear that Angela was no longer in his life. She had found someone else, and was expecting their first child. Fred tried to look as if he didn't care, but she could see the sorrow as clearly as fire in his eyes.

He had been promoted at work; without turning a hair he admitted that his skilled deception in the investigation into Eden's affair with Efraim had been a key factor in his success.

'When I was called to the first meeting, I had no idea what was coming. And when they told me, I laughed in their faces. Said you would rather die than be unfaithful to Mikael. Then I stopped laughing and got angry. Said I would tell you everything. Told them I would walk away, get another job. They let me carry on like a steamroller; then they showed me the pictures.'

He fell silent. Eden had given him her version of events, and now it was his turn. She had put all her cards on the table, told him everything.

Except the fact that Efraim was the father of her children.

'At first I thought the pictures were fake,' Fred went on. 'You with a Mossad operative? It was unthinkable. You had always been so loyal. But the evidence was unequivocal. And I was there the first time you met – do you remember?'

She did. Fred had been at the conference where she met Efraim.

'I don't recall you and Efraim speaking to one another,' she said.

'We didn't. But I saw you talking to him, and I was pleased. He made your face light up, and you'd been so low after the miscarriage.'

Eden could have wept.

So it had been obvious that he made her happy. Brightened her life. In order to crush her.

'The boss explained who he was: a Mossad operative who was well known for his ability to recruit agents. They couldn't believe their eyes when you were seen with him one day.'

'So they knew right from the start? And nobody thought of confronting me?'

'Not right from the start,' Fred said. 'But pretty early on they put together a top secret team to monitor your relationship. I wasn't brought in until about six months later. They had been waiting for you to tell your superiors that you had been the target of a recruitment attempt by the Israelis, but instead you carried on seeing him. They felt it was highly unlikely that you didn't know who he was, who he worked for.'

Eden shook her head.

'I hadn't a clue.'

Fred's expression hardened.

'As far as I was concerned, the fact that you were actually having an affair sealed the deal. If you were capable of deceiving the person you said you loved more than anything in the world, I thought you could easily be unfaithful to your employer as well, so to speak.'

Of course. That's the way friendship worked. It could be a blessing, and it could create problems. In this case it had evidently done both.

'I've explained what drove me into Efraim's arms.'

She tried to sound defiant, but she couldn't look Fred in the eye.

'You've explained now, but at the time I didn't have that information. Nor was I in a position to ask for it. Anyway, I'm still not sure I understand. I can see how you fell for him the first time round, but the second time? When you and Mikael had just had the twins? I don't get it.'

Eden fixed her gaze on a serviette on the table.

'It was a very difficult time,' she said.

As if that were a satisfactory explanation.

Fred didn't respond. Eden wanted him to tell her more. About Efraim Kiel and how she could get to him.

'You said that MI5 already knew who Efraim was. How come?'

Fred looked grim.

'These are sensitive matters,' he said. 'Top secret.'

She realised that. This was why she had come to London: to access information that would otherwise be unavailable to her.

'You have to give me whatever you've got,' she said. 'Otherwise I'll never be rid of him.'

Give me the ammunition to blow the bastard into a thousand pieces.

Fred hesitated for a long time.

Eventually he spoke:

'You know, deep down . . .'

She waited. Held her breath.

'Deep down I think I've always known that you had walked into a trap. You showed very poor judgement, but you did nothing illegal. And you're right, the only person you really betrayed was Mikael.'

She could have wept with relief.

'I'll tell you what you need to know,' Fred said. 'But not here. Let's go back to my place.'

Nothing much had changed in Fred's house, except that all the photographs that had adorned the walls of the hallway had been removed. Perhaps Angela had taken them with her, or perhaps they had been thrown away.

Fred went into the kitchen to fetch a bottle of wine, and they sat down in the living room.

'It was after 9/11,' Fred began. '2001. A lot of people thought it was our turn next. Through an undercover informant, MI5 learned that Palestinian terrorists were preparing a major attack on several British embassies around the world. A major investigation team was assembled to look into the threat, but they got nowhere. So they contacted the Israelis. The key player in the plot was supposed to be in a village on the West Bank, to which we had no access. The various attacks were to be carried out by Palestinians living in diaspora across the world.'

Eden listened carefully. She thought about the role the British had played in Palestine after the First World War, and the subsequent chaos which still reigned in 2001. Eden hadn't started working for MI5 at that stage.

'The Israelis were interested when they heard what we knew. MI5's contact on the Israeli side was Efraim Kiel. He led a special team operating on the West Bank, and they had someone in that particular village who was both reliable and willing to co-operate.'

Fred took a sip of his wine, and Eden automatically reached for her glass. She shouldn't drink; she knew that. But if Fred was drinking, she didn't want to sit there stone-cold sober. It sent out the wrong signals.

'Anyway, MI5 set up a joint operation with Mossad in order to track down the man behind the plot, and thus put a stop to it. Efraim Kiel's team were supposed to locate him with the help of a source on the West Bank. I don't know how much you remember about the situation in Israel at the beginning of the twenty-first century, but it was no picnic over there.'

Eden remembered those days very well. That was when her parents, particularly her mother, had been radicalised and eventually decided to emigrate to Israel. Eden recalled endless discussions with her mother and father, weeping with rage at the dinner table.

It had always been clear to Eden that disappointment was the strongest impetus for violence, disappointment over everything that didn't happen, or didn't happen fast enough.

The West Bank had been in flames during those years, and that was also when the decision was made to start constructing the barrier that now separated the two peoples. Running a source in a Palestinian village at that time must have been doomed to failure.

'I assume it didn't end well,' Eden said.

'To say the least. What I'm about to tell you stays between us, Eden. It's more sensitive than everything else I've told you put together.'

She nodded. She had no words to express what she was feeling.

'In February 2002, just before the Israelis moved in and reoccupied the West Bank, they thought they had a breakthrough in the source operation in the Palestinian village. Mossad contacted MI5, and we were offered the chance to be there when they went in to seize the man suspected of being behind the plot. We already had staff in Jerusalem; one of them joined Efraim Kiel's team and accompanied them to the West Bank. A high-risk project in those days. For example, sometimes Palestinian terrorists or insurgents rigged up booby-trapped buildings.'

Booby traps. Eden had never needed to worry about that kind of danger, but she knew all about them – bombs that went off when someone stood on them; bombs that could be hidden under the floor so that an entire building would collapse on top of the intruder.

'Efraim's team ended up standing outside a house they were afraid was booby trapped,' Fred went on. 'For that reason they hesitated before going in, and Kiel moved aside to request reinforcements so that they could smoke out anyone who might be inside. At that moment a child emerged, a boy aged about ten. Two members of the team went over and spoke to him, asked if he was home alone or if there were any adults in the house.'

'They did what?'

'I know – unbelievable. They didn't want him in there if they were going to use tear gas, or blow the place up, so they confronted him. But they completely misjudged his reaction. The boy panicked and pulled away from them. He was much faster than they were, of course, and he ran straight back inside through the nearest door, which evidently wasn't the one through which he had come out. And the team found out whether the house was booby trapped or not.'

The wine became impossible to swallow, stuck in her throat.

'The house went up,' Eden said.

Fred nodded, his face expressionless.

'They didn't have a chance; in two seconds the whole place was in flames. We later received confirmation that the suspect had died in the explosion. There were no attacks on British embassies. Afterwards, however, MI5 was extremely critical of the way in which the operation had been carried out. A child died that day. How many British citizens do you have to save for it to be worth the life of a Palestinian boy?'

Eden had no answer to that question. She looked down into her glass, feeling wave after wave of nausea. She realised how little she had known about Efraim's background.

'We had nothing more to do with Efraim Kiel after that,' Fred said. 'Until the day when he approached one of our brightest and best.'

He gave Eden a wry smile, and she couldn't help but smile back.

'Were you there on the West Bank?' she asked.

Fred shook his head.

'I found out about the operation when I was reading up about Kiel in order to understand who he was. Painful secrets hidden away in the archives under a bizarre code name.'

'How bizarre can it be?' Eden said. 'How do you name an operation that so obviously went against important principles that we're supposed to represent?'

'You give it the name the Israelis gave their source. And on this occasion the source on the West Bank who led Efraim Kiel's team to the main suspect was apparently known as the Paper Boy.'

The longing had been aroused deep inside him on the very first day, when the snow outside the Solomon Community was still red with blood, and the two boys were missing. He had felt his pulse rate increase, felt the surge of adrenalin. And he knew that he had done the wrong thing on the day when he walked away from the police and handed in his badge without even putting up a fight. Had he been crazy? How could he have done something so stupid?

Peder Rydh knew the answer to that question.

He had been out of his mind.

His brother had been murdered, and nothing else mattered.

But now things were different. Peder was different.

I want to go back, he thought. I really, really want my old job back.

There were so many things he missed; being around Alex was one of them. Working with such an experienced investigator so early in his career had been a blessing. Peder's success could have taken him a very long way if he had played his cards right. It wasn't just the fact that he had shot his brother's killer that had landed him in hot water; there were the women too.

So bloody pointless.

Unsatisfactory sex with women for whom he had no

respect. You just didn't behave like that. Not towards them, and definitely not towards your own wife. One thing had led to another, and eventually he had been working so hard at being a bastard that he no longer knew how to be anything else. Until now.

Peder had finally been forced to grow up. The question was whether he had left it too late.

He couldn't stop thinking about the murders within the Solomon Community. He realised he had begun to regard them as his case, his responsibility. Ylva watched with unspoken anxiety as he became unreachable, lost in his thoughts. She wondered if he was moving away from her again.

They had supper with the children and she took them off for baths and bedtime. Peder loaded the dishwasher, then fetched his laptop.

The newspapers were following the search for Polly Eisenberg. Her parents had gone to ground and were making no comment. Peder had met them only a few times, but they had made a good impression, particularly Carmen, the mother. She seemed calmer than her husband; more comfortable in her own skin.

He wanted to ring Alex, find out how far he had got with the investigation, ask if he could help in any way. Most of all he wanted to ask whether Alex wanted him back. Whether he missed him.

I'd do anything for a second chance.

The sounds from the boys' bedroom as Ylva tried to settle them reminded him that he had already been given a second chance. Things could have been much worse. He could have lost his whole family as well.

His work mobile rang. He answered quickly, not wanting to disturb Ylva and the children.

It was the general secretary.

'Sorry to disturb you on a Sunday, but . . . I have something to tell you. Something I forgot when we last spoke.'

'What's this about?'

'Efraim Kiel,' the general secretary said slowly.

Peder took a deep breath.

'Yes?'

He heard a sigh.

'I don't think this is important, I really don't. But after you asked me where Efraim Kiel was when Simon and Abraham went missing, I thought back to that afternoon. I told you Efraim was with me, but that's not the case.'

'No?'

'Everything happened so fast. First of all Josephine was shot, just after three o'clock. We were both there when the police arrived, but then Efraim went off, said he had personal contacts who might be able to help push the police a little harder. With his background he obviously knows people the rest of us wouldn't have access to, so I didn't react to what he said. And he did come back; he was there when you came in, and he was the one who made the calls taking up your references.'

Bloody hell.

'So what you're saying is that when the boys disappeared on their way to tennis coaching, Efraim wasn't in the community centre,' Peder said.

'Correct. Which doesn't necessarily mean he was lying; it's entirely possible that he had meetings that were none of my business.'

But you're not sure, because otherwise you wouldn't have called me, would you?

Peder swallowed.

Efraim Kiel no longer had an alibi for the period when the boys were abducted.

The sound of children in the house was a joy. Chatter turning into screams of delight, giggles exploding into laughter, bouncing off the walls. High voices calling out new words that made his face light up.

'Grandma!'

'Grandpa!'

Alex's son and daughter had both come for Sunday dinner with their families, a surprise that met him in the doorway when he got home from work.

His head was bursting with random thoughts and speculation about why two children had been shot dead and a third had disappeared. His grandchildren drove those thoughts away for a while. They hurled themselves at him, much less easy to elude than the adults in his company. He even managed to get through the meal before his mind was once again invaded by what had happened. What it would mean if one of the parents had lied about his alibi.

The last thing he had done before leaving Police HQ was to put Saul Goldmann under surveillance, just to be on the safe side. If he was the one who had taken Polly Eisenberg, he might lead them to her.

Diana watched him across the table. She had one of the grandchildren on her knee, holding the child close. They were not her grandchildren, but she had taken Alex's family to her heart and made them her own.

His mobile rang and he excused himself. Diana's expression was forgiving as he left the table.

It was Peder. Alex almost dropped the phone when he realised what he was saying.

Efraim Kiel didn't have an alibi.

'As you know, this is extremely important information,' he said. 'Thank you very much.'

A thank you was not enough. Follow up questions came thick and fast. Peder wanted to know what the next step would be, and whether he could be of any help.

But that was where Alex had to draw the line. Peder was not a police officer, and that was that. He could tell that his former colleague was disappointed; Peder's silence told Alex all he needed to know.

'Peder, you're not part of my team. I'm sorry, but that means I can't let you in on everything we find out.'

Peder cleared his throat.

'I know that.'

Another protracted silence.

'Was there anything else?' Alex said.

He tried to keep his tone friendly, but he was keen to call Fredrika in Jerusalem.

'I just wanted to tell you that I . . .' Peder said, then hesitated.

Alex held his breath, waiting for him to go on.

'Yes?'

'I'm thinking of trying to gain some kind of redress, Alex. I want to come back to the police. I shouldn't have had to leave.'

Alex wasn't so preoccupied that he didn't have time to say the right thing.

'That's good news. I'm really pleased.'

He meant every word, and hoped Peder could hear it in his voice.

The three grandchildren had got down from the table and came charging into the hallway, whirling around his legs like hyperactive butterflies, each trying to shout louder than the others.

'Peder, I'll speak to you very soon. Thanks again for your help.'

Alex withdrew from the children and shut himself in his study so that he could talk to Fredrika in peace. He had only just sat down at his desk when he realised what he was doing.

Making the same mistake all over again.

The same mistake, but with a new generation.

How many times, irrespective of whether it was a weekday, a weekend or a holiday, had he left his family because of work? With empty promises, assuring them that he was going to make just one more phone call, talk to one more person, stay in the office for one more hour? How much had he missed by behaving that way?

But what was the alternative? Ignore the fact that a little girl had been abducted?

That was equally impossible, and no less painful.

Fredrika sounded far away when she answered.

'Sorry I haven't called,' she said. 'I've just got back to the hotel. I've been in a meeting about the Lion with Isak and his colleagues.'

Fredrika Bergman was sitting in with the Israeli equivalent

of the National Crime Unit. Alex tried to remind himself why Fredrika had been sent to Jerusalem, rather than anyone else: because her husband was going there. But that wasn't the way things had turned out.

'Tell me,' he said.

'We have a name,' Fredrika said. 'But I'm afraid it doesn't get us anywhere.'

'Because?'

He couldn't suppress the impatience in his voice.

'There was only one occasion when the Lion had to give a name in order to be allowed to use a computer in one particular store. He said his name was Avital Greenburg.'

Avital Greenburg.

Yet another new name.

Alex felt his heart sink. This was too much to cope with.

'And did our Israeli colleagues recognise the name?'

'Yes, they did. But not in the way you're thinking.'

More surprises. It seemed there was no end to them.

'Alex, Avital Greenburg was a man who died many years ago. He became notorious in Israel when he abducted and killed two children at the end of the 70s.'

Alex didn't know what to say at first.

'Well, at least we know that the person who sent the emails was linked to the murders.'

'It definitely looks that way,' Fredrika said. 'The police here are extremely frustrated. They can't get any further with the Lion. There are no CCTV pictures, and he always paid cash for internet access.'

Alex wasn't surprised; they were dealing with a pro. A person who was fully aware of security issues. A person like Efraim Kiel.

'I've got news for you too,' he said.

Fredrika listened in silence. When he had finished speaking, she said:

'If Efraim is behind all this, then Saul and Gideon must understand why it's happening.'

'I agree. Which is what we've suspected all along – that they're keeping something from us. But we just can't work out why.'

'Perhaps through fear?' Fredrika suggested. 'Then again, what have they got to be afraid of? The worst has already happened.'

Alex nodded to himself.

'Mona Samson,' he said. 'I mentioned her to you earlier; have you found out whether she's entered the country?'

'So far the police haven't managed to identify her, but they're still looking.'

'What the hell does that mean?' Alex said. 'The police haven't managed to identify her? Mona Samson can't be the most common name in Israel. How many people using false names can there be in one inquiry?'

He could tell that Fredrika was equally frustrated. They had to make progress. Soon. Before it was too late.

'Saul Goldmann,' she said. 'Do we still think he shot his own son?'

'I've seen stranger things over the years,' Alex replied. 'But my priority at the moment is that we now have an individual who looks even more suspect since we broke his alibi.'

Efraim Kiel. Who had vanished without a trace.

Alex thought out loud.

'If Efraim is the Lion, why did he email the boys? Why not just pick them up on the street? That's what I would have done.'

If I were a killer, which I'm not.

'Because he knows their parents, realised there was a risk of being recognised,' Fredrika said.

'Bollocks. Neither of the boys had ever met him, and even if they'd seen him in a photograph, although their parents insist they don't have any pictures of Kiel, it would be more than ten years old.'

He could hear the sound of traffic in the background; Fredrika must have gone outside.

'I don't know why he emailed them,' she said. 'Possibly because it increased his chances of getting them to go with him voluntarily? Otherwise he would have been forced to take them one at a time, which would have been more difficult. Or it would have taken longer, at least.'

So many loose ends. Alex thought bitterly that it felt as if they were chasing an entire pride of lions, not just one.

'This is an endless nightmare scenario,' he said.

'Do you think so? I don't agree. This starts and ends with the Goldmann and Eisenberg families. Otherwise other children would have been taken.'

Fredrika was right, but they still had to get to the bottom of the murders, with or without the co-operation of the parents.

'Tomorrow I'm going to visit the kibbutz where Saul and Gideon grew up. Hopefully we'll know more after that.'

Alex hoped she was right.

Above all he wanted Fredrika to find the most mysterious figure in the whole case so far.

The man known as the Paper Boy.

A man who the murderer, whoever he might be, must have known about.

LONDON

The Paper Boy.

Known to some as an Israeli myth.

Known to significantly fewer people as the name of a secret source in a Palestinian village on the West Bank.

Eden Lundell was trying to digest what she had heard, while struggling with the dilemma that she now faced. Because under no circumstances could she pass this information on to Alex Recht or Fredrika Bergman. Intelligence of the most sensitive nature, which would never be admissible in a Swedish court of law. It could never be shared. She had gone to Fred for personal reasons, but now her private life had collided with her professional background, and she had no choice but to stick to the rules of the game.

Fredrika was in Israel. She wouldn't get anywhere near the information Eden had been given; the question was whether she and Alex would still be able to solve the case. Eden hoped so, because three people had died, two of them children. Justice must be done.

In one way or another.

She and Fred Banks had parted company a few hours earlier. He had looked very tired when she left his house.

'It's funny, but I always had a feeling we'd meet again,' he had said as she was leaving, a wry smile lighting up his pale face. He had given her far more than she had ever dared hope for, and for that she would be eternally grateful.

'It was good to see you,' she said.

Her voice was suddenly thick, the damp air difficult to breathe.

'When are you going back to Sweden?'

'Tomorrow morning. First thing.

She hesitated, but had to ask the question.

'If you know any more about the Paper Boy, or if you think you can find out more . . . I'd really appreciate it if you could let me know.'

His face had darkened, the smile gone in a second.

'You're asking a lot.'

She shook her head.

'I haven't told you everything. There has been a series of murders in Stockholm. Three members of a Jewish community, two of them children, and the story of the Paper Boy from Israel has come up in the investigation.'

Fred looked surprised.

'And how does that end up on your desk? What's it got to do with Säpo?'

'It's not my case; it's being investigated by a special team of detectives. But we were consulted because an Israeli citizen who is known to us is on the periphery.'

Fred opened his mouth, then closed it again.

'Not Efraim Kiel?'

'Yes.'

It was Fred's turn to shake his head.

'There's a big difference between what he did to you and killing children, Eden.'

'We don't know if he's involved. We don't think so, but

there are a number of question marks around his presence in Stockholm, and the fact that it coincides with these murders.'

Once again he reminded her of what he had already said:

'You are not to pass on what I told you, not under any circumstances whatsoever.'

'Of course not.'

He thought for a moment.

'Okay, I'll see what I can find out, although I don't know how. I'll call you if I get anywhere.'

'It would be particularly helpful to know who else was part of Efraim's team, the one that was operating on the West Bank.'

Fred let out a bark of laughter.

'You're crazy. Why do you want to know that?'

'Because there are several leads, all pointing back to Israel. And someone is watching Efraim in Stockholm. Someone other than Säpo.'

Fred grew serious.

'Take care of yourself,' he said. 'It sounds as if there's something major going on over there.'

I know. And it frightens me.

She raised a hand in farewell.

'I'll be in touch. And thanks again for your help.'

He waved back, and she turned and walked away. Once upon a time they would have hugged, but those days were long gone.

Maybe in the future, she thought when she was back in her hotel room. Maybe it would be possible to heal the past. Her relationship with MI5 was beyond repair, but she and Fred could fix things; if they tried.

It would make Mikael happy, anyway; he still talked about Fred, said how much he missed him.

He had always been better than Eden at putting his thoughts and feelings into words. She was a permanent meltdown of suppressed needs and reactions, while he was a firework, an explosion of emotions. That was both the strength and the weakness within their relationship.

She called home to say goodnight. Mikael sounded pleased to hear her voice, talked enthusiastically about what he and the girls had been up to. She listened, but told him nothing about what she had done. That was how it always was, and Mikael didn't mind. Nor did she mention that she had managed to find time to go and buy a violin for Dani; that would be a surprise.

'See you tomorrow,' he said.

'See you.'

For a second she was seized by a bottomless panic.

Dear God, please don't let me have misjudged Efraim Kiel completely.

Waking nightmares were always worse than those that came when she was asleep. She had just decided to go for an evening stroll to settle her nerves when her boss rang from Stockholm.

'I presume you're still not prepared to tell me what you're up to,' GD said, the irritation clear in his voice.

'I'll be back at work by lunchtime tomorrow.'

'Marvellous,' GD said dryly. 'But that's not why I called. We've made some progress during your absence.'

'Progress?'

'We think we've found the person who is following Efraim Kiel.'

'How?'

'The surveillance team kept one car outside the Diplomat in the faint hope that we weren't the only ones he had managed to shake off. And it seems as if their strategy worked perfectly. They identified an individual who was hanging around in the vicinity of the hotel for long periods at a time.'

'Did they get any pictures?'

'They're here in front of me.'

Eden's heart was pounding. She thought about the links to Israel, about Efraim's team operating on the West Bank: a team with which he had obviously parted company, because he had then moved on to trying to recruit agents in London.

'What does he look like? Can you send me a photo?'

'You can see the photos when you get back. But I will tell you that it's not a man. The person who is following Efraim Kiel is a woman.'

It wasn't hard to spot her. He sensed her presence as soon as he picked up her last message from reception. He knew she couldn't be far away. He had left the hotel by the same route as he had come in, slipped through the streets behind the building, then cautiously made his way back to Strandvägen. The Säpo car was still there. And a short distance away, at a bus stop, stood a figure who didn't get on any of the buses that pulled up.

To think that she had grown so careless.

It was Efraim Kiel who had trained her, spent countless hours working with her. Provided her with all the knowledge and skills necessary to survive her mission.

Now she was behaving as if she had forgotten every single thing. Or as if she simply didn't care. He took it for granted that Säpo had also seen her. Eventually she must have realised that she was making a fool of herself. As she walked away she lacked the energy he had been used to. Her head was bowed, hands shoved in her pockets.

Following her had been trickier than he had expected, because of course the car door opened and one of the Säpo goons set off after her as well. Efraim had found it difficult to shadow the Säpo guy without the other man in the car spotting him. If he could just keep his distance, he should be okay.

And so they had moved through the city, the woman first, the Säpo guy in the middle, and Efraim on the other side of the road. An unconscious troika with the unsuspecting woman as its leader. She led them down towards the central station, then along Vasagatan. At first Efraim had thought they were heading for his new hotel, which would have been most unfortunate, but the woman continued toward Torsgatan. The trail ended when she disappeared through the doorway of one of the newly built apartment blocks on the left hand side.

When the Säpo agent gave up and walked away, Efraim crossed over. Read the names of the residents, wondered which one might be hers. Going inside and ringing one doorbell after another was out of the question.

Always stay out of sight; never be noticed.

It wasn't until he was standing under the shower back in his hotel room that he understood which name she had chosen.

The realisation hit him like a thunderbolt. His hands felt numb as he turned off the water, dried himself and went into the bedroom.

Now he knew what she was calling herself.

She had taken the name of the man who was so strong that he could tear a lion to pieces.

Samson.

ISRAEL

The lion was everywhere, its image on manhole covers and flags, on ceramic ornaments and pieces of jewellery.

'The lion is the symbol of Jerusalem,' Isak Ben-Zwi explained when Fredrika asked him about it. 'There are early references to the lion's significance for the city in what Christians refer to as the Old Testament, and the symbol of the lion played a major role when we were a part of the Ottoman Empire.'

They had left the American Colony in the eastern part of Jerusalem for a late evening walk. Isak led her down Nablus Road to the Damascus Gate, set in the magnificent wall that encircled the Old City. The wall was lit up, shining against the dark sky, beautiful and uncompromising.

'During the day the Old City is a gigantic market place,' Isak said. 'We can come down tomorrow if you like; nothing is open now.'

Even though Fredrika had visited Jerusalem before, she really wanted to go to the market again. If she had time.

Tomorrow she was due to visit the kibbutzim; theoretically she would be able to go home in the evening.

'Did you find out any more about the Paper Boy?' she asked Isak. 'You said you were going to do an online search in Hebrew.'

He didn't reply. Was she imagining it, or was his expression less amiable than it had been earlier?

'This way,' he said. 'I will show you the Old City by night.'

He took her hand and led her down the stone steps towards the dark opening of the Damascus Gate. She presumed he was being a gentleman, but the gesture felt much too intimate. Discreetly she withdrew her hand, holding the strap of her shoulder bag instead.

Isak looked at her. He was clearly annoyed, much to her surprise.

So much for being a gentleman. It had been an invitation. And she had turned him down.

The Old City was both dark and deserted. The long, narrow alleyways were normally packed with traders, but now there were only endless dark walls with huge metal doors protecting the goods behind them.

'They arrive first thing in the morning,' Isak explained. 'Open the doors and set out their wares. Earlier in the year when we had a lot more tourists it was almost impossible to walk along here.'

Fredrika could easily picture the scene, in spite of the fact that it was so quiet now. A scruffy cat padded silently by, and Fredrika gave a start. She would never have ventured down here alone.

They turned left into the Via Dolorosa, walked along the road where Jesus had allegedly carried his cross, although in the opposite direction. At the end of the narrow thoroughfare the Lion Gate stood before them.

'This is where our soldiers entered during the Six Day War,' Isak said. 'And raised the Israeli flag over Temple Mount.'

His voice was suffused with pride and warmth. He was

far too young to have been around back then, but Fredrika guessed that older members of his family might well have fought in the war.

Or wars.

Because there had been so many more wars in the territory that had been known as Israel since 1948. I wonder if there will ever be peace here, she thought.

She felt slightly ashamed, and instead focused on the symbol of the lion, trying to understand how it fitted into the investigation: why someone calling himself the Lion had emailed Jewish children in Stockholm; emailed and possibly murdered them.

They walked back up the Via Dolorosa.

In silence.

Until Isak suddenly stopped. Fredrika stopped too, on her guard. She wondered what the hell she was doing between two silent walls of stone with a man she didn't know.

'I've given you almost an hour,' he said.

His voice was perfectly calm, but his expression was dark and aggressive. He moved a step closer.

'An hour. And still you haven't told me.'

Told me? What did he want her to say?

'I'm afraid I don't understand,' she said.

She backed away until she was pressed against the yellowish-white wall, with Isak far too close.

'I think you do,' he said. Still utterly calm.

The fear he aroused in her made her angry.

'I don't know what you think you're doing, but I'm going back to the hotel right now.'

She tried to sound determined, but failed. As she moved to walk away he grabbed hold of her and held her tight, pressed up against the wall with his face only centimetres from hers.

'You and your colleagues haven't told us everything there is to tell.'

The words emerged as a protracted hiss.

When she didn't reply, the grip on her wrists tightened.

'The Paper Boy,' he said. 'You know who he is, don't you? That's why you've come here. You and your subterfuge. You want our help to drive out someone you wouldn't be able to get at otherwise. Fucking liar!'

He let go of her, and she collapsed like a marionette whose strings have been cut.

What the hell was he talking about?

She made an attempt to reason with him.

'I've no idea what you mean, but I can see that you're very upset. I don't know what's happened to make you so angry, but I can assure you that neither I nor my colleagues know anything about the Paper Boy. That's why we came to you.'

Her torrent of words was interrupted by a scornful laugh.

'You've made me and my men look like idiots! Getting us to run errands that you should have asked your own security service to take care of.'

Security service?

He swore again.

'Did you think I was going to share that kind of information with you? Did you?'

Fredrika's entire body was shaking. Something had gone wrong. It was hardly a coincidence that Isak had brought her to the Old City late at night, when he knew the place would be deserted.

She was tired and frightened; she just wanted to go back to the hotel.

'I promise you, we didn't and don't know anything about the Paper Boy. That's why I'm going to the kibbutz in the morning, to find out more.'

Isak gazed wearily at her.

'And you think they'll be able to tell you something? You're obviously deluded. If you want to go somewhere tomorrow, you're on your own. I'm done with you and your games.'

With that he turned his back on her and walked away. Fredrika hesitated for a second, then set off after him. He stopped and spun around.

'Don't fucking follow me. This is where we go our separate ways. If you have any more questions relating to your investigation in Stockholm, fax them over when you get home.'

She stared after him as he disappeared into the darkness, the sound of his rapid footsteps echoing between the walls and fading away.

She stood there in the cold and the darkness without any idea of what she had done to upset him so much. Perhaps the answer lay in his assertion that he had been used to carry out tasks that should have fallen within the remit of the Swedish security service.

She hadn't a clue what he meant by that. The only thing she could imagine was that any links to the world of intelligence were stronger and more numerous than they had realised, and that they had inadvertently marched straight into affairs that were both secret and sensitive. But how? And how were they supposed to find whoever was behind the murders if even those in authority were determined to protect their secrets?

But that wasn't her biggest problem right now. Her biggest problem was finding her way out of the labyrinthine streets of the Old City, with the lights out and not a soul in sight.

Fredrika knew that she wouldn't be able to find her way back to the Damascus Gate without Isak's help. However, she thought she could find the Lion Gate, which meant she would be able to get out of the Old City and follow the wall back to her hotel.

Walking as fast as she could, her arms tightly folded across her chest, she set off along the Via Dolorosa once more.

CONCLUSION

FRAGMENT VI

The case has been like an octopus, with each tentacle representing a separate lead. The inspector remembers every single one of them. The leads that took them to Lovön. To Israel. And now to the home of a colleague.

He knows that it is over now.

That the Paper Boy has claimed his last victim.

All that remains is to understand what has happened.

And that will be impossible, because too many people are keeping quiet. Sheltering behind rules he knew nothing about.

During the past few days they have trampled on secrets they didn't even know existed. Upset people they have never met, without being able to apologise. Because how can you say sorry when you don't know what you've done?

As he stands in the apartment where a family has been smashed to pieces, he has a horrible feeling. A horrible feeling that he has missed something.

Something vital.

Something staring him in the face.

It was something I saw, something that didn't feel right.

He walks around the apartment once more. It is beautiful. Turn of the century. Stylishly renovated, perfectly in keeping with the period.

As he stands in the hallway, it suddenly strikes him. The bloodstains. They don't make sense.

He calls one of the CSIs over.

'You think the man died here in the hallway,' he says.

'It looks that way. Check out the concentration of the blood; it's all over the floor, from one side right across to the other.'

From one side right across to the other.

'But why are there no bloodstains linking the scene of the murder and the bedroom?'

The CSI has no answer to that question.

'The witness claims the man was shot in the doorway,' he says. 'Maybe he didn't die right away. Maybe he managed to get to the bedroom before he lost consciousness.'

But the inspector doesn't think so. Because there is blood in the hallway, where the first silenced shot was allegedly fired.

Then he realises what he saw.

His gaze returns to the wedding photograph. To the man's face.

His brain stops working.

It can't be true.

But it is.

He shouts to everyone else in the apartment.

'Listen to me – there's a man missing here!'

He looks at the wedding photograph again. The man smiling into the camera is not the same man who was lying on the bed with the children. He is not the children's father. And he is not married to the woman who was standing here a few minutes ago, saying goodbye to her children.

EARLIER

The Sixth Day

MONDAY, 30 JANUARY 2012

TIME: BEFORE 22:10

It was as dark as if it were the middle of the night, even though it was morning. It was seven thirty, and Alex Recht was exhausted.

Polly Eisenberg was still missing.

He had expected her to be found dead as quickly as her brother, but that hadn't happened; however, he had no idea whether that meant she was still alive.

He started the morning by asking Carmen and Gideon Eisenberg to come to Police HQ. He had run out of patience. Someone had to start talking, and it seemed reasonable to expect the missing child's parents to oblige.

Fredrika had called him late last night, sounding very upset as she told him how her Israeli contact had abandoned her in the Old City in Jerusalem. She said he had 'gone crazy' before he walked away, which could only mean that they had stumbled on highly sensitive information, without realising it. He didn't even want to think about what implications that had for their chances of solving the case.

'Go and visit the kibbutzim,' he had said to her. 'Then get back here as soon as you can.'

'I will, but I don't know if it's going to be any use; Isak seemed to think it would be a complete waste of time.'

Alex had lost track of the days, having worked all

weekend. He reminded himself that it was Monday, and Fredrika would be back the following morning. Good. He needed her. More than ever.

Mona Samson was today's project. She wasn't answering her phone, and hadn't responded to the two messages Alex had left on her voicemail.

Where the hell was she?

He picked up the notes one of the temporary members of his team had put together. Her company was fairly new; Samson Security AB had been registered in Sweden less than a year ago, which meant there was no information about company turnover or commercial activity. All they had was a brief statement saying that the firm specialised in various security systems. The homepage was equally sparse; there were no client testimonials to attract new business, for example.

Thoughtfully he read through the last section of the notes. Samson Security AB was part of a larger concern. There was also a note from the colleague who had originally been in contact with Mona Samson, to the effect that she didn't speak Swedish, but English. There was no indication as to where the mother company was based, but Alex thought he knew. In order to double check he phoned the tax office, who confirmed his suspicions.

Samson Security AB was part of Samson SecInt, or Samson Security International, and its head office was in Tel Aviv, in Israel.

Alex searched online for Samson SecInt, but found nothing. *Of course.*

He picked up the phone and called Fredrika.

'I've got another job for you. There's a firm called Samson

SecInt which is supposed to have its head office in Tel Aviv. See if you can find it, and ask about their branch in Stockholm.'

'I haven't got much time,' Fredrika said. 'I'm in a cab on my way to the kibbutzim at the moment.'

'Do your best,' Alex said.

An unnecessary exhortation; Fredrika always did her best.

He ended the call and turned his attention back to the computer screen and the homepage of Samson Security AB. The only contact information for Mona Samson was her telephone number; no address. Could the firm have several offices in Stockholm? The apartment block he had visited the previous day had looked like Mona Samson's private residence rather than business premises. Why had his colleague assumed this was her office?

He made a phone call, and his colleague said that he had been given Mona's contact details by Saul Goldmann during their first interview with him. Alex and Fredrika hadn't been involved at that stage, because they were still concentrating on Josephine's murder.

'To be honest, I didn't make much of an effort to check out the company. I had an address where Saul Goldmann said they had met, and Mona Samson confirmed that.'

'Over the phone?' Alex said

'Yes, she was out of town when I called. In Skövde, I think she said.'

That might well have been what she said, but Alex had a bad feeling about the whole thing.

After a little more digging he discovered that Samson Security AB was registered at a post box address in Stockholm. Mona Samson, however, was not registered anywhere; the apartment in which she was living was presumably a sublet.

Alex thought things over. Regardless of whether or not Mona Samson could provide Saul Goldmann with an alibi, they must know one another. Goldmann had given the police both her address and telephone number, and claimed they had had a business meeting, which had apparently taken place at her private residence. Unless of course her office was there too, but why would an overseas company that had invested in a branch in another country go for such an unprofessional set-up?

After a certain amount of hesitation, he called Saul Goldmann. Saul sounded tired when he answered, almost apathetic.

It was now four days since his son had been found shot dead out on Lovön, barefoot in the snow with a paper bag over his head. That could drive any parent crazy. Or leave them feeling tired and apathetic.

'I'm sorry to bother you,' Alex began. 'But we're having problems getting in touch with Mona Samson. Do you know how we can contact her?'

'I gave her details to another officer last week. I thought you'd already spoken to her?'

His tone was sharper now, as if Alex's question worried him. Just as he had reacted during the interview.

'We have, but I'd like to get in touch with her again, and I'm getting nowhere. Do you happen to know whether Samson Security has an office in the city? You gave us the address of her private apartment, and she's not there.'

He was risking everything on one throw of the dice, hoping his bluff would work.

It did.

'Oh, right, yes. We met in her apartment instead of her office. I happened to be nearby, so it was easier. Well, I say I happened to be nearby, but we did have an appointment. However, I had another meeting beforehand. In Kungsholmen.'

Saul Goldmann was wobbling. Gabbling.

Alex was surprised; Saul Goldmann had not given the impression that he was a person who was likely to do either of those things.

So what was he hiding?

'Saul,' Alex said, choosing every word with care. 'If there's something you'd like to tell me, something you think could improve our chances of finding the person who killed Abraham and Simon, then please talk to me. Because time is running out for another child. We still haven't found Polly Eisenberg. And I'm afraid she will suffer the same fate as Abraham and Simon unless we track her down very soon.'

Saul's silence was unbearable.

Say something. For fuck's sake, say something.

'I've told you everything I know. I have nothing to add.'

'Okay, if you insist. But perhaps you remember where Mona Samson's office is located?'

'Of course. Samson Security has a rented office on Torsgatan.'

ISRAEL

The landscape around Jerusalem was just as dramatic as the history of the city.

They were driving south along the main road towards Tel Aviv. Fredrika was in the back of a cab reading through her notes. The kibbutz she was heading for was called Jeich Tikvha, and according to the map lay not far from Netanya, a town thirty kilometres to the north of Tel Aviv. The other kibbutz had closed down some years ago.

Fredrika was still shocked at the way the previous evening had ended. She had left the Old City alone via the Lion Gate, then she had followed the wall until she reached the Damascus Gate. She hadn't heard from Isak, nor had she expected to. Her suitcase was in the boot of the cab, and she wanted nothing more than to go home. Leave Israel and forget that she had ever been there.

Alex had called her and given her yet another job. She hoped she would have time, but had to admit to herself that her desire to visit an Israeli security firm was minimal. Anything she did from now on lacked legitimacy since the Israeli police had disowned her, and she didn't think Israel was a very good country in which to play at being a police officer.

The hotel had helped her to book a cab; it was expensive

but practical. The driver said something she didn't hear, and pointed through the windscreen.

'Sorry?'

'Rain,' the driver said in English. 'It's going to rain.'

Dark clouds had come rolling in over the coast and were moving east. The first heavy drops began to fall as they turned off for Netanya.

Fredrika was tired. The peace and quiet of the hotel had allayed the fear she had felt when she finally got back, but not the paranoia. She had the sense that someone was watching her, and before she went to bed she checked several times to make sure the door was locked. She had called Spencer to say goodnight, but that had been a mistake. He knew her so well that after just a few words he could tell that something had happened.

'I wish I was there with you,' he had said. 'Hurry home.'

He didn't need to ask more than once; she had absolutely no desire to stay.

'Here we are,' the driver said. He pulled up; forest on one side of the road, a high fence on the other. Up ahead she could see an entrance with a guard post.

'Jeich Tikvha,' the driver said, pointing. 'It means "There is hope" – did you know that?'

She didn't, but took some consolation from the words. She certainly needed hope.

He dropped her off and drove on. Fredrika picked up her case and walked over to the guard. What the hell was she doing here?

This whole thing was a lunatic project in a country which was one of the most challenging in the entire world in terms of security. It would have been much easier with Isak by her side.

The rain was falling heavily now, and she increased her speed. The guard stared at her with suspicion.

'Good morning,' she said. 'I'd like to speak to the Gold-mann and Eisenberg families, if they're available. It's about their sons.'

Being on unfamiliar ground with a task that was far from clear wasn't ideal. Fredrika realised this when she was shown into David and Gali Eisenberg's house. The place where Gideon Eisenberg had grown up.

'I'm sorry to turn up unannounced and at such an early hour,' she said once they were seated at the kitchen table. 'But we really need your help with our investigation.'

It was nine o'clock; she had left Jerusalem at seven thirty.

'Is this about Simon and Polly?' Gali asked

She looked as if she were on the verge of tears. Fredrika shuffled uncomfortably; this was an impossible situation.

'It is. And I have to begin by saying that you are under no obligation to talk to me. I am with the Swedish police, and I don't have the authority to conduct an investigation in Israel. But I was here on another matter, and wanted to take the opportunity to meet you.'

'We're happy to help the police in any way we can,' David assured her.

They seemed like decent people. Calm and collected. And so sad.

'Do you have other children apart from Gideon?'

'A daughter,' Gali said. 'She lives in Haifa.'

Not too far away; that must be some consolation when their son had moved all the way to Stockholm.

The house was small and simply furnished. If Fredrika

understood correctly, everything on a kibbutz was owned collectively. Therefore, the house was not theirs, but had been allocated to them as a place to live. The very thought of not owning her home, or at least having a contract with the landlord, made Fredrika's head spin.

She began by asking a question to which she already knew the answer.

'How long is it since Gideon left Israel?'

Gali sighed.

'It's exactly ten years.'

'Do you remember what motivated the move to Stockholm? I understand they left at the same time as the Goldmann family.'

There was no mistaking the reaction. As soon as Fredrika mentioned the name Goldmann, both Gali and David stiffened.

'It was just a coincidence really,' David said. 'The fact that they moved at the same time.'

'It all happened so fast,' Gali said. 'One day the decision was made, and we didn't understand it at all. They left just a few weeks after Simon was born.'

'So something must have happened, something that meant they didn't want to go on living here,' Fredrika said.

'Gideon always found it very difficult to talk about his job,' David said, with some hesitation. 'And we respected that. As far as we know, the decision had something to do with his work, but we never found out what happened.'

Gali shook her head sorrowfully.

'They just disappeared. We've been over to visit them many times, of course, and they've been here, but things just aren't the same.'

'You said Gideon found it difficult to talk about his job,' Fredrika said, turning to David. 'What did you mean by that?'

'It seemed as if everything he was involved in was top secret.'

'You mean at the firm where he worked?'

David looked confused.

'Firm? Gideon didn't work for a firm. He was employed by the military until he moved. Just like the others.'

A thought flitted through her mind. The others?

David straightened up.

'If you want any more information, you need to ask Gideon,' he said. 'He's in the best position to know what he can and can't reveal about his past.'

He realised he had said too much, and Fredrika knew she wouldn't get any more out of him.

She tried a different tack.

'Of course. We've already spoken to Gideon, and will be doing so again. A moment ago you said "just like the others". That he was employed by the military just like the others. I assume you were referring to Saul and Daphne Goldmann?'

They'd said they stayed on in the army for a year or so after their military service, hadn't they? A year or so. But if Fredrika was right, it now seemed that they had stayed on until they left Israel.

'That's right,' David said.

He had looked relieved when Fredrika started talking; he didn't need to feel as if he were betraying his son.

'And Efraim Kiel,' Gali said.

'Efraim Kiel?'

'Gideon, Saul, Daphne and Efraim did their military ser-

vice together, then pursued a career in the army. Efraim was
the only one who stayed in Israel.'

'That's probably because he was the most successful,'
David said with a melancholy smile. 'He was always a
winner, always the leader.'

'Did he also grow up on this kibbutz?'

'No, his parents lived in Netanya, but the boys went to
junior and high school together.'

One thread after another was woven together, the pattern
growing clearer all the time.

Efraim Kiel had come up yet again. Efraim Kiel, who
didn't have an alibi for the murder of the two boys. The man
Alex couldn't track down.

And once again it was apparent that Simon and Abraham's parents had lied. None of them had revealed that they
had gone to school with Efraim, and spent time in the army
together; they had said only that they did their military service with him.

As an investigator, Fredrika had to ask herself why. She
also wondered if they were lying for reasons relevant to the
inquiry, or because of something completely different. The
sense of chasing lost souls became stronger the more she dug
into the past. Was it because their work had been top secret?

'Do Saul Goldmann's parents live nearby? I'd really like to
speak to them too.'

A shadow passed across the kitchen table. The rain hammered against the window pane, and the Swedish cold felt like
a distant memory. In Israel it was like the Swedish summer.

'Unfortunately they are no longer with us,' Gali said. She
looked sad, but Fredrika could see something else in her eyes,
something indefinable that had nothing to do with sorrow.

Something that looked a lot like relief, in fact.

'Were they very old?' she asked.

David cleared his throat.

'Aida died in a car accident last year. And Avital . . . Avital took his own life.'

Silence fell in the small kitchen.

Avital? It was a coincidence, of course. The Lion had called himself Avital Greenburg. But Saul's father was Avital Goldmann.

'It must have been very difficult for Saul, losing both his parents when he's so young himself,' Fredrika said. Saul was only forty-five; most people don't expect to lose their parents until much later in life.

'I shouldn't think he misses them,' David said, getting up from the table. 'He didn't even come to his mother's funeral.'

Gali stroked his back as he passed her on his way to the sink.

'David, we know nothing about all that,' she said.

'If he wasn't close to them in the past, perhaps he's thinking about them now that he's lost his own son,' Fredrika said, trying to smooth things over.

David switched on the coffee machine, and it came to life with a series of noises. The atmosphere in the kitchen was oppressive, as if the air was full of unspoken words.

'I shouldn't think Saul cares about the boy either,' he said.

At that Gali slammed her fist down on the table.

'I just said we know nothing about all that!'

'Nonsense!' David said, turning to face the two women. 'I'm sure everyone knows the situation.'

What situation?

'May I ask what you're talking about?' Fredrika said.

'The fact that Abraham wasn't Saul's son.'

'David!'

'The boy is dead, Gali. What does it matter?'

Gali began to cry, silent, heart-rending tears.

David softened.

'What are you saying?' Fredrika said, looking at him.

David couldn't meet her eye.

'Well, that's the rumour. That Saul had had a vasectomy. One of our neighbours who's a doctor arranged for him to have it done in Haifa, and then along comes Daphne a few years later and announces that she's pregnant.'

'But why didn't Saul want children?'

Fredrika didn't understand. He must have been so young when he made the decision not to be a parent.

David didn't respond.

Fredrika gently placed a hand on Gali's arm.

'Why didn't Saul want children?' she repeated.

An eternity passed before Gali wiped her eyes and answered the question, her voice no more than a faint whisper.

'Because he was afraid that the Paper Boy would take them.'

One of the earliest flights from London took off at seven o'clock in the morning, and Eden Lundell was on board. The night had been an endless torment of sleepless anxiety. The story Fred Banks had told her had triggered a chain of thought she was incapable of stopping. Every time she closed her eyes, she saw the Palestinian boy who had died in the explosion on the West Bank. Half dozing, half awake she pictured him running towards the house where he thought he would be safe. Yanking open the door and standing on the trigger mechanism for the bomb that someone had concealed in the entrance to keep enemies away.

But why had no one told the boy he must never, ever use that door?

The whole thing was insane, and Eden couldn't get her head around it.

And now two more boys had died. Ten years later and in a different part of the world.

The fate of the Palestinian boy was the key to the mystery into which the police investigation had developed, she was sure of it.

She left her hotel at five thirty in the morning and travelled out to Heathrow. She was hoping that Fred would have more to tell her, that he would call.

And he did.

The plane had barely touched down at Arlanda when Eden switched on her phone. Fred called as the plane taxied in.

'Can we meet?' he said.

'No, I've just landed in Stockholm.'

'We need to talk. I have more information for you.'

She closed her eyes. Thought for a moment.

A plane wasn't the best place to conduct a top secret conversation, but she had no choice. She tried to remember what the missing child was called.

Polly Eisenberg.

Time was running out for her.

It was for Polly, and for those who had already died, that they had to bend the rules.

'It will have to be now,' she said.

'I've checked the minutes from meetings on the joint operation with Mossad. On one occasion a couple of representatives from Efraim Kiel's special team were there; I have their names here.'

Eden had spent her waking hours during the night trying to piece together the puzzle.

The boy who died in the explosion was important.

So was the secret source who led them to the suspected terrorist.

The source known as the Paper Boy.

Even before Fred told her the names of the other team members, she knew what he was going to say.

'Saul Goldmann and Gideon Eisenberg. I've read one or two articles online; they're the fathers of the boys who were murdered, aren't they?'

'They are,' Eden said.

The plane had arrived at its gate and the passengers were beginning to disembark. Eden stayed where she was in her window seat.

This was nothing but pure revenge.

An eye for an eye.

The most classic principle of all, which never seemed to go out of fashion.

'We have to find out the name of the boy who died on the West Bank,' she said. 'Otherwise we'll never find the murderer.'

'I know,' Fred said. 'But I'm afraid I can't help you there. His name isn't in any of the records, nor any explanation as to why he was in that house in the first place.'

'Could he have been the suspect's son?'

'More than likely. But he died in the explosion.'

'Who else was in the house?'

'It doesn't say; it just says that three bodies were found inside, the boy and two adult males. As far as MI5 were concerned the matter was resolved, however tragic the outcome. We have no information about how Mossad chose to follow up what had occurred.'

Eden worked through what she had heard.

Efraim Kiel had led a team recruiting sources in the Palestinian enclave of the West Bank. Saul Goldmann and Gideon Eisenberg had been part of that team. After the disaster of the boy's death, both Saul and Gideon had immediately left the country and moved to Sweden. That was back in 2002. And now, ten years later, when their own sons had reached the same age as that Palestinian boy, at a guess, someone was taking revenge.

It was hardly surprising that the Goldmanns and Eisenbergs weren't co-operating, according to Alex. They were keeping quiet because they weren't allowed to talk about what had happened. An episode that still haunted them, a decade later.

The question was what she should do now. Because officially the information she had been given did not exist.

'They must realise what's going on,' Fred said.

'Of course.'

'I imagine the most likely scenario is that they'll get in touch with their parent organisation in Israel and ask for help.'

Eden didn't think that was going to happen. By leaving Israel, Saul and Gideon had turned their backs on their former employer. There had to be a concrete reason why those two, but not Efraim who had also been there, had felt compelled to move.

It was painful to think of Efraim's name.

You fucking lunatic, you're not mixed up in all this, are you?

She didn't believe he was. Not as a killer, anyway.

Nor did she think that he just happened to be in Stockholm when everything kicked off. Could Mossad have sent him to keep a watchful eye on his former colleagues? Could they have had some kind of warning about what was going to happen?

If so, then Efraim had failed spectacularly.

'What are you going to do now?' Fred asked.

The anxiety in his voice gave him away.

There would be devastating consequences for his career if it emerged that he had passed on classified information, particularly as he had given it to a woman who had once been accused of working as a double agent.

Eden had never been good at gratitude or being in someone's debt, but she would never forget this.

'I don't know,' she said.

Honest and gentle.

'Don't burn me,' he said.

'Not for anything in the world.'

She was the last to get off the plane. She called GD and told him she was on her way in. She tried to assemble far too many fragments to form a whole. If the motive was revenge, then who was the avenger?

The Paper Boy, she thought. Is that what this is all about?

A little while later, in a cab on the way from the airport, she realised that there were only three people who could answer that question:

Saul, Gideon and Efraim.

If they even knew.

Because something was missing from this story. She felt strongly that it was all related to the boy who had died in the house, but could there be alternative scenarios? She didn't know how many men had made up Efraim's team; were there more men and women who had been punished by having their children murdered? Could there be more victims in Israel? If so, the Israelis should have made the connection by this stage, and got in touch with the Swedish police.

Eden shifted impatiently in the back of the cab.

It was through the victims that the perpetrators were found. If her basic theory was correct, if Simon and Abraham had been murdered in revenge for what had happened in that Palestinian village, then none of those involved were safe. Unless they were childless. Could Efraim have a family, and if so, where were they? Eden had no idea what kind of life he led. Perhaps he had already had a family back in the day, when he and she first met.

Bastard.

It wasn't until the cab was driving through the city streets that she realised what she had ignored. Consciously or unconsciously.

Because of course Efraim Kiel had children.

At least two of them.

Eden's daughters.

It was vital to act quickly. First of all Alex Recht drove over to Samson Security AB's office on Torsgatan and rang the bell. He banged on the door and eventually tried the neighbours. No one knew where the woman who usually occupied the office might be, but one man said he had seen her only the previous evening.

Alex called Mona Samson twice from the pavement outside, then drove back to Police HQ, contacted the prosecutor and asked for a warrant to search the premises of Samson Security AB.

'Why?' the prosecutor wanted to know.

'Because I'm wondering if Mona Samson might have fallen victim to our killer, and I want to make sure she's not lying there dead.'

The thought had struck him as he stood there hammering on the door.

So far he had assumed that the woman he was looking for was somehow involved in what had happened; the indentations on the roof indicated that a woman had played a part in the murders, and Mona Samson was the only woman who had emerged as a suspect. But what was to say that she couldn't also be a victim? In this tangle of loose ends where nothing was what it appeared to be, wasn't it possible that Mona Samson had somehow been drawn in and exploited?

Standing in her office a little while later, he didn't know what to think.

The place was spartan, bordering on desolate. Or perhaps the company hadn't been there very long. Two desks, a bookcase, a computer, a few books and brochures. And a mattress on the floor. That was all. Cold and sparse. Alex stood in the middle of the room, the snow that had landed on his coat melting and dripping onto the floor.

'Empty,' said a colleague who had come with him. A technician was there too. In films the cops always had a skeleton key in their back pocket; in reality, it was the police technician who opened doors.

They had no mandate to remove anything, so they had to leave the computer where it was. As for the next step . . . Alex gazed around despondently.

'Let's put the building under surveillance,' he said. 'See if she comes back. It looks as if she sleeps here sometimes.'

His colleague glanced up.

'But we don't know what she looks like.'

'In that case we'll put someone on the door asking everyone who goes in to show their ID,' Alex said. 'We have to find her.'

Fifteen minutes later he was back at Police HQ, sitting at his desk reading the latest surveillance update on Saul Goldmann's activities. He was travelling only between home and work. Sometimes Daphne was with him, sometimes he was alone. There was a photograph of the couple standing on the pavement outside their home; they had their arms around each other, and it looked as if Daphne was weeping on her husband's shoulder.

Alex swallowed hard and put down the picture.

There was a certain kind of grief against which there was no defence. Daphne's crumpled face expressed that particular sorrow, and it was painful to see.

He forced himself to look again, knowing that he had seen something important.

Saul's face.

Barren and closed.

Not distorted with anguish like his wife's. Alex knew he was on thin ice, that he couldn't or shouldn't draw conclusions from a single snapshot, a brief moment. But it actually looked as if Saul wasn't grieving at all. He seemed annoyed, if anything.

Alex went down to the technicians' department and managed to get hold of Lasse, who had helped them with the Super Troopers forum.

'Saul Goldmann's mobile,' he said. 'Have we got a location for the occasions when we want to know where he was?'

'In other words when the teacher was shot, when the boys disappeared, and on the morning when they died?'

'Yes.'

'No. We haven't asked the phone company for that information.'

'In that case I'll fill in a request and sign it right now,' Alex said. 'And I want a list of calls for the relevant days.'

He was about to leave when Lasse said:

'However, I've just got a GPS on Mona Samson's phone. The guy who called her to confirm Goldmann's alibi asked me to do it last night. He was probably worried in case you thought he hadn't done a good enough job.'

Too right.

'What did you find out?' he said, desperate to know.

Lasse waved him over, wanting him to look at the computer screen.

'At two o'clock on the afternoon when the boys went missing, she received a call. We can see that she was definitely in Kungsholmen then, but look where she was when the phone rang at three.'

Alex peered at the screen.

The mobile had been up by the bridge, Djurgårdsbron. In Östermalm.

'Bloody hell,' he said.

'The teacher was shot just after three, wasn't she?'

'She was.'

'But at that time Mona Samson, or her phone at least, was by Djurgårdsbron.'

'She could have been separated from her phone,' Alex suggested. 'It might have been in her car, for example. Do we know if she actually has a car?'

'I checked, but I couldn't find one. Of course she could have hired one that day, or borrowed one from a friend.'

'True,' Alex said. 'But given the location of the phone, I think we can assume that she definitely wasn't in Kungsholmen with Saul Goldmann. Where did she go after that? When did the next call come in?'

'Hang on,' Lasse said. 'Look at this. So she had a call at two o'clock, which she didn't answer. I don't know who that was from. But guess who called her at three o'clock?'

'I haven't time to play guessing games – just tell me.'

'Saul Goldmann. But she didn't answer then either.'

Alex let out a whistle.

'Bloody hell,' he whispered.

Lasse smiled with satisfaction.

'The next activity is half an hour later, at three thirty. She called Goldmann, and they talked for just over two minutes.'

Alex stared at the map where Mona Samson's trail ended. At Djurgårdsbron. Which wasn't far from the building on Nybrogatan, where someone had lain on their stomach on the roof and shot a teacher in the back. He thought about what the CSIs had said: that the person on the roof had been no more than one metre seventy tall.

And then he thought about the theory that the boys had been picked up by someone they knew. Perhaps Efraim Kiel, if he was the one who had sought them out online. Even if they hadn't met before, it wasn't unreasonable to assume that the boys might have been curious and gone with him if he referred to their exchange of emails. But it could also be much simpler than that; it could have been Saul Goldmann who had picked them up.

What a team they would have made, if that were the case. Saul and Mona. Providing one another with an alibi. Helping one another with the murders in order to fragment the investigation, make the police's job so much more difficult.

They're not a team; they're a couple.

The realisation made him go cold.

That was why they had lied, why they had met in her apartment rather than her office.

'They're in a relationship,' he said, hardly conscious of the fact that he was thinking out loud.

'Who?' Lasse said.

'Samson and Goldmann.'

'So they got rid of the kid so they could make a fresh start? Is that what you're saying?'

Was it that simple? Alex hesitated. 'Something along those lines.'

'But why take Simon Eisenberg as well? And what about Polly?'

Alex had no answer to that, but his brain had gone into overdrive. If he could just gather together all the scraps of information and odd circumstances that had rained – or snowed – down on them over the past few days, a clear picture would emerge. Because the Eisenbergs and the Gold-manns had a history that they were keeping from the police. A reason why they no longer spent time together, in spite of the fact that the men had been in close proximity for decades.

Alex had no idea how deep the conflict was, but he sin-cerely hoped that Fredrika would have found out something about their background in Israel. Because by now Alex was certain they were close to a resolution of the case.

Very close.

If they could just work out why Simon and Polly Eisenberg had to die as well.

ISRAEL

The rain had stopped, but the cloud cover remained. They were walking through the kibbutz as Gali and David Eisenberg took Fredrika on a guided tour of Gideon and Saul's youth.

'Gideon was always so cautious,' his mother said. 'Anxious and nervous. He was an easy target for Saul's vivid imagination.'

David Eisenberg shook his head.

'If I'd realised Saul was the one filling his head with rubbish I would have done something about it earlier.'

'This is where the Goldmanns lived,' Gali said, pointing to a house only fifty metres from their own.

The kibbutz was idyllic, with its lush greenery. A little community cut off from the rest of the world. Fredrika couldn't work out how they supported themselves; fruit cultivation might have carried the economy in years gone by, but these days they must have another income stream.

So this was where Saul and Gideon had spent their childhood, crawling among the plants and shrubs, running from one house to the other.

'Does Saul have any brothers or sisters?' Fredrika asked.

'No,' Gali said. 'And that was a great source of sorrow, above all to his mother.'

Fredrika could understand that. She was very glad she had two children, even though her son had been unplanned. But no less welcome for that.

'The Paper Boy,' she said. 'Where does the story come from?'

She could see by the look on Gali and David's faces that this was a sensitive subject. Gali slipped her hand into her husband's.

'It was Avital, Saul's father, who told me the story first,' David explained. 'When we were children. We didn't live here then, we lived in a village in the south of Israel. The story grew and became a legend, and after a few years its origins were forgotten. And eventually Saul told Gideon the tale. When we heard about it, we thought it was a very practical idea, to be honest. You're familiar with the history of Israel – full of conflicts and difficulties, in spite of the fact that the state has existed only since 1948.'

'You mean it was useful if the boys stayed indoors after dark?' Fredrika said.

'Not necessarily indoors, but we didn't want them going off on night-time excursions outside the kibbutz with the older kids,' David said. 'Teenagers can be incredibly irresponsible. Once two of them hitched from the kibbutz to Netanya. It could have ended very badly, because it turned out that the guy who picked them up was a wanted criminal.'

'We were keen to make sure that our boys stuck to the rules when it came to late evenings and nights, so we didn't dispute the story of the Paper Boy, who came and took children while they were sleeping,' Gali said. 'It sounds stupid now, but as we said, at the time it was practical.'

'The myth spread to the neighbouring kibbutz,' David went on.

That was where Daphne Goldmann had grown up. Unlike Carmen Eisenberg, she had heard about the Paper Boy when she was a child.

'But then something dreadful happened,' Gali said, an anguished expression on her face.

'Children actually began to disappear,' she said in a voice that was no more than a whisper. 'One from our community first of all, then one from the neighbouring kibbutz.'

Fredrika shuddered, pulling her jacket closer around her body.

'Were they found?'

'Yes,' David said. 'Each of them was missing for only a few days, then they were found naked by the roadside, with severe lacerations. It looked as if someone had simply pulled up in a car, thrown them out and driven off.'

Children disappearing. One at a time. Found naked by the roadside.

Fredrika ran her fingers through her hair; she was finding it difficult to breathe.

'Do you know what had happened to them?'

Gali couldn't speak. She was weeping silently, her head resting on David's shoulder.

'It looked as if an animal had tried to rip them to pieces,' David said, his voice breaking. 'I was there when the first child was found. Someone had attacked him with a knife – not deep stab wounds, but scratches and slashes. It almost had a ritualistic feel. But the actual cause of death was a bullet in the chest, fired from a distance. It was eventually established that the children had run for their lives before they died. The murderer first caught his prey, abused it, then let it go in order to hunt it down and kill it.'

Fredrika's head was spinning.

The only thing she could think about was the children who had been shot on Lovön; who had been chased barefoot in the snow in freezing temperatures.

'The police and the press called the killer the Hunter, but the children on the kibbutzim believed it was the Paper Boy who had taken them.'

The Hunter and the Paper Boy. Fredrika blinked up at the sun, which had broken through the cloud cover for a little while. She chose her words with care.

'When the children were found, were they marked in any way? Apart from their injuries, I mean.'

Gali straightened up and wiped her eyes.

'Both children had a paper bag over their head, with a face on it,' David said. 'The police kept that detail to themselves at first, but the rumour spread in no time because so many of us had been involved in the search. Needless to say, that fuelled the children's fear of the Paper Boy.'

The strain was clear in every line of his face.

'Did they catch the killer?' Fredrika asked, thinking back to a case she had worked on a few years ago. The murderer had used a grave site in Midsommarkransen, returning to it over a period of many years. God forbid the same thing was happening again: a killer who had moved from Israel to Sweden. Please let it not be true.

'They did,' David said.

She let out a long breath. Thank goodness.

'He made a mistake,' Gali said. 'Another child went missing, a boy. He managed to get away, and was able to tell the police what had happened to him, and who had taken him.'

'He came staggering in through the gate,' David said. 'The guard took care of him and made sure the police were called right away.'

'He was from this kibbutz?' Fredrika asked.

A shadow passed across David's face. His eyes filled with tears, and he could barely speak.

'Yes. And he was never the same again. He said he was fine, but we could see the change. But at least they caught the person responsible, which was a blessing in the midst of all the sorrow.'

He fell silent, watching a bird as it flitted from tree to tree.

Gali didn't say anything either; she waved to a neighbour passing by.

They had more to tell, Fredrika could feel it. *A lot more.* She waited until the neighbour was out of earshot.

'So what happened to the murderer? I assume he got a long prison sentence.'

Gali looked as if she was about to start crying again.

'Life,' David said. 'Which was only right after what he had done.'

But?

There was an unspoken 'but' that they were avoiding, refusing to touch.

'It was just so terrible for his family,' Gali whispered. 'We did our best to support them, but it was difficult. Especially for us.'

'His family? You knew them?'

David nodded. Fredrika gazed at the idyllic surroundings, tried to work it out.

'The murderer came from here? He was one of you?'

Another nod, and Fredrika was beginning to understand.

'He killed himself in prison,' David said. 'His son was particularly badly affected by the whole thing. I'd say he was every bit as damaged as the boy who got away.'

Gali wiped a tear from her cheek.

'Avital was the Hunter and the Paper Boy,' she said. 'Now do you see? Saul Goldmann's father was the murderer.'

Fredrika didn't know what to say. Saul's father had subjected other children to the same horror that had now claimed his own grandchild. The Paper Boy had travelled from the past to the present.

Someone had brought him to life.

'Although in those days the family was called Greenburg, not Goldmann,' David said.

Fredrika stopped dead. For a second, time stood still.

'Avital Greenburg. Was that his name?'

'Yes, but when it was all over, Aida changed the family name. For Saul's sake, so that fewer people would remember his background.'

But someone still remembers.

Whoever had called himself the Lion had known exactly what he was doing.

The Lion was a chameleon, who had taken the devil's name without hesitation.

'Did you ever get an explanation for what he'd done?' she asked. 'Why he'd killed those children?'

David sighed.

'Not really. Back in those days people weren't so fond of psychological analysis as they are now, but he was obviously sick. It would be absurd to think anything else.'

'We knew so little about his past,' Gali said. 'Both his parents died in the Holocaust; only Avital survived. Very few children came out of the concentration camps alive, but he was one of them. He was four years old when the war ended, and he was placed with foster parents who left Europe and came to Israel. I have no idea what that kind of start in life does to a person, but it's obvious that he too was badly damaged.'

It was hard to disagree. Fredrika had just one more question.

'Who was the boy who survived? Does he still live here?'

Gali turned and started walking back towards her house.

David didn't move, but he couldn't bring himself to look at Fredrika.

At that moment she realised what he was going to say.

'It was Gideon,' he said. 'Gideon was the Hunter's last victim. It was Gideon who put Saul's father in prison.'

Twice he had been to her apartment block. On both occasions he had seen the tall man emerge with the girls. On the Sunday they had gone to Vasa Park, on the Monday to day care. But he had seen no sign of Eden, which led Efraim Kiel to conclude that she had gone away.

And that worried him. Because Eden ought to be shaken up by what had happened, by the fact that he now knew he was the father of her children, yet she had taken the risk of leaving her family alone. Admittedly her husband looked more than capable of defending his children if he had to. Efraim had seen him once before, in London. It had been a bad idea. Feeling over-confident, Efraim had gone to Eden's house. He had been standing in the street when they came out hand in hand.

Eden had watched him to the very last second. That was when he realised she had fallen in love with him.

But right now Efraim had bigger problems than Eden. The woman who was following him was one of them. She wasn't sticking to the rules. She wasn't keeping out of the way. And what the hell was she doing in Stockholm? Efraim couldn't shake off the feeling that he had seriously misjudged the situation. Made a mistake, in fact.

Or several mistakes.

Because now he was caught up in an unpleasant dilemma, and he couldn't see a way out.

I have to get out of this country. Fast.

But that wouldn't solve the problem of the Paper Boy. There were certain things you couldn't run away from, however much you wanted to.

He also had to work out what to do with the girl, Polly. Time was running out, he had to act.

They called when he was in his hotel room getting changed. He had walked over to Torsgatan in the hope of spotting the woman he had followed the previous day, but instead he had seen the police entering the building. Plain clothes officers, instantly recognisable to Efraim's trained eye. Right in front of the Säpo goons, who were also watching the woman's apartment. He couldn't understand why Säpo and the police apparently didn't know about each other; why weren't they working together?

His phone rang as he was pulling on his jeans. He stopped dead. It was his dedicated work mobile, the one only his employer knew about.

'Yes?'

'Can you talk?'

'Yes.'

His boss got straight to the point.

'We have a problem. There's a Swedish police officer over here asking questions about the Paper Boy.'

He had been expecting this, and had an answer ready.

'It's a different Paper Boy,' he said. 'Not the one you're thinking of.'

'Excuse me – there's more than one?'

His boss sounded irritated.

'Yes. The original. A child killer from a kibbutz outside

Netanya. And then there's the one both you and I are familiar with,' Efraim said.

'And it's the first one the Swedish police are interested in?' his boss said with a certain amount of relief.

'I think we can assume so. There's no reason to believe they would know about the Paper Boy on the West Bank.'

It sounded as if the boss was tapping away on his keyboard.

'Nothing would make me happier than to be absolutely certain you're right,' he said. 'But there are complications.'

'Like what?'

'The Swedish police have also been asking questions about Mona Samson. If you're not familiar with the name, let me inform you that she used to be known as Nadia Tahir. Now do you understand what's worrying me?'

Efraim didn't answer immediately; he wasn't sure what to say.

Oh yes, I knew that Nadia had changed her name.

'They don't know what they're asking about,' he said. 'Believe me, the only Paper Boy they're interested in is the child killer.'

'I still think they're too bloody close.'

Efraim went over to the window and gazed out at the wintry landscape.

'I made it clear to our friends in the police in Jerusalem that they must stay away from the Paper Boy,' his boss went on. 'That his fate was a matter for the Israeli security service and no one else. Not our own police force, and definitely not the Swedes. I'm aware that I humiliated them. My actions may well have had a negative effect on the way in which they subsequently dealt with their Swedish colleagues, but to be honest I don't really care.'

Efraim watched a mother and two children on the other side of the street. The little ones kicked at the snow, laughing as it swirled around their feet.

'I'm sure it'll be fine,' he said distractedly.

The Stockholm police had surprised him with their creativity, travelling all the way to Israel to ask questions about the Paper Boy. And Nadia, or Mona as she was calling herself these days. Efraim knew perfectly well that his own behaviour had been less than cautious. It wouldn't surprise him if the police started asking questions about him too.

Perhaps he should send them off in another direction.

A plan began to take shape. It wasn't pretty, but nor was the reality he had to deal with.

'Is it Alex Recht who's gone to Israel?'

'No, it's a woman – Fredrika Bergman.'

Fredrika Bergman. Efraim had never heard of her, but now his curiosity had been aroused. And he was annoyed.

'I assume you've been following the investigation in Stockholm?' his boss said.

'To a certain extent. It's difficult to get hold of information without seeming too pushy. I don't want to draw attention to myself.'

'Very wise. But what worries me most of all is the murdered boys' surnames.'

Efraim closed his eyes and rested his forehead against the cold window pane. Remembered what the cool metal had felt like in his hands before he threw the gun into the Baltic Sea.

'Eisenberg and Goldmann,' he said.

'It's hardly a coincidence, is it? Gideon and Saul must be their fathers.'

'That's right.'

'And you still maintain this is about a different Paper Boy from the one we got to know on the West Bank?'

'I don't know. But the Paper Boy the Swedish police are asking questions about is an imaginary figure in a tale told in a couple of kibbutzim outside Netanya.'

'Saul Goldmann and Gideon Eisenberg haven't made contact with us, but surely they must see the connection?'

'Presumably,' Efraim said. 'But once again – the murders have an equally clear link to the Paper Boy I referred to as the original.'

He outlined briefly what had happened to Gideon and Saul when they were young. He had only heard their story himself when they did their military service together. They had formed an unbeatable quartet: Efraim, Saul, Gideon and Daphne, who became Saul's wife. It was Daphne who had confided in Efraim, explained why Gideon had so many terrible scars on his body, and told him about the role Saul's father had played in the events of the past.

It had been Saul's suggestion that they should call their source on the West Bank after their shared childhood trauma, and no one had objected.

'I did actually know that story and how it had affected Gideon and Saul,' his boss said when Efraim had finished. 'But I didn't know that the residents of the kibbutz had their own nickname for the murderer.'

He sighed, and went on: 'I don't like this. It stinks of revenge, and we can't allow that.'

'Saul and Gideon turned their backs on us,' Efraim said. 'I stayed, but they went away.'

'I know, but we can't set a precedent, looking the other way when someone attacks Israeli citizens in another country.'

'Of course not.'

He waited, wanting the call to end.

'The Paper Boy,' his boss said. 'By which I mean "our" Paper Boy. Do you have any idea where that person is right now?'

'No.'

'Do you think he's involved in these murders?'

'That would involve making the assumption that he's in Stockholm, and I have no reason to believe that he is.'

'But I have,' his boss said, and Efraim froze. 'Or at least I have information indicating that the person in question has travelled to Stockholm on a number of occasions over the past year. And has stayed for quite long periods.'

Breathe in, breathe out.

'I didn't know that.'

'There was no reason why you should. But now things have changed. There's one last thing I want you to do before you leave Stockholm, Efraim. I want you to track down the Paper Boy in order to confirm that he has nothing to do with these murders. Can you do that?'

Efraim sank down on the bed. That was exactly what he had been doing for the past few days.

But the Paper Boy found me before I found him.

'No problem.'

'Good. In that case I shall expect a rapid resolution of the matter.'

'I'll do whatever is necessary,' Efraim said.

'Excellent. If this really is about what happened in Gideon and Saul's childhood, then I shall feel happier. Sorry for their sake, of course, but happier. Otherwise we have a major problem.'

And with those words he ended the call.

Efraim remained sitting on the bed, his mobile in his hand.

The Paper Boy refused to rest, refused to leave him in peace.

Which actually suited Efraim Kiel very well.

Because he had never loved anyone as much.

Like most other people, Eden Lundell had always assumed that when she had children, it would be with the love of her life. Ironically, that was exactly what she had done, in a way.

Because for several years, years she would prefer not to remember, Efraim Kiel had been just that. The biggest thing that had ever happened to her. The most overwhelming love affair. The very thought of how willingly she had accepted him made her feel sick.

She went straight to her office and closed the door when she got in just before lunch. Mondays always involved a long series of meetings, which she loathed. Meetings were for people who didn't have enough to do. Eden's agenda was always packed, and today she had no intention of turning up at a single meeting. She had more important things to think about.

A threat to her family.

Apart from Eden, only one person knew that Efraim was the father of her children.

And that was Efraim himself.

If it was Efraim who had murdered Simon Eisenberg and Abraham Goldmann, there was no reason to assume that he would attack his own daughters. But Eden was convinced the boys had been killed in revenge for the boy who had died on the West Bank, and she couldn't see why that revenge shouldn't encompass Efraim's children too. After all, he had been there too when the boy died in the explosion.

Her heart was racing, exhaustion creating ghosts in her mind.

She told herself to calm down. Reminded herself that the only two people on earth who knew the truth about her daughters were her and Efraim.

Why would he have told anyone else?

And in such a short time.

She took off her jacket. Why could they never get the heating right in this place? Sometimes it was too hot, sometimes too cold. Today it was suffocating.

She ran a finger over one trouser leg, smoothing out a crease.

Her mother's voice echoed faintly in her head:

'*You must always make sure you're neat and tidy, Eden. That will get you a long way in life!*'

As if her mother had got anywhere to speak of.

'*Your life has stood still ever since you got married, Mother dear.*'

An assistant knocked on her door.

'Yes?'

'GD asked us to keep a lookout for you. He expressly said that he wanted to see you as soon as you came in.'

Did he indeed.

'I'll go and see him in a minute.'

The question was what she was going to say to him.

Everything Fred had told her was in confidence; she had to keep it to herself, even if it meant that the investigation ground to a halt. And even if it meant going behind GD's back.

'By the way,' she said to her assistant. 'I'd like you to book one of Säpo's apartments for me, please.'

'Have you joined the ranks of the homeless?' her assistant said with a smile.

Eden forced herself to smile back.

No, I just want to make sure my family has somewhere to hide from a lethal killer.

'We're having some work done at home and we need a place to sleep for the next few days. I'd really appreciate it if you could sort that out for me.'

I'd really appreciate it. Please. Words that Eden often forgot, with predictable results.

Her assistant nodded and disappeared.

Eden followed her out of the office and headed for the lifts. She had decided to tell GD as little as possible. There was no logical reason to think that Efraim had anything to do with the murders; however, it still bothered her that he had been sent to Stockholm at the same time. She just couldn't come up with a satisfactory explanation.

Which left her with another alternative: it really was pure chance that Efraim's visit to Stockholm coincided with the murder of his former colleagues' children.

The problem with that theory was that Eden Lundell didn't believe in chance. Could this be an exception? She realised she had to call Alex, check how the investigation was going. Find out whether he was anywhere near the truth and a solution. It would be an indescribable relief if Alex had discovered a completely different reason behind the murders.

I won't be that lucky.

Eden was standing outside Buster Hansson's office when it struck her.

She was paralysed with shock at the realisation that she had missed the obvious.

The person who had killed Simon and Abraham had also known about the Paper Boy, and left a reference to the source on the West Bank. Which significantly reduced the number of suspects, because source names were classified.

In certain cases not even the source knew what his or her name was within the organisations he or she worked for.

Suddenly she couldn't breathe.

If the killer was someone who knew who the Paper Boy was, then he must be part of Mossad. Therefore, it could be Efraim.

Or the father of one of the boys.

Modern man seemed incapable of grasping or accepting that he always left a trail – electronic if not physical. It was difficult to avoid making mistakes, which was some small consolation for the police; without all those mistakes, many crimes would never be cleared up. Alex Recht knew that only too well.

He heard from Lasse in the tech department less than two hours after they had last spoken.

'You asked about Saul Goldmann's mobile.'

'Yes?' The tension was unbearable.

'You wanted to know where he was when he called Mona Samson's mobile at three o'clock: Karlaplan.'

Alex's chest felt tight. He rubbed his forehead.

'They live near there,' he said. 'Although that doesn't change anything. If he wasn't the one who killed Josephine and picked up the boys, I hope he has a good explanation for why he lied in a police interview.'

'What about his alibi for the morning when the boys were shot?'

Alex thought for a moment. Had they even checked? All the parents had an alibi for the time when the boys went missing, so it hadn't occurred to them to look into what they were doing on the morning of the murders.

Then he remembered.

'We didn't ask for alibis because the fathers were involved in the search, and the mothers were in the community centre, ringing around the boys' friends and classmates.'

'Okay ... Had the parents organised themselves into groups, or were they searching individually?' Lasse wondered.

'Individually.'

'So Saul Goldmann was alone all night and all morning?'

Unfortunately, he was right. Saul could have been doing anything during those hours. Alone in his car. Free to go wherever he wanted. Out to Lovön, perhaps, to set up the murders of his son and his son's friend.

'To be fair, Gideon Eisenberg was alone too,' Alex said. 'But we've got nothing on him. What about Goldmann's phone traffic for the rest of the night?'

'There were lots of calls, of course. He spoke to his wife a couple of dozen times, and to Gideon, and several other people.'

'Did he also speak to Mona Samson?'

Lasse laughed dryly.

'He did. No fewer than five times.'

'And where was she when she took those calls?'

'Kungsholmen.'

They took the boys in the afternoon, Alex thought. Took them somewhere and kept them there overnight. Drove them out to Lovön in the morning. Let them go, one at a time, then hunted them down and shot them.

'I think I know how you believe all this fits together,' Lasse said. 'And I tend to agree with you. I also think Goldmann and Eisenberg have a lot more going on together than they've told us so far. The only problem is that we can't link either of them to Lovön, nor have we found the vehicle that must have been used to transport the boys to the place where they died.'

'And we don't have a murder weapon,' Alex said.

He felt a sense of mounting frustration. The resolution was so close, and yet so far away. What worried him most was the fact that Polly Eisenberg was still missing. His opinion on her chances of survival had shifted slightly; if she had been dead, they would have found her. The ritual of the paper bags was too important to the murderer for him – or her – to miss the chance of displaying the latest victim. If Mona Samson was involved, that could explain her absence.

'What's going on with Samson's phone traffic at the moment?' he asked.

'Her mobile is switched off. Calls aren't being put through, so there's no link to the mast when we try the number.'

There could be a thousand reasons why Mona Samson was unavailable. She could be away. She could be ill. But Alex didn't think that was the case. He was convinced that her radio silence was connected to the murders.

They're up to their ears in crap, and we still can't get to them.

'I'll speak to the prosecutor,' he said. 'I want to bring Saul Goldmann in again.'

He was largely talking to himself; that wasn't something Lasse could help him with.

'Good luck,' his colleague said. 'I'll let you know if Mona Samson switches on her phone.'

'Thanks.'

Alex thought grimly that he could do with all the good luck wishes in the world, because if he summarised the investigation so far, it wasn't just full of holes; it was a huge castle in the air.

They couldn't link any of the suspects to the final crime scene on Lovön.

They had no leads on the vehicles that had been used to pick up Simon and Abraham, and to transport them to the island.

They hadn't found the murder weapon.

All he had was a father who had lied about an alibi, and didn't have one for the time of the murders. Saul Goldmann, who might be having an affair with Mona Samson. Which was the possible motive he had come up with, but it was pretty pathetic for such a speculative crime.

Saul had murdered his own son so that he would be able to spend the rest of his life with Mona Samson. Alex didn't know whether it had been his own idea or Mona's, but that was less important at this stage.

But why kill Simon Eisenberg too? And why take Polly?

To hide the real motive. That kind of thing happened sometimes; a murderer camouflaged one crime by committing several more.

It's too weak, he thought. It won't stand up.

Shit.

At that moment Fredrika called from Israel.

'I'm catching an earlier flight,' she said. 'I'm in a cab on the way to the airport.'

'What time do you land?'

'Eight o'clock this evening. There's a stopover in Zurich. But there are things I need to tell you right away. Saul Goldmann's father was the Paper Boy. He murdered two children and abducted another before he was caught.

Gideon Eisenberg was his last victim, and as a result Saul's father was given a life sentence. And another thing: Saul Goldmann is probably sterile. He wasn't Abraham's biological father.'

If Alex hadn't been holding onto the phone so tightly, he would have dropped it.

'I've just left Tel Aviv,' Fredrika went on. 'There's no company there or anywhere else in the country called Samson SecInt.'

The story that had led to the shooting of the two boys on Lovön came over to Alex as clearly as the colours of a rainbow. Fredrika's account was long and detailed. She wept as she described the meeting with Gideon's parents.

The Paper Boy was not just a myth.

He had existed.

Saul Goldmann was his son.

And Gideon Eisenberg had been his last victim.

'How come they remained friends?' Alex asked.

'I mentioned that to the parents, and they said they weren't sure they would describe their relationship as friendly. According to Gideon's mother, it was as if the events of their childhood created a bond between them that neither was able to break, possibly because of politeness, or sorrow over the past. As far as the move to Sweden is concerned, I got the feeling that something happened when they were in the army, something they can't or won't talk about, and that's why they decided to leave the country. I've no idea why they chose Sweden in particular.'

Alex didn't think he needed an answer to that question. He briefly outlined what he had come up with.

'I was wrong about the motive, but I think I'm right about our killer,' he said.

'I agree. Saul Goldmann is our man. What do we do now?'

There was only one possible response. As if in a trance, Alex turned and gazed out of the window. Even more snow, even lower temperatures.

Where was Polly Eisenberg?

'We go to the prosecutor and we bring in Saul Goldmann.'

'And Mona Samson?'

'I'll put out a call on her. I want an end to this.'

The tempting aroma of coffee found its way into Peder's office. He had just been out, and there was snow on his clothes and in his hair. If it hadn't been so warm in the community centre, he would have been worried about getting sick.

They were still taking plenty of calls from anxious members of the community. The idea of temporarily closing the Solomon school had been discussed, but Peder had advised against it. Instead he had increased security at the school entrance and had held a meeting that morning to go through safety issues with the staff.

Peder Rydh hated being on the outside. And he had probably never been more of an outsider than he was right now. He had heard nothing from Efraim Kiel. Contact with Alex was sporadic. His former colleagues in the National Crime Unit didn't answer when he called.

And yet it was Peder who had cracked some of the key issues in the investigation. If they had listened to him earlier on, they might have had the chance to move Polly Eisenberg to safety before she was taken.

Peder didn't understand the background to what had happened, nor did he know whether the police had any suspects in mind at this stage. They should have, in his opinion, because they were running out of time. He was certain that

Polly didn't have many hours left to live – not if she had been abducted by the same person who had killed her brother.

As far as Peder could see, the idea that they were dealing with two perpetrators was beyond all reasonable doubt, otherwise the timeline just didn't work. Two killers with very different temperaments. One took his time. Planned a structured approach. Abducted his victims, then murdered them at a later stage. The person who had shot Josephine from the roof hadn't had that kind of patience, which worried Peder.

Why had the attempt on Polly Eisenberg's life been so different from the murder of her brother?

Shot in the street, in broad daylight. Protected only by the falling snow.

It just wasn't logical, bearing in mind how the perpetrator had acted the second time he approached Polly. She had been in the park, tobogganing with a friend. Why not try to shoot her there? Or had the killer abandoned his attempts to end her life in front of witnesses after the previous failure?

Peder went into the kitchen to make himself another cup of coffee.

He still believed they were looking for two killers, one who had concentrated on the boys, the other on Polly. Or was it just his imagination? If he thought about how the crimes had actually been carried out, it seemed more likely that whoever had abducted the boys had also taken Polly. Perhaps he or she had disapproved of the actions of the sniper on the roof and decided to go it alone.

But in that case, why hadn't they found Polly?

Her brother had been killed less than twenty-four hours after he disappeared. Peder thought the idea that the perpetrator might have murdered Polly then hidden her body was out of the question. That wasn't how either of the killers operated.

Which meant she was still alive.

He took his coffee back to his office.

If Polly was still alive, it was necessary to ask a difficult question: why wasn't she dead?

Because it was never the intention that anyone other than the boys should die.

Intuition could lead anyone astray, but this time Peder was sure he was right. Polly's abduction just didn't fit in.

The first incident was so neat and tidy, so symmetrical. Two boys of the same age. Both abducted at the same time, both found shot dead in the same place. Polly wasn't part of that picture, unless you took into account the fact that the Goldmanns had only one child. If the aim was to leave both sets of parents childless, then Polly had to be dealt with.

But why such a different MO in each case, if the children were going to be killed with the same gun anyway?

It didn't make sense. It just didn't.

Almost without realising what he was doing, he picked up his phone and with practised fingers found Alex's number.

Alex sounded stressed.

'Peder, I haven't got time to talk right now.'

He could feel the pulse, the adrenalin coming from Alex, and felt a fresh surge of envy. He was so tired of being on the outside.

'I can call back later – it's just an idea I had.'

'You know I'm happy to listen to you, but things are a bit hectic here. Was it something important?'

Peder hesitated, unsure whether what he had to say would qualify as important.

'It's just something that occurred to me. About Polly Eisenberg.'

He noticed a sudden stillness in Alex.

'Tell me.'

Peder put his doubts to one side; he had nothing to lose by saying what he thought.

'I believe she's alive. That's why you haven't found her.'

'Right.'

Alex sounded disappointed, as if he had expected Peder to come up with something better.

'Actually,' he went on, 'I've been thinking along the same lines. That we still have time.'

'You misunderstand me. I don't believe she was meant to die at all.'

'You've lost me,' Alex said. 'You were the one who came up with the idea that the sniper hadn't meant to kill Josephine.'

'Exactly. But I'm wondering if you're looking for two perpetrators, with a different agenda.'

He was already starting to wish he hadn't made the call. His ideas were too premature to share with someone else; they sounded ridiculous when he put them into words.

'A different agenda?' Alex said. 'Peder, if you know who these people are, you have to tell me.'

'Are you crazy? Of course I don't know who they are,' Peder said, his cheeks flushing with a sudden spurt of anger.

What the hell was Alex thinking?

I'm on your side, Alex. I've never been anywhere else.

He tried again.

'I've been thinking about how the different crimes were committed. There was an enormous margin of error for whoever lay on the roof and shot Josephine. The weather was terrible; it was snowing and visibility was poor. Only a real sharpshooter could have taken on a task like that and succeeded.'

He could tell that Alex was listening now.

'Go on.'

Peder went over what he had come up with so far. How well planned the murder of the boys seemed in comparison with the attempt on Polly's life. How strange it was that Polly still hadn't been found.

When he had finished, Alex remained silent for a little while.

'I will get back to you,' he said eventually. 'And I'm glad you called. But right now the evidence is pointing in a different direction.'

'Can you tell me anything?' Peder said, with a certain amount of pessimism; he knew what Alex was going to say.

'Not at the moment, but we'll talk later. Your support has been invaluable, Peder. I won't forget that.'

Peder suddenly realised why Alex sounded so stressed.

'You're about to arrest a suspect, aren't you?'

He heard a rustling sound at the other end of the line.

'I'll call you,' Alex said. 'Bye.'

And he was gone.

Peder sat in his office with his coffee, still convinced that he was right.

Two killers had shared the same gun, but not the same vision. He didn't even want to contemplate what consequences that might have for the way in which the story currently being played out in Stockholm might end.

It was late afternoon by the time the police went to pick up Saul Goldmann. He was under surveillance, so they were well prepared for any sudden movement or an attempt to leave town. But nothing happened; he was arrested at work, where he had been all afternoon.

Alex Recht decided to stay at Police HQ; he was going to conduct the first interview with Saul, and wanted to make sure he was absolutely ready.

Fredrika had written a summary of what Gideon Eisenberg's parents had told her, and she had managed to send it to him before she boarded the plane in Tel Aviv.

Mona Samson was still notable by her absence. Alex was annoyed that she had managed to slip under the radar before they realised she was involved. Perhaps she was hiding wherever they were holding Polly Eisenberg. Perhaps she too was being held against her will. But in that case the question of who had been lying on the roof still remained; it certainly wasn't Saul Goldmann, because he was taller than the indentation in the snow suggested.

At the same time as Saul was being arrested, a search would be carried out at his home and his office. The prosecutor had agreed only when they were able to prove that Saul's mobile had been in Östermalm when Saul claimed he had been in Kungsholmen.

Alex leaned forward, resting his chin on his hand as he made a mental list of what he was hoping they would find.

A pair of size 43 boots. Or something that would reveal how the boys had been transported, perhaps a receipt for a hire car or something similar. Their attempts to find out whether a person by the name of Zalman had rented a car in Stockholm around the time of the murders had proved fruitless.

But most of all Alex wanted to find the murder weapon.

The prosecutor had been very clear. Without a confession or further proof, he would never be able to take it to court.

A confession seemed highly unlikely, but they ought to be able to find further proof.

Otherwise it would be back to square one, and in that case Alex had no idea how they were going to save Polly Eisenberg.

At first glance Saul Goldmann didn't appear to be particularly bothered by the situation, although he had requested the presence of his lawyer throughout the interview.

'Do you understand why you're here?' Alex began.

'Because for some unknown reason you think I killed not only my own son, but his friend as well. It's an utterly ridiculous idea, and I hope we can clear this up as quickly as possible.'

Alex studied him closely.

His facial features were as neat and tidy as the clothes he wore. He seemed to be handling his son's death much better than his wife, who had broken down completely as she watched her husband being led out of the office.

'You say your own son,' Alex said, 'but he wasn't yours, was he?'

He rarely opened an interview with a straight right, but this time he had decided to go for it.

Saul Goldmann couldn't hide his surprise. His lawyer gave him a quizzical look, but said nothing.

'What? Of course he was my son.'

'According to our information, that isn't the case. You had a vasectomy many years ago.'

'I'm sorry, but I really don't see what this has to do with anything.'

'Then you'd better think again, because obviously we are interested in your relationship to the child we suspect you killed.'

Alex could see that Saul was already seething, which was a good thing. Those who lost control were often the easiest to manipulate, even if they would never admit it themselves.

'Abraham was my boy,' Saul said, emphasising every word. 'I loved him deeply, and I am bereft without him.'

His voice held until the very last word, then broke. Alex wasn't sure whether that was down to grief or anger.

'Who's the Paper Boy?' he said.

'You asked me that the last time we met.'

'And now I'm asking you again. Who's the Paper Boy?'

Saul's expression was defiant.

'An Israeli myth.'

'Invented by whom?'

'I have no idea.'

'Who first told you the story?'

'I can't remember.'

'Did he really exist?'

'No, as I've already told you, he was an imaginary figure.'

Alex leaned back in his chair.

'My colleague is currently on her way back from Israel, where she visited the kibbutz where you and Gideon Eisenberg grew up.'

The colour drained from Saul's face.

'Are you sure the Paper Boy didn't exist in reality?'

Saul blinked, but said nothing.

Patience was an undervalued virtue when it came to interviewing a suspect. Alex allowed time to work for him and wondered how long it would be before Saul gave in. As expected, it didn't take many minutes.

'I assume you want me to say that my father was the Paper Boy.'

'Wasn't he?'

'No. It was just something we made up as kids.'

'But he did abduct and kill children?'

Saul sighed.

'Yes.'

'How was he caught?'

There was another long silence, and Saul's expression changed. He scratched his forehead and let out a low groan.

'This is pure fantasy. You know that Gideon was my father's last victim, and you think I attacked his child as an act of revenge. And that I killed my own son as well because I'm not his biological father.'

He shook his head wearily.

Alex refused to lose heart.

'Good guess,' he said. 'But I'm afraid it only covers part of our theory. Where were you when Simon and Abraham disappeared on their way to the tennis centre?'

'I've already told you – in a business meeting with Mona Samson from Samson Security.'

'And where was this?'

'In her apartment on Hantverkargatan.'

'Why were you in the apartment instead of her office?'

'Because I was in Kungsholmen anyway.'

'So she stayed at home rather than going into work, just so that she could meet you?'

'She said she could just as easily work from home.'

'But you've been to the office on Torsgatan?'

'Yes.'

'How did you get to know one another, you and Mona Samson?'

Saul shifted in his seat and glanced at his lawyer, who still hadn't said a word.

'We met at a conference in Brussels last spring.'

Classic.

'How would you describe your relationship?'

Saul's expression grew wary.

'Professional.'

'And that's all?'

'Yes.'

Really?

It was Alex's turn to sigh.

'I'm going to give you one more chance to answer my question. Where were you when Simon and Abraham disappeared on their way to the tennis centre?'

Saul leaned forward across the table.

'I was in Kungsholmen with Mona Samson.'

Alex also leaned forward, meeting Saul halfway.

'How come you rang Mona Samson at three o'clock that afternoon?'

A rapid blink, but otherwise Saul remained impassive.

'I can't answer that.'

'Can't or won't?'

'Can't.'

'Because?'

A thin smile played around Saul's lips.

'Because I'd left my phone at home that day. Abraham might have used it and called the wrong number by mistake. Or it could have been my wife. I don't know, because I wasn't at home.'

Fuck.

But Alex hadn't finished.

'When you called Mona Samson's mobile, it was near the bridge – Djurgårdsbron. Had she also left her phone somewhere?'

The lawyer decided to speak up.

'It's hardly up to my client to explain where Mona Samson's mobile phone was that afternoon.'

Alex backed off.

'Where is Mona Samson at the moment?'

'I haven't a clue.'

'Are you in a relationship with her?'

Saul burst out laughing.

'I'm sorry, are you serious?'

'Yes.'

'Okay, no. No, no, no – I am not in a relationship with Mona.'

The lawyer cleared his throat and looked demonstratively at his watch.

'If this is all you've got, I think we're just about done here,' he said.

Pure rage surged through Alex's body, putting all his senses on full alert. No fucking way was Saul Goldmann getting off so easily.

At that point the interview was interrupted as a colleague knocked on the door and came in.

'Can I speak to you for a moment?' he said to Alex.

Alex got up and left the room.

'This had better be good news,' he said.

'It is. Mona Samson has been in touch. She's retracted her previous statement. Saul Goldmann left her apartment at two o'clock.'

The plane was cruising at thirty thousand feet. Fredrika Bergman was in a window seat, feeling stressed because she wasn't on the spot in Stockholm, where everything was happening, but calmed by the fact that as long as she was in the air, she was isolated from the rest of the world.

With the help of what she had been told by David and Gali Eisenberg, they now had a viable theory.

Saul Goldmann had become the Paper Boy.

He had murdered Abraham, who was not his biological son.

He had also, after waiting for many years, taken his revenge for the loss of his own father when he was a child. That was why he had targeted Simon and Polly Eisenberg, the children of the man responsible for sending Saul's father to prison.

But something was bothering Fredrika; she wasn't completely satisfied with their conclusions. There were still several unexplained loose ends.

Mona Samson, for example. Was she the person on the roof who had shot Josephine? And was it to conceal her involvement that she was hiding behind this peculiar security company that seemed to be little more than a facade?

And then there was the Lion. Who might be Saul Goldmann. Or Efraim Kiel. But if Saul was the Lion, then Fredrika didn't understand why he had chosen to make contact with the boys via email. The Lion was definitely linked to the murders in some way; if she hadn't been convinced before, there was no doubt left in her mind when she found out about the name he had given in one of the internet cafés. Therefore, the exchange of emails must have served a purpose – but what was it, if not to enable him to approach the boys without arousing their suspicion?

Fredrika usually slept whenever she flew, but this time her body rebelled, refused to give in to tiredness.

Because she knew something was wrong.

They had stumbled on something when they started asking the Israeli police questions, and Fredrika couldn't work out what it was. The only thing she knew for sure was they had come too close to information that the state of Israel wished to protect.

There was nothing strange about that; such information exists in every country with self-respect. This time, however, it had jeopardised an important police investigation through a refusal to co-operate. She recalled what Isak Ben-Zwi had said to her: that she wouldn't learn about the Paper Boy on the kibbutz. That she was deluded if she thought she would find what she was looking for there.

He had sounded as if he knew who the Paper Boy was.

But he obviously didn't, because otherwise he would have known that Avital Greenburg had once been called exactly that: the Paper Boy.

Could there be more than one Paper Boy?

Of course not. The whole thing must be a mixture of classified information and a misunderstanding.

Fredrika still couldn't shake off the feeling of unease that was steadily growing stronger.

Evidence was being withheld, for valid or invalid reasons. And that was damaging the investigation, leading them to the wrong conclusions.

Gideon and Saul had lied about their professional background. They had also lied about their reasons for leaving Israel, either because they thought none of this was relevant in the hunt for whoever had murdered their sons, or because they had no choice, regardless of whether they believed that this tragedy was linked to their past.

The latter alternative worried Fredrika more than anything, because it could mean that the parents knew exactly why someone had chosen to murder their children in particular, and that they had decided to handle it themselves, without involving the police.

In which case the drama could well have a more apocalyptic resolution than any of them could imagine.

'The apartment is on Mariatorget. I want you and the girls to go there right away. Pack a bag and get a cab. I'll be there later this evening.'

Eden Lundell was talking as she walked from Säpo HQ to Alex Recht's office in another building.

'Eden, I'm just about to start cooking tea for the girls,' her husband Mikael said wearily. 'What are you talking about?'

Her heart skipped a beat. She didn't have time to be gentle and diplomatic; she just wanted him to do as she said.

'I can't explain what's happened, but we won't be able to stay at home for the next few days. Please do as I say. Get a cab to Police HQ in Kungsholmen and pick up the key in reception, then go to the apartment and wait for me there.'

She would have spoken to Mikael earlier in the day, but hadn't been able to get hold of him. That was fine; the girls were safer in some anonymous day care centre than in the apartment.

Thank God they weren't at the Solomon school.

She heard the sound of clattering in the background, along with her daughters' non-stop chatter.

Eden's everyday life; all too often she was much too small a part of that existence.

'I'll call you when we've eaten,' Mikael said.

Eden stopped dead.

'Mikael, for fuck's sake, this is important. Just do as I say. Get in a cab. You can order pizza when you arrive.'

She had raised her voice because of fear and frustration. It didn't matter if there were only two people in the entire world who knew that Efraim Kiel was the father of her children; right now that was one person too many.

'In that case you need to come home and explain why it's so urgent,' Mikael said. 'Because I am not about to drop everything on some whim of yours.'

Eden could have wept. She hardly ever felt that way, and it frightened her.

'Can't you just do as I say? This is important. Really important.'

Her tone was calmer now, and she had lowered her voice to its normal pitch.

Mikael said something to one of the girls.

'Okay,' he said. 'Okay. But tonight we need to have a proper discussion, because I can't cope with this. You take off on some secret mission, then you call home and want us to turn our lives upside down. You just don't do that. Not if you're a family.'

She nodded eagerly, overwhelmed with relief. She didn't care how angry he was as long as he got out of that apartment.

'Absolutely,' she said. 'We'll talk when I get there. See you later.'

She slipped her mobile into her pocket and ran the rest of the way to Alex's office, straight up two flights of stairs without waiting for the lift. She had called him a little while earlier, and he had said he would be there for fifteen minutes, but no longer.

He was alone at his desk when she walked in.

'Bloody hell, did you run all the way?'

She sat down.

'I read online that the police had arrested the father of one of the boys as a suspect for the murders. Is that true?'

'Yes.'

Alex looked wary, as if he wasn't sure how much he was prepared to tell her.

'May I ask which of them it was, and why?'

Alex glanced at his watch, then folded his arms.

'We've just taken a break in the interview. I need to be back in ten minutes. Would you mind telling me why this is important to you?'

What could she say to that?

'As I told you, Säpo has a certain amount of interest in Efraim Kiel,' she said, choosing her words with care. 'I just want to rule out any additional links to our operations in your investigation.'

It was a weak answer. Why would she have come hurtling over here to find that out?

But Alex didn't seem to have time to ponder such an anomaly.

'Do you remember my asking you about the Paper Boy?' he said.

Eden nodded.

'We now know who he is,' Alex said proudly.

Eden couldn't believe her ears. How was that possible? Surely the Israelis wouldn't have shared such sensitive information with Fredrika Bergman?

'A deranged child killer,' Alex said.

She waited for him to tell her the rest: that the Paper Boy

had been a secret source working for the Israelis, but instead he told her a completely different story.

Fifteen minutes later Eden Lundell was standing on Polhemsgatan, smoking a cigarette.

Two Paper Boys.

Two stories.

Alex's theory was more convincing than hers. It wasn't perfect, but it was better. Kudos to Fredrika for her efforts in Israel. She had found out an astonishing amount in a very short time, information they would never have got from anyone else.

She felt the weight of her mobile in her pocket and thought about calling Mikael again, telling him they could stay at home.

But that would annoy him even more. Mikael wasn't the kind of person who could deal with mixed messages. Better to let them go to the apartment in Södermalm.

Eden stubbed out her cigarette and went inside. It wasn't until she was in the lift on the way back to her office that she realised what she had done. That cigarette was the first one she had smoked since she arrived back in Sweden. She hadn't missed them for several hours.

The decision was made before the lift doors opened.

She yanked the packet of cigarettes out of her pocket, dropped them in the waste bin along with her lighter.

Eden Lundell had smoked her last cigarette.

Interview rooms were always too small. The air was always too stale, the light always a little too bright. They had started the second session, and Alex Recht didn't care if he had to stay there all night. Saul Goldmann was going to start talking, and soon.

'You can carry on telling me you left your phone in your apartment. You can carry on telling me that you can't be responsible for the location of Mona Samson's phone when you called her. But let me make one thing clear: Mona Samson has retracted her previous statement. She says you left her apartment at two o'clock. And guess what? We believe her.'

Alex left the words hanging in the air, waiting for Saul Goldmann's counter-move.

He had changed during the short break. He was a broken man.

'Is she here?' he said. 'Mona – is she here too?'

'No. But you are.'

Mona Samson's whereabouts were still unclear. She had told the police she was on a business trip to Norway; she had called from a different mobile on a withheld number, said if they wanted to get hold of her they could use the number they already had. It would take time to find out the new number and track the location of the phone. After speaking to her they had tried the old number, but the phone was switched off. They had asked her to come to Police HQ at her earliest convenience, but Alex suspected that wasn't going to happen any time soon.

Saul Goldmann held up his hands in a defensive gesture.

'Okay. I lied. I admit it, I lied. But I had nothing to do with Abraham's murder. Nothing at all.'

He swallowed hard, clasped his hands on the table. Looked down and paused for a moment before continuing.

'It's true, Abraham wasn't my biological son. And it's true that my father was the so-called Paper Boy. It was because of him that I had a vasectomy when I was only twenty; I was obsessed with the idea that I might be like him, that I would never be a good parent. It took time to get over what had happened, but my mother made sure I got help. Professional help. When Daphne and I moved in together I tried to have the vasectomy reversed, because I'd heard that was possible. But not in my case.'

He looked very sad.

'They said complications must have arisen, and there was nothing they could do. So we went down the IVF route with donated sperm. It was a mutual decision. We both longed for children, and Abraham was very much a wanted baby when he was born.'

The words simply flowed; no prompting was necessary. Alex listened in silence.

'Daphne and I have been together for over twenty years. There is no woman in the world that I love more, but you know how it is; things get a little . . . dull. That's what happened to us, and then Mona turned up. Very attractive, expressive, vibrant. She worked for an Israeli company in the process of setting up branches in Sweden. Mona is half-Israeli, half-Palestinian. I can't explain why, but I fell for her. Slept with her the first time we met, then carried on in Stockholm.'

He shrugged, looking slightly puzzled, as if he couldn't quite understand why he was telling the police about his private life.

'We met at her apartment last Wednesday. Had some sushi, went to bed. I left at two, but I was so tired I went home and had a sleep. She has that effect on men. You give her what she wants, and you can hardly remember a thing afterwards. When I got home I realised I'd left my iPad in her apartment. That was why I called her, to find out when I could pick it up. Abraham would wonder where it was, and I didn't want to end up in a situation where I had to start coming up with a whole load of explanations. But she was difficult to get hold of, and when I did speak to her she said she was tied up with meetings, and wouldn't be available for the next few days. She sent me the iPad by courier later that evening. Not exactly discreet.'

He changed position on the uncomfortable chair, seeking the right words for what he wanted to say next.

'Although of course nobody reacted to the business with the iPad, because by then we realised that something had happened to Abraham. Daphne went over to the Solomon Community, and Gideon and I began searching for the boys. We started near the tennis centre, then moved further and further away. The police wanted to speak to us, of course, so we had to interrupt the search for a while. And I was in a complete panic.'

Another defensive gesture, and this time he glanced at his lawyer.

'I didn't want to tell anyone why I'd been at home having an afternoon nap when Abraham went missing. I'd told Daphne and my work colleagues that I had a meeting, so I stuck to that and asked Mona to say the same if you contacted her. She was reluctant at first, but I persuaded her that it was the best thing to do. For the sake of the investigation. If you had to waste time following up a lot of unnecessary minor leads, you would lose the rhythm, and might not find the boys.'

Saul's shoulders slumped.

'But that's what happened anyway,' he said.

And that was the end of his account.

Alex remained silent, taking in what he had heard. He felt completely at a loss; he didn't know what to think.

The story worked. Saul Goldmann still lacked a confirmed alibi for the time when the boys disappeared, but Alex knew he was telling the truth. Saul had shown different aspects of his character; the lack of that information had led Alex to judge his reaction to his son's death as abnormal.

But he still had questions.

'Mona Samson – do you have a picture of her?'

'Our relationship isn't, or wasn't, the kind that involves going around with photographs of each other in our wallets.'

No picture. But Alex had a picture. Not of Mona Samson, perhaps, but of the woman who had brought a chrysanthemum to the Solomon Community after Josephine had been shot. And he had brought it with him to the interview room.

'Is this Mona Samson?'

He handed Saul the sketch. Saul gazed at it for a long time.

'Hard to say, but it could be her.'

Alex took back the drawing. 'It could be her' wasn't definitive enough, but it had been worth a try. He changed tack.

'What do you know about her company?'

'The basics. We never actually did business together.'

'Would you be surprised if I told you that the mother company in Israel, which she used to register with the Tax Office, doesn't exist?'

Saul's eyes widened.

'I didn't check,' he said. 'I didn't think it was necessary.'

He was more co-operative now, and Alex wanted to make the most of that.

'Why did you leave Israel in 2002?'

'I've already told you.'

'I'd like you to tell me again. And this time you can cut the crap about the firm you were working for, because we know that both you and Gideon were employed by the Israeli military until you moved.'

Saul's expression changed. His posture grew more erect as he stood guard over his past.

'There are clearly defined limits when it comes to what I can tell you about my professional background,' he said. 'It's true that I was in the Israeli armed forces, but I can't go into which branch or what my work involved.'

'Not even if it has something to do with your son's murder?'

No answer.

'Tell me why you moved.'

'Because of something that happened on duty. An accident, you could say. Both Gideon and I had had enough after that. The risks and the level of personal commitment were too great. We were both going to become fathers, and in 2002 Israel was literally in flames. A cavalcade of suicide bombers had turned the country into hell on earth, and the Israeli counter-offensive wasn't exactly moderate, of course. But we just wanted to get out of there, so we moved to Stockholm. We had both been here before, and knew one or two people. We thought we would be able to establish ourselves in Sweden, and we were right.'

'Efraim Kiel – how well do you know him?'

'You've asked me that before as well. Efraim has the same background as me and Gideon. And Daphne. We worked together. But he chose to stay, both in Israel and in the military. I have no idea what he's doing these days.'

'Have you had any contact with him while he's been in Stockholm?'

'No.'

'Do you think he has anything to do with the deaths of Simon and Abraham?'

For the first time Saul dropped the mask completely.

'Efraim? No, definitely not. Why would he do such a thing?'

Suddenly Alex had had enough.

'That's my fucking point! *Why would someone do such a thing to you and Gideon?* I don't believe for a moment that you have no idea.'

Saul's reaction was not what Alex had expected. He became completely calm. Relaxed a fraction, looked Alex straight in the eye.

'Of course I have an idea,' he said. 'What astonishes me is that you apparently don't.'

Alex felt control shift over to Saul, and there was nothing he could do about it. Saul realised what was happening, and grew in stature.

'I was intending to deal with the matter myself, but if you'd like to help, then of course I would welcome your input.'

Deal with the matter myself?

'Gideon,' Saul said, uttering the name like a swear word. 'Have you put the same energy into checking his alibi as you did with mine?'

Alex would like to think that was the case, but he didn't know.

'Yes,' he said.

'Liar!'

Saul Goldmann slammed his fist down on the table.

'You've done no such thing. Gideon said he was in meetings all afternoon, but that's not true. When I was driving home from Kungsholmen, after I'd been with Mona, I saw him walking along Strandvägen and turning off onto Nybrogatan. It was about twenty past two. I asked him about it, but he said I was mistaken, and that he'd been in a meeting with the bank then. No fucking way – I saw him from the car!'

Alex's mouth went dry. This couldn't be true. How many false alibis could these two come up with?

'We'll double check what you say, but I'm not expecting to find anything,' he said, well aware of how feeble it sounded.

But Saul hadn't finished.

'Do you know why we don't hang out together any

more? Because we couldn't have him around once we had a child. Gideon had more reasons than I did to leave Israel. There were rumours that he had been so damaged by what had happened to him that he had started molesting boys – hitting them, threatening them with knives. Now do you understand? I defended him, said it was slander. But then I saw him with a young boy one night when we were in a bar in Tel Aviv. And when I say a young boy, I mean a child who hadn't yet reached puberty. They were standing out in the street, and it looked as if Gideon was trying to give him money, but the boy ran away. After that I was more careful.'

Alex saw a chance to regain the upper hand.

'But you let Abraham and Simon spend time together.'

'Never at their house, unless Carmen was at home.'

'So you think Gideon murdered both your son and his own? Because he is so damaged by what happened to him as a child?'

Saul's eyes filled with tears.

'You should see him without clothes. My father made a good attempt at turning his skin into a patchwork quilt. I think he said he has over fifty scars. You can't go through something like that and remain sane. It's just not possible.'

The tears spilled over, and Saul dashed them away.

'That night when we were searching for the boys, I saw Gideon. He was sitting in his car, staring into space. He had parked near the television centre. Do you know how many times I drove past him? Five. He sat there all night; he never moved.'

Alex went cold inside.

'And Polly?' he said. 'What has he done with Polly?'

'The question you should be asking is why she's not dead,' Saul said.

Alex didn't understand.

'It's not Gideon who's taken her – it's Carmen. Because she knows what a sick bastard she's married to, and she's hidden the only child she has left.'

It was evening. Efraim Kiel suddenly realised he was kicking up the snow as he walked along; he had seen small children doing it, and he could understand why.

His heart was heavy as he remembered other children's feet that had made the snow swirl up. Bare feet that grew cold, weakening their bodies.

He was a man with no religious conviction. Everything he had done throughout his life had been based on his own internal compass, his own perception of what was right and wrong, good and evil. The occasions when he felt with hindsight that he had done the wrong thing were few.

It took him only a few minutes to walk from the hotel to the address on Torsgatan where he had seen the woman enter the building. And this time neither Säpo nor the police were there. He peered into the dark stairwell. No movement out on the street or inside the building. He assumed the block housed mainly offices, which were now empty. Most people had probably set off home through the darkness.

To make dinner, or see what was on TV.

Put the children to bed, if they had any.

Things that Efraim knew others did, while he travelled far and wide to make sure that his people were safe and secure.

The light came on; someone was on their way out.

Excellent. He wouldn't have to waste time trying to break in.

A young woman emerged, smiling at Efraim as she held the door open for him. He smiled back and quickly stepped inside. Allowed the door to close behind him.

The noise was unexpectedly loud.

Efraim set off up the stairs. If he had read the plaque by the door correctly, the office of Samson Security AB was on the third floor.

Samson.

Her new surname. It suited her; she had always admired the lion for its strength and invincibility.

Efraim took two steps at a time. Increased his speed, reducing the distance between them. If she was in the apartment, of course, which he thought unlikely.

But oh, how he wished she was.

Then he was standing outside her door. He rang the bell and waited. No one came. He rang the bell again. Waited again.

She obviously wasn't there.

He took out the necessary equipment to open the door, and in seconds he was in the hallway. He smiled in the darkness. Anyone who knew anything about locks would realise immediately that this couldn't possibly be a company that specialised in security.

He didn't switch on the main light; instead he went over to the windows behind the desks to see if they had curtains. Indeed they did; she hadn't missed that detail. You had to be able to turn on the light without anyone being able to see it from outside.

Efraim was virtually certain that no one was following him, but just in case he'd got it wrong, he wanted to make sure he minimised any possible damage.

Once the curtains were drawn, he switched on the desk lamp. He glanced around the room. Took in the sparse furnishings and thought that with such an unimpressive facade he would be surprised if she'd managed to attract a single client.

There was a computer on one of the desks. Presumably the police hadn't had a warrant to remove it.

Efraim started it up and went through the files on the bookshelf while he waited. Empty. He laughed out loud, then sat down and grew serious, reminding himself that he didn't have much time. Because he had one more job to do before he went to bed.

He was going to pay Fredrika Bergman a visit.

Make sure she understood the importance of not getting mixed up in things that had nothing to do with her.

Every war claimed its victims.

As far as Efraim was concerned, no war had been more significant than the one in which he was engaged right now. And he was ready to do whatever it took to emerge victorious from the conflict.

The computer turned out to be just as easily accessible as everything else in the room. No password was required. He clicked his way around the system. The police would probably have needed some time to realise how empty the document files were, if they had opened them, because everything was written in Hebrew.

There was no internet connection.

No word processing program.

It was rare that anyone made such an effort to embrace the minimalist approach.

He moved over to the document handling program. To his surprise he found an ordinary text file there.

Efraim felt as if he had suddenly developed tunnel vision when he read the name of the file.

'To Samson'.

He knew that this time he was the lion.

He didn't hesitate; he had to see what she had written. He opened the document, read the short lines she had left behind in the empty office.

> I have seen the girl
> I know who she looks like.
> You said you suffered as much as I did.
> But that's impossible.
> You went on to have two more children.
> Congratulations.

Efraim couldn't take his eyes off the screen. He read the words over and over again.

She had seen the girl.

Realised she was his.

But I didn't know.

Efraim read the message one last time, then deleted the file. She hadn't written one word about Polly, who had disappeared. Just his two newly discovered daughters.

As he left the building on Torsgatan, he thought about what that meant.

It was only when he was back in his hotel that he realised what she was telling him.

The knowledge made him go weak at the knees; he had to sit down on one of the sofas in the lobby.

Not only had Efraim deprived her of the victim she had selected.

He had also provided her with two new ones.

Sometimes Mikael Lundell thought that Eden lived in a parallel universe.

One which bore no relation to his or anyone else's.

'Pack a bag and get a cab.'

They had two children, one of whom suffered from a number of allergies. You couldn't just pack a bag and take off. You had to plan, work things out.

This time Mikael had got it all wrong. He had abandoned the cooking and started packing, which had been a mistake. The girls were hungry, and they were also starting to get tired, while Mikael himself was so furious he felt like standing in the middle of the floor and screaming.

Why was there never any peace and quiet?

Why did Eden constantly come up with new ways of stressing out her family?

Tops and trousers, underwear and pyjamas. Comfort blankets and toys.

A furious yell from the kitchen sent him hurtling through the apartment.

Dani was sitting on the floor sobbing hysterically. Her sister was standing next to her, patting her on the head. Blood was pouring from Dani's forehead.

'She fell over,' her sister said, pointing to the angular edges of the table leg.

Mikael picked her up, as always astonished at how light she was, even though she had been alive for such a long time.

He examined the cut on her head. Did it need stitches? No. Had she knocked out any teeth? No.

'Does your head hurt?'

Dani howled something that might have been a yes.

'Do you feel sick?'

Apparently not. He carried her to the bathroom where he had started packing a toilet bag. He cleaned the cut, found a plaster with a bear on it. When Dani had calmed down, Mikael carried her back to the kitchen. Both girls were obviously tired, and kept glancing over at the stove; Daddy had promised to cook their favourite tea.

Fuck Eden and her whims and fancies.

'Okay girls, guess what we're going to do?'

Two expectant little faces.

'We're going to order pizza and eat it here before we leave. What do you think about that?'

Their eyes lit up. Mikael picked up the phone; he had no intention of leaving the apartment until the girls had food in their stomachs.

Half an hour later, the pizzas still hadn't arrived. Mikael called the restaurant again, and was told the pizzas had been sent out.

'But they're not here,' he said, unable to hide the irritation in his voice.

He threw down the phone and went back into the kitchen.

'I'm sorry everything's such a mess,' he said to the girls. 'Daddy will fix us something to eat.'

He took some mince out of the fridge. They would have spaghetti Bolognese as planned, and if Eden had a problem with that, she could bloody well come home from work.

Yet another alibi had cracked like a window pane hit by a stone. This time it was Gideon Eisenberg's.

Getting hold of someone with access to the bank's database of clients and visitors wasn't easy, particularly at seven o'clock in the evening.

'I don't care how they do it,' Alex Recht bellowed. 'This is an emergency. We need that information.'

Eventually they managed to contact an administrator who was still on the premises and was able to access the list of clients. She then called Alex personally to confirm that Gideon Eisenberg had indeed had a meeting with a deputy manager at the bank between two thirty and four thirty the previous Wednesday, just as he had said.

'Do you know whether the meeting actually took place, or whether it was just booked in?' Alex wanted to know.

'You mean could it have been postponed?'

'Yes.'

'Unfortunately I can't tell from the records; sometimes staff forget to make a note if a meeting is cancelled or postponed.'

'In that case I want to speak to the manager in question. Right now.'

The administrator realised the seriousness of the situation, and said that she would contact her colleague immediately and ask him to call the police.

Alex's phone rang a few minutes later.

'I have a very simple question,' he said. 'According to your admin staff, Gideon Eisenberg was in a meeting with you at the bank between two thirty and four thirty last Wednesday. Can you confirm that the meeting actually took place?'

The answer came immediately.

'No, it was postponed. Did I forget to make a note in the visitor database?'

Yes you did, you fucking idiot.

'Why was the meeting postponed?'

'Gideon rang and said he was ill.'

Alex ended the call with a brief thank you, and ran out into the corridor. He gathered his colleagues in the Snakes' Nest. They listened as he explained the latest twist in the case.

'We need to bring in Gideon and Carmen Eisenberg,' he said. 'Right away.'

He thought he ought to call Peder, tell him he was partly right: someone else had taken Polly.

He wished Fredrika was there. She would have been a godsend when it came to interviewing Carmen, but then again she could do that when her plane landed. It wouldn't do any harm for Carmen to sit and wait.

'Are we sure that Gideon is the guilty party?' one of his colleagues said. His expression said it all; he was far from sure.

'No,' Alex said. 'But we now know that he doesn't have an alibi. And we have Saul's account, which I'm inclined to believe. So we have to bring Gideon in; anything else is out of the question.'

They were out of the Snakes' Nest as quickly as they had assembled there.

Alex went in one of the cars to the Eisenbergs' apartment in Östermalm. Sitting in his office waiting from them to return wasn't an option; there was too much adrenalin coursing around his body.

He texted Diana from the back seat:

'Will be late again. Love you. See you later.'

The car skidded on the snow which had not yet been cleared from the road. They were driving insanely fast, blue lights flashing, sometimes in the wrong lane facing the oncoming traffic. A younger colleague was at the wheel, still hungry for the kicks everyone thought were a daily part of police work, but which in fact very rarely came along.

They couldn't go fast enough for Alex. He was convinced they were running out of time.

They raced along Strandvägen towards Djurgården, then turned onto Styrmansgatan. As they passed the theatre and Nybrogatan, Alex thought about Peder, and his idea that they were looking for two perpetrators who were at odds.

Alex wasn't sure he understood what Peder meant. At this stage he wasn't even convinced they were looking for two perpetrators. Gideon Eisenberg was no taller than one metre seventy; he could easily have been the person who lay on the roof and shot Josephine, then worn shoes that were too big for him out on Lovön. The CSIs had said that while it looked as if the boys had slithered and stumbled in the snow, the killer's tracks were even and controlled. That could work if he had been wearing oversized shoes, making him move more slowly.

They had found absolutely nothing when Saul Goldmann's

office and apartment were searched. No murder weapon, no shoes. Alex hoped they would have more success with Gideon Eisenberg.

They pulled up half a block away. No one had forewarned the Eisenbergs; they had just assumed Gideon and Carmen would be at home.

Which they were, fortunately. Carmen answered the door, and Alex and two colleagues stepped into the hallway. Carmen was paler than any living person Alex had ever seen.

'Have you come to see Gideon?' she whispered.

Alex nodded.

'He's in the living room.'

They walked through the wide hallway to the living room door, and stopped dead.

'I found him when I got home.'

Carmen's voice was barely audible.

Gideon was hanging from a hook on the ceiling. Someone had taken down the chandelier and hanged him with a noose. CSI and forensics would determine if he had done it himself, but that was Alex's instinctive reaction.

'He left this.'

Carmen handed him a sheet of white paper.

'It was on the kitchen table.'

Alex took the paper and read the brief message.

Forgive me.

The plane landed twenty minutes ahead of schedule. The passengers got to their feet as soon as it stopped moving, and Fredrika Bergman took out her mobile phone. Her first call was to Spencer; she missed his voice. Missed being close to him.

I'm home, darling.

He still sounded hoarse:

'That was a short trip.'

'It was no fun without you, so I hurried home to Sweden.'

He laughed quietly.

'Did you manage to play your violin?'

Fredrika thought about the instrument she had taken with her; she hadn't played it once.

'The trip would have been a complete fiasco without it.'

Spencer laughed again, but subsided in a fit of coughing.

'Will you be home soon?' he said eventually.

'I won't be long, but I just have to call in at work first.'

How many times had she said that over the past few days? Feeling incredibly guilty, she called Alex. He answered right away, and she listened to what he had to tell her without saying a word.

They had arrested Saul Goldmann.

Gideon Eisenberg had hanged himself.

And Carmen had been taken to the custody suite at Kronoberg.

'I'd like you to interview her,' Alex said. 'There's a chance she might know where Polly is.'

'If that's the case are we really going to lock up the only person who knows where she is?'

'Too bloody right we are, to put her under pressure, if nothing else. Besides, I don't believe Carmen is the only person who knows where Polly is. You don't just leave a five-year-old; she has to be with another adult. And don't forget, Carmen and Gideon were with us when their daughter went missing, so if she is involved, she must have had help.'

Fredrika was picked up by a patrol car at the airport, and driven into the city with blue lights flashing. She had never made the trip from Arlanda at such speed. Trees and buildings were lost in a blur. She sat in the back seat, trying to gather her thoughts and work out what she wanted to ask Carmen Eisenberg.

Where is your daughter?

Where have you hidden her?

She thought about David and Gali Eisenberg in Israel, and wanted to weep. Now they had lost not only a grandchild, but their son too.

It was more difficult to drive fast once they reached the city. The streets had still not been cleared properly, and the car skidded several times. Eventually they arrived, dropped Fredrika off outside the entrance on Kungsholmsgatan and sped away.

She picked up her bags and went inside, into the warmth.

Alex was in his office. He got up and gave her a hug. Held her tight, as if he wanted proof that she had survived the trip.

'Can you cope with this?' he asked.

'No problem. I'll just take off my coat.'

Her office looked exactly as she had left it a few days earlier. The next time she went to Israel she would stay longer. The sense of being away had already left her; the only thing on her mind now was how to begin the interview with Carmen.

'What kind of shape is she in?' she asked Alex on the way down to the room where Carmen was waiting.

'She's in shock.'

Which was only to be expected when someone had lost her son and her husband within a week.

Alex was going to sit in on the interview, which was a good thing; Fredrika wasn't sure if she could remember all the details he had given her.

Carmen was a shadow of the woman Fredrika had met before.

Pale and gaunt.

She had never seen a more weary expression.

'How are you feeling?' Fredrika asked when she had sat down.

Carmen didn't answer immediately. This isn't going to work, Fredrika thought. We're going to have to ring the emergency psychiatric service and take her over there.

'Terrible,' Carmen said. 'I feel terrible.'

'We understand that, but as I'm sure you realise, we have questions to which we need answers. Right away.'

Silence.

'When did you find Gideon?'

'When I got home from work. I was only in the office for a few hours. I couldn't stay there. People just sat there staring at me; they didn't know what to say.'

'A lot of people find it difficult to deal with another person's grief,' Fredrika said. 'Which means they sit and stare instead. What time did you get home?'

'Five o'clock.'

Which meant she had been alone with the body for over two hours.

'You didn't try to get him down? To save him?'

'No.'

'Why not?'

'Because I could see that he was dead. I've seen dead bodies before.'

'So what did you do?'

Carmen ran a hand through her hair. She looked as if she was about to burst out crying, but had run out of tears.

'I don't really remember,' she said. 'I went and sat on the sofa. Looked at him. Kept him company.'

Fredrika was edging her way forward, unsure of how to move on.

'Were you surprised when you found him?'

'Not really. Gideon hasn't been feeling too good. He never has, to be honest. You know what happened to him when he was a child?'

Fredrika nodded, and Carmen looked relieved. No doubt she was glad to be spared the ordeal of putting the indescribable into words.

'I don't think he was ever normal after that. When we met I didn't notice it at first, and we had so much in common. Fun. We had fun. I saw the scars when he took off his clothes, of course; there were so many of them, like the runs in an anthill, all over his skin. But he said he was okay, he told me he'd had help. It wasn't until we had children that he changed.'

'In what way?'

'He suffered from periods of depression. He was never really happy; he always seemed anxious and miserable. Overprotective. He got worse and worse, in spite of the fact that we were living in Sweden, where I thought we could feel perfectly safe.'

Fredrika remembered what Saul Goldmann had said, according to Alex: that Gideon had shown an interest in young boys.

'You didn't suspect that Gideon had been damaged in other ways by what had happened to him – psychologically, I mean?'

Carmen looked blank, then she got angry.

'I know what you're talking about. There were rumours that he liked little boys, but none of that was true. It was just something Saul spread around. He's the very antithesis of a good friend. He's a complete bastard.'

'Why would Saul say such a thing if he didn't believe it was true?'

'How should I know? To turn the spotlight on someone else, perhaps. A lot of people looked at Saul and wondered if he had emerged unscathed from his own childhood, or if he was as sick as his father. But there was nothing wrong with Gideon, not in that way. That wasn't what Saul's father subjected him to.'

Fredrika decided to change the subject.

'Do you know where Gideon was when the boys went missing?'

Once more Carmen was silent.

'I know he said he was at the bank,' she said after a little while. 'But he wasn't.'

'No?'

'No, he'd gone for a walk.'

Fredrika and Alex looked at one another.

Gone for a walk?

'At least that's what he told me,' Carmen whispered. 'And I believed him, because he often did that to shake off a migraine. But we didn't think you would understand, or believe him, so we agreed to say he'd been at the bank as arranged.'

Carmen took a sip of water from the glass in front of her.

Alex stepped in.

'Carmen, do you know where Polly is?'

She gave a start.

'Polly? No, how ... Why are you asking me that? Polly's missing!'

Indeed she is.

'Perhaps you were afraid of losing her too,' Fredrika said. 'So you hid her away?'

Carmen shook her head so violently that Fredrika was afraid she might hurt herself.

'No, no, no! No, I don't know where my Polly is!'

She started crying, quietly at first, then louder and louder. Until the crying became a scream, filling the entire room.

'Please, help me. Help me to get my daughter back. Because I don't know what I'll do if I lose her too.'

Fredrika and Alex exchanged despairing glances. They were in agreement.

Carmen didn't know where Polly was.

And nor did they.

CONCLUSION

It wasn't the coldest evening he had ever experienced, but it was the longest. He was hidden in the shadows behind the entrance to the underground station, which gave him a clear view of the stairs he was watching. If everything went as expected, he would soon have company. The thought of what he had to do filled him with horror.

It was only a question of time before she appeared.

Nadia.

The woman who had been recruited by Efraim for Mossad as a secret source on the West Bank. Who had been known as the Paper Boy. And who had given birth to Efraim's child.

Benjamin.

He had reached the age of ten by the time he rushed into a house and activated an explosive device hidden under the floor.

He had been running away from Gideon and Saul, while Efraim stood to one side, phoning for reinforcements. He had never been able to forgive Gideon and Saul for what they had done. He had sworn that one day they would pay. The fact that they didn't know Benjamin was his son and therefore wouldn't understand why their sons had to die was irrelevant. Revenge was still necessary.

It had seemed so simple. If Efraim Kiel looked back, he had

made only one mistake: he had told her what he intended to do.

'Next year a decade will have passed,' he had said. 'And then I am going to go to Stockholm and end the lives of Gideon and Saul's sons, in return for what they did to Benjamin.'

He had wanted to leave Gideon's second child, Polly, out of the whole thing.

And that was where it had all gone wrong.

Because Efraim had told Nadia, who called herself Mona Samson these days, that there was another child. And she wanted him to take both, because she had no children left. The discussion had turned into a full-blown quarrel, but he had thought he had emerged as the victor. Until the day he received a message from the Paper Boy at his hotel.

He had been stupid. Unbelievably stupid. He realised that now. He had sent her a message before he left Israel, said he was on his way to Stockholm to put things right. That his plans were in place, the time had come.

He had hoped the message would bring her peace.

But it hadn't.

She must have put a considerable amount of effort into her own preparations. Set up a new identity, created a dummy company. And, if you believed the media reports that had reached Israel by now, she had also embarked on a relationship with the father of one of the dead boys. They didn't mention her name, but Efraim knew.

Nadia with Saul or Gideon. The very thought made him feel sick.

It couldn't be true.

Efraim's preparations had been rigorous and time consuming. He had got in touch with the boys via Super Troopers, an online forum he had heard about on a visit to Stockholm the previous autumn. If he hadn't found them there, he would have contacted them some other way. He wanted to make sure they came along voluntarily the day he abducted them; he didn't want to kill them on the spot. That would destroy half the point of the murders.

The rest of the operation had been relatively simple. Getting away from Lovön after shooting the boys hadn't been a problem; the response from the authorities had been anything but rapid. The tracks left by the wheels of the van had obviously failed to lead the police in any particular direction, which didn't really matter anyway. The vehicle had been stolen and fitted with false number plates. He had also used a car for the abduction itself, because he thought the boys would be less inclined to go with a stranger driving around in a van. Everything was possible, as long as you had patience.

But it seemed that Nadia hadn't given up on the idea that Gideon deserved to lose both his children. At first Efraim couldn't work out how she knew where he was staying, then he remembered that he had mentioned the Diplomat. A long, long time ago, when Benjamin was still alive and they still had a viable relationship. The first time Efraim visited Stockholm.

'It's right by the water,' he had said. 'You can see boats when you look out of the window.'

Why the hell had he gone back there?

The simple answer was that he liked it. The staff didn't ask unnecessary questions, and they already knew him by the alias he usually used.

Unfortunately Nadia had also stumbled upon his alias; she had once heard him on the phone, booking a flight. He hadn't noticed her until he had hung up. He should have thought about that incident when he was planning his trip to Stockholm, and he cursed his own carelessness. If she hadn't known his alias, she wouldn't have been able to play her little game.

He had been surprised that she had gone to the hotel and left him a message, but that was nothing compared to the fact that she had got into his room and found the gun he had acquired in order to kill the boys. He had trained her well in the skills needed to survive as a source on the West Bank for over ten years, and now he was paying a high price. She wasn't a good enough shot to hit a small child from that distance, and as a consequence she had shot a teacher instead.

If only she had said something.

Then he would have got rid of the gun immediately, used a different one to shoot the boys.

Instead he had to live with the fact that all three victims had been shot with the same gun.

Whatever – they would never find it. It was resting safely at the bottom of the Baltic Sea.

A far more serious problem was his decision to save Gideon's daughter, and that was only possible if he took her away. Therefore, Efraim had kidnapped Polly when she was in Tessin Park with her friend and the friend's parents. He had given her a sedative, and she had been hidden in the van when he drove onto the ferry that would take him to Finland. The same van he had kept the boys in overnight on Lovön; he had to get rid of it anyway.

In Helsinki he had had to push the boundaries, make use

of contacts he had developed through his job, contacts who agreed to look after the child until the danger was over. And to get rid of the van.

Perhaps he had already realised by that stage that he couldn't stop the avalanche that had been set in motion. That it would crush everything in its path.

Including himself.

Suddenly he saw someone approach the doorway, peer inside, then step back.

The darkness swallowed her up before he had time to react, but he knew he hadn't been mistaken. He wasn't the only one watching the apartment block. Nadia was there too.

Efraim hunched his shoulders against the cold and waited for Nadia the Paper Boy's next move.

Another late night at the office. It was almost half past nine. Shit. She really had meant to leave earlier, join her family in the temporary apartment. Not waste time in yet another meeting with GD, whose imagination appeared to be running riot about what she had been up to during her brief absence.

'So you're saying that Efraim Kiel has nothing to do with the murders?' he said again.

'In my opinion,' Eden Lundell replied.

Yet again. They had already gone over all this at lunchtime, but GD had insisted on another meeting. Säpo had been closely following the police investigation into the murders.

'But you're not prepared to tell me what that opinion is based on?'

'I can't. I'm sorry.'

GD was starting to look annoyed, which wasn't a good sign. Eden was too tired to argue in a civilised manner. She had spent hours catching up with work since she got back from London, and now she just wanted to go home. She had also spoken to Alex Recht and Fredrika Bergman. The case had taken a new turn; it seemed that Gideon Eisenberg was the guilty party, and he had hanged himself in his own living room.

Fucking coward.

She was ashamed to admit that she felt a certain sense of peace at the thought that he was gone. At least he wouldn't claim any more victims, thank God. Everything could get back to normal.

Or not.

Because Eden had made a decision. She had stopped smoking for good. A habit was a weakness, and she couldn't afford any sign of frailty. And she was going to go on holiday with her family in March. The girls would soon be starting school, and there would no longer be any room for that kind of spontaneity.

'I'm taking a week off in March,' she said. 'A family holiday.'

'I didn't think you went in for that kind of thing,' GD said.

'I do now.'

She didn't even have the energy to sound defensive.

'Okay, so if Efraim Kiel has nothing to do with the murders, then why can't we find him?'

'Because he's better than us. Because he doesn't want to be found.'

'Why not? What's he doing that he doesn't want us to see?'

How was Eden supposed to know that?

'I've no idea.'

'Mossad have got a nerve if they've started up a new operation in Stockholm,' GD said. 'I was very clear about our views on unauthorised intelligence activities.'

Eden suppressed a sigh.

'He could be keeping a low profile for personal reasons. There doesn't have to be a Säpo-related reason why he doesn't want to be under permanent surveillance.'

GD's expression was grim.

'I'd feel better if we hadn't lost the woman who was following him as well. Did I tell you we tracked her down to a place on Torsgatan? An office block.'

'No, you didn't.'

Eden was only half listening; in her mind she was already at home with Mikael.

Things will be different from now on. I promise.

'In that case I haven't mentioned that we haven't seen her since. She just disappeared. Went into the building and never came out again.'

'I assume she used a different exit. Or our surveillance guys missed her. That kind of thing does happen.'

GD ignored her comments. Eden wondered how come GD was better informed about the latest surveillance reports than she was. Officially Efraim Kiel's case was being handled by the counter-espionage unit, but GD was obviously following developments in minute detail – possibly because he, unlike the head of counter-espionage, knew that she and Efraim had been an item.

'We've been watching the block on Torsgatan,' he went on. 'The strange thing is, they said they were almost certain they saw police officers enter the building today, but our guys decided against making themselves known.'

Eden was immediately alert.

'Were they from Alex Recht's team?'

'I don't know. Counter-espionage were supposed to check as discreetly as possible, but I haven't heard from them.'

Of course not. Eden couldn't think of anyone who worked more slowly than the counter-espionage unit. Impatiently she took out her mobile and called Alex. GD raised an eyebrow, but said nothing.

'Alex, it's me, Eden. Sorry to bother you again, but I'm just wondering if your team has been involved in an operation on a property on Torsgatan over the last couple of days.'

She listened in silence to Alex's response.

Then sat for a long time with the phone on her knee.

Lost for words.

Back to square one.

'The woman who's following Efraim is wanted in connection with the murder inquiry,' she said eventually. 'They think her name is Mona Samson, and that she was in a relationship with the father of one of the boys. Some of that information has already been leaked to the media.'

'How does Recht know she's shadowing Kiel?' GD said in surprise.

'He doesn't, but as far as I can see we must be talking about the same woman.'

She was almost grinding her teeth in frustration.

What is it I'm not seeing? What is it that we're all missing?

Alex had mentioned that they could be looking for two separate perpetrators. If Mona Samson was the person who had helped Gideon Eisenberg, she was still out there. And she was a threat to Eden and her family.

But how would she know that Efraim had two children?

'I have to go home right now,' she said firmly. 'We can talk about this in the morning.'

'Good idea. Try to get some rest – you look tired.'

Eden felt her knees crack as she got to her feet. She was back in her office pulling on her coat when Mikael rang.

'Where are you?'

'I know, I'm late. But I'm on my way right now, and I've got lots of good news.'

She picked up her bag and Dani's new violin.

'Sounds promising,' Mikael said. 'We could certainly do with some good news here; it's been one hell of an evening.'

'I'm really sorry you had to leave in such a rush. But it will only be for tonight, if that's any consolation; we can move back home tomorrow.'

'Eden, we're not in the other apartment. We're still at home.'

She stopped dead.

'What?'

'Everything went wrong, and the girls were absolutely worn out.'

She wasn't listening any more. Fear flooded her body. Not because something had happened, but because she was thinking about what could have happened.

'For fuck's sake, Mikael, this is serious. You have to do as I say when I ring and . . .'

'No, I don't,' he interrupted her, sounding furious. 'If it's so important, then you can bloody well come home like a normal person, explain what's going on instead of creating havoc like you did this afternoon.'

At that moment Eden heard a sound in the background.

A sound she couldn't place.

It came again.

The doorbell.

The doorbell.

'Mikael, don't open the door!'

'It's only the pizzas I ordered about a hundred years ago. I got so angry when they didn't arrive that they promised to send them over for free. We can have them with a glass of wine when you get home.'

She heard his footsteps moving through the apartment.

'Mikael, I mean it. Tell them to leave the pizzas outside the door. Don't open it!'

'For pity's sake, Eden. I'm not going to frighten the life out of a pizza delivery boy just because you're paranoid.'

She set off again. Started to run.

'Please, Mikael, please . . .'

'Eden, it's the pizzas. He's got the boxes in his hand. Love you, see you later.'

He was gone, leaving her alone.

Pizza.

Of course he was right.

Of course it was the pizza delivery boy.

She called him back.

Her heart was pounding like a jack hammer.

Unnecessarily.

The pizzas had arrived, Mikael had just opened a bottle of wine and was about to lay the table.

A stray tear of pure relief trickled down her cheek, and she dashed it away.

'By the way, can you pick up some milk on the way home? I've just noticed we've run out.'

'No problem.'

She decided to call in at an ICA supermarket that she knew was open late. There was always a queue, but it didn't matter. After all, she wasn't in a hurry any more.

Everything was under control.

He was running out of patience. Something had to happen soon. She had to show herself again, and next time he wouldn't miss her. He couldn't, because otherwise he knew it would be too late.

Efraim Kiel had believed he had a well thought out plan. If he hadn't been given the task of recruiting a new security chief for the Solomon Community in Stockholm, he would have found another reason to come to Sweden.

Because now it was time to put things right.

Time to wreak the revenge he and Nadia had spent ten years waiting for.

Nadia, the amazing woman he had managed to recruit as a Mossad informant. A Palestinian woman whose great secret was that her father had been an Israeli Jew; her mother had never told anyone else.

Nadia had been recruited because of her husband. She was married to a man the Israelis suspected of being involved in Palestinian terrorist activities. Not only involved; he had been one of the operational leaders. Nadia had had integrity; she wouldn't sell out just any Palestinian to the Israeli side, but the fact was that the man she had fallen in love with and married had deceived her. He wanted to pursue an armed battle against the Israeli occupying forces, which she was happy to go along with. But not if the violence was directed exclusively at the civilian population. She had made it clear at an early stage that she was only prepared to be with him if he and his comrades attacked military targets.

He had given her his word. And broken it.

That had provided Efraim with the key to a successful recruitment, and soon Nadia was one of the Israeli security service's most important sources.

In his defence, Efraim often told himself that he had tried to resist. That he had never meant to fall in love, but had been forced to capitulate. Efraim had never felt for any woman what he felt for Nadia. She became pregnant almost right away, said that she knew it was Efraim's child she was carrying.

'You can't do this,' Efraim had said. 'Your husband will kill you if he finds out.'

'Which is why it will be our secret – yours and mine,' she had replied.

Therefore, he was not inexperienced when it came to being the father of another man's child, but in Nadia's case he had known about it, and it had caused him great pain. Because Efraim had wanted the impossible: a normal life with Nadia.

There were a thousand reasons why it was out of the question, but only one counted.

They would die, all three of them. Even if they left Israel.

'He knows people everywhere,' Nadia had said. 'They would find me and kill me.'

Therefore, the husband had to go. Somehow.

It wasn't an easy operation to put in place. Months passed, turning into years. Nadia said she needed a break from Efraim, and those words led to a hiatus of several years. They met only to exchange information, and she had something to offer less and less often. Her husband was lying low; he had lost influence within the organisation. Efraim didn't see his son, but had to make do with the photographs Nadia gave him. The boy was too old; he would start asking questions if he was suddenly introduced to an Israeli man.

Then MI5 got in touch. They were trying to track down a terrorist who was planning attacks on British embassies.

He stamped his feet up and down on the spot. He followed the news on his phone. Apparently Gideon Eisenberg was dead; he had killed himself.

It had been Saul's idea to call one of the Palestinian sources the Paper Boy. At first Efraim had thought it was a bad idea, but then he had changed his mind and said he wanted to use the name for his newest recruit. Nadia the Paper Boy had become Efraim's project. No one else was allowed to meet her, even though they knew of her existence. No one but Efraim and his boss knew her identity. Gideon and Saul ran their own sources in Palestinian towns and villages.

Efraim's bosses felt that taking out Nadia's husband would be too destructive, so they let him carry on, but made sure they sabotaged every plan that Nadia was able to tip them off about.

When the joint operation with MI5 got under way, everything was suddenly heightened – both the exchange of information and their love affair. Nadia's husband was the key player in the plot to launch a series of attacks on British embassies, and the Israelis decided they had had enough. Nadia's husband had to go.

Efraim had not been involved in the strategic planning, otherwise there would never have been so many of them there on the day his life came to an end. The team had stood outside the house where Nadia's husband was that afternoon, wondering if they dared go inside.

He had moved a short distance away, said he was going to call for reinforcements. Which he had done, but first he had called Nadia to make sure she was nowhere in the vicinity.

He could still remember the panic in her voice.

'You have to abort the whole thing! Benjamin is with him!'

Efraim hadn't seen his son emerge from the house.

He hadn't been there when Saul and Gideon, those stupid bastards, had decided to approach him. A ten-year-old kid who had been scared of Israeli men all his life. Who knew it was almost never good news when they came calling.

The boy had run for his life.

Back to the house.

Which was booby trapped.

It had been over in seconds. There was nothing Efraim could do. But later, as he wept with Nadia, he had promised her vengeance.

Saul and Gideon had been badly affected by what had happened. They had both said they could no longer justify what they were doing. Efraim realised that their past was haunting them; when children were involved, they wanted out.

So they had left the country, but Efraim had kept tabs on them. He had never forgotten what they had done, and that there was a debt to be paid. Both Gideon and Saul were blessed with a son; Efraim couldn't accept that such an outcome was fair.

'I'll give them ten years,' he had said to Nadia. 'Then I will take from them what they should never have been granted.'

But it was all over between Efraim and Nadia. She didn't want him any more.

'You gave me the best thing I ever had,' she said. 'But you also caused me the greatest pain I have ever known. I can't reconcile those two experiences. I just can't.'

Therefore, Efraim had lost not only a son, but the love of his life, and for that Gideon and Saul would pay the highest price imaginable.

Nadia made a new life for herself in northern Israel. They met occasionally, but briefly. She would remind him of what he had promised, and Efraim would assure her that he would never let her down again.

That promise rang hollow as he saw Nadia approach the door of the apartment block for the second time. Everything happened so fast. Before Efraim could take one step, she was inside. The door clicked shut behind her.

Shit.

Efraim raced across the road, afraid that every second was vital.

It took him ninety seconds to get the door open.

And that was all the time the woman known as the Paper Boy needed.

Her case was too heavy to carry in the snow. Fredrika Bergman had been indoors for far too many hours; she needed some fresh air, which was why she wanted to walk home.

She glanced at the suitcase, decided she could pick it up the following day.

But not her violin.

She was determined to take it with her so that she could play for Spencer.

She put on her coat, picked up the violin case and called in to see Alex on her way out.

'Are you sure it's okay if I go home? You don't need me?'

Alex looked exhausted.

'No, you get off. I won't be long myself.'

Fredrika felt lost. Sad. Almost resigned.

'It's over,' she said. 'And yet it isn't.'

Alex pulled a face.

'As far as I'm concerned, there is absolutely no doubt: Gideon is the killer we've been looking for. And until we've had a proper conversation with Mona Samson, I'm not prepared to eliminate her completely from our inquiries, in spite of the fact that she's finally condescended to get in touch.'

Fredrika agreed.

'She could have been the person on the roof, if it wasn't Gideon. When is she supposed to be coming in?'

'Tomorrow. I hope she turns up, because otherwise she'll be in real trouble.'

Alex picked up the copy of Gideon Eisenberg's brief suicide note, which had been on his desk.

'I wish he'd left a longer message,' he said. 'So that we could understand why he did what he did.'

But Fredrika had learned that it just wasn't possible to understand some things.

'He must have been so badly damaged by what Saul's father did to him.'

Slashes and scratches inflicted all over his body with a knife.

A road map of scar tissue.

A daily reminder of what he had gone through. She tried to shake off the image.

'That might be an explanation, but it's hardly an excuse,' Alex said.

He was right; as far as Fredrika was concerned, there was no excuse for shooting two ten-year-old boys and leaving their bodies barefoot in the snow.

'We'll find Polly tomorrow,' she said.

Alex nodded.

'We will. I'm sure she's alive.'

'Me too. Goodnight.'

She raised a hand and left.

She walked out of Police HQ, out into the fresh air.

It wouldn't be a long walk, but she didn't need one. She just wanted to feel the cold night air on her face, to stretch her legs. She decided to go via Sankt Eriksplan and Vasa Park, which would extend her route slightly.

She called home to tell Spencer that she was on her way.

He didn't answer.

Perhaps one of the children had woken, and needed his full attention.

She put away her mobile, enjoying the winter chill even though it was snowing once more.

Across the street she could see the figure of another woman, who also seemed to be carrying something resembling a violin case. Fredrika followed her through the falling snow and saw her head towards the ICA supermarket on the corner. She was swallowed up by the store's glass doors, and Fredrika carried on walking.

He ran twice as fast as he imagined his son had run on the day he died.

He glanced at the list of residents, because he couldn't remember whether Eden lived on the second or third floor.

Third.

From a purely logical point of view, he should have realised that it was already too late.

That he wasn't going to get there in time.

That she would not allow him to prevent the completion of her task.

When he reached Eden's floor, there was nothing but silence.

The absence of sound made him feel sick.

He grabbed the door handle. Pulled it. Hard.

And found that the door was open.

Surprise made him lose concentration, just for a second. Then he could see once more. With terrible clarity.

Eden's husband was lying on his stomach in the hallway. Efraim crouched down automatically and felt for a pulse.

He felt the faintest throb against his fingertips.

Erratic, but it would have to do.

He stepped over the body and carried on into the apartment.

He had expected a fight. An attack. Loud screams and

vicious blows. To her head and neck, arms and knees. Whatever he had to do to put her out of action.

But she was one step ahead of him.

And Efraim realised he would never catch up.

She was standing in Eden's bedroom.

He could see her in profile.

The main light was not switched on; only the street lamps cast a faint glow into the room.

That was all the light he needed.

He could see what there was to see. The two girls, lying in their parents' double bed. Fast asleep. As peaceful as only children can be when they are asleep.

'Don't do it,' he said.

He saw the gun in her hand.

He tried to play for time.

'Was it you who murdered Gideon?' he said.

She was taken aback.

'He's dead?'

'They say he killed himself.'

'I'm not surprised. I always thought he was weak.'

Efraim wondered how she knew. Was it Gideon she'd had an affair with, or Saul? He no longer cared.

Instead he looked again at the gun she was holding. Saw the extension to the black barrel.

A silencer.

That was why he had heard nothing when she shot Eden's husband.

Surely she hadn't already shot the girls, had she?

He took a step closer, his hand closing around the gun in his pocket.

Looked at the sleeping girls.

'Don't do it,' he said again. 'This is nothing to do with them.'

She turned to face him.

Slowly, as if she had all the time in the world. As if she knew, better than he did, that he would never be able to bring himself to shoot her.

'Indeed it is,' she said. 'And you're late.'

He couldn't stop himself.

He hurled himself at the bed, tore off the covers. And saw the blood on the children's pyjamas.

He stared at the darker of the two girls, the one who looked so much like his sister.

Tears filled his eyes, blurring his vision. He walked around the bed, positioned himself opposite her.

'For fuck's sake. *What's the point of this?*'

'You know that as well as I do. And now my work is done.'

Efraim shook his head.

Pulled out his gun. Took aim, knowing that she wouldn't have time to shoot him first.

'You're going nowhere,' he said.

'You think we should stay here? And do what? Wait to welcome home the rest of the family?'

He forced himself not to take his eyes off her, not to look at the girls again. Perhaps it would be just as well to wait for Eden, because what did she have to live for now? What was left when everything had been taken away?

'I don't think so,' she said.

She raised her gun, and there they stood.

Two people who had once loved each other enough to create another person.

There was nothing left of what they had had.

Not one iota.

'I promised to take revenge,' Efraim said. 'And I did.'

Nadia's face contorted in sorrow.

'You envisaged a lesser revenge than I did,' she said. 'Much lesser. You wanted to spare Gideon's daughter.'

'I believed in a just revenge. I didn't know we thought so differently.'

The gun shook in her hand.

'You can't do it,' she said. 'You can't shoot me, can you? Not even now.'

He opened his mouth to say that she was wrong.

He could do it.

But he didn't want to.

She got there first.

'But I can, Efraim. I can.'

And she did.

Efraim twisted and fell, landed on his back on the bed and automatically began to shuffle away. His strength quickly failed. He was unable to raise his gun and fire. The last thing he saw in this life was Nadia's face as she bent over him. She appeared to be crying.

'Forgive me,' she said. 'Forgive me.'

And with that she rested her head on his chest and felt him draw his final breath.

AFTERWARDS

The alarm was raised by the neighbour in the apartment opposite. He had been on his way out when he heard a door open – first once, and then again. Curiously, he peered through the spy hole. And saw Mikael Lundell, the priest, standing in the doorway facing a woman.

Who took a gun out of her pocket and shot the priest in the chest.

Without making a sound.

The neighbour edged as far away from the door as possible, then called the police.

Alex Recht was still in his office, so he was informed about the call that had come in minutes earlier from Sankt Eriksplan. Suspected shooting in the stairwell. Could it have anything to do with his case?

'Why should it?' he wanted to know, thinking that enough was enough.

'The residents of the apartment in question are Eden and Mikael Lundell,' his colleague said. 'Have those names come up in your inquiry?'

Four minutes later Alex was in a car heading from Kungsholmen to Sankt Eriksplan at speed, blue lights flashing and siren screaming.

Not Eden, he thought. Anyone but Eden.

He called Fredrika.

'Suspected shooting at Eden Lundell's apartment on Sankt Eriksplan. Come if you can.'

The apartment door was closed but not locked when they arrived. The stairwell was quickly filled with police officers and a team from the National Task Force, who by chance happened to be on exercise nearby when Eden's neighbour called the emergency number.

They had their guns at the ready, heavy boots thumping on the hard surface of the stairs.

Alex waited outside, the snow falling on his face and clothes.

He didn't even feel the cold.

He stood there without moving a muscle.

Until someone shouted that the apartment was clear.

He could come up.

There were two children and a man in what must be the master bedroom. The children were lying in the man's arms.

Alex Recht, the inspector who thought he had seen it all up to now, dropped his gun on the floor and wept.

His prayer had been heard.

Eden Lundell had not been shot. But her entire family was dead.

Eden arrived.

No one could stop her.

And why should they?

She must be allowed to see with her own eyes.

Because Alex didn't have the words to tell her.

She was carrying a violin case. She put it down on the floor. It remained there after she had left, when they discovered that one of the children was still alive. The other child was dead. Just like her father.

Eden disappeared.

According to the officers on the street, she might as well have gone up in smoke.

At the same time, Alex realised that the man who had been lying on the bed with the children didn't bear the slightest resemblance to the man posing with Eden in the photographs on the bedside table.

'Listen to me, there's a man missing here!' he shouted. 'Eden Lundell's husband, the priest who was shot. We have to find him! Fast!'

The angels had shown Eden their mercy for a second time tonight, because Mikael Lundell was found in a closet in the hallway, carelessly hidden under a pile of blankets. The CSIs had missed the fact that the bloodstains smeared across the floor led to the closet door. Eden's husband was tall and well-built; whoever had shot him had only just managed to push him inside.

'He's lost a lot of blood,' the paramedic said. 'We don't even know if he'll survive the journey to the hospital.'

'Do what you can,' Alex said.

He hoped the priest had God on his side.

And he wondered why Eden hadn't said anything.

Because she must have known it wasn't her husband lying on the bed.

*   *   *

Alex called the morgue where the bodies were being kept overnight.

'The man who was brought in a little while ago – did he have any ID on him?'

'I thought you knew who he was.'

'We were wrong.'

He waited while the technician went off to check what had been found among the man's belongings.

At that moment Fredrika Bergman walked into the apartment, ashen-faced and with tears in her eyes.

'Sorry I didn't get here earlier. I should have realised; I heard the sirens when I was walking home.'

Alex reached out and stroked her arm.

The technician came back.

'I found a passport,' she said. 'He's not Swedish.'

'Israeli?'

'Yes, his name is Efraim Kiel.'

Alex let out a long breath. Slowly he lowered the hand holding the phone.

'We've found Efraim Kiel,' he said.

Fredrika looked bewildered.

'What was he doing here?'

Alex shook his head. He knew that Eden had kept a vital piece of the puzzle from him.

He knew that he still didn't have it.

And that terrified him.

Because now he understood why Eden had refused to go to the hospital with her daughter.

'Eden knows who did this,' he said. 'She's going to take this city apart if we don't stop her.'

'According to the neighbour, it was a woman who shot Eden's husband,' Fredrika said.

They looked at one another, both well aware of who that woman must be.

'Mona Samson,' Alex said.

He immediately sent a patrol to the office on Torsgatan and her apartment on Hantverkargatan.

'She won't be there,' Fredrika said.

'I don't think so either,' Alex said gloomily; he still didn't understand what had happened. If Gideon was the killer who had taken the boys, did that mean Mona Samson was his partner? The person who had lain on the roof and tried to shoot Polly Eisenberg? Who was still missing . . .

Alex pressed both hands to his head.

'I'm going mad,' he said. 'What the hell is all this about?'

Fredrika looked at the blood on the sheets.

'It's as if this doesn't concern us at all,' she said. 'As if the players in this game are following their own rules, with their own referee and linesmen.'

'I can't accept that. I want to know what happened.'

'So do I, but who's going to tell us?'

'Eden,' Alex said.

'Do you really think she knows? If she does, then surely she would have been able to prevent this.'

Alex spread his hands in a gesture of resignation.

He felt like crying, but managed to hold it together.

'Where do we think Mona Samson might be? She can't have got very far,' Fredrika said.

Alex forced himself to think.

Where would someone like Mona Samson go?

'She's on her way out of the country,' he said, unexpectedly sure of himself.

'By plane?'

'Yes.'

He ran out of the apartment, sent a patrol car straight to the airport. Fredrika followed him.

'Alex, we have to be prepared for the possibility that we might not find her. We know her name isn't Mona Samson, for a start.'

'We've got a sketch. We'll put that out.'

Fredrika had seen the sketch, and knew it was worthless. So did Alex.

'We have to find her,' he said. 'We have to.'

They looked at one another, both at a loss. They reached a silent mutual agreement: they didn't want to wait in Eden's apartment.

To the relief of the CSIs, they left the building and went and sat in one of the patrol cars which was parked up with its engine idling.

Alex thought about what Peder Rydh had said: that they were looking for two perpetrators who couldn't agree; who had fallen out.

He told Fredrika as she leaned back against the headrest, utterly exhausted.

'So what we saw here tonight is the result of two killers who couldn't agree?'

She sounded dubious.

'I don't know what we saw here tonight,' Alex said. 'How does Eden fit into all this? Why did her daughters have to die?'

'Because they were in the wrong place at the wrong time?

This is such a mess; I can't see a single clear thread that runs through the whole case.'

'You think it's a coincidence?' Alex said, gazing out of the window. 'That there was no logical reason for the murderer to come to Eden's apartment? There just happened to be some kind of confrontation?'

It was his turn to sound hesitant now.

Fredrika pulled off her hat, dotted with snow crystals.

'I think we missed Efraim Kiel's part in all this,' she said. 'Given what I learned on my visit to Israel, I'm wondering if the Israelis know more than they're letting on, and if Efraim Kiel was on some kind of mission over here.'

'You mean the Israeli police might have asked him to look into the murders, as he was here anyway?'

She nodded.

'Something along those lines. That would explain why he was so interested and why he asked so many questions. And why he's been avoiding the Swedish police; since all those involved have an intelligence-related background, he wanted to run his own race.'

She threw down her hat.

'I'm not saying that's definitely the case,' she went on. 'It's just an idea, and it could explain things.'

Alex shifted in his seat, feeling a fresh surge of energy.

'I think it's a bloody good idea,' he said.

For the first time a coherent picture was slowly beginning to emerge. Eden had said that Säpo had its own reasons for keeping Efraim under surveillance. Could that have led him to Eden's apartment? Had Mona Samson followed him there?

That must be what happened.

He was just about to share his thoughts with Fredrika when a colleague yanked the car door open and shouted:

'A woman's just been killed on Odenplan. She stepped out in front of a car – there was nothing the driver could do. We think it's Mona Samson. In fact we know it is; she had a gun fitted with a silencer in her pocket, and several Samson Security AB business cards. Plus her appearance matches the sketch.'

Alex didn't know what to feel; every emotion drained away, leaving him empty.

'So she's gone,' Fredrika said.

'Yes,' their colleague replied.

'Good.'

There was nothing more to say.

Fredrika and Alex simply sat there in the car, waiting for life to begin again.

During the first week in February, a little girl came wandering into the Swedish embassy in Helsinki. She was crying so hard that at first it was difficult to work out what she was saying, but eventually they managed to get her name.

Polly Eisenberg.

She had been driven to a street nearby and told which way to go.

Nobody knew who had dropped her off, including the child.

Nor did she know where she had been.

Carmen Eisenberg had been sitting in her apartment overwhelmed by apathy, having lost both her husband and children within a week; Polly's return brought her back to life.

Gideon's parents came to Stockholm to collect their son's body. He was laid to rest in the country he had left ten years earlier. Carmen and Polly were there too; Polly wore a pretty dress and played with her doll. Her mother sat beside her, pale and silent. She didn't move a muscle throughout the entire ceremony.

Slowly the truth emerged, until eventually the only thing missing was the murder weapon.

Through Gideon Eisenberg's employer, they learned that he had had two meetings with the woman known as Mona Samson. The meetings had taken place a few months earlier, and as far as the employer knew, had not led to any definite collaboration.

At least not on a professional basis.

When the police went through Gideon's computer and personal diary, it turned out that he had met Mona on numerous occasions afterwards. In bars and restaurants. Outside working hours.

'Gideon had a lot to apologise to his wife for when he died,' Fredrika Bergman said acidly. 'He was cheating on her.'

'So Mona was having relationships with both Saul and Gideon,' Alex said. 'Can we draw that conclusion?'

Fredrika thought so. 'Perhaps she and Gideon wanted us to think that Saul was the perpetrator. And we almost fell for it; if we hadn't managed to discredit Gideon's alibi, we would never have believed Saul's story.'

Two Israeli passports were found on Mona Samson, one in the name of Mona Samson, the other Nadia Tahir. They didn't know why she had two passports, and the Israelis couldn't – or wouldn't – explain it. Around her neck she wore a pendant with the inscription 'Benjamin's mum'. They had no idea what that meant either.

They also found out that Gideon had been on a business trip to Israel during the week when Abraham and Simon were exchanging emails with the Lion.

'He was responsible for the email correspondence,' Fredrika said. 'He came up with the Lion, probably to distract attention from himself in a subsequent police investigation. I don't suppose we'll ever find out who picked up the boys on their way to their tennis coaching session; it could have been Gideon, or it could have been Mona Samson.'

The whole idea was sick, but it was logical in spite of that. It bothered Fredrika that both Gideon and Mona were dead; she couldn't shake off the feeling that they hadn't managed to reveal the whole truth about the murder of the two boys.

Another thing that bothered both Fredrika and Alex was Mona Samson's role in the murders. The secretary at the Solomon Community was shown a picture of her, and confirmed that it was Mona who had delivered the chrysanthemum in a bag with a face on it. What had driven Mona to help Gideon? Could it really be just because she loved him?

'I don't understand what made her go up on that roof and try to shoot Polly Eisenberg,' Fredrika said.

'There's so much we don't understand,' Alex said. 'We don't even know for certain that it was her. Gideon wasn't very tall, remember. It could have been him up there; maybe Mona changed her mind and tried to save Polly. Someone must have taken her to Finland, after all.'

But Fredrika wasn't happy. Regardless of whether or not Mona Samson had tried to kill Polly Eisenberg, she had shot Efraim Kiel and Eden's husband and children. No one would commit crimes like that without a personal motive. Unfortunately, Polly didn't remember anything about the person who had abducted her.

And so the quest for information continued. They tried turning the thumbscrews on the only person they had left.

Saul Goldmann.

But he consistently refused to talk about his past, about how he knew Efraim Kiel, about the work they had done, and what had happened to make him and Gideon leave

Israel. He swore that he would have helped them if only he could have done so; he said that he was sure all this had no connection to his years in the military. Fredrika got the feeling that he was partly telling the truth, and that this was causing him considerable pain.

There was some light in the darkness: Peder Rydh had gone to the Labour Court, and was trying to get his job back. It looked as if he was likely to succeed. Alex and Fredrika didn't often discuss it, but they were both hoping he would rejoin the team.

Fredrika was finding it difficult to sleep. The death of Eden Lundell's daughter, and the boys who had died out on Lovön, gave her no peace.

The silence from the Israelis was deafening. The official line was that from their point of view, the matter had been resolved. The perpetrators were dead, and would claim no more victims. That was the important thing.

In the centre of everything that had happened stood Eden Lundell.

Fredrika couldn't help feeling that she knew more than she was prepared to say. When questioned, she had said that she had met Efraim in London a few times, but that he had been no more than a passing acquaintance. She had no idea why he had died in her apartment, along with one of her daughters.

Her other daughter survived. So did her husband.

Fredrika knew that the family had moved abroad; perhaps that would help the healing process.

'She seemed so worn down when we interviewed her,' Fredrika said.

Alex glanced away, mumbled something she couldn't quite hear.

On the evening when she walked away from the crime scene, they had found her at the hospital, by her daughter's side. She had stayed there until the child regained consciousness.

Fredrika had seen Eden once more before the family moved away. They had met on Kungsholmsgatan. Eden was pale and gaunt, but calm. Almost serene.

And that was what eventually saved Fredrika Bergman's nights: the fact that Eden, who had come so close to losing everything, seemed to be one of the few who knew why.

There were days when she didn't cry. Days when they went on short outings, her daughter played, and her husband wasn't tired or in pain. But those days were few and far between. As a rule she had to make do with brief periods of peace of mind. The nights were long and silent, the days equally long and light. She had begun to grow accustomed to a fragmented daily rhythm. When it came down to it, she could get by on just a few hours' sleep at a time.

Israel had been Mikael's idea, and this time Eden had said yes. They didn't know how long they would stay.

Until they were whole again.

Until they could cope with everyday life.

Mikael said very little. Asked too few questions. Eden thought she would go under if she wasn't given the opportunity to unburden herself.

When she brought it up and wanted to talk about what had happened, Mikael shook his head, withdrew into himself, said they could discuss it some other time. She told the police, and her parents, no more than necessary. The only person who pinned her down was her boss at Säpo.

'This game stops right now,' GD said. 'You tell me what you know.'

But Eden kept her counsel.

'You have to believe me when I tell you it's over,' she said. 'There will be no further consequences.'

'What the hell was Efraim Kiel doing in your apartment? You must realise that I can't simply overlook such a thing, not when I know your history.'

She had gazed at GD for a long time.

'How do you know I was telling the truth when I said that Efraim and I had an affair? How do you know I didn't allow him to recruit me? How do you know I'm not exactly what you thought I was in the first place – a Mossad double agent?'

GD had looked at her sorrowfully.

'I just know, Eden.'

At which point she had burst into tears yet again.

She had offered to resign, but GD had suggested she take a year's leave, with immediate effect.

Dani was laid to rest the following week. If Eden so much as brushed against the memory of her daughter's funeral, she broke down and wept for hours, particularly during the night. Sometimes she had to bury her face in the pillow in order to smother the scream that was trying to get out. The grief never loosened its grip, refused to release her.

Eden thought she understood what had gone on. The press wrote about Gideon Eisenberg and the woman who had been his lover. They made much of his past and his childhood experiences. But Eden knew better. The attack on her children confirmed that she had been right all along. The murders that had devastated the Solomon Community were related to the events on the West Bank all those years ago.

The only thing she couldn't work out was who Mona Samson was, and why she had followed Efraim to Eden's apartment.

Eden could not leave these questions unanswered. On her second day in Israel she made contact with Mossad. She explained her business in one sentence, and was given an appointment to meet the man who had been Efraim Kiel's boss.

'I want to know why Mona Samson wanted Gideon Eisenberg and Saul Goldmann's children dead,' she said.

'You're asking for information that I am not at liberty to give you,' he said. 'You must realise that, even though I obviously have the greatest sympathy for you and your family in view of the tragedy that has befallen you, and the pain it has caused you. I really am very sorry for your loss.'

Eden had never been so close to killing another human being.

'Give me one reason why I shouldn't go to the press with the whole thing,' she said. 'Or to my employers in Sweden.'

The man thought it over. For a long time.

'You're playing a dangerous game,' he said eventually. 'And I will allow you to win. But everything I tell you stays between us. I have a question for you first of all: what was the connection between Efraim Kiel and your children?'

Eden accepted his rules without hesitation.

'He was their father,' she said.

She could see that the answer was unexpected, in spite of the fact that it should have been obvious, given the circumstances.

'I understand. Did Efraim know that?'

'I answered your question. Now you answer mine.'

Efraim's former boss gave a wry smile, then told Eden what she had already heard from Fred Banks in London. It was only when he reached the end of the story that she found out who Mona Samson was.

'Mona Samson, or Nadia Tahir to give her her real name, was the Paper Boy,' he said. 'The source Efraim ran in the Palestinian village on the West Bank. And it was her son who died in the explosion.'

He spread his hands wide.

'It's a terrible story from start to finish. Gideon and Saul left Israel after that, which was a sign of weakness, if you ask me. But I suppose everyone makes their own judgement.'

Eden wasn't interested in making a judgement. She was trying to feel something after what she had just learned, but she couldn't. The fact that the woman who had murdered Eden's daughter had lost her child herself was of no importance.

'How come she was carrying Israeli passports?' she asked.

'That was down to Efraim. Her life would have been in danger if she had stayed on the West Bank after the deaths of her husband and son; she was at considerable risk of being exposed as a source. We offered her the chance to disappear in another country, but she wanted to stay in Israel, so she was granted Israeli citizenship. It was no big deal; her father was an Israeli, after all. A year ago she contacted us and asked for a new identity; she said she thought she was being followed. It was then that she became Mona Samson.'

'Do you think Efraim was involved in the murders?'

The man's expression hardened.

'Of course not. Nadia was behind all this, and she persuaded Gideon to go along with her by exploiting the terrible

experiences he had been through as a child. I can guarantee
that he didn't know what her real motive was: to avenge the
death of her son. Efraim was the only one who had met her;
Saul and Gideon had no idea who she was, what the Paper
Boy looked like.'

'So the fact that Efraim was in Stockholm when this all
kicked off – that was pure coincidence?'

He nodded.

Eden thanked him for his help, and got to her feet. The
man she had come to see also stood up.

'We'd still really like you to join us, Eden,' he said. 'Any
time.'

She didn't answer; she just turned and left.

Mikael was still signed off so that he could recover from the
bullet wound. Saba was the one who had healed the fastest,
although she often asked about her sister Dani. Time and
time again they explained that she was gone.

'She's not coming back. Ever,' Eden said, feeling as if she
was about to fall apart.

How many times could one heart break?

An infinite number of times.

Tears poured down her face without her even noticing.
When she was driving the car. When she was out shopping.
When she was watching TV. When she was cooking.

She exercised as frequently as she could, often twice a day.
Physical exertion and pain became a balsam for her soul.

'You have to forgive yourself,' was the last thing GD had
said to her. 'You couldn't possibly have foreseen this.'

But that was exactly what she had done, and still she had
failed to act decisively enough. If only she had explained to

Mikael why they had to get out of the apartment, why they weren't safe there. She also hated herself for the misjudgement she had made when she first walked in; she had simply assumed that Mikael must be dead, since Efraim was lying on the bed with the children.

Mikael was haunted by the same demons. He blamed himself because he hadn't done what Eden said. Their anguish grew into a monster that threatened to destroy everything they had left. It was as if they were caught in a raging torrent, and neither of them had the strength to stay afloat.

They were being carried away from all their routines, away from one another.

Until the day when Eden realised she was pregnant, and saw a light flicker in Mikael's eyes. A faint light, but it was there.

And she knew that she couldn't wait for him any longer. He had to know what she hadn't been able to bring herself to tell him for five long years.

She told him one night when they were both lying awake. Her voice was no more than a whisper, and she couldn't look at him as the words left her mouth.

'You're not Dani and Saba's father.'

Her whole body was shaking.

She could feel the tears trickling down her cheeks, seeping into her hair.

Mikael lay there motionless.

On his back, his gaze fixed on the ceiling, he reached out and took her hand in his.

'I've always known that,' he said.

AFTERWORD

AND ACKNOWLEDGEMENTS

To begin with there was only the title. The very first time I visited my publisher, Piratförlaget, I said that the title of my fifth book would be *The Chosen* [*Davidsstjärnor*]. Looking back that seems completely incomprehensible. I never even thought that I would write five books. Or six, actually – I've started writing children's books too.

I am sitting at my desk trying to remember what it felt like to write *The Chosen*. It isn't particularly difficult, because I have never enjoyed writing something so much in my whole life. I have been fascinated by the history of the Jewish people and the creation of the state of Israel for such a long time; how could I resist the temptation to write a book with that title at some point? When I had finished, I wept; the sense of loss was so overwhelming. You can write a book only once. Everything that follows – the re-reading, the revision – is something else. Something that, for me, doesn't have much to do with writing. So when *The Chosen* was finished, I felt bereft. There was only one cure: to start a new project as soon as possible, because it is when I am writing that I feel best of all.

I thought we could have a little chat about that, dear reader.

About the importance of feeling good. And about where I was in my life when I wrote this book.

A few years ago I wrote a piece that was published when *Unwanted* [*Askungar*] came out in paperback in Sweden. I said that we must get better at following our heart, at devoting ourselves to things that give, rather than take, energy. I differentiated between what we do because it is right and strategic (or 'good for our career'), and what we do because we want to. And writing was – and is – exactly that: something that I want to spend time on because it is so much fun. Because it makes my life better on so many levels.

Yet for a long time I insisted on marginalising my writing, keeping it as a leisure activity. In spite of the fact that I was producing a book a year, and had been published in a dozen countries, I carried on working full time, often in locations in a constant state of re-organisation, with almost comically poor leadership which suppressed both creativity and productivity. I used to say that I would never be able to resign. This was based on the erroneous assumption that if I stopped working, I would also lose contact with the politics of international security, and to be honest I can't imagine my life without that contact. As time went by, it became clear that I had been wrong. I could integrate what was going on in the world with my writing, as long as I had the courage to expand my authorship to include non-fiction texts and per-haps journalism. And if I missed having a job, I could always apply for a new one.

So since January 2012 I have been a full-time author, and at the moment there is very little from my old life that I miss. The transition between old and new was actually supposed to happen at the end of 2010 / beginning of 2011, but then I got another allegedly good job. In Vienna. As a counter-terrorism expert. That was something I couldn't say no to, and so 2011 became yet another year when I worked and wrote at the same time.

I had so much fun that year!

And I was utterly exhausted.

Another dysfunctional workplace, where I was sapped of strength and energy. My airways hated the dry air in Vienna; I had a permanent cold. On top of that I did too much travelling, slept too little, wrote at night, worked during the day, had visitors from Sweden at the weekends. Eventually I had had enough. I am too smart to carry on like that. I had to stop doing two jobs at once, and I had to catch my breath. So that's what I did. The autumn of 2011 was a long wait for my contract in Vienna to come to an end so that I could return home to Stockholm, where my new life would begin.

And then everything went wrong. To cut a long story short, less than a week after I moved back to Sweden, I ended up in hospital, more ill and more terrified than I have ever been in my life. Then I got better. The long version of the story doesn't belong here, but I remember the feeling so well. The feeling that I was rotting from the inside. I lost every scrap of energy in just a few days. My body felt like a small town where the lights were going out in one area after another. I was drowning. Try taking a deep breath with water in both lungs. It's impossible.

Becoming aware of your own mortality is a good way of starting to examine both your lifestyle and life choices. When I looked back at the way I had lived over the past few years, it wasn't difficult to see that I had spent far too much time on things that I didn't really value, but hadn't had the courage to say no to. There was a cruel irony in the fact that when I had finally dared to make the leap, I was doomed to fall at the final hurdle. I couldn't reconcile myself to that. Not under any circumstances.

And I didn't have to, as it turned out. Apparently I had brought a souvenir back from Vienna: streptococcus. Physically I recovered quickly; mentally much more slowly. I had seen my own fragility, and to a certain extent I had become a different person, someone who was suddenly in a hurry. If I was ever struck down by a serious illness again, or affected by something else that threatened my existence, I was determined not to stand there regretting a whole lot of important stuff.

In many ways, 2012 was one of the best years I have ever known. That was the year when I sat in the historic American Colony Hotel in Jerusalem beneath a clear sky studded with stars, and wrote *The Chosen*. Something I had dreamt of for so long: to spend time in Israel and write a book. It was magical, the most perfect writing experience ever.

It's hardly surprising that I grieved when it was over, or that I love being a writer on a full-time basis. Because this is what I have come to realise: if you sort out the big things in life, the small things will follow.

A year has passed, *The Chosen* is about to be published, and I am sitting here trying to come up with a sensible afterword. I don't really have much more to say.

I have to add the obligatory disclaimer:

This story is entirely fictional.

I have even taken the liberty of inventing a completely new Jewish community in Stockholm, because I didn't want to involve any of those that already exist.

The legend of the Paper Boy is also entirely my own invention.

I would really love to return to Jerusalem to write more books.

Because there will be more books. I feel calmer now, I no longer race through life like a sprinter. My head is already full of ideas for lots of new books.

At Piratförlaget they think I'm crazy when I keep on turning up with yet another new manuscript, but that's fine. Dear Pirates, you have a very special place in my heart! What would have become of me if we hadn't found each other? Thank you for continuing to publish my books, and thank you for helping me to become a better writer. Special thanks to my publisher Sofia and my editor Anna. I always put that sentence in my acknowledgements, and it is equally true each time.

I also have agents, at the Salomonsson Agency. You are wonderful and you are crazy! I only have to poke my nose around the door of your office for twenty seconds, and I have enough energy to run a marathon in under two hours! I am so proud to be represented by you. Thank you for the enormous amount of effort you put into promoting my books overseas, and an extra big thank you to my agents Jessica and Leyla.

In my personal life it is impossible to mention everyone by name; there are far too many people to thank. First of all: my wonderful, reliable friends. How do you thank so many people at once? Without you there would have been no good books, particularly in 2012. It is you who give me strength and energy, and it is mainly with you that I share my everyday life. I try to keep you as close as I can, because whatever twists and turns my life may take, you are always there.

Thank you.

And then there are my siblings, who continue to rejoice in my successes, and who are always happy to help me celebrate them. Thank you! We have found a whole new meeting place through my writing, which is terrific; I cannot tell you how much I value it.

Finally I must express my heartfelt thanks to my mother and father; they too are always there. It is wonderful to have such devoted and loyal parents. Who come to the Gothenburg Book Fair every year to listen to me talking about my latest book. Who fly to Vienna to be with me when I am celebrating the publication of my books in German. And who drive right across Sweden in a blizzard when I call from the hospital in tears.

Thank you.

Kristina
Stockholm, 18 February 2013